D0547493

Infinite Loop

Meghan O'Brien

Yellow Rose Books

Nederland, Texas

Copyright © 2005 by Meghan O'Brien

All rights reserved. No part of this publication may be reproduced, transmitted in any form or by any means, electronic or mechanical, including photocopy, recording, or any information storage and retrieval system, without permission in writing from the publisher. The characters, incidents and dialogue herein are fictional and any resemblance to actual events or persons, living or dead, is purely coincidental.

ISBN 1-932300-42-2

First Printing 2005

9 8 7 6 5 4 3 2 1

Cover design by Donna Pawlowski

Published by:

Yellow Rose Books
PMB 210, 8691 9th Avenue
Port Arthur, Texas 77642-8025

Find us on the World Wide Web at
http://www.regalcrest.biz

Printed in the United States of America

Acknowledgments

I'm bound to forget someone, so first let me lay out a blanket thank-you to everyone who read the initial drafts of *Infinite Loop*, offered encouragement, gave me advice, or otherwise contributed to the long, slow evolution of this project. I truly appreciate it.

I'd first and foremost like to thank my partner Ty, who is incredibly understanding about being ignored when I'm "in the zone". Without her love and support, I wouldn't be the person I am today.

I'd also like to thank the friends who make my life richer. Kathy Young, who is always willing to read my rough drafts and give me invaluable feedback. Angie Williams, who makes me laugh and allows me to love her, and who also doesn't mind reading my stuff over and over again. Jodi Justice-Williams, for always offering encouragement. My sister Kathleen, for believing in me and being proud of me.

And to those who helped me get here: Jennifer Knight, for being a tough editor and teaching me a hell of a lot. Lori Lake, for all her advice and assistance, and for being a great role model. I also want to thank Radclyffe, who has always answered any writing/publishing question I've directed at her. And certainly not least, McJohn, who helped me get going on an initial rewrite of this story, and who made suggestions that helped shape it into a much better novel.

Finally, thanks to everyone who reads. Without you... well, this would be pointless.

For Ty, who is my life, and who first taught me about real love

For my sister Kathleen, because I always told her I would dedicate my first novel to her

And for the rest of the family I've made:
Angie, Jodi, and the baby boy tentatively known as Ryan

Chapter
One

"I HATE GODDAMN straight bars." Regan took a swig of her beer and glowered at a frat-boy type walking by their table hand-in-hand with a vapid-looking girl.

From the proliferation of pool tables and dartboards in the lung-burningly smoky bar, and nary an arcade game in sight, Regan knew that she wasn't amongst her own kind. *And sexuality's got nothing to do with it.* She sensed her companions' sighs before she heard them.

"Yes, Regan," Dan said, raising his beer and his eyes to the ceiling. "We're perfectly aware of your aversion to heterosexual mating grounds. Now be quiet."

"Thanks. I appreciate the sympathy."

Dan grinned at her, and Regan couldn't help but smile back at the warmth in his eyes. "I tease because I love," he said.

Adam leaned across the table. "In a minute I'm gonna tease 'cause I'm annoyed." He turned to Dan and gave him a serious look. "Didn't I tell you that this place was going to offend her tender lesbian sensibilities?"

Dan stroked his chin, nodding thoughtfully. "Right you were, too. And you know how I hate to offend anything that's tender and lesbian."

Regan shot a self-deprecating smile at her friends. "I thought I should at least pretend to have a social life that doesn't involve video games or the Internet." She tugged self-consciously on her Atari T-shirt. "I guess I should have worn something trendier. I know I'm a fashion plate at the office, but the geek thing doesn't play well in dyke bars, let alone in this Abercrombie and Fitch ad."

Adam scanned the crowded bar over Regan's shoulder, then raised his eyebrows at something she couldn't see. "Oh, I'm not sure you'd have a problem getting laid, if you were so inclined."

Regan tried to resist the urge to look behind her, but failed. An attractive blond-haired man stood at the bar, staring at her.

When he saw that she was returning his gaze, he grinned and gestured slightly with his drink. Regan frowned and turned back around to face her co-workers, who didn't bother to hide their amusement.

"Oh, please." She drained the rest of her beer.

Adam looked across her shoulder to offer her rejected suitor a sympathetic shrug.

"I think you just broke his heart." He stood up on unsteady legs. "Want another beer?"

"Might as well." Regan's eyes followed him as he lumbered towards the bar, cutting an easy path through the crowd thanks to height and bulk. She sighed and looked around. Yeah, she was out of place all right.

The bar was filled with people, the men cocky and flirtatious and of no interest whatsoever to her. The women were impeccably dressed and made up, far more feminine and eager than she. She gazed at a giggling group of them, seated at a nearby table, and felt like Jane Goodall observing chimpanzee behavior.

How do they do that? she wondered, taking in the tiny shirts, the skin-tight jeans, and the craftsmanship of perfectly coiffed hair and made-up faces. *Jesus, being straight would kill me in a week, tops.* She ran a hand through her short auburn hair, and adjusted her wire-rimmed glasses. *Thanks, ladies, but I'll stick to the baggy jeans and ringer T-shirts.*

An awed "Wow" from Dan intruded on her reverie, and Regan followed his lustful stare into the crowd. She nearly laughed aloud when the dancing bodies parted as if by scripted command, and a powerful dark-haired woman in a form-fitting black T-shirt and blue jeans stepped into the breach.

This is the part where the music fades away, time slows down, and we ogle the most beautiful woman we've ever seen, Regan mused, then she stared at the stranger and her internal cynic fell silent. *Holy shit, she* is *the most beautiful woman I've ever seen.*

Something about her made the other women in the bar pale by comparison. Maybe it was her eyes; Regan wondered how it would feel to be the focus of their intensity and tried to see what color they were—*blue, and I'm hers forever.* Maybe it was her mouth. She had a confident grin just shy of lopsided, and it caused her face to fall a bit short of perfect, but endeared her to Regan in an instant. Her stride was self-assured, feline, almost predatory, and for a crazy moment Regan felt as if she were the intended prey. Her very willing prey. *Who am I kidding? I'd be hers forever no matter what color her eyes are.*

A half-remembered line of poetry flitted through her brain.

Ah me! I cannot sleep at night. She shook her head at the errant thought. Had the sight of a woman — however gorgeous — ever inspired poetry in her before? She was a programmer, damn it, and not given to starry-eyed flights of fancy. With a pained groan, she picked at the label on her empty beer bottle. *I really need to get out more.*

Moments away from embarking upon a spontaneous — and no doubt deeply satisfying — sexual fantasy about the alluring stranger, Regan released a strangled gasp and lowered her eyes to the table. *No fucking way. Oh, sweet God, is she coming over here?* She kicked Dan sharply under the table.

"Jesus." He tore his lustful eyes away from the vision, fixing them grumpily on his companion. "What the hell is wrong with you?"

Regan scowled. *Perfect. Just perfect. Not only am I stuck at a straight bar, but now I get to watch Dan get picked up by my living, breathing dream girl, and all because he has a Y chromosome.* She squirmed in discomfort, woefully aware that her raging libido would not be sated tonight. *Or rather, I'll be playing to an audience of one. Again.*

Dan's face lit up with what Regan assumed was supposed to be a charming smile, and he raised an eyebrow in cocky greeting, more poised and self-assured than any code monkey in a "W00t!" T-shirt had a right to be. Regan envied his easy confidence, and wished she could steal some for herself. She was already sweating at the sight of the sexy woman.

"Hey." The woman's deep voice carried easily over the pounding music that filled the bar. She ran a casual hand through dark hair that reached just below her ears, mussing it slightly. Her gaze moved from Dan to Regan, and the corner of her mouth lifted in patient amusement.

Regan's heart thumped madly in her chest. She raised her eyes to offer a timid nod and immediately wondered, *Where's that beer I ordered?* The woman's steady gaze drew hers. *Grey*, she confirmed. *Blue. Grey. What the hell's the difference, anyway?* Their eyes locked and for a moment Regan forgot that she was in a straight bar. A feeling of connection, heat, and pure desire engulfed her. It was so intense and overwhelming that she imagined the other woman had to feel it as well. *Yeah, you wish.*

"Hey, yourself," she said, hoping she sounded confident. *So far, so good. Just keep breathing and don't act like an idiot. She's incredible, yes, but straight. No reason to be nervous.*

"How're you doing?" Dan piped up.

Regan gave him a dirty look. *Eye contact, man, and you ruined it.*

"I'm okay." After a moment of hesitation, the heart-stopping woman added, "Actually, I'm hoping to be a little better."

"Oh, yeah?" Dan gave her a flirtatious wink.

Regan failed to suppress a snort of amused disgust. She fiddled with her empty beer bottle and wished again that Adam would return with her refill. She spotted his head above the crowd of people. He had a shit-eating grin on his face and, predictably, a petite blonde smiling up at him. *Bastard! If I ever needed a beer, it's right now.* She scuffed the toe of her boot against the floor and winced when she kicked the table accidentally.

"Look, I don't know the situation here and I apologize if I'm out of line—" The woman broke off, casting a glance over her shoulder into the crowd. It struck Regan then that she seemed a little nervous.

"We're not together," Dan said.

Regan snorted a little. *I'll say.* To her shock, those incredible grey eyes eagerly sought her confirmation. She mumbled something to the affirmative and the woman gave her a warm— actually, almost hot—look.

"Oh, great. In that case," she asked Regan, "do you want to dance?"

Under different circumstances, Dan's slack-jawed expression would have sent Regan into a fit of uncontrollable guffaws. As it was, she could only manage to open and close her mouth in mute surprise.

The dark-haired woman seemed momentarily diminished somehow by nervousness, jamming her hands into the pockets of her jeans. "If I'm out of line, or if I've offended you, I'm sorry. I don't normally approach women in straight bars. I mean, I don't normally even come to straight bars. But my friends," she gestured to a table somewhere behind the throng of dancing people, "asked me to come with them and I've been feeling a little miserable all night. I noticed you and thought that maybe you also looked a little miserable...and definitely very cute. And so I thought I'd come see if maybe you were in a similar situation. I apologize if—"

Pull yourself together before she apologizes her way right back across the bar! Regan squeezed her hands into fists, working up her nerve. "You didn't, uh...you're not out of line."

"No?"

Hell, no. Regan offered her a smile. "As a matter of fact, you're right. I think we are in the same situation."

With a glance at Dan's bemused face, the woman offered Regan a tanned hand. "I'm Mel, by the way," she shouted over the music.

Regan wiped her sweaty palm on the leg of her jeans and took Mel's hand, making sure to give a confident squeeze in greeting. "Regan."

Mel promptly pulled her to her feet and Regan found herself nearly face-to-face with her unexpected dance partner. She wobbled a little on her feet, nervous and tipsy and already painfully aroused. A strong hand reached out to steady her.

"So, Regan," Mel leaned forward to speak in her ear. "Shall we?"

Regan cast an anxious look around the crowded bar. "You don't get embarrassed easily, do you?"

"Me?" Mel laughed out loud. "No. Listen, if anyone's got a problem with two women dancing—"

"No," Regan shook her head. "What I mean is, I'm not exactly light on my feet."

"Ah." Mel gave her hand a squeeze. "No worries. I'll lead."

Regan's heart was pounding. No matter how many times she'd wished and prayed for just this kind of scenario, she was scared to death now that it was happening. She was also thrilled beyond words. As Mel pulled her towards the dance floor, she glanced over her shoulder at Dan and grinned at his playful glare.

Mel led them to an open spot on the dance floor, amidst the crowd of warm, moving bodies. She turned around without releasing Regan's hand. After a moment of silent appraisal, she nodded at Regan's shirt and said, "Are you really an Atari fan?"

"Yeah," Regan answered. *Are we actually talking about antique game consoles now? Could this night get any more surreal?* "I actually have a 400 that I still play."

She blushed the moment the words left her mouth. *Smooth,* she scolded herself. *Not two minutes into this and you've exposed yourself as nothing more than a pathetic geek.* She waited for a familiar look of condescension from Mel, and was shocked when she received a sultry smile instead.

"I remember playing Shamus as a kid. That was an awesome game."

Oh, my God, Regan thought, *I've found her. She's the one.*

A fast-paced song began pumping through the bar's sound system, rousing the people around them into enthusiastic motion. Regan broke out of her stupor at the realization that they were the only two people not dancing. Mel saved her from the awkward job of finding a rhythm. Snaking a muscled arm around Regan's waist, she pulled her close, moving them together with the beat of the music.

At first Regan felt stiff, almost robotic, and then she closed her eyes and concentrated on letting her body go. Soon she began to feel the effects of her drinks, as well as the effect of the supple, feminine body pressed against her own, and she relaxed. She didn't feel the self-consciousness dancing usually elicited; she lost awareness of the many people moving around them. All she was aware of were Mel's hands on her waist, and on her stomach; Mel's hips pressing into her bottom; Mel's eyes, hungry and intense. If they had captured anyone's attention, Regan was totally oblivious to it, lost in a world of sound and sensation. Time lacked meaning, and her body transitioned from one beat to another as if by instinct.

She only came back to herself when she realized how tired she was becoming. And how wet. She ran her hands down Mel's back in awed reverence. *If I don't find something to lean against, I'm going to fall down.* When the song ended a few moments later, she leaned into Mel and said, "I think I need to sit down. Can I buy you a drink?"

Mel gave her a slow smile and moved forward to press the whole length of her body against Regan's. "A drink sounds great," she said.

Regan shivered at the feeling of full breasts pressed against her own. It was the most action she'd gotten in two years. She felt dangerously short of breath, unable to speak. At a loss, she headed for the bar, her hand entwined with Mel's. *Please, God,* she begged, *let me seem interesting and sane enough to spend some time with her. Quality time. Amen.*

At the bar they waited in silence for their drinks. Trying to converse so close to the dance floor seemed like more effort than it was worth. Mel was having a Coke because she was driving. Regan had ordered a Long Island Iced Tea, hoping to soothe her nerves. It was time to pull out the big guns and get nice and relaxed, she decided, glancing surreptitiously at the dark-haired woman. *With any luck at all, she'll be my designated driver, anyway.*

"I think there's a room in the back where we might actually be able to hear each other," she yelled.

"Lead the way," Mel answered, picking up her Coke. She caught the straw between lush, full lips, and took a slow swallow of her drink.

The erotic display was even more jarring than the roller coasters Regan had long ago sworn off, and her stomach flip-flopped in response. She needed to think of some way to appear cool and calm and irresistibly sexy, and fast. Smiling and nodding was going to get old quickly.

The small poolroom in the back of the bar was moderately quieter than the dance floor, and they managed to find a table in the corner. Mel set her glass down and gave Regan an easy smile. "So what's a nice girl like you doing in a place like this?"

Regan laughed, grateful that her beautiful companion had taken the lead. "Straight co-workers. They wanted to come here, and for some odd reason I was the only one who wanted to be surrounded by dykes instead. Majority rules, I guess."

"Not a bar person?"

"Not usually. I don't think I do very well in the bar environment. Honestly, I feel a little...out of place in these situations."

"You're doing just fine right now," Mel said. "In fact, you're the most compelling reason I've ever seen to hang out at a straight bar." She cocked an eyebrow playfully.

Regan felt herself drawing from some deeply buried wellspring of confidence, inspired by this woman's interest. "Oh, I bet you say that to all the girls you pick up in straight bars."

Mel reached across the table to take Regan's smaller hand in her own. "Only the ones I find absolutely adorable."

Regan grinned then, feeling most of her tension melt away under warm eyes and even warmer skin. She interlaced her fingers with Mel's and squeezed.

"So those guys were your co-workers." Mel rubbed her thumb over Regan's knuckle. "What do you do?"

"I'm a software developer. The computer-nerd garb isn't just a fashion statement."

"Wow," Mel blinked, and Regan was surprised to see admiration in her eyes. "I'm impressed. I took a first-level programming course in college, but it never really clicked for me. I'm always amazed by people who can understand that stuff."

"Well, I've had a lot of practice. While my peers were out partying in college, I was writing little shareware programs to pay my way through school."

"Where'd you learn?" Mel continued to rub her thumb in distracting patterns over Regan's hand.

Is she actually interested in this stuff? Regan stared uncertainly across the table. *Just don't start talking her ear off about your geeky hobbies. How many women have you bored to tears with that stuff?*

"I taught myself in high school," she said, keeping it brief. "I spent a lot of time in my head during my formative years. Do you like computers?"

"I love them. I mean, I don't know much about software or anything, and I'm baffled if it stops working, but I have a kind of ignorant fascination with them. They're not a big part of my job, though, so I don't get to use them very much."

She might just be the perfect woman. It was possible. Regan wasn't looking for a total geek, just a woman who could appreciate that her hobbies didn't make her an insufferable loser. Unwilling to push her luck despite the encouraging signs, she changed the subject. "What do you do?"

"I'm a cop," Mel answered. Her voice was a bit short, and no further information was forthcoming.

"If you tell me you've got the uniform and the handcuffs and all that jazz, you'll become my personal sexual fantasy." Regan startled herself with the declaration.

"Oh. A girl who appreciates the usefulness of handcuffs?"

Regan's boldness all but evaporated under the heat of Mel's seductive gaze. "So do you like being a cop?" she asked feebly.

Mel chuckled a little at this obvious attempt to steer the conversation in a different direction. "I guess so," she said after a moment. "My dad was a cop. So was my uncle. I didn't really think about doing anything else, from the time I was a kid."

"Well, I'm also impressed. I don't think I could do it...it must be tough."

"Yeah." Mel's eyes darkened. "Sometimes."

Regan sensed a definite lack of enthusiasm from her companion. *Great. Maybe now you can start talking about nuclear warfare to brighten the mood a little.* "So you never told me what you're doing in a straight bar," she said. *New subject.*

Mel's eyes brightened. Clearly, social trivia was more to her liking. "My college roommate is getting married in a month and a half. She wanted to get together with some of her girlfriends before the big event. I think we're supposed to be having fun here. To be honest, this kind of gals' night out is highly unusual for me."

"Must be fate, huh?" Regan giggled and tossed back the rest of her drink in two big swallows.

"Hey, now." Mel traced her fingers over Regan's outstretched arm. "You're not going to get drunk on me here, are you?"

At the casual question, the taste of the alcohol finally registered in her brain. "No, I'm done. I've reached that point where I realize how much I can't stand drinking."

"So why do it?"

"I'm a little nervous right now." *Of course, that whole arm-stroking thing helps.*

"Please don't be nervous." Mel's fingers closed lightly on Regan's forearm, and she leaned forward and pressed impossibly soft lips to hers.

The impetuous move shattered Regan's reservations, and she returned the slow, easy kiss without hesitation. Mel broke the sweet contact after only a moment and wrapped strong arms around Regan, who returned the hug with unthinking gratitude. She was perfectly aware of the thrill of full breasts pressing against her own, of the firm suppleness of Mel's body, but it was the unexpected tenderness of this gesture that struck her most forcibly.

Easing back slightly, she teased, "I'm guessing you don't have any problems finding dates, do you? I'm not sure you could be any more charming if you tried."

Mel smirked, waggling lascivious eyebrows. "Baby, you ain't seen nothing yet."

A hand on Regan's shoulder stopped her reply.

"Hey, Regan, can I talk to you for a minute?" Adam stood above her, giving her a goofy smile. He shot a brief glance at Mel, obviously agog.

"Sure." Regan gave Mel an apologetic smile. "I'll be right back."

"Sorry to interrupt," Adam said as they moved out of earshot.

"You should be. What happened? The blonde wasn't interested?"

"Maybe *I* wasn't interested."

"Uh-huh. So what's up?"

"Well, Dan and I were kind of thinking of leaving. We're not exactly having your luck, and Dan wants to get up early to start working on his game, so..." He shifted, looking a little awkward.

"And me without a designated driver..." Regan supplied.

"Unless you do have one." He nodded towards Mel, who was leaning back in her chair and twirling her straw between lazy fingers.

She looked relaxed and achingly sensual, and Regan despaired at the idea of leaving now, before she could live out the rest of this amazing dream. "Can you give me a couple of minutes?" she asked and didn't bother to wait for Adam's response.

Eyes locked to Mel's, she returned to the table and sat down in the chair next to her.

"Problem?" Mel reached out to tuck an errant lock of auburn hair behind Regan's ear.

"My friends are ready to call it a night, and my designated driver is summoning me."

"Do you want to leave?"

"Not really." She offered Mel a shy smile.

"Well, I can drive you home. That is, if you think your friends will feel comfortable entrusting your virtue to me."

"I'm the guardian of my own virtue, lady, and I can assure you it's the least of my concerns." Regan turned and signaled Adam that she would be remaining.

"Have I told you lately how absolutely darling you are?" Mel asked.

"Not nearly enough. Have I told you lately what an insufferable flirt you are?"

"You love it," Mel drawled. "You just tell me you don't."

"Was I complaining?" Regan answered in as innocent a voice as she could muster.

Mel broke into a too-wide grin. "Banter, even. You're good."

I've never bantered with someone I've just met in my entire life. Sure, I'm kinda drunk, but this still seems so...easy, so...not that scary. "It takes two to banter," Regan said. "And to tango, as well, or so I've heard."

Mel chuckled at this and slid a hand forward until she touched Regan's fingers. "I like you," she said and smiled at her.

Regan almost stopped breathing. She couldn't believe her dorky joke had earned her such a smile. Not playfully flirtatious, not seductive, not even compassionate; this smile was something else entirely, open and genuine and deeply, deeply warm. "Thank you," she said.

Mel broke their eye contact, and looked down at their clasped hands as if she had surprised herself. When she met Regan's eyes again, something passed between them, a kind of tenuous, unspoken bond, as close to a miracle as Regan had ever experienced. She felt like falling to her knees and thanking the universe for it.

"So do you want to get out of here?" Mel asked softly.

More than anything. Regan leaned over and kissed her cheek. "Yes."

"LEAVE IT TO you to find the one other lesbian in this place."

Mel smiled at Jane, the bride-to-be responsible for dragging her to the straight bar she was now anxious to leave. "Oh, I'm sure there are plenty of women with latent lesbian tendencies here tonight," she drawled, glancing around.

The bar was near closing and a steady stream of people filed out the door, not far from where she was standing with her tipsy friend. About twenty feet away, Regan waited next to Mel's motorcycle.

"Latent until you're through with them, right?"

"What can I say? I like helping people get in touch with themselves." Mel threw an arm around Jane's shoulders and gave her a friendly hug, conscious of several pairs of eyes burning a hole through her cheek.

Jane's annoying friends stood a few yards away, near a row of parked cars, pretending not to eavesdrop. *That's right, ladies. Stare at the dyke sideshow. Step right up.* Mel didn't bother to give them a look.

"So did you have a completely horrible time?" Jane asked.

"Nah." Mel cast a quick apologetic look at Regan for the delay. "I can't say I'm sorry I came."

"You're just saying that because of the redhead, aren't you?"

Mel grimaced. *Am I a complete asshole for taking off with a one-night stand that I met at Jane's little gathering?* "I'm sorry," she said, aware that she was treading on thin ice. She and her former college roommate were distant at best, but Jane was still the closest thing that Mel had to a friend. She wasn't certain how she'd managed not to alienate her yet. "I swear, I hadn't planned on —"

"I'm not upset," Jane said. "You are who you are, right?"

A surly bitch who sits in silence all night until she spots a tasty prospect for the evening? Mel had repeated the same mantra throughout an endless string of casual affairs: *I am who I am, right?*

Jane stood on her tiptoes and gave Mel a kiss on the cheek. "She's waiting for you. Go get 'em, tiger."

How many times had Jane said that to her in college, an encouraging send-off as yet another conquest beckoned? Leaving her friend, she joined Regan, who was staring at the Harley Sportster like it was going to reach out and bite her. Mel smiled at the trepidation in her eyes, and at the way she bit her lip. Regan, she acknowledged, was a woman she wouldn't normally consider her type. In fact, if she'd been at one of her favorite bars, Mel doubted she would have approached the redhead. Mel's "type" ran the gamut of physical appearance and personality, but usually excluded shy women. Then again, shy had never looked so good on anyone before.

"I promise you, I'm a good driver," she said. "I've only hit little old ladies...oh, hell, once or twice."

Regan flashed her an uneasy grin. "It's not the little old ladies I'm worried about. It's the trembling young computer geek."

"I promise I'll take good care of her." Mel rested a hand on the seat of her bike. She wrapped her free arm around Regan and drew her close, leaning to whisper in her ear, "I have plans for her, after all."

"You do?" Regan squeaked.

Mel grinned. *Yeah, she's a little drunk.* "I do."

She had decided she wanted to spend the night with Regan while they were dancing and, anticipating what was to come, she felt a strange mixture of desire and tenderness. The desire was familiar, the tenderness, not so much.

Mel pulled on her helmet and climbed onto the bike, planting her feet firmly on the ground. She reached out and took Regan's hand, instructing, "Put your left foot on the pedal." Regan did as she was told, tottering unsteadily. "Now swing your right leg over the seat and, you know...straddle it."

Regan gave her an admonishing look. "Don't enjoy this so much."

"Sorry." She wasn't.

A pink tongue poked out from between full red lips, as Regan concentrated. With surprising agility, she eased herself onto the motorcycle and hovered above the seat for a moment before settling down. Once in position, she rocked her hips back and forth a couple of times to get comfortable.

Mel was beyond turned on. She needed to get this woman home, quick. "Put your helmet on," she managed. "And hang on tight." She kick-started the bike, grinning as it roared to life and Regan's arms grabbed her around the middle. Glancing over her shoulder at the panicked redhead, she yelled, "You ready?"

"As I'll ever be," Regan shouted back.

Mel drove the bike out of the parking area, turned onto the street, and opened the throttle wide. Regan's house was less than a couple of miles from the bar and the route was familiar; a good knowledge of Detroit and the surrounding suburbs was one of the few perks of her job.

Regan's arms wrapped even tighter around her waist in reaction to yet another sharply taken turn and Mel reveled in the feeling of soft breasts pressed against her back. Regan didn't need to know how safe and slow Mel was making the trip, not when a full-body hug was the reward every time she leaned into a turn a little more than was necessary. The first time had been unintentional, but the sweet contact she'd received as a consequence had been all the motivation she needed.

Jesus, what was wrong with her? Had she ever smiled this much before? She liked Regan. She really did. And while she knew that fact wouldn't give most people pause, it was earth-shattering for her. She couldn't remember the last time she'd bedded someone she actually liked. Hell, she couldn't remember the last time she'd met someone she really liked.

It was scary. Regan was the most real person Mel had met in as long as she could remember. It seemed almost wrong that she would soon end their evening together the same way she ended so many others with women she would never see again.

If she was the type to spend more than one night with a woman, Mel decided Regan would be the kind of woman she'd choose, without a doubt. The feeling unnerved her, and she blew out a breath, ordering herself to snap out of it. Regan was cute, goofy, and unknowingly sexy and if Mel was lucky, she'd turn out to be one of those shy girls who were amazing in bed. She made the turn onto Regan's street, slowing down as they entered the subdivision.

"It's the third house on the left, thank God in heaven," Regan said, relief evident.

Grinning, Mel steered the Harley into the indicated driveway, slowing to a halt next to a small Colonial-style house. The silence was heavy when she turned off the motorcycle and lowered the kickstand with a gentle foot. She eased herself off the bike and turned to face Regan, who was still sitting on the seat, eyes closed and face pale.

Mel stared at her for a moment, something unfamiliar tugging at her lips. "Delivered in one piece, as promised." She reached out and caressed a cool cheek with her hand. "That wasn't so bad, was it?"

Regan opened her eyes. She looked rattled. "So I've decided that maybe motorcycles should remain safely within the realm of my lurid sexual fantasies."

"Oh, come on. You're not going to tell me that wasn't at least a little fun?"

Regan appeared to give the question careful consideration. "If by fun you mean starkly terrifying, then, yeah, maybe."

She moved to dismount, but Mel stopped her with a firm hand to the chest. "Motorcycles *are* fun. Let me show you."

Regan glanced around at the dark houses in her neighborhood, then looked back up at Mel. "Show me?"

"Yeah." Mel climbed back onto her bike, sitting backwards on the seat to face her dubious companion.

Regan eyed the silent rows of houses again. "How? I mean, show me, how?"

"You ask a lot of questions." Mel closed the distance between them, capturing Regan's lips in a fiery kiss.

Regan tasted slightly of alcohol, and just as she had when they'd danced, she seemed stiff at first, then she relaxed and gained confidence, moaning into Mel's mouth, sliding her tongue along her upper lip. She wrapped slim arms around Mel's shoulders, scooting forward on the seat to press her body into Mel's powerful frame.

Mel burned with arousal, her fingers tingling with the need to touch Regan. She could feel the same need coursing through the woman in her arms. Regan's hands traced dizzying patterns over her shoulders and down her back. Her own hands explored soft hips and the gentle swell of a breast. She took Regan's lower lip between closed teeth and tugged a little, unleashing a moan from Regan that nearly made her come right there. Jesus, if they didn't slow down Regan would bring her off right in the driveway.

With considerable effort, Mel pulled away and gulped some much-needed air. She shifted on her seat, trying to alleviate some of the throbbing between her legs. Opposite her, Regan breathed raggedly, eyes closed and lips swollen.

Mel reached out to trace her thumb over Regan's eyebrow, her fingers curling around to tangle in auburn hair. "See," she said.

Regan stared back at her with unveiled tenderness. It was not the kind of look Mel was used to getting from women. She was used to seeing desire, and playfulness, and occasionally coy innocence, but never the genuine warmth she now saw.

Mel lowered her eyes, for some reason feeling less relaxed than she usually did in these situations. "Why don't we go inside and start our night?" she asked.

Regan's silence lasted just long enough to make her really nervous. "I...yes, but does it...I mean, um..."

God, the shy thing was cute. "What?" Mel asked. "Does what?"

"Does it have to be just one night?"

It wasn't that Mel had never been asked the question before. But women usually waited until after an evening's passion had been spent before springing it on her, at which time she never had a problem telling them the truth. *Yes, it does. No, we can't. I never promised you anything more.* What staggered Mel now was the answer she wanted to give: *I don't want it to be.*

Panic kicked in. *I need to get out of here. I need to go be alone for a while.* "Listen, I..."

Regan's eyes shone with stormy emotion, and the blush that rose on her cheeks was visible in the moonlight. "I just fucked this up, didn't I?"

Mel flinched at Regan's naked vulnerability. Christ, that was a pretty brave thing she just did, wasn't it? Mel felt about three feet tall. The woman she was with had just taken a chance because she felt something—something maybe Mel could feel, too. But instead of facing those feelings, she wanted to escape as fast as she could, betraying the trust she'd just been shown. *Way to be an asshole, Laney.*

Mel sighed and steeled her nerve, not sure what the hell she was doing. "No, you didn't fuck anything up."

"Just forget I said anything, okay? I just—"

Mel shushed the redhead, placing her fingers across pouty lips. "It's okay." *I don't want to be an asshole anymore. Not with her.* "But I think we should stop for tonight, okay?"

Regan gave a small, defeated shrug. "I'm sorry. I really do want to spend the night with you, you know." She gave a sad little chuckle, shaking her head before dropping it into her hands. "God, this alcohol is making me honest."

Mel climbed off her motorcycle and held out her hand to Regan. "I like honest. It's refreshing."

Regan snorted but took her hand, standing up to clumsily dismount the bike. "Refreshing, huh?"

As she stepped away from the bike, she stumbled a bit, and Mel caught her in an impromptu embrace that surprised both of them. "You're very refreshing, Regan."

"So, do you want to come inside?"

Mel gripped Regan's elbows and stepped out of their embrace with a regretful smile. "No, I meant what I said. I think we should stop for tonight."

"Okay." Her disappointment was plain.

"Hey." Mel reached forward to tilt Regan's face up. "I said that we'd better stop for *tonight*, okay?" She paused, uncertain. "If this isn't just going to be a one-night stand, we probably shouldn't start it out like one."

Regan raised doubtful eyes.

"I mean it," Mel insisted. She wasn't certain she meant anything. The only thing she knew for sure was that she couldn't sleep with Regan now for reasons that eluded her. She wanted Regan so bad she could taste it, but here was her conscience deciding to introduce itself just in time to screw up the evening. She knew she'd felt something different with this woman tonight, but she hadn't counted on this. But no matter how much her reactions unnerved her, something told her to take a chance—her feelings were too unfamiliar not to explore. Aware of the silence dragging out between them, she said, "Why don't you give me your number? I'll call you, we can go get dinner somewhere."

"Are you sure?" Regan gave her a serious look. "If you're not interested, I'd really rather just—"

"Regan, be quiet and get me your number, okay?"

Regan broke into an awkward smile, then took a step back and adjusted her glasses. "Okay. I'll be right back."

Mel leaned against her bike and watched Regan open the side door of her house. A light appeared in the window moments after she disappeared inside, and Mel exhaled a shaky breath. Her mind was awhirl; she wanted to stay just as much as she wanted to leave, but she was afraid to make a mistake.

Are you actually going to call her? She thought back over the evening, and especially about the unexpected tenderness, even protectiveness, she felt for Regan. Maybe she would call. Maybe she would do something different.

After a couple minutes, the door opened and Regan approached. Mel shifted on her feet, covertly straightening her clothes and trying to maintain a neutral expression. She even managed a small smile, and felt the smile grow slightly when Regan returned it.

"Here. I wrote my home number on the back." Regan handed her a thick business card, the letters visible in the moonlight.

Regan O'Riley, Software Developer. Mel grinned. "Regan O'Riley, huh?" She realized that she probably hadn't known the last names of at least half the women she'd slept with. "That's very cute."

"One crack about the blarney stone or leprechauns, and I'll smack your mouth," Regan said with a playful scowl. "I've heard it all."

Mel laughed out loud at Regan's warning. She was so adorably non-threatening that Mel couldn't help but lean over and, still chuckling, kiss the tip of her chin. "Thank you. It feels good to laugh like that." She couldn't remember the last time someone had really made her laugh.

"You're welcome," Regan said. "I had a really good time tonight. For a straight bar, you know."

"I know. Me, too."

"Cool." Regan planted a quick, shy kiss on Mel's cheek. "Goodnight, then."

Mel slipped the card into her back pocket. "Goodnight."

With one last smile, Regan turned and ambled up to the side door, then disappeared inside, taking the brilliant promise of the evening with her.

Deflated, Mel got back on her bike. This had been one fucked-up, surreal night, from beginning to end. She placed the palm of her hand flat against the cheek that still burned from that small kiss. *Will I call her?* She looked back over her shoulder at an illuminated window, wishing she could catch sight of the woman inside. *I hope so.*

Chapter
Two

"BURNING THE MIDNIGHT oil?"

Adam's question barely penetrated the wall of sound being pumped directly into Regan's ears. She considered pretending that she hadn't heard him, engrossed as she was in the crafting of a particularly vexing function. *But if I don't answer, he'll just do that annoying flicking at my ear thing until I do.* Regan fumbled with her iPod to stop Pink Floyd, and removed the listening pieces.

She turned in her chair and looked up at him. "I just know there's a good reason you're interrupting my flow here."

"I thought you were almost finished with Thompson Automotive." He propped himself against her desk with his arms folded. "You know, it's not good for you to spend so many late nights slaving over the keyboard."

Regan snorted. "What are you talking about? How do you think I spent my college years?" *Oh, hell, let's be honest here.* "Or my high school ones?"

"And look where that got you." Adam gave her a smug grin and made a sweeping gesture around their funky industrial office. "Come on, let's go out and see a movie or something."

Regan sighed and leaned back in her chair. "That would mean dealing with people. I'm not really in the mood."

Adam migrated further onto her desk, sitting and swinging his legs back and forth in lazy rhythm. He looked around at the empty workstations, long since abandoned for the evening. "You work too much."

"What else is there to do?"

"I don't know. Go out, socialize." Adam gave her a careful look. "Get laid."

Regan pulled off her glasses and rubbed her eyes. *Please don't ask about Friday night.* Now that Tuesday evening was here and she had yet to hear from Mel, she had decided to chalk the entire episode up as a humiliating example of why she shouldn't drink anymore. Who said honesty was the best policy?

"I'm fine," she said. "There's nothing wrong with wanting to get a little lost in my code."

Adam's heel banged against her desk. "As long as you find your way back to the real world every once in a while, no, there isn't."

Regan lifted her eyes to his. "I'm not *that* bad."

He leaned over and clapped her on the back. "Regan, they've stopped banking your comp time. Paul knows that if you ever came collecting, we wouldn't see you for six months."

Regan smirked at the thought of her project manager panicking if she ever took advantage of the fruits of all her overtime. "Dude, you know I spend plenty of time slacking off, playing video games. I'm not exactly a chronic workaholic." She spun her chair back around to face her monitor and typed a fast line of instinctive code. "So you're going off to your thrilling and exciting night, then?"

"Hey, I never claimed that my night was going to be particularly thrilling. That was what you were supposed to provide by hanging out with me. The thrill."

Regan tilted her head to raise amused eyebrows at her tall friend. "I provide thrills for no man," she told him.

"Don't be so sure of that." Adam chuckled. "I was pretty thrilled by the concept of living vicariously through you Friday night."

Regan released a deep sigh. *Great, he's brought it up.* "You give me way too much credit."

Adam's grin faded. "So, it didn't go well?"

Regan shrugged. "Well, yeah. I mean, we didn't—" She sighed again. "I don't know. I guess not."

Adam answered with a soft groan. "I'm sorry. I should have taken the hint when you refused to talk about it yesterday."

"I think I fucked up."

"How?"

"I thought it might be something more than it was." She let her disappointment seep to the surface. "She was really amazing."

Adam rested his hand on her shoulder. "I'm sorry, Regan. Someday some woman out there is going to realize how cool you are, you know that?"

Regan snorted. "You think?"

"I know." Adam slid off the desk and grabbed the backpack he'd set on the floor beside him, hefting it over his shoulder. "In the meantime, though, have fun with your code."

"I will." She looked over at her glowing monitor, at the

formatted lines of well-commented code. *I always do.*

"Want me to lock the door on my way out?" Adam called out to her as he walked away.

"Yes, please," she called over her shoulder. To herself, she mumbled, "I might be here awhile."

Programming was the ultimate escape. Regan supposed she looked at writing code like most people probably looked at reading books; it was her opportunity to leave herself for a little while, to become absorbed in pure creation and problem-solving. It gave her great satisfaction, and somehow she was less lonely when she was banging away at her keyboard. Of course, the loneliness always came back when she returned from her self-imposed isolation.

Regan took a break about a half hour after Adam left, eyes straining from her already full day of work. Sliding her glasses off, she pinched wearily at the bridge of her nose, then put them back on and looked around the empty office.

"Time to get serious," she said aloud, speaking just to hear a human voice.

Regan had her late-night coding routine down pat. She rose to her feet, lifted her hands above her head, and rose up onto her toes. Twisting her torso slowly from side to side, she managed a soft groan, then dropped her hands to her sides. *I need to learn to drink coffee,* she mused as she retrieved her empty water bottle from her desk and refilled it at the company water cooler. She glanced at the coffee machine the rest of her co-workers could not live without. *I'm not sure I'm a real programmer if I don't worship caffeine. Too bad it tastes like hot garbage.*

She returned to her desk and set the bottle carefully beside her monitor. She'd been quite paranoid about that little maneuver ever since the infamous water-spilling-into-the-keyboard incident of September 2002. Adam and Dan hadn't let her forget about that debacle for weeks.

Regan dropped into her comfortable desk chair and set her feet squarely on the floor, swinging the chair this way and that. Then, after only a moment's hesitation, she pushed off with her toes and propelled her chair into the open space away from her desk. Another moment, and she set herself spinning in mad circles. All part of the routine.

The room blurred around her, objects blending into one another. She waited until she could feel her head whirling before she tried to catch up with the visual input surrounding her, then planted her feet hard.

The ensuing head rush was ample inspiration to begin a marathon night of coding.

OFFICER MELANIE RAINES sat in the passenger seat of her patrol car and stared out the window at nothing. She was thinking about Regan O'Riley. Again. *I should just call her,* she told herself for the millionth time. She wanted to call her; every day that passed made her more certain that something important was slipping away. Why was it so hard to do this?

"If someone had asked me last week if it were possible for you to be any quieter, I'd have told them no way in hell," a deep voice startled her. "Apparently I'd have been wrong."

Mel blinked and turned her head. Her partner glanced at her with gentle brown eyes, and then turned back to look at the road.

She managed a sheepish smile. "Sorry."

"Nothing to be sorry about," Peter Hansen said easily. "Just thought maybe you needed to talk about something. Or not."

Mel sighed. More than three years as partners and not once had she taken him up on that offer. Was he ever going to get the hint? Did she really want him to get the hint? She liked knowing that Hansen cared, even if she didn't know quite how to respond to that caring. One day he would give up, and how would she feel then?

She made a decision. "Damn, you're persistent."

"I'm a cop. I'm supposed to be persistent." Hansen eased their car to a stop at a red light and flicked a cautious glance at her. "You seem...darker than usual this week."

Mel studied the people crossing the street in front of them, the dreary, drizzling sky that hung over Woodward Avenue and their stopped car. *Darker than usual.* How dark was she most days?

"Would you believe that I've spent more time with you, Hansen, in the past three years than I have with any one person for almost ten years now?" Mel surprised herself with the admission.

"Sounds lonely."

"No, it hasn't been. I mean, it never felt lonely." She wondered if that was the truth.

"But it does now?"

"I don't know. Maybe."

"Why maybe?" Hansen sounded as if he were trying to approach a scared animal he feared would bolt at his presence.

Amazed by the infinite patience he always seemed to have for her, Mel brought her fingers up to rub at her throbbing temple. Maybe the way to stop being so miserable was to try something different. She drew in a breath, then pushed forward before she lost her nerve. "I met a woman last weekend."

Hansen looked surprised. Not surprised that she was a lesbian, surely—she'd told him that two years ago, after unleashing barely controlled fury at a couple of fellow cops who had been making homophobic jokes about a mugging victim. Rather, he was surprised by the fact that she was saying anything at all. It wasn't her style to bare her soul to anyone.

Hansen laughed, a deep, sonorous rumble. "I should've guessed. Isn't it always a woman?"

Mel shot him a cautious grin, unsure of how to proceed, whether to keep talking or to shut the hell up already. But what did she have to lose, really? "See, that's the thing." She felt like she was about to reveal a dirty secret, and she tried to choose her words carefully. "It never really has been for me."

"No?"

"What I mean is, I, uh...I don't generally become preoccupied with women. I mean, a particular woman." Mel wished she'd never started this. "The truth is, I'm not usually occupied with any woman for more than an evening or two."

"Ah," Hansen said.

Mel waited for a moment, then realized the older man wasn't going to say anything more. She slouched a little further into her seat and stared out the window. So much for the heart-to-heart.

"You know what my favorite thing is?" Hansen said after a long moment.

"No." It was the truth. She hardly knew anything about her partner outside their car and the precinct and the miserable uniform.

"I like the way that my wife knows when I've had one of those days." Hansen's voice grew tight. "Like a couple weeks ago, with that Rogers kid."

Mel sucked in an uneasy breath, refusing to react to his words. She struggled to keep her face impassive as she was assailed with images from that day; the seventeen-year-old kid lying on the hot, cracked sidewalk in a pool of his own blood and urine, an honor student in the wrong place at the wrong time, two months from high school graduation and the promise of a full-ride scholarship to the University of Michigan. Nathan Rogers's mother, shaking with hysterical sobs behind yellow police tape, there to watch her son being carried away with a sheet over his face because he was shot not thirty feet from the front door of his home.

Mel couldn't suppress the shudder that ran through her body at the memory of those cries, at the senseless loss of potential and her own feeling of empty impotence when all she could do was try and help clean up the mess.

Yes, that had been a bad day.

"Somehow she just knows." Hansen was still talking. "I don't know how, even if I don't say a word. And she knows just what I need. To make me forget, to remind me of the good things. Even if it's just a cold beer waiting for me, or a story about something Katie learned at school that day, or a hug." He trailed off then, sounding a little embarrassed.

"Yeah," Mel said, totally out of her league with this touchy-feely stuff.

"I guess all I'm trying to say is there's nothing wrong with wanting that," he continued. "I think everyone needs someone to remind them of the good things. Even you, Officer Hard-Ass."

Mel snorted at the nickname. She wanted to ask him what the good things were, but didn't. She couldn't admit to him that she didn't know anymore. She stared out the passenger window again, arms folded over her stomach. Could Regan remind her of the good things? She'd felt pretty good when she was with her.

"Maybe," she murmured, as much to herself as to Hansen.

She continued to look at the passing buildings, the foot traffic, anything but Hansen's face. She was done talking, exhausted from the turbulence of her emotions and unwilling to lose her composure while on the job.

Hansen must have sensed that the subject was closed because he fell quiet. The only sounds in their car were the low guitar melody coming from their radio and the hum of the city streets beneath their tires. After their uncharacteristically open conversation, the silence no longer felt comfortable, as it normally did, and instead bore down upon them, making Mel feel close and cramped within the confines of the vehicle.

"So, you taking the detective test soon?" he asked after a few minutes. His voice was light, his attempt to change the subject pitifully obvious.

From one shitty topic to another, she thought, and kept her answer brief and non-committal. "Not sure."

"I remember the twenty-two year old kid who couldn't stop talking about making detective. When she talked, I mean." She raised an eyebrow at him, and he added, "What's stopping you? The Lieutenant has even started asking me about it."

With a vague sense of unease, Mel remembered the words that would have elated her only three years ago. *You're a good cop, Raines, and you'll make an excellent detective.* Lieutenant Jackson was wondering why she wasn't taking the test; now she knew that Hansen wondered, too. She didn't know how to explain why the thought of making detective now made her feel so empty. Falling back on humor, she gave her partner a mischievous wink. "Maybe I'm just not ready to leave you yet, Hansen."

"Can't say I blame ya." He changed lanes as they approached a cluster of familiar fast food places. "What do you say? Lunchtime?"

"Sounds good to me."

"Tacos?" He shot her a wide-eyed look of innocent hope.

Mel groaned. "Tacos? Are you kidding me?"

"It's your pick tomorrow if we can have tacos today."

Mel felt a grin appear without her consent. "Hansen, it was supposed to be my pick today. You had a real craving for greasy cheeseburgers yesterday, remember?"

"Tomorrow and Friday, then," he offered. "You can have the next two."

"I'm such a sucker."

"And that's really a very fine quality in a partner." Chuckling, Hansen flipped on the turn signal. A garish sign advertised the taco joint Mel had frequently sworn never to visit again. Mel stifled further protest when he pulled into the driveway of the restaurant and guided the car into the drive-thru. As was his custom, he fell into a state of deep and silent concentration while he studied the colorful, glowing menu.

She was grateful for the reprieve, and her mind immediately returned to Regan. *I'll call her tonight,* she decided. Her heart began to jackhammer in her chest, and she brought a hand up to rest on her throat. *Nothing's ever going to change unless you change it.* She studied her shoes, balling her fists in her lap. *It doesn't have to mean anything more than a second date.*

The thought, meant to comfort, only scared her.

REGAN WAS DROWNING her sorrows in good, old-fashioned hedonism. It was seven o'clock on Wednesday night, and she was ensconced in her favorite easy chair, a thick down comforter wrapped around her pajama-clad body even as she enjoyed the chill of air conditioning. Stretched in front of her, her feet moved back and forth on the footrest in time to the music that poured from her television screen. Her eyes were fixed on the fast-paced video game in front of her, hands moving in practiced motion over her controller. On one side of her was a full bottle of water, and on the other was a half-empty bag of gummy bears. *Oh, yeah, it don't get much better than this.*

She let out a triumphant yelp as she executed a perfect 1080 Swiss Cheese in what was quickly becoming a record-breaking game of SSX on her Playstation 2. "I am a *goddess!*" she crowed, pumping an exultant fist into the air. "Who needs sex when I have video games?" she asked no one in particular.

She was trying to take Adam's advice. Working late every night *was* kind of pathetic. She reached a quick hand over to snatch a gummy bear from the bag while her snowboarder sped down a straightaway. *Unlike this right here, of course.*

The sound of the phone ringing jarred Regan right out of her zone. She whipped her head around in a frantic effort to locate her cordless phone — *over there, on the table* — then turned back to watch in horror as her digital snowboarder smashed face-first into the snow. *Shit!* There was no time to mourn her high score. Regan sprang from her chair and raced over to half-vault, half-stumble over her couch. Her mind was racing as she grabbed the phone. It could be her. She turned on the phone and brought it to her ear with such force that she nearly clocked herself in the head. "Hello?" she gasped.

For a moment she heard only silence, then, "Regan?"

It was instantaneous — a Pavlovian response to the sound of a beautiful woman's voice. Regan's heart began thudding madly in her chest. Her throat tightened, trapping her voice before it could reach her lips. Her cheeks were hot and flushed. *It's her! For Christ's sake, you moron, say something! She actually called you. Let her know it wasn't a mistake.*

"Yes, this is. It's me...I mean, I'm Regan," she stuttered.

"Hey, this is Mel...um, from the straight bar. Did I interrupt you or something?"

"Oh, no!" Regan shouted, and then clapped her hand over her mouth. Wincing, she explained, "I, uh...I was in the middle of a video game and it took me a minute to find the phone." She blushed at her unthinking honesty.

Mel's chuckle helped to alleviate some of her distress at the admission. "Cool. And you can stop blushing, okay? I still think you're adorable."

Regan disobeyed by turning even redder. The throaty voice on the other end of the phone made her legs weak. She sat down on the floor and pulled her knees up to her chest, leaning back against the couch. "And what makes you think I'm blushing?" she asked.

"They don't call 'em 'powers of deduction' for nothing," Mel replied. "I happen to know that you always blush when you talk about something you think is nerdy."

This insight did nothing to slow her pulse. "I find that most adult women aren't overly impressed by my geeky toys."

"I'm not most adult women. I suspect you aren't, either."

Regan laughed. "No, I'm not."

"For the record, I like video games." Mel's voice was friendly, conversational, and it set Regan at ease. "I'm sure you could kick my sorry ass at almost anything, but I have been known to play."

"*Almost* anything?" Regan grinned at the patterned wallpaper in front of her, and then closed her eyes, trying to picture what Mel would look like with a phone in her hand.

"Nobody beats me at Tetris," Mel said.

Regan's grin widened until her cheeks hurt. "Oh, that sounds like a challenge."

"Consider the gauntlet thrown."

Regan laughed. Now that her nervousness had eased a bit, her body began to relax. She bit her lip and made a confession. "I wasn't sure you were going to call."

There was dead silence for a moment. "I wasn't sure I would, either." Brutal honesty.

"Why did you?"

"I..." Mel sounded off-balance at the question. "I couldn't stop thinking about you."

Regan's heart thumped hard, erratic. She brought a hand up to rest on her breast, a sense of euphoria. *She thought about me?* "I'm so glad I'm not the only one," she breathed, and sensed that her words hit Mel just as hard.

Mel's voice changed when she spoke next. "I want to be honest. I don't have much experience with this."

"Experience with what?"

"Calling women. Dating. Whatever this is."

"What do you want it to be?" *This absolutely gorgeous woman sounds just as nervous as I do. Does she realize how much that helps?*

A pause. "I want it to be dinner tomorrow night, to start."

Regan beamed at the wall in front of her and wiggled her toes with the excitement. "I'd like that."

"Yeah?"

"Yeah. I would. I'm really glad you called."

She heard Mel's smile in her voice. "I'm glad, too." She cleared her throat. "Well, unless you want to ride my bike again, we'd better meet someplace or you can come pick me up."

Regan shuddered at the memory of that motorcycle ride, and what had happened after it. "How about I pick you up? I'm hell with directions, so I'll never make it to an agreed-upon meeting place."

Mel snorted. "Then why do you think you can make it to my place?"

"Incentive," Regan replied. "Now give me the directions."

Mel's answering laugh reminded her of just how attractive the incentive was.

Chapter
Three

MEL SMILED ACROSS the table, chin resting in the palm of her hand. Her elbow was planted on the table, and her eyes were stuck on Regan's red hair and pale skin. *Beguiling*. Mel had never wanted to use the word before, but that's exactly what she was.

Regan was wearing an army green ringer T-shirt that proclaimed *There's No Place Like 127.0.0.1* — presumably some kind of computer geek thing — and low-rise cargo pants. Her hands were clasped in front of her on the table, and her foot tapped audibly on the tile floor. She was chattering away, obviously nervous but trying hard not to show it.

Mel looked around at the intimate surroundings of the restaurant Regan had chosen; a dozen crowded tables lit with candles surrounded them, and brightly colored paintings adorned the walls. "Um...this is a nice place," she offered when Regan paused to catch her breath.

"I have an unhealthy addiction to their breadsticks," Regan said.

"Ah, so you had an ulterior motive in bringing me here? And here I thought you were catering to my love of Italian food."

"Let's just say I figured this could be a win-win situation."

"I'm sorry it took me so long to call," Mel said without thinking. She dropped her eyes to the table, feeling vulnerable for having said it. "I swear I must have taken your card out of my wallet a hundred times, looked at it, then put it away again."

"You were nervous?" Regan sounded incredulous.

Mel gave a shaky laugh. "I'm still nervous." In fact, this was scaring the hell out of her.

Regan reached across the table to take Mel's hand. "As a good friend of mine once said, please don't be nervous."

Mel cocked her head at Regan, staring into tender green eyes. "Friend, huh?"

"I'd like to be," Regan said in a soft voice.

"Ladies." A sandy-haired young man appeared at their table,

pen poised over a pad of paper. "Are you ready to order?"

Mel was glad for the interruption and let Regan order first. Why was this so hard? She'd spent all week thinking about Regan. The shy redhead was the only thing that felt good to Mel right now, and this was the first time anyone had ever affected her like this. That had to mean something, right?

She scanned her menu, at a loss to decide what qualified as good date food. Spaghetti sounded messy. Scampi would give her killer breath. "I'll have the lasagna."

"Good choice," Regan commented after the waiter walked away. "My second favorite meal here."

Mel took a sip of her water, studying her date over the rim of the glass. Maybe next time she wouldn't be so nervous. She clasped her hands together on the table, slightly freaked out when she realized that she was already thinking about "next time."

"I'm a lot less nervous in bars," she said.

Regan laughed. "I noticed. I don't understand it, though. The more I get to know a person, the easier it is for me. Being surrounded by strangers kind of undoes me."

"I guess I feel more comfortable around strangers."

"But everyone needs friends."

Regan's quiet certainty brought Hansen's words to mind: *I think everyone needs someone to remind them of the good things.* Mel wondered why what seemed patently obvious to Hansen and Regan was so elusive to her.

"I guess I'll have to take your word for it." She looked past Regan to the profile of a man sitting near them, careful to avoid eye contact with her date. Their conversation was unnerving her, as was her growing compulsion to be totally honest.

"Oh, come on," Regan said softly. "I can't believe that someone like you doesn't have friends."

Mel shifted her gaze to the hand clasping hers. "I don't. My choice, really." God, she sucked at this.

Regan stared at her a moment, then withdrew her hand from Mel's to gesture at the space between them. "So is this...okay?"

"This is *very* okay." Needing something to do with her hands, Mel unrolled her napkin, freeing the cutlery within. "I was telling the truth when I said I liked you the other night," she said. "I had a really good time."

Regan beamed at her. "I had a good time, too."

Mel couldn't help but return Regan's happy expression. She wasn't sure she had ever seen such honest emotion from a person before. Regan, once at ease, was so unpretentious and genuine that Mel could only sit in awe of her. She was beautiful.

"So." Regan rested her arms on the table. "Now that you have me here, my friend, what *will* you do with me?" She gave Mel a mischievous smile.

Mel could see her wanting to come out of her shell, struggling to overcome her reserved nature, and found she wanted to do the same thing. She felt desperate to connect with her new friend, to stop being so guarded. "I don't know," she answered, more serious than Regan probably expected. "But I look forward to figuring it out."

The waiter returned with their salads and Mel picked up her fork, thankful for an excuse not to talk for a few minutes.

Regan had other ideas. "So what about those women who took you to that bar? They're not your friends?"

Still on the friend thing. Mel finished chewing a crouton, then said, "Jane—the blonde, about my height—she's the closest thing I have to a friend. We probably talk on the phone once every few months. That was the first time I've been out with her in about a year, though. The others are her friends." She gave Regan a playful grin. "I didn't pay a lot of attention to them. I don't think they knew quite what to make of me."

"A seducer of ostensibly straight women?" Regan suggested.

Mel snickered. "Oh, please. Nobody ever thought you were straight."

Regan wiped her forehead with the back of her hand, sighing in exaggerated relief. "Thank God."

They concentrated on their salads by silent mutual agreement, occasionally looking up to smile at one another over the lit candle at the center of their table. Mel couldn't believe how much like a real date this seemed, and how little she suddenly cared about that fact. It felt good. So far. After a couple minutes their waiter turned up with a basket of steaming breadsticks.

"Ah. Your fix," Mel teased.

"Oh, happiness." Regan retrieved a hot breadstick from the basket the instant it was deposited on the table.

Mel watched with amusement as she took a healthy bite, closing her eyes and moaning contentedly as she chewed. There was nothing like the sight of pleasure on a woman's face.

With a wholly satisfied expression, Regan gasped, "God, these are good."

Mel picked up a breadstick, raising an eyebrow at Regan before taking an experimental bite. She chewed a moment and then sighed. "You're right. These should be illegal. You have to promise not to bring me to this joint too often or you'll be rolling me out of here."

She tensed slightly as she realized the implication of her statement. Already she could see a future that included Regan. It was time to stop getting ahead of herself.

"I promise. Besides, I have plenty of other vices I can introduce you to."

"I'm counting on it."

Regan chewed for another moment before giving Mel a curious look. "I have to admit, I'm surprised you like video games."

Mel felt startling heat rise in her cheeks. "And I have to admit that my motives haven't always been pure. My favorite bar in college had a Tetris arcade game and I found that being the constant high score had a strange aphrodisiacal effect on women."

"Man, you'll have to show me where *that* bar is."

"Nah. I'm not going to toss a total babe with your gaming prowess to those wolves. I'd rather keep you to myself."

Regan's mouth curled. "Total babe, huh?"

"Totally." Mel felt her confidence returning as they ventured away from serious topics into the light banter that had so intrigued her their first night together.

"So, where did you go to college?" Regan asked in an obvious attempt to divert attention away from herself.

"Michigan State. On a softball scholarship."

"Oh, no, not a Spartan!" Regan bemoaned. "We're rivals!"

"U of M, huh? I won't hold it against you."

Regan sputtered. "So says the couch burner?"

Mel scowled playfully. "Stupid rioting kids. We'll never live that down."

Before Regan could come back with another zinger, their waiter bustled up to the table with their order. Regan met Mel's stare from across the table, and they held the eye contact as the young man arranged their dishes.

Regan had ordered spaghetti. As soon as the waiter departed, she poked at it with her fork and asked, "So, what did you study?"

"Besides women, you mean?"

Regan leaned back and assessed Mel with an amused expression. "Yes, besides women."

"Criminal justice." Mel didn't mean to be short, but talking about her life was such an unfamiliar thing that it left her struggling for words. It was exciting to be here, though. Mel felt the same energy thrumming through her body that she got when she drove up north to find deserted country roads where she could open her throttle. Did Regan feel this connection, too? Was it making her heart feel like it could pound out of her chest?

"I guess that makes sense," Regan said. "Did you grow up in Michigan?"

"No. I was born in Oklahoma. I came to Michigan to go to school and then joined the department in Detroit when I graduated."

"Did you know people out here or something?"

"Not really. I'd just met Jane in college, but like I said, we've never been extremely close."

"What about your family?"

"What about them?" It always came back to family. Mel could feel her defenses stirring, and tried to remain calm and open. Regan was just being polite. People talked about their families in social settings, didn't they?

Regan seemed unaware of Mel's discomfort and continued her innocent questioning. "I mean, are you close to them? Were they upset when you moved out here?"

"Not really." Mel kept going despite the fact that she wanted to run and hide at the topic. *Haven't I let it ruin too much already? I refuse to ruin this thing with Regan.* "I have a brother, Michael. We're not very close. My dad and I...well, we don't get along. And my mom died when I was eight."

"Oh." Regan pushed some noodles around with her fork. "I'm sorry."

Mel held her face rigid. "It was a long time ago." To lighten the mood, she said, "So what did you study at Michigan? Computer science?"

"Ironically, women's studies." Regan's tone became self-mocking. "I say ironically because, unlike you, I didn't actually spend a lot of time studying women in college."

"No?" Mel flirted. "I'll bet they were studying you."

"Is everyone this charming where you come from?"

Mel winked. "I guess you just hit the jackpot when you found me." She took a sip of water and said, "You majored in women's studies and became a software developer. How does that happen?"

Regan rolled her eyes. "The major was a rebellion against my parents, and the career is a concession to the real world."

"What did your parents want you to do?" Mel asked, trying to imagine what it must be like to defy parental expectations.

"Something lucrative, I guess. Something respectable. I don't think they cared to think about my life deeply enough to get specific in their expectations."

Whoa. Mel flinched at the barely veiled bitterness. *I guess I'm not the only one with an uneasy relationship with her upbringing.*

"I don't see them very often," Regan continued. "I mean, they're good parents and everything. I always had everything I wanted—well, except tuition after I declared my major. They're just really distant. They don't really know me, and I don't think they want to." Her eyes grew sad and Mel extended her hand to enclose one of Regan's.

I can't stop touching her, she realized, staring down at their hands, her own olive complexion a sharp contrast against her date's pale pink skin. "It's their loss," she said, and her voice was rough. "You're an amazing woman."

Regan's cheeks turned an immediate flaming red, and she rocked in her chair for a moment before leaning forward and planting an impulsive kiss on Mel's temple. "Thanks," she breathed.

Mel shivered at the contact and struggled to maintain some semblance of the stoicism that she normally wore like a mask. More than three years on the force, seeing the things she'd seen, and what finally undoes her is a 5'3" self-professed computer nerd? Disbelieving, she stroked the inside of Regan's wrist. Everything about the evening felt revelatory.

"So your parents actually stopped paying for your school over women's studies?"

"Sort of. My dad threatened to withdraw my tuition to try and make me see his point of view. That pissed me off, so I called him on it. I told him that he could have his tuition, and I'd have my women's studies degree."

"Wow." Mel felt her respect for Regan grow by leaps and bounds. "Just like that?"

Regan leaned across the table and lowered her voice to a conspiratorial whisper. All lingering shyness seemed to have disappeared. "It wasn't as ballsy as it sounds. Remember I told you that I wrote shareware programs to pay my way through school?"

"Yeah."

"I'd actually just completed a pet project of mine a couple of months before my little 'disagreement' with my parents. I'd released it as shareware for fun, you know, to see if anyone would like it. And by the time my father threatened me, I'd already made a couple thousand dollars." Regan shrugged her shoulders, the picture of nonchalance. "Hell, I had just started receiving payments and they were coming in fast. I figured if I was careful and saved what I made, I could at least pay for the rest of the school year."

"I bet your dad was surprised."

"Oh, my God, you don't even know," Regan laughed. "Once

he realized that I was challenging him, he couldn't back down. I couldn't, either. I'm pretty sure he thought I'd come running back, begging for help after a few months. I don't think he's ever quite gotten over the fact that I didn't need them anymore, that they didn't have a say anymore."

"God." Mel picked up another breadstick and took a careful bite. "That's awesome—writing software that earned you a couple thousand dollars is a big deal."

"Seventy-five thousand dollars," Regan mumbled.

Mel nearly choked on her breadstick. "What? Holy shit! Seventy-five thousand?" Damn, that was impressive.

"It was pretty successful. I even released a couple of later versions."

Could she be cooler? "What the hell did you write?"

"Um." Regan's cheeks blazed impossibly hotter.

Mel couldn't stop a slow grin. "Spill it," she commanded in her very best interrogatory voice.

"Well, this was back before all the peer-to-peer stuff they have today and, well, you know, the Internet wasn't nearly as easy to navigate, so there was a certain demand..." She grinned as Mel poked her in the arm. "I called it PornSpider. It was basically a big old porn search engine."

Mel exploded into loud laughter, then clapped a hand over her mouth as a few diners craned around to stare.

"So *anyway*," Regan gave Mel a pointed look, "it was just a little application that let you search the Internet for pictures and videos based on keywords and stuff. Had a built-in media player to display what it found...it was pretty popular for the lazy porn connoisseur. Not bad for its day, if I do say so myself."

"My, my, dear Regan, and I thought you said you weren't studying women in college."

"Not real ones."

"I find that hard to believe."

"Well, one," Regan admitted. "I had my first and only relationship during my junior year. Sarah. We lasted about a year, parted as friends."

"And since then?"

"Not much to talk about. No relationships, a couple of casual things. Honestly, despite my porn industry ties, I'm pretty boring."

"I doubt that," Mel drawled. "The boring part, I mean."

"And what about you?" Regan asked, her voice becoming bolder as she challenged the other woman. "How many women have you seduced with that Oklahoma charm?"

Mel could feel her face flood with heat. "Um..."

"That bad?"

Mel resisted the urge to curl a finger beneath the collar of her shirt and pull it away from her overheated neck. "I've never really lacked for company. It's just that I haven't had a lot of experience seeing women more than once." She told herself to stop acting guilty. There was no reason to feel bad about her past. It wasn't so long ago that she had been proud of it. "That sounds terrible, doesn't it?"

"It doesn't sound terrible. It sounds honest." Regan was holding her napkin in one hand, tearing at the corner with the other. "I'm not sure why I'm any different, but I'm glad you thought I was."

"You are different." Mel met her earnest stare. What was it about this woman that weakened her defenses?

"So, how intimidated should I be?" Green eyes flashed with anxiety despite the playful tone. "Got a rough estimate?"

"Regan, there's no reason for you to ever be intimidated by me. I may have slept with a lot of women, but there are plenty of things I haven't experienced." She paused, looking down. "Honestly, I should be intimidated by you."

"By me?" Regan looked startled.

"Yeah, I mean, I don't actually even know how to be in a relationship."

Regan smiled, an expression that started at her gorgeous mouth and traveled all the way to her eyes, which sparkled with warmth. "I'll teach you if you'll teach me."

Mel felt familiar panic start to rise at the words, an instinctive reaction from years of shutting herself off from everyone and everything around her.

Regan frowned a little and reached over to stroke her arm. "You seem bothered. What is it?"

"I don't know." Mel blushed at how transparent she was. "Doing something wrong. Disappointing people. Getting hurt."

"I wish I knew what to say to make you feel better." Regan propped her chin on a fist. "I don't know what will happen, honestly. All I know is that you've yet to do anything wrong, and I can't imagine anything about you that would disappoint me. And I promise to do my best never to hurt you."

Mel's vision blurred. She cursed under her breath, wiping her traitorous eyes with the back of her hand. "I'm sorry." She barked out a sharp laugh. "You must think I'm insane."

"Not at all," Regan said. "I think you're wonderful."

"And you impress the hell out of me."

Regan looked as if she wasn't sure what to say for a moment, seeming both pleased and embarrassed. Then her face brightened. "Wait a second...don't think you're getting out of it that easy!"

"Out of what?"

"You never answered me when I asked how many women there've been. And now I'm dying of curiosity."

Mel hesitated. "Um, you first."

Regan produced her own total without hesitation. "Three. Now you."

Jesus, Mel thought. Three? "I don't know. Sixty. Seventy." Quickly, she added, "I've always been safe."

"Holy moly!"

"Holy moly? Did you just say holy moly?"

Regan arched an eyebrow. "Yes, holy moly! You're a veritable strumpet!"

A wide grin accompanied the gently teasing words and Mel relaxed as she realized that Regan didn't seem put-off. In fact, she looked downright amused. "Yeah, well, strumpethood isn't all it's cracked up to be."

"It's a tough gig, huh? I'll try and remember that the next time I'm alone on a Saturday night."

"I'm serious! It gets boring after, oh, number fifty or sixty."

"My poor baby," Regan cooed. "I'll have to be sure to make life interesting for you again, won't I?"

Coquettish, Mel thought. *I've never had the urge to use that word, either, but she definitely sounds...coquettish.* "I'd say you're off to a really good start."

REGAN TOOK HER second wrong turn of the night just three blocks from Mel's apartment. She cast a surreptitious gaze at her passenger, who was studying every CD she had in the truck. *God, I hope she doesn't notice that I keep getting us, quote unquote, lost. What a sad little ploy to prolong our date.*

"What the hell is this?" Mel held a CD case with two fingers as if it might contaminate her.

Regan tilted her head to read the title. "The Spice Girls! It's a classic!" She shot Mel a haughty look. "Put it down if you can't appreciate it."

"Classic, huh?" Mel snorted, tucking the CD back into its spot. "Let's just put this away and I'll pretend I never saw it."

"Good idea," Regan came to the end of the unfamiliar street, and braked at a stop sign, flipping on her turn signal. *I can't take another wrong turn, can I? I mean, that would be too obvious, wouldn't it?* She could feel Mel staring at her.

"I still think you're adorable," Mel said. "And so is the whole driving us around in circles thing."

God, kill me now. Regan cringed.

"I don't want this evening to end, either." Mel's voice was low and so quiet that Regan cursed the pounding in her ears that overwhelmed it.

Maybe it was the night sky; maybe it was the gentle fragrance on the breeze that blew through Mel's rolled-down passenger window; or maybe it was just the way Mel made her feel like the kind of person she never thought she would be. Whatever it was, something infused Regan with a powerful wave of unexpected courage.

Okay, now or never, she thought, and asked, "Does it have to end?"

Her heart dropped into her stomach when this was met only by uneasy silence. Regan turned her truck on to a dark side street. Mel's street. *Why isn't she answering me?* She swallowed the lump in her throat, willing her face not to betray her humiliation. *She doesn't feel the same way.*

"I want to say that it doesn't." Mel sounded uncomfortable. "But I think it does."

"I understand." Her voice was steady and calm, an absolute lie when she shook inside. "You don't have to explain."

She steered her truck into the driveway of Mel's apartment complex and parked in an empty spot next to Mel's motorcycle. She couldn't meet Mel's eyes. *I thought she was feeling the same way.*

"Regan, look at me."

Mel's gaze was full of warmth, affection, and, unless Regan was mistaken, powerful lust. "You know that I'm attracted to you, right?" She tilted Regan's face toward her, two fingers under her chin. "I'm also interested in you. I want this — whatever this is — I want it to mean something."

Regan held her breath when she saw the genuine feeling that shone from Mel. "So do I," she whispered.

"But I don't think I'm ready to make that kind of promise yet."

"I'm not asking for a promise," Regan said. "I'm not saying that to try and change your mind or anything, I just want you to know that it doesn't have to be a promise."

"But it does." Emotion was raw and visible on Mel's face. "I care about you, already, and I haven't made love with anyone I cared about for a long time. So, for me, it's going to be a kind of promise." Her eyes dropped. "And I hope for you, too."

Regan was stunned silent by Mel's naked vulnerability. *She's taking this seriously. She's taking me seriously.* "I understand," she said. "And I respect that. I was just feeling a little insecure. I want for it to mean something, too...for us to mean something."

"You don't play games, do you?" Mel touched Regan's cheek, as if in awe. "You don't know how much I appreciate that."

Regan wrinkled her nose. "Life's too short to play those kinds of games. What's the point in not being honest?"

Mel broke into a grin, unbuckling her seatbelt so that she could wrap strong arms around Regan. "Don't ever change," she murmured.

"I think that's the nicest thing anyone has ever said to me. Thank you."

"Do you think I could get a goodnight kiss?"

Regan laughed and unbuckled her own seatbelt. *You could get anything you want.* She leaned forward and kissed Mel. Hard.

At first Mel seemed surprised by the fierce passion of the kiss, allowing herself to be moved backwards by the force of Regan's body. After a moment she regained control and pushed back, exploring Regan's mouth with her tongue. A warm hand slid up over Regan's collarbone, and possessive fingers curled around the curve of Regan's neck. Regan had never been so turned on in her entire life. They broke apart gasping. Mel's hand was still on Regan's throat; Regan could feel her pulse racing beneath those fingertips.

"I need to get out of this truck before I throw you down and take you right here." Mel fumbled behind her back for the door, eyes dazed and face flushed with arousal.

Regan groaned and let her eyes slip shut at the thought. "Not a good thing to tell me when I'm in this state. I won't be responsible for my actions."

"Moan like that again and I won't be responsible for mine." Mel found the door handle.

"I'm sorry." It didn't sound very genuine.

The corner of Mel's mouth twitched. "Oh, please. Like I ever want you to apologize for being sexy."

Sexy? Regan tried to decide how someone like Mel could ever find her sexy. *Really?*

Mel leaned in close and kissed the bridge of her nose. "Yes. You're very sexy, Regan."

Regan felt herself blush to the tips of her toes. "Likewise," she managed.

Mel opened the door and got out of the truck. Sliding a hand into the back pocket of her jeans, she withdrew a battered leather wallet and fished around in it. "Call me, okay?" she said, passing Regan a business card.

Regan took the card without looking at it. "Count on it."

The look Mel gave her—shy, excited, and anxious all at the same time—caused a funny feeling in the pit of Regan's belly. It wasn't a feeling she was used to, though she had felt something similar once before, back in college. The feeling lingered after Mel closed the truck door and walked up to her apartment. It was still there when Regan could no longer follow Mel with her eyes. She drew a deep breath and then exhaled very slowly. She felt shaky and thrilled and scared out of her mind. She knew what that feeling was.

I could fall in love with her. Easily.

Chapter
Four

MEL WOKE UP with a frustrated groan. Her alarm clock was buzzing and her right hand was trapped in her pajama bottoms. She blinked in sleepy confusion, then remembered. *Oh, yeah, I never did finish.*

She slapped the alarm clock into silence and turned her face into her pillow. Right in the middle of the best fucking dream, too. Mel closed her eyes and tried to recall the fading details. Five more minutes and she would've had Regan completely naked.

"Goddamn alarm clock," she complained to the print of Magritte's *La Magie Noire* that hung on the wall. It was the only point of color in an otherwise spare room.

She sat up and swung her legs over the side of her bed, feeling the sleep-warmed skin of her bare torso pebble with gooseflesh in the cool morning air. It was 5:06 a.m. Not too bad. Her date with Regan the night before had thrown off her sleep schedule by a good hour and a half, and she felt it. She always felt it when something disrupted the order in her life.

It was only the inevitability of her morning routine that forced her out of bed. Rummaging in her dresser, she retrieved a variation of the same outfit she wore every morning: a pair of athletic shorts and a snug white sports bra. She got dressed on auto-pilot, and ambled into the room her apartment complex had obviously intended to be the master bedroom, but which she had converted into an exercise room. It wasn't like she'd ever needed a big bedroom, especially when ending dates was easier if they didn't wind up here.

Mel thought about Regan as she lifted weights. She didn't usually think about anything of consequence. Most times, the challenge of lifting, of pushing past her pain, had the pleasant effect of clearing her mind of all thought. Not so this morning. She couldn't get red hair and that shy smile out of her head. *There's no place like 127.0.0.1.* What the hell did that even mean? Mel chuckled out loud and swiped the back of her hand across her sweaty forehead. Never had she thought so hard about a woman's T-shirt.

God, I hope she calls me. The errant, anxious thought stopped her cold for a moment. *I hope she calls me?* What the fuck was she thinking?

After a session on the treadmill, Mel pulled her sports bra off and walked down the hallway towards the bathroom. She paused at her computer and stared at the screensaver, a barely clad actress who shot her a sultry grin, but despite the eye-candy, all she could think about was Regan. When a smile came swift and unbidden to her lips, Mel knew nothing would be the same anymore. She launched her sweaty sports bra into the laundry basket, and decided to deviate from her schedule.

How hard could it be to write a quick e-mail?

She bit her lip and thought hard. *Dear Regan,* she typed, then began a furious backspacing. That sounded weird, saying "dear." Resolved, she typed *Regan...*then sat in silent contemplation for a couple torturous minutes. Finally, she sighed in exasperation. Was this what writer's block felt like?

"Regan," she rehearsed out loud. "I can't stop thinking about you. Between the sex dream and almost falling off the treadmill because I was daydreaming, you're honestly freaking me out."

Mel laughed. She did feel freaked out but really great at the same time. How was that possible? She drummed her fingers on her abdomen. Maybe because she knew something had to give, and Regan was the best reason she'd ever had to change. Inspired by the thought, she typed out a few lines with confident ease before rereading the e-mail and blushing as she looked at her own words.

"What's happening to me?" she whispered and read the short message again. "What are you doing to me, Regan O'Riley?"

She clicked the "Send" button before she lost her nerve, and headed for the shower, trying to remember what she used to think about before she thought of Regan.

Work? She watched the water sluice down her stomach. No, she was glad to have a distraction from that. Sex? She closed her eyes as Regan immediately sprang back to her mind. Her bike? She could almost feel Regan on the seat behind her. Forget it. She was doomed. She felt like a crazy person. If this was what falling for someone was like, she wasn't sure if she was up to it. Yet, she seemed to have little choice in the matter. She was hooked.

Her stomach clenched at the thought. Goddammit, this was scary as hell!

Mel opened her eyes and looked up at the shower massager over her head. She hesitated only a moment and then, with a defeated little grin, reached up and snagged it from its cradle.

"It's either this or be distracted all day," she said aloud, and looked around. Nobody could dispute that logic.

When she came, it was with Regan's name on her lips.

MELANIE RAINES. THAT'S what the business card said. She'd been repeating that name in her head since dropping the cop off at her apartment the night before. *She wants me to call her.* Regan grinned. *She gave me her number and everything!*

Regan grabbed her glasses and hurried down the hall to the bathroom, ready for her whirlwind morning choreography. Bed to shower in 53 seconds. Not bad. Sleeping naked eliminated precious seconds most people would spend stripping off.

Standing beneath the hot jets, she squirted shampoo into the palm of her hand and thought about Mel and their date with a goofy smile on her face. *I never expected things to go so well*, she mused. She wasn't used to feeling an instant connection with another person. It happened so rarely that she knew to take it seriously; the last time had been with Adam in college, and he had been her most loyal friend ever since. That she now seemed to have something real with such a beautiful woman, with someone who made her heart pound every time she looked at her, amazed her.

Melanie Raines. Getting dressed, after she'd towelled dry, she saw herself as she imagined Mel might see her—the way Mel made her feel when she pinned her with those smoky grey eyes. She looked good. Regan smiled at herself in the mirror, tucking her wet hair behind her ears. She suspected that Mel had a lot to do with the radiance that shone from within her, so clearly that even she could see it. *I could definitely get used to feeling like this.*

Intellectually, Regan was aware that she wasn't an unattractive woman. She was short and pleasantly symmetrical, if not classically featured. But she had been self-conscious about the way she looked for as long as she could remember. She pulled on a pair of baggy jeans. *Thank God for a casual office.* The next choice was her T-shirt. *Always an important decision.* Most of hers had humorous, and usually geeky, phrases emblazoned upon them. Regan finally chose one that read "SELECT * FROM *users WHERE clue > 0...0 rows returned.*" It was a favorite.

E-mail was the most important step of her morning routine. Before breakfast, even before putting on her shoes, she had to check in with the world. Regan scanned the names and subjects of her unread messages, impatient to open the most interesting one.

There was an e-mail from Adam, with the subject "Official

plea for a Halo rematch," which Regan bypassed with a smirk. Another message from her father, something about financial planning, which she knew she'd never read and therefore ignored upon sight. She stopped searching when she reached her most recently received e-mail, eyes glued to the name of the sender. Mel Raines.

"No way." Regan's heart began a steady thumping and her cheeks grew warm. "No fucking way." *If she's not careful, I'm going to fall head over heels for her.* She clicked on the e-mail, holding her breath as it opened. *E-mail! She's the perfect woman!*

The note was short and unimaginably sweet. *Regan,* it read, *I haven't stopped thinking about you since you dropped me off last night, and I decided that you might like to know that.* Regan grinned. The note went on, *I also decided that I'd like to tell you so that I can imagine the amazing smile that I know is on your face right about...now.*

"Clever deduction, officer," she murmured. "You're just full of surprises."

For long minutes, she stared at the note, trying to remind herself that she had sworn not to let her expectations spiral out of control. But that was before the e-mail. Regan sighed and rolled her eyes at herself. *Now I'm planning the wedding.*

As much as she didn't want to feel so optimistic, well...there it was. She was optimistic. Regan sighed at her own idealism. *I can't help it if I haven't been burned enough to be scared of the fire.* Such were the hidden perks of crippling shyness and adolescent unpopularity. Regan had a bold thought then, an unfamiliar craving to break free of her reservations and make a connection with another person. *Tonight maybe I'll call Mel, and ask her if she wants to go out.*

The way she felt—the way Melanie Raines made her feel—Regan just might do it. She just might summon the courage to pick up the phone.

Maybe.

AND I LET her go home. Am I crazy? Mel stiffened her lower lip and concentrated on looking surly.

No way was she going to sit through an entire morning briefing grinning like a lovesick kid. Glancing around at the uniformed cops surrounding her, she was satisfied that nobody was paying any particular attention to her or her good mood.

Even when she managed to let a few minutes pass without conjuring up Regan's face, it wasn't long before some inconsequential thing brought those delicate features into focus.

Aside from making her feel a little embarrassed and exposed, convinced that everyone could see the change in her, this distracting train of thought was not as annoying as she would have expected. In fact, it was exciting to have something beyond the monotony of her daily life to visit inside her head.

Even this miserable fucking job couldn't bring her down today, she mused.

As soon as the briefing was over, Mel searched out the duty cop for cruiser keys and her radio, then walked out of the Detroit Police Department's 14th Precinct building into the warm May sunshine.

For a moment she just stood there and looked around at the parking lot, surprised anew by how content she felt. Today everything seemed right. She sent a small rock skittering across the rows of parked cars with a sharp kick of her boot. Would it be totally pathetic to call her tonight? Did she care if it was? She squinted up at the sun, surprised to realize that no, she probably didn't.

Mel reached the patrol car and slipped on her sunglasses. Not yet wanting to leave the fresh air, she leaned back against the hood, arms folded, and allowed herself to enjoy a sweet memory of Regan's passionate kiss from the night before. She knew her happiness was still obvious when Hansen walked toward her with a stupid grin on his face.

"Who are you, Captain Happy, and what have you done with my partner?" he called out and casually tossed a bagel in her direction.

Mel caught her breakfast and nodded her appreciation. "What's that supposed to mean?" she asked. "I'm incapable of smiling?"

"Well, no, you're surely not. But my partner, on the other hand..."

Mel raised an eyebrow at Hansen as she thumbed the keyless entry and opened the driver's side door of the patrol car. Hansen climbed into the passenger seat and stuck his bagel in his mouth so that he could struggle with his seatbelt. Fastening her own with one hand, Mel fought back a smirk at his clumsy maneuvering. When he managed to lock the strap across his waist, he looked at her and chewed.

"Stop looking at me." She started the car, immediately reaching out to flip on their favorite oldies station at a low volume. "It makes me nervous."

She backed out of the narrow parking space and shifted into drive, taking a bite of her bagel before navigating their car out on to the street.

"Let's head down to Washington first," Hansen said.

"Sounds good." Vandals had been targeting businesses in a three-block radius for the past two weeks; they'd learned in roll call that a bakery on Washington had been hit late last night. Another day, more pointless destruction.

Mel remembered the Spice Girls CD and numerous wrong turns and broke into another involuntary smile. After a moment, she realized that Hansen was staring at her again. "What?" she growled, eyes on the road.

"It's the woman, right? Isn't it always a woman?" he answered himself.

This was weird, Mel decided. She could see from his kind brown eyes his desire to have this kind of conversation with her. Maybe it had something to do with Regan, but Mel found that she wanted it, too. Ah, Christ, it was just Hansen, she thought. Three years together now, maybe she could let him see her happy. Maybe she could share a tiny part of herself for a change.

"Yeah, I guess it is," she said.

"I'm glad. The smile looks good on you."

Mel didn't say anything, uncertain of how to respond to his compliment and horrified when she felt her face flush. She was grateful when Hansen turned to look out the front windshield, away from her, and began to munch on his bagel again.

She glanced down at the car's clock as she turned down a narrow side street. 9:27 a.m. Only eight and a half hours to go. It took an effort to hold her happiness in check. God, it was a beautiful day. The thought lasted at least ten minutes before the Friday jinx kicked in and they got their first domestic violence call.

The address was only four blocks away on Detroit's east side. Run-down houses lined both sides of the block, some of which appeared to have been abandoned long ago. Their destination was a small, battered white house on the far corner of the block. An old Ford truck was parked haphazardly in the driveway and the front yard was littered with trash. One light was visible through the front window of the house, but Mel couldn't see anyone moving inside.

"Don't worry, we'll make this quick," Hansen said as they bailed out and scanned the surroundings. The only sound in the air was that of birds chirping.

They walked swiftly up to the house, casting cautious eyes around. Mel dropped her hand to rest against the butt of her Glock, the motion almost unconscious. When they reached the front porch, she and Hansen positioned themselves on either side of the door.

At her nod, Hansen raised his fist and pounded hard on the door. "This is the police!" he shouted. "Open up!"

There was no answer. Quietly, Mel spoke into her shoulder mic, appraising the dispatcher of their situation. "Frank Calleja," she relayed the responses to Hansen in a low voice, "35-year-old Hispanic male, priors for assault with a deadly weapon and domestic violence. Cops have been called to this address twice before." She tossed him a meaningful look. "Let's be careful in there."

Hansen pounded on the door again. "This is the police, Mr. Calleja!"

Mel took a step back and angled her body slightly towards the door, the palm of her hand resting on the handle of her gun. Listening for any sound, she flexed her fingers, tense. When none came, she took another step back and glanced sideways towards the windows. Tattered curtains prevented her from looking inside. Hansen's large fist paused in mid-air as soft footfalls approached from the home's interior. The sound of various locks being disengaged made Mel stiffen with tension. Prepared for the worst, she relaxed slightly when the door swung slowly open to reveal a little blonde girl no more than six years old.

She looked like any of the dozens of little blonde girls Mel had encountered during her three years as a cop. Nose running, hair long and tangled, she looked up at Mel and Hansen with big blue eyes. Tear tracks were visible on her dirty cheeks.

Mel softened her face into a patient smile and spoke quietly to the girl, aware that Hansen was still alert, watching the hallway beyond for signs of her parents. "Hi there," she said. "We're police officers. We're here because we heard that people were fighting and that they need our help. Are your mommy and daddy fighting, honey?"

"Mommy and Frank are having a fight," the girl answered.

Mel made brief eye contact with Hansen, then asked, "Do you think your mommy can come to the door, sweetheart?"

The girl shook her head and fat tears began to roll down her cheeks. "No," she whispered.

From somewhere in the house came a loud slapping sound, and then a muffled male shout. "Fucking bitch! If you don't shut the hell up, I'll kick the shit out of you!" Another scream, and then silence.

"Take the kid to the cruiser," Hansen said. "I'll call for backup."

Mel held out her hand, giving the girl a warm smile when she reached out and took it with sticky fingers. "What's your name, sweetheart?"

"Molly."

"Come on, Molly. You can wait in my car while we talk to Frank, okay?"

Mel walked the trembling child to their cruiser as quickly as she could, tossing frequent glances back over her shoulder at Hansen. Her partner talked into his shoulder mic in a quiet voice, relaying the situation to dispatch, his eyes pinned to the front door.

Mel helped Molly into the backseat, and asked, "Where are Frank and your mommy, honey? What room are they in?"

"The bedroom."

Mel reached out and stroked tangled hair. "That's down the front hallway?"

Molly nodded. "At the end."

"I'll be right back, Molly." She shut the little girl in the car and jogged back up to the porch.

"There's definitely an assault in progress," Hansen said as she climbed the stairs. "A lot of shouting and punching."

"The girl says they're in the bedroom, last room down the hallway."

One hand on his Glock, Hansen stepped inside the house. "Backup's coming. Five minutes, maybe. Let's go."

They walked down the hall, Mel trailing after Hansen, until they reached the last door on the left. Inside, she could hear muffled sobbing and angry whispers.

Hansen knocked hard on the bedroom door. "Sir, ma'am, this is the police. Would you please come out, hands where we can see them?"

The harsh whispering stopped; for a moment they could hear continued sobbing, but then even that was silenced with a choked cry. Nobody came to the door.

Hansen knocked again. "We've received a complaint about a domestic disturbance," he yelled. "Why don't you two come out here and we can talk about this, sort it out?" He paused a moment, his head tilted towards the door. "How about that?"

There was still no response.

Mel flicked her eyes down the hallway, back towards the open front door. Their backup had yet to arrive.

Hansen knocked again, harder this time. "Listen, you're either going to come out here and talk to us, or we're coming in there and then we can all talk back at the precinct. How do you want to handle this situation?"

For a moment there was silence, and then a woman called out, "Please—" before being cut off with a sharp slap.

Mel exhaled through her nostrils, tensing her jaw. She kept her hand firmly on the handle of her gun, looking up at Hansen.

He gave her a nod and put his hand on the doorknob. "We're opening the door," he warned. "We want your hands where we can see them."

Mel stepped to the side of the door and Hansen pushed it open and immediately moved to the side, craning his head to try and see inside the bedroom. From her vantage point, Mel couldn't see if anyone was there.

"Come on, man," Hansen called out. "All you've got to do is come out here and talk to us. It doesn't have to be this way."

He had barely finished his sentence when a large dark-haired man burst out of the bedroom door, slammed into Hansen and took a few running steps down the hallway before turning to face them. A woman screamed from the bedroom and at the same time Mel saw the gun in the man's hand. She was already pulling her Glock from her holster when he surged forward, his weapon raised.

Loud gunfire filled the air and Mel felt a stinging pain on her face. She hit the floor, rolled, and came up on her knee. Vaguely aware of Hansen on the floor near her, she raised her weapon and took a single shot at their assailant.

The man's shoulder jerked backwards and he reflexively dropped his weapon. Mel was on her feet and moving as the gun clattered to the floorboards. She kicked the weapon away and forced the wounded man to the floor.

"Fucking bitch cop, you shot me!" He writhed, clutching his injured shoulder.

"Face down!" Mel shouted at the snarling man. "It's over, pal. Put your hands where I can see them!"

After cuffing his wrists, she retrieved his handgun and removed the clip, ejecting the unfired rounds and pocketing the ammo.

"Hey, Hansen." She got to her feet, glancing around for her partner. "You wanna Miranda this asshole?"

She stopped speaking, almost stopped breathing. Hansen was still on the floor. Staring up at the ceiling, he was making wet, gasping noises that turned her stomach. She stumbled over to him and dropped to her knees next to his body.

"Oh, Jesus, Hansen," she whispered.

Blood flowed freely from a large hole in his neck and he stared up at her with frightened brown eyes. Mel pressed one hand to the gaping wound and activated her shoulder mic with the other, reporting an officer and suspect down and requesting ambulances.

From the bedroom doorway, a sobbing blonde woman stared at her. Blood streamed from a cut on her forehead, and her mouth was slack from shock.

"Go sit down," Mel told her. "There's help coming." She placed her free hand against the one that was already on Hansen's neck, desperate to hold his life inside. "Hold on, Hansen," she murmured, hearing sirens. "You're going to be fine. They're coming right now."

Chapter
Five

REGAN WAS CURLED up in her favorite chair in her favorite position, feet dangling over one arm and back propped against the other. *The Princess Bride* played on her television, perfect entertainment for the lonely night to come. She had just popped another gummy bear in her mouth, eyes fixed on Inigo's sword fight with the man in black, when the doorbell rang. It was 6:30 p.m.

Damn it. I told Adam I wasn't in the mood for video games tonight. She rose from her chair and walked to the door. *God, I wish it were Mel.*

She looked out the peephole and gasped at the sight of her visitor. Mel was standing on the front porch, eyes downcast. Heart pounding, Regan unlocked the door and pulled it open. Mel didn't seem like the type to just show up unannounced. And she had company. A dark-featured man stood next to her, looking awkward.

"Regan, hey." Mel looked up. A bright white bandage covered her cheek, and her grey eyes were haunted, accented by dark circles that added years to her face. She radiated pain.

"Mel. What happened?"

"Ms. O'Riley?" The man beside Mel spoke. "I'm Detective Morales. Officer Raines was involved in a shooting earlier today."

Regan turned to Mel with frantic eyes. She looked her up and down, scanning a plain white T-shirt and dark navy sweatpants emblazoned with a Detroit Police Department logo. "Mel, are you all right?" She stepped forward before Mel could answer, reaching out to take her cold hands in her own.

Mel's lips twitched. "I'm okay. Look, I'm sorry to barge in on you in the middle of Friday night."

Regan glanced over at Morales, then slid her right hand up the back of Mel's arm to grip her above the elbow. "It's no big deal. I was just watching a movie. I'm glad you came. Are you sure you're all right?"

Morales cleared his throat, drawing Regan's attention to his grave face. "She disabled the shooter after her partner was wounded by gunfire. She did real good, and everyone got out alive."

"For the moment," Mel muttered darkly.

Impulsively, Regan pulled her into a tight hug. Mel was tense in her arms for a moment before she melted into the embrace. "How badly wounded?" Regan whispered into Mel's ear.

Mel shook her head, tickling Regan's cheek with her hair. "Pretty bad. They're worried about spinal cord damage."

Regan tightened her arms around Mel. "Thank you for bringing her," she told Detective Morales.

Morales nodded. "Hey, Raines, we'll call if we hear anything more tonight."

As he walked away, Regan tugged gently on Mel's hand and didn't release it until they were in her sitting room, standing next to the couch. She let go then only because she was not certain the contact was appreciated; as far as she was concerned, she never wanted to let go of Mel again. *She could have died.* Regan watched Mel lift her hands to her face and press the heels of her palms against her eyes. *She shot someone tonight. Someone shot at her. I can't even begin to understand that kind of bad day at work.*

As if she were in a daze, Mel sat. "I'm sorry to bother you with this."

"You know you're not bothering me." Regan reached out and let her hand hover in the air over Mel's bandaged cheek. She blinked stinging tears from her vision; her fingers were a pale blur pushing dark hair out of Mel's face. "I'm glad you came here. I mean it. You shouldn't be alone after something..."

"I didn't want to be alone." Mel gave a humorless smile. "What a prize, right?" She snorted in self-deprecation, and dropped her face into her hands. "Aren't you so lucky that I asked you to dance?"

Regan felt her lower lip quiver in frustration. "That's how I've been feeling, if you want me to be honest. Lucky."

Mel raised her eyes, the disbelief frozen on her face almost comical in its magnitude. Regan was caught somewhere between laughing and crying at that look, unsure of whether to grab Mel tight or smack some sense into her. When she stood abruptly, Regan sprang up beside her, fearing a skittish retreat even though her visitor had nowhere to go without a car.

"I'm sorry," Mel mumbled. "I really shouldn't have come

here. I don't know why I..."

Regan gripped Mel's upper arm with her free hand. "Why shouldn't you have come here? I want you here."

"I just shouldn't do this to you." Mel stared at her, blinking rapidly. "We've only had one real date."

Regan didn't want to hear it. She stopped Mel's lips with a finger. "Don't say it." She took a step closer and caught Mel's fingers in hers, the contact light and non-threatening. "I'm here, Mel. Why don't you let me be here for you?"

Mel's full lower lip began to tremble. "I just—" She took a deep breath, and the words spilled out of her in a rush. "I just wanted—God, I don't know...I wanted to be in your life, somehow. But you don't need me. Jesus, you don't want me. Please, trust me on that."

Regan paused, shocked at the candor of Mel's words. *She wants me in her life?* Her mouth hung open, and she had to shake her head to move past the moment. "You don't know what I want. Or what I need."

Mel studied her face, and Regan hoped that she understood what she was saying. "I'm so fucked up. God, I'm just starting to realize how fucked up I really am. And I don't need to drag you down with me." Mel squeezed Regan's hand in hers. "You deserve so much, and I don't know if I can—"

"Stop." Regan planted her other hand on Mel's upper chest. "It's too late. I'm involved. There's nothing you can do about that."

Mel stared at her for a long time, her frank gaze making Regan squirm. Eventually a shy smile transformed her weary features and Regan's control snapped. She leaned into Mel fast and without thought, wrapping her arms around Mel's lean body in a hard hug. Mel barely hesitated before returning the embrace, burrowing her nose into the soft skin of Regan's neck. For a moment they stood, simply breathing. Neither said a word.

Mel broke the silence. "Nothing I can do about it, huh?" Warm breath tickled Regan's throat.

"Nope. Nothing."

Regan smiled against Mel's hair, and then, only when it seemed absolutely necessary, she pulled away from their hug. "Do you want to talk about it?" she asked in a low voice.

Mel tugged at the collar of her T-shirt, a grimace on her face. "No, I really don't."

"Then we won't. Why don't you take a shower and I'll get you something to change into?"

Mel's relief was telegraphed across her face. "A shower would be great."

Regan led her down the hallway to the bathroom. "I'll get you a towel," she said, flicking on the lights and stepping forward to retrieve a bath towel from the small closet next to the shower.

She turned back around to find Mel pulling off her T-shirt. In another motion, she discarded her bra. Regan stood, towel forgotten in her hands. *She's not shy, is she? In fact, I think she's the opposite of shy.* Hastily, she averted her eyes. *Just what exactly is the opposite of shy, anyway? Anti-shy?*

Mel cleared her throat, and Regan thrust the towel out blindly. "I'll leave something for you to change into right outside the door." Keeping her eyes to the floor, she left the room, closing the door behind her.

Jesus God, I don't care what anyone thinks, I'm a saint for keeping my eyes down.

AFTER A QUICK search in her bedroom, Regan had a T-shirt and a pair of boxer shorts for Mel. The shower was running when she dropped them outside the bathroom door. Unsure of what to do next, she groaned when she finally realized what she was wearing: a faded Fraggles T-shirt, worn thin with age and love.

"I should change," she whispered.

As if on cue, the shower stopped. *Well, I guess the damage is already done.*

"Want a beer?" Regan shouted at the bathroom door.

She heard the curtain drawn back and Mel answered, "Yeah, sure."

Resigned to her fashion statement, Regan went to the kitchen for two beers. She returned to the sitting room and waited for Mel, staring at the bottles sweating on the coffee table. *So, what now?* She folded her hands over her stomach, a little queasy with nerves. *This is so definitely not a situation for a social retard.*

When Mel walked into the room minutes later, she was plucking at the boxer shorts she wore. "I like these. I just might have to steal them." Her voice was light, almost playful.

"You should," Regan said, studying the expanse of bare legs before she could stop herself. *Great. Sensitive.* Embarrassed at her lapse, she forced her eyes to Mel's face.

"They look much better on you than they do on me."

"I doubt it." Mel dropped onto the couch beside Regan, and looked her up and down. "Though I gotta tell you, the Fraggles shirt is fucking *hot*."

She couldn't have stopped the blush if she'd tried. "Shaddup."

Chuckling, Mel reached out to touch the neck of one of the bottles of alcohol. "Is this for me?"

"If you want it."

"Thanks." Mel took a long, slow swallow, and sighed heavily. "I don't usually drink, but I think I'll make an exception tonight."

Regan took a small sip and set her own bottle down on the table. "Any particular reason why? That you don't drink, I mean?"

Mel's grey eyes went steely. "My father's an alcoholic. It normally doesn't appeal to me."

The admission was nearly emotionless, but Regan could see Mel searching for a reaction. Sensing she wasn't looking for sympathy, Regan simply nodded her head. "Understandable."

After a few silent moments, Mel sniffed loudly and fixed Regan with a plaintive stare. "I just keep thinking, why now? You know? Things were just starting to be different, and then this—"

"What was different?"

"Hansen and me. We were just starting to talk. Really talk, I mean. I felt like we were working towards something more. I don't know."

Regan filled in the blanks. "You guys aren't close?"

Mel wrapped her arms around her knees, still holding her beer. "We never had been. Until recently. I told him about you."

She told him about me? "You did?"

"Yeah. And the bastard was just starting to give me all this sage wisdom about women, and now..." She left her thought unfinished.

Sage wisdom? Rather than ask, she took Mel's hand and played with long tan fingers. "Things can still be different. How serious is it?"

Mel cast a faraway look at the wall. "They're not sure yet." She took another long pull of her beer, nearly emptying the bottle. "That...fucking...*prick*. That fucking *asshole* shot Hansen in the goddamned *throat*, and he just lay there bleeding...he was awake, but he just kept *bleeding*, and I had my hands over his throat..." She choked on a sudden sob, and turned her face away. "I don't know what any of us can take from this. I don't know what Annie Hansen will take from this if he—God, if Hansen fucking *dies*—"

"He's not going to die." *You could have died, and I've only just found you.* Regan took Mel into her arms, pulling her close and squeezing her for all she was worth. "I'm so goddamn glad you're okay."

Mel's shoulders shook beneath Regan's hands, and she began to weep in earnest, as if something had broken inside of her and wave after wave of carefully repressed feeling and anxiety was being violently unleashed. The outpouring of raw emotion overwhelmed Regan, and she held on to Mel, almost scared to let go. *How can I care about her so much so soon?* She kissed Mel's forehead again, feeling her sobs begin to abate.

Mel seemed content to remain in Regan's embrace and made no move to leave. In time, after her breathing had stilled, she spoke again in a muffled voice. "You make me feel so safe." A long pause. "No one has ever made me feel like that before. God. And I thought being shot at was scary."

The nervous honesty of her words touched Regan. Sensing the admission had not been easy to make, she said, "I'm not scary."

Mel withdrew slowly from the embrace and sat up, turning red-rimmed eyes to her. "But feeling this way is."

"You're scared to feel safe?"

"I'm scared of getting used to it, I guess. Of needing it." Mel picked at the fingernails of one hand with the other. "I'm not sure if I can go back to where I was before, already, and I don't know—"

"Hey," Regan interrupted. "Stop worrying so much about going back. I'm not going anywhere. You're stuck with me."

"Even if I'm fucked-up beyond your wildest dreams?"

Regan managed a laugh at that. "You have no idea how wild my dreams are, Mel."

"Not *that* kind of wild." Mel's attempt at a smile quickly faded.

"I'm serious," Regan said. "We're friends. Don't worry about all the rest of it right now; that'll work itself out. We're friends, for as long as you want it."

Mel studied Regan with eyes made silver from the tears she'd shed. "Thank you. For everything. I'm so glad you were home."

"Me, too," Regan whispered.

"I just didn't know what to do when Morales asked where he should drive me. I didn't want to go home." Grey eyes pinned Regan with an intense gaze. "All I wanted was to be with you."

"For the record, all I wanted tonight was to be with you, too."

Mel lit up at her admission and, after a beat, leaned forward to press a chaste kiss on Regan's lips. The kiss was friendly but brief, merely a moment of reconnection amidst the turbulence of the evening. It calmed Regan in a way that defied explanation.

"I'm exhausted." Mel leaned back against the arm of the couch. "Too exhausted to think any more, about anything."

"Do you want to go to bed?" The instant the question left her mouth, Regan blushed at the unintended suggestion in her words. "I mean, uh—"

With sparkling eyes, Mel leaned forward and captured Regan's mouth in a slow kiss. Regan let out a desperate moan into the joining of their mouths, closing her eyes in utter relief. *She could have died tonight.* She couldn't stop thinking it, even as she stroked Mel's tongue with her own and tried to memorize the sweet flavor of her mouth. *But she didn't. She's all right, and she's right here.*

Regan brought her hands up to grip Mel's biceps. Her only desire was to affirm the solid presence of Mel beside her, and so the kiss wasn't about passion. It was about friendship and trust, and deep longing, and it left Regan staggered.

"Wow," she said when Mel pulled away.

"Yeah. Wow." Mel's lips twitched into a little smile. "After a kiss like that, I suppose this is the part where I tell you that maybe I should go. Except it's kind of late, I don't have my bike, and I really, really don't want to leave."

Regan ignored the nervous fluttering in her stomach. "Stay the night. Please."

Mel gave her a steady look. "I don't think I could—"

"I want to hold you tonight. Just sleep here with me tonight, okay?" Regan stood and pulled Mel to her feet. "Not that I don't *want* to drag you into bed, you understand, for something other than sleeping. But that's not a decision for tonight." She led them to her bedroom.

"I agree. Despite my almost...crippling interest," Mel snaked an arm around Regan's waist, and turned to look her up and down. "And I'm pretty sure I shouldn't be having sexual thoughts about women in Fraggles T-shirts, anyway."

Regan nudged Mel with her shoulder, throwing her slightly off-balance. "Get used to it, sweetheart. I love this thing, and it's not going anywhere."

"And since I'm not, either..."

Regan tried to hide her smile at the tentative comment as she led Mel into the master bathroom. "Exactly."

Regan opened up her bathroom closet and found an extra toothbrush, still boxed, to give to Mel. Mel took it with a delighted smile.

"I've never had a toothbrush at someone's place before."

"Ah," Regan said. "I'm your first?"

Mel tipped her head. "I'm starting to think in more ways than one."

Just when I think I'm over the blushing. Regan watched Mel in the bathroom mirror, brushing her teeth in silence, then turned to the sink and busied her own toothbrush. *How someone can make me so comfortable and so thrilled at the same time is beyond me.*

They stood next to one another and performed a bathroom routine that was surreal in its familiarity. It felt like they had been doing the same thing together for years. Regan caught Mel's eyes in the mirror more than once, and they shared pleased looks with one another.

Regan escaped to her bedroom while Mel was finishing up in the bathroom. Quickly, she stripped off her jeans and pulled on a pair of comfortable boxer shorts before climbing into bed. Mel was going to sleep in her bed. This was the last way she'd pictured ending the evening when she'd settled down to watch *The Princess Bride.*

The bathroom door opened and Mel flipped off the light as she exited. She stood next to the bed for a moment and fiddled nervously with the hem of her boxer shorts, as if she wasn't certain what to do or say, then she crawled in beside Regan.

"It's been a while since I slept in the same bed as somebody," Regan said to break the tension.

Mel gave her a wary sidelong glance. "Me, too."

Regan lifted an interested eyebrow. "You mean—"

"Yeah, yeah." Mel looked embarrassed. "I'm something of a cad. I'm not exactly proud of it."

Regan broke into a careful smile. "So we both admit we're a little awkward with this sort of thing?"

"Grudgingly. I'll grudgingly admit it."

Regan tugged on her upper lip in an effort to stave off the full-blown grin that threatened to take over her mouth. Keeping her voice even, she said, "Well, we're both intelligent, functional adults, right?"

"Define functional."

"You're functional enough."

"I was wondering about you."

"Shaddup." Her body began to relax at the return of the banter that just seemed to happen between them. "I'm just saying, I'm sure we can figure this out."

"Sleeping together?" Mel smirked. "I'm sure you're right."

Regan stretched out her arm in invitation. "So c'mere."

Mel moved into Regan's embrace after only the briefest hesitation. She rested her head on Regan's shoulder and slid an awkward arm across her stomach. Overwhelmed, Regan planted an impulsive kiss on Mel's forehead, and for a moment Mel just lay there, tense. Then she seemed to melt into Regan's arms, nuzzling her face into Regan's neck with a contented sigh. The arm across Regan's belly relaxed and gentle fingers began tracing patterns over her side. Seconds later, Mel eased a leg over one of Regan's.

"Oh, my God." Mel's voice was muffled against Regan's neck. "I can't believe how good this feels."

Neither can I. Regan tightened her arms around Mel and kissed her hair. "Something else to add to the list of stuff that feels good in bed."

Mel snorted and gave her an indulgent squeeze. "Goofball. Say good night, Regan."

"Good night, Regan."

Chapter
Six

MEL TORE INTO wakefulness with a startled gasp, her body tense and frozen on the bed. She kept her eyes closed as the last tendrils of the nightmare she couldn't remember drifted away on her shaky exhalation. She was slowly aware of three things — she was not in her own bed, she was not wearing her own clothes, and she was definitely not alone.

In fact, she seemed to be a pillow. She shifted slightly, eliciting a sleepy groan from the body that pinned her to the mattress.

Jesus Christ. Hansen. Mel's eyes flew open and she nearly sat up, but was stopped by the heavy weight lying across her chest. It all came back to her. Hansen, lying in a pool of his own blood. Morales's dark eyes and sympathetic gaze. Ruined flesh and beige-ugly hospital hallways. And Regan — relaxing into Regan's embrace and feeling as if nothing could hurt her there.

Mel looked down at the top of Regan's head. Red hair tickled her chin, and the comforting weight of Regan's arm was tucked under her breasts. Mel blinked, feeling a slight burning ache in her eyes from the crying she had done. A wave of shame rolled over her when she remembered breaking down in Regan's arms.

She thought she'd given up crying. Hadn't her father broken her of that habit when she was nine?

"Crying is for babies. Are you a baby, Laney?"

She cringed in the closet where she sat huddled with her favorite stuffed dog. Its fur was damp with her tears. Her father was a giant looming shadow above her, angry eyes and clenched fists. She could smell the alcohol on his breath.

"I..." She was scared of him even then, and it hadn't been a year since her mother died. "I miss mommy."

He left a hand-shaped bruise on her upper arm when he yanked her to her feet. The second blow caught her across the face and sent her back to the floor in agony.

She had made a promise that night that she would never cry again. Ever. And she had kept that promise until yesterday evening, only ever shedding a few hastily concealed tears.

The fact that somehow Regan had coaxed sixteen years of carefully repressed emotion to the surface with a hug and a few words left Mel feeling awed and frightened. Regan, she decided, was very powerful.

The powerful one emitted a sleepy mumble and shifted to bring a hand up to cup Mel's breast through her T-shirt. Mel moved her own hand, finding the soft skin of Regan's lower back where her T-shirt had ridden up in her sleep, and stroked her with gentle fingers.

Regan moaned. The sound was deep and low, and Mel thought it must be the product of a particularly erotic dream. Mel squeezed Regan tighter against her side, and surrendered herself for a moment to dreamy possibility. She could really fall in love with this woman. In fact, it had already started. She felt her nipple tighten under the heavy weight of Regan's hand and gasped in a combination of pleasure and dismay. What the hell was wrong with her? What kind of screwed-up, sex-obsessed freak got turned on at a time like this?

She turned her mind to Hansen. Would he even walk again? He was all she liked about her job; even he might not be enough to keep her on the force, and if he wasn't there, she didn't know what she would do. Attempting the first relationship of her life amidst all of this turmoil didn't seem ideal. However, it also didn't seem like a choice.

As terrifying as it was, trying to be with Regan was the only option that appealed to her. *I'm just really scared I'll fuck this up. God, I hope I don't fuck this up.*

She shifted beneath Regan, trying to dislodge herself. Regan barely moved, except to whimper and flex her hand against Mel's breast, making it even harder to concentrate on her escape. Mel cleared her throat, willing Regan to wake before she was driven completely crazy. A moment later green eyes opened and blinked up at her in sleepy confusion.

"For a minute there I was wondering why my bed was moving," Regan mumbled, raising the corner of her mouth in a small smile.

"Sorry," Mel lied. "Leg cramp. I didn't mean to wake you."

"S'all right." Regan settled her head back on Mel's shoulder, then stiffened slightly, staring awkwardly at her own hand, still cradling Mel's breast. "Well, this ranks right up there on my most mortifying moments list." She moved as if to withdraw the offending hand, but Mel caught her and pressed it down again.

Mel gave her a beatific smile. "Did you hear me complain?"

It wasn't flirtatious, it wasn't a come-on; it was simply permission to be comfortable. They lay silently for a moment, still curled into their nocturnal embrace. Regan stroked her thumb along the swell of Mel's breast, reaching up to brush across her still hard nipple. Mel bit back a gasp, and Regan glanced up at her with curious green eyes. She flattened her palm against Mel's breast, soothing, then removed her hand and rolled over onto her back.

"Did you sleep well?" she asked.

"Very well." Mel leaned forward and pressed a soft kiss to Regan's temple. "Thank you."

"You're very welcome." Regan stretched her arms above her head then gave Mel a serious look. "Checked your voice mail yet?"

"Lieutenant Jackson called around five-thirty this morning." At Regan's surprised look, she smiled. "I took it in the other room. I didn't want to wake you up."

"How is your partner?"

"Out of surgery. Stable. They'll be able to tell us more about possible spinal cord injury later today when he wakes up."

Regan shuddered a little. "I guess we just wait and see."

Mel closed her eyes and nodded, a tiny smile tugging at the corner of her mouth. It was then she realized that she had no idea how to behave. This was the first morning-after where her first thought hadn't been about walking out of the woman's life. The trouble was that she didn't know how to stay in Regan's life, or even where her own life was going. Her stomach twisted in knots when she thought of what she had to do today, and how she didn't know what to do tomorrow.

"I've got to go be interviewed again by Internal Affairs at the precinct this morning," she said. "Maybe do a walk-through. I'm doing that before I go see Hansen."

Regan nodded, propping herself up on her elbow. "Is there anything I can do?"

"No. Just...be my friend."

Regan gave her a sober nod. "Done." She caught Mel's hand and dropped a soft kiss across the knuckles. "What happens now with work?"

Mel shrugged, shifting further onto her back to stare at the ceiling. "Mandatory three-day suspension of duty. Pending a psych evaluation and an official investigation of the incident, some desk job. After I'm approved by the department psychiatrist, back to street duty." Her voice was hollow and her recitation of regulation was dispassionate. "No matter what happens, I doubt Hansen will be back."

"Are you worried about that—about what's going to happen at work?"

Mel bit her lip, struggling with how to answer that. Maybe the truth? "I hate my job, and the last thing I want is a new partner." Embarrassed, she cast her eyes up at the ceiling. "I don't know what I want right now. All I want is Hansen better."

Regan blinked at the confession. "How long have you hated it?"

"A while."

Regan touched Mel's arm. "This wasn't your fault, you know."

Mel blinked back the tears that stung her eyes. "Yeah." She wished she could believe that. Maybe if she'd taken the other side of the bedroom door. She was usually on the left, so why did she take the other side? Or maybe if she'd pulled her gun a little faster. Or if she didn't spend so much time hating her job.

She slipped out from beneath the covers. "Hey, I should probably get going. It's going to be a really long day."

Regan sat up and gathered the thick comforter to her chest. "You gonna be okay?" she asked.

She looked completely irresistible and Mel wanted nothing more than to stay in bed with her rather than face the real world. Crawling over the bed, she gathered Regan in a tight hug. *Remember that she really cares about you. Remember how amazing that is.* "I'll be fine." Planting a sweet kiss on her forehead, she whispered, "Thank you. For everything."

MEL FOUND ANNIE Hansen sitting on an ugly mauve-colored couch outside of the hospital cafeteria. She had her purse in her lap, hands splayed out on top of the black leather. An older white-haired woman sat beside her, a wrinkled hand resting on Annie's.

Mel approached with a timid smile. "Mrs. Hansen?"

Her partner's wife turned at the sound of her voice, and directed an amused look up at Mel as if they were already friends. "It's Annie, please. Mrs. Hansen makes me feel like an old schoolteacher."

"Yes, ma'am." Mel tried not to show her surprise at the warmth of this greeting.

"Ma'am, even!" Annie interrupted her, sharing a chuckle with the older woman. "That's not much better."

Mel hooked her thumbs into the pockets of her jeans, shooting the two older women an apologetic smile. "Sorry about that. Annie."

Annie turned to the white-haired woman beside her. "Mom, this is Peter's partner, Mel Raines. She's the one who went on the call with him and who took care of him until the paramedics arrived." Annie gave Mel a grateful smile. "Mel, this is my mother, Margaret James."

"It's very nice to meet you, ma'am," Mel said. "I wish it was under better circumstances."

The white-haired woman gave her a kind nod. "Officer Raines, I can't thank you enough for what you've done for our family. Peter's a wonderful man, and I'm very glad you're here for him."

Mel swallowed, nodding. Her face burned hot at what felt like very undeserved praise. "Me, too." She directed a cautious look at Annie. "I heard he did well in surgery."

Annie beamed at her. She looked better than she had when Mel saw her briefly the night before. Her cheeks had regained some of their color, and though her eyes were still watery red, they sparkled with renewed life. "He did. The bullet didn't hit his spinal column, and there's no paralysis."

Mel fought back her emotion. "Good."

"He was awake for a little while this morning. He wasn't very coherent, but he managed a few words to me."

Looking at the obvious love in Annie Hansen's eyes, Mel remembered Hansen's words about his wife. *And she knows just what I need...to make me forget, to remind me of the good things.* Mel felt lucky to be in the presence of something like that; it gave her hope for her own life.

"He asked after you," Annie said. "He was worried about you, couldn't remember what had happened exactly."

Mel blinked back the tears that stung her eyes. "Will I be able to see him today?"

"He's sleeping right now, but I know that you're one of the first people he wants to see when he wakes up." She leaned forward, reaching out to take Mel's hand. "Maybe later this evening? Do you want me to call you when he comes around?"

Mel gave her a vigorous nod. "Please." She cast nervous eyes around, suddenly uncertain. There had to be something else she could do to help, other than hanging out at the hospital. She remembered Hansen's weekend plans. "Hans—" Mel stopped, shooting Annie an apologetic look. "Peter was going to refinish your deck this weekend, wasn't he?"

Annie's face threatened to fall, but she held it together. "Yes."

"Would you mind if I did that for him today?" At Annie's look of surprise, Mel explained, "I don't really have anything planned for today, and I don't feel like going home right now. I'd really like..."

Annie reached out and clasped Mel's hands in her own. "I understand, and I know Peter would really appreciate it, just like I would." She lowered her voice to a playful whisper. "He's been dreading that project for weeks."

Mel chuckled. "I could tell."

"Well, I was going to stop by home, anyway, to get some of Peter's things for him. I can give you a ride, or you can follow me. "

"I brought my bike. I'll just follow you."

Annie lifted her purse strap over her shoulder then stepped forward and slid an arm around Mel's waist. "I see why he cares so much for you," she whispered into Mel's ear. She squeezed her once more, then released her, turning again to help her mother to her feet.

Astonished, Mel followed them out of the hospital in a strangely pleasant haze. Hansen cared for her? She looked back over her shoulder, then up at the ceiling at where she imagined Hansen slept somewhere above them. Maybe it was time she let him know she cared for him, too.

ADAM ARRIVED ON Regan's porch at five o'clock sharp, carrying a six-pack of Mountain Dew under his arm. He gave Regan a broad grin when she answered the door.

"Ready for a little Halo action?" he asked.

Regan groaned. *I forgot all about the pre-work week ritual video-gaming tournament.* She wrinkled her nose, stepping aside to let him into her house. "Not really."

Adam gaped at her as she closed the door behind him. "For real?"

"Unloading countless rounds of ammo into digital enemies doesn't hold its normal appeal at the moment."

Adam looked at her blankly for a moment. "Oh, yeah." He winced. "Mel, huh?"

Regan gave him a pained smile. "Yeah. Mel."

Adam followed her into the living room, dropping his six-pack on the coffee table and collapsing onto his favorite spot on her couch. "Wow. I didn't even think about it like that. Halo, I mean."

Regan twisted her lips into a tight smile, dropping into her favorite chair and drawing her legs up beneath her. "Trust me, I never thought about it like that, either. Wanton video game violence has kinda lost its charm for the time being, now that I've gotten a taste of the real thing."

Adam leaned forward, elbows on his knees, and gave her a steady look. "So how are you doing with that?"

Regan tugged at a lock of her hair. "I wish I knew that her partner's okay. She's pretty worried about him."

"That answers my next question. I wondered if you'd heard anything."

Regan shook her head. She'd told Adam everything over instant messenger after Mel left that morning, but hadn't heard from her since. Never had hours felt more like days. "Not yet."

"Why not call her?" Adam snagged a can from his six-pack, cracking it open and taking a long swallow.

Regan picked at the knee of her blue jeans with nervous fingers. "I hate the phone." Adam gave her a pointed look that made her hackles rise. "She's going through a lot right now. She's never been in a relationship before, or had someone asking after her like that. I don't want to push her. I'm not very smooth with stuff like this in general. I'm afraid I'll sound like a moron."

Adam laughed at her outburst. "Regan, you are *anything* but a moron."

"You know what I mean—a social moron."

Adam laced his hands behind his head, and leaned back against the couch. He studied her so intensely that Regan squirmed beneath his gaze. "She likes you, right?"

You know that I'm attracted to you, right? Mel's words rang through her head. Her own internal voice followed. *You know that she wouldn't have let you see her cry if there wasn't something there, right? You feel it. She feels it, too.*

"Yes," she mumbled.

"So, stop worrying about how you'll sound, then, and recognize that if it's going to work, it's not something that can be undone by a phone call." He gave her a meaningful look. "Not by a phone call, not by stuttering, and certainly not by blushing."

"I know," she whispered. *I'm trying to remember that.*

"So call her," he concluded. "Let her know that you're here for her. And that you haven't been scared away yet."

Regan stared up at the ceiling, studying the subtle texture of the paint that covered it. "Do you think I should be scared away?"

"Because you nearly lost her just as you found her?" Adam's question was quiet and sympathetic, but the words sent a chill through Regan's body. When she didn't answer, he said, "I know that you don't do this stuff often—dating stuff. You know.

Relationships. And this sounds pretty heavy."

Regan managed a tremulous laugh. *That's an understatement.* "Do you think I'm making a mistake?"

"Not if it's the real thing."

"I don't think it's a mistake." The tears she had been fighting spilled over onto her cheeks. *Jesus, now I'm crying in front of Adam. This falling in love stuff is crazy.*

A big hand settled on her knee. Adam looked anxious about offering the comfort; it wasn't the way they normally related. "Then I'm very happy for you," he said. "You deserve someone who can appreciate you in all your geeky glory."

Regan laughed, happy for the levity. "Truer words, my friend..."

"What?" Adam asked. "The geeky part?"

Regan shoved Adam's hand off her knee. "The 'glorious' part."

"*Glory*," he said. "Geeky glory."

"Either way, you give really good advice. For a straight guy and everything."

"I know." He looked over at her television, gazed longingly at her various video game consoles, then turned back to her. "So..."

I guess he deserves something. Regan thought for a moment, then gave her friend an evil grin. "Tony Hawk?" she asked. Skateboarding was safe. *The fact that I can kick his ass is just the icing on the cake.*

Adam leaned back on the couch, stretching his arms and giving her a shit-eating grin. "Only because you've had a rough weekend."

MEL WAS BACK at the hospital by seven o'clock that evening. Her arms and face were sunburned and her muscles ached; the smell of varnish lingered in her nostrils and left her a little light-headed. She was flush with the satisfaction that comes from a day of hard work, and ready to talk to Hansen for the first time since she held him on the floor of that horrible, broken-down house. There were a fair number of people sitting in the waiting room with her, some with plain expressions of anxiety or sadness on their faces, others with their noses in books and magazines. Mel sat ramrod straight in her chair, impatient and anxious at the same time.

When Annie finally returned from Hansen's room, she looked weary-happy. "Peter would like very much to see you now. It's room 813."

Mel stood and ran a nervous hand through her hair. "He's up to this?"

Annie put a reassuring hand on her arm. "He's weak, but he knows you're coming and he wants to see you."

Mel strode through the hallways to Hansen's room with confidence, her head held high. It was a trick she'd learned as a kid; when you're at your most uncertain, face the world as if nothing can shake you. Showing vulnerability can be a costly mistake. That was a lesson her father had taught her. He'd taught her a lot of things, some more painful than others. If only he'd taught her how to deal with the way almost losing Hansen was making her feel.

When she found the right room, she paused to take a deep, calming breath, then entered quietly. Hansen looked like shit. She hated thinking it, but it was the truth. He lay, startlingly weak and pale, in the center of a wide hospital bed, tubes and monitors attached to various parts of his body. A sterile-looking neck brace immobilized his head, a large bandage protruding from beneath it. What she could see of the bandage was bright white, a stark contrast from the red gore she still saw when she looked at his neck. Her stomach churned as she remembered clamping her hands over that very same spot just a day ago.

A sound from the deathly still form on the bed made her jump. It sounded like a hello.

"Hey, partner." She approached the bed to look down into foggy brown eyes. Hansen blinked and focused on her face, giving her a slow smile as she dropped into the visitor's chair. "Nice place you got here. How you doing?"

"Hanging...in there." His eyes sought out her own bandage, modest against her cheek. "You? Were you hit?"

"It's nothing."

"Thank God," he breathed. An ugly purple bruise covered his temple, and his upper lip was scabbed over with dried blood.

Mel gave him a careful smile and tried not to gaze too long at his injuries. "I'm glad to see you awake. You had me worried there for a little while."

"I've got it...under control. Annie said you refinished...our deck today?" He spoke slowly, deliberately. His breathing was labored and his voice rough.

Mel gave him an embarrassed nod. "Seemed like the least I could do. I think it turned out pretty well. You've got a beautiful house."

Today had been the first time she'd seen it, and the thought shamed her. For all the times he'd invited her to dinner, she'd always had an excuse not to go. It took him nearly dying to get her there. Mel looked down at her feet before meeting his eyes again.

"Annie's been after me...to patch up the roof. Guess I'll have to...trip and break my ankle or — "

"Don't," Mel whispered.

Hansen managed a quiet chuckle. "Thought...you had a...hot date this weekend."

"Looks like you're it."

A weak grin. "And my wife...says I'm not a...a ladies man." He stared up at her, intense and statue-still. "They interview you?"

"Yeah. Last night, and then again this morning. We did a walk-through and everything." Mel interlaced her fingers in her lap. "I think it's okay. I'm suspended for the next few days, at least, but Lieu keeps telling me that I did the right thing. My reactions, you know..." *But no matter how many times Jackson reassures me, I'm always going to wonder.*

"I talked to...Jackson, earlier."

"I hadn't realized."

"Yeah. I told him I don't remember...a lot of it." He paused. "It happened so fast." His voice was a rough whisper, a surreal sound coming from larger-than-life Hansen.

She leaned in close to hear his quiet words. Tears stung her eyes. "It did. Too fast."

"Don't...you...dare blame yourself."

"I'm trying," she whispered, and placed her hand on his arm. "I promise I'm trying."

Since when did he know her so well? The most unnerving part was that she suspected he probably knew her more than she'd like to admit.

Hansen regarded her for some time. "So about that date," he said, and took a breath. "About the woman..."

Mel chuckled and shot him a dirty look. "You're not gonna give up on that one, are you?"

"The least...you could do is answer. One thing I do remember about that day, you said you needed...my advice." He gave her a pointed look. "Right?"

Mel recalled her frantic pleading to Hansen as she waited with him for the ambulances to arrive. *You're gonna be okay, you hear me? You're gonna be okay, and you're gonna keep giving me advice about women. I'll even take it, I swear.* She sighed. Of course he remembered that part.

"Right." She reminded herself that yesterday afternoon, she would have given anything to talk about women with him. And Regan was right — things could still be different between them. "I stayed with her last night."

Hansen's eyes shone. "Stayed with her?"

"Nothing happened," Mel said. He shot her an affectionate look, sending her headlong into embarrassed stammering. "She just...she just listened to me. She...made it better somehow."

"Good. That's a good thing."

Cheeks burning, Mel said, "Yes. It is." She met his steady gaze, and realized how nice it would be to talk to someone about her turbulent feelings. The words tumbled out when she saw the unrestrained warmth in his eyes. "I don't know, though. I don't know right now."

"Don't know about what?"

"A lot of things. I don't know how good I'd be for anyone, and especially someone like Regan."

"Regan, huh?" Hansen smiled.

"Yeah. Regan."

"Well, maybe you ought to let...Regan decide that?"

Mel looked away. "I don't want to hurt her."

"You don't want her to hurt you," Hansen shot back, his voice suddenly stronger.

Mel struggled not to retreat behind her defenses. *He cares about you. That's all this is.* "What's wrong with that? I think that's reasonable, not wanting to get hurt."

"What's wrong, is that life...is too damn *short*...and uncertain...to miss it because you're scared."

Mel shifted in her chair. Damn, it was uncomfortable. And she didn't want to talk anymore. She stood up quickly and opened her mouth, a ready excuse at the back of her throat.

Hansen reached out and brushed at her arm with feeble fingers. "You sit down," he wheezed, "and you listen to me. I can't get out...of this bed to chase your stubborn ass...down the hall...if you walk away from this. So please...don't do it."

Mel snapped her mouth closed, the wind taken out of her sails. "That's not fair."

"You're telling me."

Mel took her seat again.

"I told you I'm glad I have...your attention. I'm glad because...I want to talk to you...*really* talk." There was a strange urgency in his eyes. "You don't talk, ever...do you?"

Mel shrugged and studied her shoes. Her inability to communicate her feelings was becoming a recurrent theme. She looked up at him with a humorless smirk. "I have this weird feeling that you and Regan would get along very well."

"We've got something in common," he said with a pained smile. "We care about you."

Mel saw the truth of his words in his eyes. Between Regan

and Hansen, she was almost afraid that things were too good to be true.

Hansen sank into his pillows and released an exhausted breath. He closed his eyes with a grimace, and it took some time before he relaxed.

Mel looked down at the hand that rested beside his hip, noticing that his thumb was shakily pressing the self-administering morphine pump he held. "I should really let you rest."

Brown eyes opened, dazed. Hansen focused on her with some effort, blinking slowly. "I am...kind of tired."

She gave his bicep a tender squeeze. "Sleep now, okay?" He opened his mouth as if to speak, but she cut him off. "I'll be back tomorrow. And we'll talk. I promise we'll talk about whatever you want."

Hansen smiled at her as his eyes slipped shut again.

Mel returned his smile and realized, all at once, that she was seeing him as a genuine friend for the first time. Whether or not he returned to the force, she wanted him in her life. Against all instinct, she had grown to trust the second person in recent days to penetrate her defenses. It was scary but it felt good, too. And it left her as exhausted as Hansen looked.

Chapter
Seven

REGAN SAT IN her favorite chair with her cordless phone in her hand. *I can do this.* She had been psyching herself up for nearly fifteen minutes, though she felt no closer to dialing the number than she had fourteen minutes ago. *Stop freaking out. Be realistic. She likes me. We've definitely connected. She wants me in her life — she said so. Once I call her, I'm sure I'll just know what to say — it seems like I never have to struggle for words when she's around.*

The ringing of her cordless phone pulled a startled squeak from her throat and she dropped the trilling object into her lap, then fumbled to pick it up and answer it.

"Hello?" She sounded breathless and panicked and, God, how she hated that.

"Hey, Regan."

She knew the voice instantly, and it thrilled her and relaxed her at the same time. "Mel...how are you? How's your partner?"

"I'm doing okay. Hansen's a lot better. The surgery went well and he's awake and talking. I've been spending a lot of time at the hospital, keeping him company."

"That's great." Regan's body hummed with nervous energy. "I'm so glad to hear it."

A pregnant pause. "I'm an ass for not calling sooner." Mel's voice grew rougher. "I'm sorry."

"You've got a lot on your mind right now."

"True," Mel said. "But I can't stop thinking of you."

Regan closed her eyes, feeling as if she would melt at the words. "Me, too." She relaxed back against the pillows behind her, picking her feet up to stretch down the length of the couch. "I've been thinking about you, too. Quite a lot."

"I'd like to see you again. Soon."

"Oh, yeah?" Grinning, Regan rubbed her hand back and forth over her stomach, pushing her T-shirt up a bit and trailing her fingers over bare skin.

"Maybe Tuesday night?"

I can make it two more days, Regan reasoned. "Sure. Want me to make dinner for you? Or we can go out somewhere, if you want." *Whoa there, tiger. Let's take it down a notch.*

Mel gave her an affectionate peal of laughter. "You can cook?"

Regan wrinkled her nose. "I don't do it very often, but yes, I can manage. What do you like to eat?"

"Too easy." Evil chuckles met the unintended innuendo. "I won't even go there."

"You won't?" Regan feigned disappointment. *I know I'm comfortable around her already. Moments like that turn me on instead of freaking me out.* "Really?"

"Oh, don't worry." Mel's voice was silky smooth. "I promise not to ever leave you disappointed or...unfulfilled. When it really counts, I mean."

"I'm glad to hear that." Regan trailed her fingers along the waistband of her jeans. She felt a smile play on her lips as she thought of how Mel might look at the other end of the line. "You haven't disappointed me so far, after all."

"Imagine that," Mel commented, then, as if she consciously made an effort to go easier on herself, she said, "I wanted to thank you again for letting me stay with you on Friday night. Hansen thinks you're just what I need."

Regan blinked at the statement. *Wow.* "Still giving you advice on women?"

"Yeah. Every chance he gets."

"Is it good advice?"

"I think so. He's helping me not be stupid and mess this up."

Regan laughed. "Don't you know by now that it's not so easy to mess this up? You befriended me, so now you're stuck with me."

"You have no idea how much I appreciate that."

"So how are you doing—in general?"

A shaky sigh came over the line. "I'm a little overwhelmed."

"About work?"

"Yeah," Mel answered. "I know I don't want to ride with anyone else, and I feel like I should just go ahead and take the detective test, because it's what I used to want to do..."

"But?" Regan prompted.

"But it's not what I really want. The trouble is, I don't know what else to do. I'd feel like such a failure if I just quit."

"You want to quit?"

There was a long moment of silence, and Regan tipped her head to strain for Mel's answer. It came after another few breaths. "Yes. I feel like such an asshole...a fucking weakling, but I just can't. I can't do it anymore."

Regan kept her hand still on her stomach, feeling the distant echo of her heartbeat through her fingertips. "It's okay, Mel. Not everyone is meant to be a cop."

"I am," Mel asserted. Her tone left no room for argument.

"Family tradition?"

"I guess so. Ever since I was a kid, it was all I wanted."

"What you wanted or what your dad wanted?" Regan guessed.

It took Mel so long to answer that Regan began to think she wouldn't. "I always wanted him to be proud of me. I used to ride around with him in his patrol car before Mom died, and I remember how we'd laugh. All I wanted was to grow up and be my dad's partner, to ride around with him all day long. After my mom died, everything changed. It was like I lost both of them." Her voice broke. "We could never do anything right, Mike and me. That didn't stop me from trying, though, and I knew Dad wanted me to be a cop, so—" She faltered for a moment, then whispered, "Nothing worked. He's never—"

"It sounds like he's the one with the problem," Regan said. "It's not your fault, and you can't spend your life trying to please someone who will never be pleased."

"I know you're right. But that doesn't stop me from feeling like a failure."

Regan expelled a harsh sigh, frustrated. "Listen to me. Not being a cop isn't equivalent to being a failure. There are other ways to be successful."

"I feel like it's too late."

"How old are you?" Regan asked. *How can I not know that already when I feel like I've known her for years?*

"Twenty-five," Mel said.

"Twenty-five? God, Mel, you're a year younger than me! What do you mean, *it's too late*? Are you calling me old?"

Mel rewarded her with a tentative laugh. "I mean, not ancient or anything, but—"

Regan interrupted her before she could complete that thought. "Listen to the wisdom of your elder. It is *not* too late to do something else."

"I wouldn't know what to do."

"Well, what do you like to do? Besides drive women mad, that is."

"You mean you don't think I can have a career driving women mad?" There was a strained edge to her teasing, as if she were trying to lighten up.

"On the contrary," Regan said softly. "I think you'd be wildly successful. I'm just not sure I'm willing to share you."

"Fair enough." Mel hesitated. "I really don't know what I could do."

She knows. For some reason Regan felt sure Mel was holding back. "Now tell me what you actually wanted to say," she said.

"It's stupid." Mel's voice turned shy. "Unrealistic."

Regan smiled. "Try me."

"I like drawing."

She sounds like she's afraid I'll belittle her or something. Regan wondered at the source of Mel's insecurities. "Are you good?"

"Yeah," Mel chuckled, bolder now. "I'm pretty good."

"So why is it unrealistic?"

Mel sighed. "I'm definitely too old for the starving artist thing."

An idea began to take hold in Regan's mind. "But you like computers, right?"

"Well, yeah, of course."

Of course! Regan silently crowed. *She says 'of course'! The perfect woman!* After a few moments of silent thanks to the universe, she focused on the topic at hand. "So what about graphic design? Or web design? Or Flash development? You could learn animation, or computer graphics, or God, Mel, anything!" Regan couldn't suppress the excitement in her voice. *Yeah! Nerdy stuff! Come to the dark side, it's fun!*

"You think so?"

Regan was surprised at the whispered question. The last thing she had expected was the fearful hope in Mel's voice. "Well, yeah. I know guys who do amazing stuff. Almost anyone can learn the technical part of it. But you're very lucky if you have natural artistic ability."

"Maybe," Mel murmured.

She sounds...optimistic? Contemplative? Mel wore her moods so plainly, Regan could already read her face. She wished she could see her now. "You don't have to figure it all out right now. It's something to think about, though."

"You're right. It is." Mel sounded distracted. "I've got a lot to think about right now. I'm just...overwhelmed."

A wounded partner, career on the rocks, Regan inventoried. And where exactly did she fit into Mel's life? She closed her eyes, hating what she was about to do. *Of course she's overwhelmed, dopeshow. What's more overwhelming than a new relationship?*

"Listen, Mel," she said. "I know that what's happening between us is just another thing that's coming at you from out of nowhere right now. And if you're overwhelmed by it, or we're just moving too fast..." *Why am I doing this?* "I'm just trying to say that there's no pressure from me, okay?"

"Regan, you're the one thing in my life that feels totally natural right now. I'll admit that it's overwhelming, but..." Mel paused, and her voice seemed lighter somehow, as if sharing of her worries had unburdened her of a great weight, enabling her to speak freely. "It's overwhelming in the most amazing way. When we're apart I get scared and I start thinking too much, but when we're together you just make me feel so good." A shaky breath followed the soft confession. "I've been so torn up about everything the past few days, but just calling you has made me feel like maybe everything will be okay." Regan opened her mouth to respond, but remained silent when Mel continued. "It always makes me feel better to talk to you."

"Talking to you makes me feel better, too."

Neither spoke for a couple of minutes.

"I wish everything else could just disappear for a while," Mel finally whispered. "I wish I could just spend time with you and let you make me feel better. I'm so tired." She sounded drained. "I just want to get away from real life for a while, you know?"

Regan thought of countless nights spent slaving over her code while wishing that she had something greater out there calling her. "I know what you mean." She smiled as an old college fantasy popped into her head. Impulsively, she said, "We should just toss a couple of bags into my truck and take off for a week or so. Get lost in America, and, in the tradition of all the great road movies...you could find yourself." It sounded so corny, she laughed.

"Where would we go?"

Regan indulged in her fantasy for another few moments. "I don't know. Maybe the Southwest? I've always wanted to see Monument Valley. It'd be very 'Thelma and Louise'. Except the driving into the Grand Canyon part, preferably." *Wouldn't that be amazing?*

"Really?" Mel sounded hesitant. "Do you really want to take a road trip?"

Yes! Regan had said it on a lark and she'd expected it to be dismissed as pure fantasy. *Does she actually sound interested?* She struggled for a safe reaction. *Please don't let me embarrass myself.* "Well, uh...no. I mean..." Why was she making this harder than it needed to be? "Yes." *Perfect, Regan. Just perfect.*

"I've never taken a road trip with another person before," Mel said after a long silence.

"It's fun," Regan said. "Think about it. Okay?"

"Okay. I'm so glad I called. I miss you."

"I miss you, too."

"So I'll see you Tuesday night?"

"Yes! Yes, definitely." *I don't even care how desperate that might sound. A thousand times yes!*

"Cool. I can't wait."

"Very cool, yeah." Regan's face hurt from smiling so hard. "I look forward to it."

They said goodnight and Regan hung up, casting a satisfied smile at the ceiling. After a moment her smile tightened a little in concentration and she furrowed her brow.

A road trip, huh?

MEL NEARLY MADE it through her next visit with Hansen without discussing Regan or the road trip idea. She held the information inside of her so tightly that her teeth were clenched with the effort. Hansen seemed to sense something was up because he kept shooting her curious looks.

"Drunk driver killed two elderly sisters last night," she commented, scanning the newspaper. "Driving on a suspended license, no less."

Hansen groaned, shifting in his bed. "Christ, Raines. I'm in the goddamn hospital here. You think you could talk about something a little less depressing?"

Mel grinned. The good-natured complaint was a sure sign that her partner was slowly regaining his strength. The subtle reemergence of his ruddy color and gentle humor confirmed it. Only four days earlier, she'd thought he would never give her a hard time again. She had to hand it to modern medicine.

Mel folded the newspaper and deposited it on the tray that was positioned over Hansen's bed. She'd read through the sports and editorial sections at his request, and continued with the news headlines to avoid casual conversation. Hansen had an uncanny ability to zero in on the things she least wanted to talk about.

"When are you going back to work?" he asked.

Mel sighed. "Lieu told me to take the rest of the week off. I go back to a desk on Monday."

"Get to visit the shrink, all that good stuff."

"Yeah." Mel felt dangerously close to sulking at the thought of having to talk to a psychologist. "I can't wait."

"Don't worry about it." Hansen waved a dismissive hand in the air. "It'll be a piece of cake."

Mel shrugged. The last thing she wanted to do right now

was to go back out there. The thought made her feel weak, but it was the truth. *I can't do it anymore.*

"I appreciate your spending so much time here the past few days," Hansen offered in a quiet voice. "I know Annie's appreciated it, too." He looked down at the white sheet that covered him. "It's not easy for her right now, especially with Katie."

"How's she doing?" Mel asked. Katie was ten years old. Old enough to know that her father had almost been killed.

Hansen blinked, eyes bright with sudden emotion. "She's scared. Annie says she's having nightmares."

Mel leaned forward and touched Hansen's wrist. She couldn't stand to see the quiet pain. "She'll be okay. This was scary for everyone."

"What about you? What are you going to do after the shrink clears you? You know I won't be back."

Mel cast her stinging eyes down to the floor. "I know. I don't want to ride with anyone else. I think my only option now is to take the detective test." Further and further into what she hated. What a great idea. She met his eyes once more. "It's about time I did, anyway."

Hansen stared at her hard. "You don't like the job, do you?" At her intake of breath, he added, "You haven't for a while."

Mel's throat felt dry. "You get shot and that gives you the right to be as blunt as humanly possible?"

Hansen gave her a smug grin. "That's how I see it."

Mel sighed. "No, I don't like the job anymore. But, what can I do?"

"The detective test isn't your only option."

Mel brought her hands up to cover her face. Hot tears burned her eyes, elicited by Hansen's gentle words. "Yes, it is," she answered, keeping her voice steady. "I'm not riding with someone new. The detective test is the next logical step in any event. I've just been putting it off."

"You know it's not the *only* option," Hansen reiterated.

"You mean just quit?"

Hansen shrugged, fumbling for his bed control with one hand. When he found it, he lowered himself into a slightly reclined position and sighed in relief. "I'm just saying, life is too short to be unhappy. It doesn't make you a lesser person if you decide you want something else. I see what this thing has done to Annie, to Katie, and I'm finding that it's not what I want, either."

Mel studied her partner. His face was earnest, his voice insistent. She got the sense that Hansen was desperate to relay his realizations to her. "I don't blame you," she said. "Your family needs you."

"And I need them. It's about what I want, too. I'm not disappointed to be facing life behind a desk. I know cops are supposed to be macho—begging to get back on the streets after something like this." He shook his head. "Screw that. I understand now what's important. I just want you to understand, too."

"I get it," Mel said.

"Good." Hansen lay back on his pillow. "So you'll think about all your options?"

"I'll get through this," Mel said, non-committal.

Hansen gave a weak bark of helpless laughter. "You're so frustrating, Raines. Who's going to think less of you for doing what you really want? Tell me that."

"I will."

"Bullshit," Hansen answered in a quiet voice. "I don't believe that."

"Can we drop this?" Mel snapped. She looked at her mentor lying in bed, tubes and wires still stretched out around him. The thought crept into her head, a slow and startling realization. *I respect his opinion more than my father's.* She softened her tone. "I mean, can we talk about something else now?"

"Sure," Hansen said. "How's your girl?"

Mel chuckled as she raised her eyes to the ceiling. "You're so predictable. You know that, right?"

"You find that comforting about me," Hansen told her.

Mel laughed even louder. "I guess I do," she admitted. A grin stayed on her face at the thought of Regan being "her girl." "She mentioned going on a road trip."

"A road trip?" Hansen pushed aside the meal he'd been contemplating during their conversation. "Really?"

"Yeah. She said I should get away from things, take some time to think."

"That's not a bad idea." Hansen's slow grin grew so wide it looked like it would split his face. "You should go," he told her. "Call her. Don't blow it!"

God, he was a pushy bastard. For some reason she found that trait more endearing now.

"What are you waiting for?" he urged.

She sighed and picked up the paper again. "I just don't know if I deserve her, especially right now. I don't know if I'd just be leading her on, doing something like that. I don't know if I'll even be able to figure out how to...be with her."

Hansen gave her a gentle smile. "So you'll find out."

The thought made Mel exhale shakily. Could she handle finding out? "I just feel like my life is falling apart around me right now, and I don't know if it's the right time — "

"Raines," Hansen interrupted her. "Sometimes life falls apart. What's important is not letting that stop you from taking the opportunities as they come. If you don't pursue this thing with Regan, are you going to wonder what could have happened and regret missing out?"

Mel didn't have to search hard for a response to that. When she was away from Regan, she got worried and pessimistic. But when they were together, it was like none of that mattered at all. It felt like everything was going to be okay.

As if he had guessed exactly what she was thinking, Hansen said, "You're going."

"Excuse me?" Mel sputtered.

"Where are you headed on this trip?" he asked, ignoring her indignation.

"Monument Valley," Mel answered, in a total daze. "But we're not driving into the Grand Canyon."

Hansen gave her a strange look. "Good."

A tentative knock on the hospital room door tore Mel's thoughts away from redheads and road trips, and Hansen's eyes away from her. Annie Hansen smiled at her from the open doorway. She looked tired, but happy. Mel's attention was immediately drawn to the small hand Annie held in her own; she followed a thin arm back up to gaze at the little brunette girl who stood next to her mother, looking just as nervous as Mel suddenly felt.

"Hello, Mel." Annie took a step inside, pulling Katie gently behind her. Smiling towards the bed, she greeted, "Peter."

I want someone to say my name with that kind of love. Mel felt like an intruder all of a sudden. Hansen managed to sit up to welcome his family with an adoring grin.

"Hey, sport," he said to Katie. Looking up at Annie, he murmured, "Sweetheart."

"Hi, dad," Katie whispered. Fretful eyes darted over the equipment surrounding Hansen, and the little girl stopped to stand a few feet away from the bed.

"She's a little nervous about the hospital," Annie explained.

Despite the fact that she felt like she should leave, Mel felt compelled to say something to Hansen's daughter. "I understand. I've hated hospitals ever since I was about your age, too." Looking at Katie was like looking at a memory of herself when she would visit her mother.

"Katie," Annie said as she placed a hand on her back, and

gestured at Mel. "This is your dad's partner, Mel. She's the one who saved his life."

Mel opened her mouth to protest, but stopped when serious hazel eyes swung up to stare at her with reverent awe.

Much of Katie's unease seemed to disappear. "You did?"

Hansen nodded and shot Mel an affectionate look. "Yeah, sweetie. She stopped the bad guy and arrested him."

Mel shifted in discomfort, unsure that she deserved the attention she was receiving. Her heart thumped in her chest, and she eyed the door. She was shocked when Katie stepped forward and wrapped tentative arms around Mel's waist.

"Thank you," the girl murmured.

Mel raised startled eyes to Hansen and his wife. Both gazed back at her with bemused smiles and misty eyes. "Well, it was the least I could do." Mel gave Katie an awkward pat on the back. "Your dad is always helping me when I need it."

With something akin to hero worship in her eyes, Katie released Mel and returned to her mother.

"Do you want to give your dad his present, sweetie?" Annie took a folder from the large bag she carried over her shoulder.

Katie reached into the folder and withdrew a thick sheet of white paper. Hesitating just a moment, she walked to the bed and offered the paper to her father. "I drew this for you."

Mel blinked rapidly at the soft statement to force down sudden emotion. Once again, it was like looking back at her younger self. She watched Hansen's brown eyes sparkle with delight as he accepted the drawing.

He held the paper out and studied it with a serious gaze. "I think this is the best I've seen yet," he said. "Someday I'll be looking at your art hanging in a museum somewhere." He grinned at Mel, and turned the paper around to reveal a pencil drawing of what was most likely the family cat.

"That *is* very good," Mel said. "I'm impressed." And she was. The kid was good, and with a supportive dad like Hansen, there was a good chance she could learn to be great. A loving parent made so many things easier. Clearing her throat, she said, "I should really get going. I've got some things I need to do."

Hansen swung his eyes over to pin her with a meaningful stare. "Does that mean you've made a decision?"

Mel hooked her thumbs in the pockets of her jeans. "Yeah."

MEL DROVE TOO fast to Regan's house, rehearsing what to say the whole time. *So about that road trip, were you seriously serious?* She shook her head. *Take me away from all of this, Regan.*

Help me find myself again. She rolled her eyes. She didn't have one goddamned worthwhile thing to say.

The sun was hanging low in the sky when she pulled into Regan's driveway, causing everything to glow in the kind of orange light that had once seemed so magical to Mel as a kid. It felt magical again as she parked her bike, scared and nervous and so excited she could hardly stand it. She swung her leg over the seat, planting her feet solidly on the ground and taking a deep breath to center herself.

This was going to change everything. *I want everything to change.* She marched up to Regan's front door, hands jammed in her pockets, chuckling at how utterly out of control she felt. *So take control.*

It only took a minute for Regan to answer the door, and her green eyes lit up in unselfconscious pleasure at the sight of Mel standing there. "Hey," she said. "I wasn't expecting you for another hour or so."

"I'm sorry. I couldn't wait." Mel closed the distance between them, pulling Regan into a tight hug. She turned her head to inhale the scent of auburn hair and her eyes slipped shut in pleasure. The embrace calmed her, grounded her; it narrowed her focus down from all the things that scared her in life to just the two of them, pressed tightly to one another. How had she ever managed without this before? On this level, nothing else mattered.

"I've been doing a lot of thinking," she whispered, her voice shaking. "And the thing is, I need you in my life. That's the only thing I know for sure right now."

"I'm here." Regan slid one hand down to rest on the small of Mel's back, pressing their lower bodies together even more.

Realizing they were still standing in the open doorway, Mel tightened protective arms around Regan and slowly backed her into the house, kicking the door shut behind them. She continued walking until Regan's back was pressed up against the wall.

"Were you serious about the road trip?" Mel asked.

"Yes."

The grin was an unstoppable force, exploding onto her face without conscious thought. She moved her hands to grip Regan's shoulders. "Let's do it."

"Are you serious?"

"Completely." Mel leaned forward and kissed Regan hard, feeling all of her fear and anxiety and desire condense in her belly and explode into passionate force. With trembling hands, she pressed the smaller woman against the wall and growled a little as she plundered her mouth with her tongue.

Regan gave as good as she got, returning the kiss with vigor. They both released muffled sounds of pleasure—from Regan a series of whimpers, from Mel a rumbling purr. Regan reached her hands up to grip Mel's biceps, and Mel hooked one of Regan's legs, lifting it to curl around her thigh for balance. She kissed her again, very deeply, then drew back to gaze at her with unfocused eyes. "May I take you to your bedroom?"

Regan nodded, a dark blush suffusing her face. "Please."

REGAN STOPPED IN front of her bed and turned around to face Mel. "This is the first time I've had someone in my bedroom. Like this, I mean."

Mel traced her fingers over Regan's jaw. "Really?"

"Well, I only bought this house a year and a half ago," Regan said, then immediately dropped her face into her hands. "Why am I always so honest about the embarrassing stuff?"

Mel laughed and reached out to thread her fingers through silky auburn hair, cradling the back of Regan's head in the palm of her hand. "I'm honored," she said. "I'm so very honored, that I'm the first and that you feel you can be honest with me."

"It's like I don't have a choice." Regan grasped the hem of her shirt in both hands, and hesitated only a fraction of a second before pulling it up and over her head. She tossed her T-shirt to the floor and folded her arms low over her stomach, leaving her bra-encased breasts uncovered for Mel's eyes. "There's no part of me that wants to hide from you."

Mel inhaled swiftly, her nostrils flaring with powerful emotion that threatened to overtake her. Regan's trust sent an almost crippling flood of arousal through her, and she walked them to the edge of the mattress. They tumbled down onto the bed, and Mel hovered over Regan on her hands and knees, offering a tender shield to the smaller woman. Her stomach was poised inches above Regan's, and she was careful not to rest her weight on the body below hers. The pose was protective, and she liked how it made her feel. She gazed down into aroused green eyes, lifting an eyebrow when small hands pressed hard against her back.

"I want your weight on me," Regan complained with a petulant frown, the pressure of her hands not even making an impact on Mel's willful position. "I want to feel all of you against me."

"And I'm supposed to give you what you want?" Mel teased.

"Yes." Regan wrapped two strong legs around her hips, all four limbs joining in the effort to unite their bodies. She hissed her pleasure when Mel suddenly gave, lowering her body to rest on top of Regan's.

Their mouths met in a hungry kiss; Mel felt her whole body begin to relax, to cleave to Regan, to fill in the redhead's dips and hollows and to accept the gentle curves offered into her own empty spaces. Sensation stalked and pounced on her like a stealthy jungle cat, overwhelming any second thoughts.

Regan pulled away from the kiss, gasping. "Too many clothes." She stroked the side of Mel's face. "Help me fix that?"

"Okay." Mel sat back on Regan's hips and straddled her body. She tugged her T-shirt off and tossed it on the floor, feigning a casualness she didn't quite feel.

"That's a good start." Regan's hands came up to caress the warm skin of Mel's stomach. "May I help with the next step?"

The corner of Mel's mouth twitched with amusement. Incredibly, she couldn't stay nervous. She reached up and touched her own throat, then trailed her fingers down over the curve of her breast, dipping slightly into the cup of her bra. "Sure."

Regan sat up slowly, reaching around Mel's back and pressing her face into the spot between two full breasts. Mel's eyes slammed shut at the painful sensuousness of the caress, and she felt an impossible flood of wetness between her legs. With agonizing slowness, Regan dragged her hands up the length of Mel's back, from the dip just above her bottom to the curve of her shoulder blades. Another pass of small, soft hands and her bra was unclasped and Mel was left bare and unbelievably aroused. Her nipples grew so tight beneath Regan's gaze that it brought an involuntary grimace of pleasure to her face.

"You're amazing," Regan murmured.

Mel resisted a girlish urge to cross her arms over her breasts, choosing instead to stare down at Regan with the bravest eyes she could muster. She traced gentle fingers from Regan's eyebrow to her cheek, then down over her throat to the tip of one cotton-covered breast. "So are you."

Regan's quick movement took her by surprise. Wrapping strong arms around Mel's solid middle, she wrestled her down onto the mattress.

Mel laughed as she allowed Regan to manhandle her. "Pretty impressive," she complimented as their positions were reversed and Regan straddled her hips.

Leaning over her, Regan planted a kiss on the corner of Mel's mouth then sat up and unhooked her own bra.

"I wanted to do that." Mel stared at Regan's full, pale breasts with a slightly dazed smile. "You're beautiful."

"And you're still overdressed." Regan eased herself off Mel's body, and Mel began to sit up only to be stopped by a hand on her bare chest. "No. Let me." She pulled down the zipper of Mel's jeans with nimble fingers. "I could get used to this whole undressing you thing."

"What a coincidence."

Grabbing the jeans in both hands, Regan drew the material down over long, tanned legs and finally tore them from Mel's ankles.

"Impatient?"

Regan ran her hands up the length of Mel's legs, trailing her thumbs over the silky skin of her inner thighs. "Desperately."

"Me, too." Mel felt like she was about to explode.

Regan curled her fingertips over the band of Mel's panties and slid them down, sending a flood of liquid desire straight to Mel's center.

Mel groaned. "You can't even understand what this is doing to me."

Regan quickly removed her own jeans and panties, then slid down onto her belly between Mel's thighs.

"I'd like to find out," she said, and kissed her way up Mel's stomach to her breasts. She covered an erect nipple with her hot mouth, and Mel was torn between savoring that sensation and concentrating on the feeling of Regan's hand easing between their bodies to find her wetness.

Of all the ways Mel had imagined their first time, she had never envisioned Regan taking the lead. She also hadn't pictured herself being the nervous one. Mel squeezed her eyes shut as Regan's fingers slipped through the slick arousal that had pooled between her legs.

"Well," Regan stroked slick folds, circling swollen flesh with teasing fingers, "it feels like it's doing the same thing to you as it's doing to me."

Mel groaned in pleasure, unable to do anything else. She spread her legs even further apart in silent encouragement. Regan lowered her mouth to Mel's breast once more, and she arched her back into the intimate caress. It was so fucking intense, she felt like she might burst with wanting. She squirmed and Regan slowly released her nipple. Mel opened her eyes and moaned in protest when exquisite fingers abandoned their task between her thighs. The disappointment vanished when Regan brought her right hand up and stared at glistening fingers before bringing them to her mouth.

Watching Regan extend her tongue to sample the wetness that she had gathered wrenched a painfully aroused noise from

Mel's throat. "You're too fucking good at this," she breathed.

Regan beamed in answer, and shifted down to settle between Mel's spread legs. She looked up at Mel with a playful gaze as she hooked her arms around muscled thighs. "At this, too, I hope."

Warm, wet lips licked and kissed a blazing trail across her belly, down to her abdomen, and over her sensitive inner thighs. For long moments Mel gasped and panted as Regan teased her mercilessly, always coming close to touching her where she throbbed and ached for contact, but never quite making it.

"God, Regan," Mel whimpered. "Please."

Regan dropped a chaste kiss on top of the dark curls covering Mel's sex. "Since you asked so nicely." She gave her a mischievous grin, then lowered her mouth to slide her tongue across Mel's wetness with a low moan of satisfaction.

Mel felt as if she were dying and being born at the same time. Regan's tongue played over her swollen folds with instinctive precision, eliciting shuddering gasps of pleasure. Completely devoid of any thought, any worry, Mel reached down and cradled Regan's head. Holding her in place, she stroked her auburn locks in reverence.

Mel's legs began to shake, her hips thrusting upwards of their own volition. She pushed herself unashamedly into Regan's mouth, crying out when a firm tongue slid down and penetrated her. "Regan."

Regan lifted her head so that her mouth hovered only an inch above Mel's center. "You taste so good," she groaned. Hot breath splashed across Mel's overheated flesh, sending a racking shudder through her body. Regan lowered her head to return to her task.

When she felt Regan start to moan against her, her mouth vibrating in a groan of sheer bliss, Mel finally lost control. The incredible pressure that had been building inside since their kiss in the front hallway exploded and she cried out, the orgasm so intense she felt her head swim.

Regan's arms grasped her thighs, holding her firmly against the tongue that still laved her. Almost as soon as she began to recover from her climax, she felt herself crest again and threw one arm over her eyes, nearly overcome. Stunned by the intense feelings, both physical and emotional, Regan aroused in her, she placed a limp hand on Regan's cheek.

For long moments, they were still, then Regan finally drew back, placing a gentle kiss between Mel's legs before laying her damp face against Mel's inner thigh. That had been absolutely amazing.

"Come here." Mel tugged weakly on Regan's shoulder, drawing her up to lie next to her. She couldn't help but grin when Regan settled by her side and stared at her with amorous green eyes.

"I'd been wanting to taste you since the moment I saw you. You're even better than I imagined."

Mel placed a gentle kiss on her lover's swollen lips, running her tongue across them to sample herself. "Thank you," she whispered. "I can't...I've never... That was incredible."

"Really? I mean, coming from a connoisseur and all — "

Mel silenced her with a passionate kiss. Pulling back after a few moments, leaving Regan panting, Mel said, "It's never been like this for me before."

Cheeks pink, Regan gazed at Mel's throat. "Good."

Mel sat up and leaned over to wrap strong arms around Regan, adjusting their bodies so she was poised over the other woman's soft body. They were belly to belly, their breasts pressed together and their legs entangled. Mel traced Regan's mouth with trembling fingers, biting her own lip as the task of making love to another human being suddenly weighed down upon her.

Regan stared up at her without reservation. Her expression was one part desire, cheeks flushed and eyes hooded, the other part almost painful openness. The trust and affection Mel saw there left her breathless, and something totally indefinable in Regan's eyes tugged very deep inside Mel's belly, thrilling her and terrifying her in equal measure. She opened her mouth to speak, but was unsure of what to say.

"You're shaking." Regan lifted a hand to push a dark lock of hair away from her face.

Mel struggled for words. "I'm nervous...a little."

"Why?"

"I'm not used to this...showing someone how I'm feeling."

"Don't be." Regan ran a warm hand up Mel's side, fingertips lingering on the swell of her breast. "You're the most beautiful woman I've ever touched."

The whispered confession touched Mel in a way that defied explanation. "Likewise," she said and captured Regan's mouth in a brief, hard kiss before moving down Regan's chin, her neck, and her collarbone, never leaving pale skin for an instant.

Regan moved gently beneath her, an incoherent stream of soft noises falling from her lips like an incantation. Mel savored every inch of her lover that she could consume. Regan was an uncontrollable addiction. Pulling an erect nipple into her mouth, she rolled it between gentle teeth, growling her need. Regan unleashed a moan that sent a rush of wetness to cover Mel's inner thighs.

Mel pulled away from Regan's breast, impatient to sample the rest of her lover's body. Her lips slid from belly to pubic bone to hip and on down trembling thighs. The soft kisses were thorough enough to properly express her appreciation for the part upon which they were placed, but not concentrated enough to do more than ratchet Regan's arousal to a frantic level. Mel only gradually became aware that her caresses were driving the other woman towards the edge, and fast.

She placed a final, gentle kiss on the damp curls between Regan's legs. Leaning back on one elbow, Mel nudged her lover's thighs apart with her hands and stared into half-open green eyes. With undisguised tenderness, she trailed her fingers across an impossibly silky inner thigh before lowering her gaze to take in the sight of Regan's center, now exposed to her scrutiny.

Mel had seen a lot of women since she first discovered her love for them in high school. She had been amazed the first time she had been allowed to explore another woman, the peaks and valleys of that feminine landscape, the most mysterious and glorious place of which was all soft pink skin, swollen folds, and inviting depths.

But when she stared now at Regan, she swore she had never seen anything as amazing before in her life. "You're beautiful." She lowered her fingers to the liquid heat. "And so wet."

Consumed by a sudden, fierce desire to touch Regan everywhere, to possess her completely, Mel slid a gentle finger inside her body, drawing forth a small keening sound.

"Yes," Regan gasped, her hips thrusting into Mel's hand eagerly. "More."

Mel added a second finger, pressing them both back into her with excruciating slowness. She filled her lover with firm strokes, taking her rhythm from the rolling movement of Regan's hips. Without stilling her hand's motion, she crawled up beside Regan and claimed her parted lips in a heated kiss.

"I want to hear you come," she whispered. "Are you going to come for me?"

At Regan's weak nod, Mel blazed a hot trail down her body with mouth and tongue, stopping momentarily to suck firmly on an erect nipple before continuing on to her final destination. When Mel's lips came once again to Regan's pubic bone, her control broke and she moved to envelop hot, swollen flesh in her mouth and stroke the pulsing skin with a firm tongue.

Regan cried out and bucked her hips beneath Mel's upper body. Mel shifted to hook one of Regan's legs over her shoulder.

She closed her eyes and sucked Regan into her mouth, groaning at the sweet taste of her, at how it felt to pleasure her. Regan came hard and fast, tightening around Mel's fingers, throbbing and jerking in Mel's mouth. The sound of her loud cries, the feeling of shaking hands tangling in her hair, the quivering of pale thighs cradling her head, nearly sent Mel over the edge again. She continued to lap as Regan rode out her pleasure. *I made her feel this way. This is all mine.*

When Regan's cries finally quieted and the motion of her hips stilled, Mel slowly withdrew. The movement elicited a mournful sound and Mel dropped a final kiss between those pale legs, then crawled up to take the trembling woman in her arms.

"Thank you," she whispered.

"No," Regan whispered back. "Thank you."

And like that, Mel's uncertainty vanished. There was no place for it. Lying with Regan in her arms felt too natural to question. She closed the distance between their faces to drop a string of languorous kisses across that pale temple.

"You make me feel so beautiful," Regan mumbled into Mel's shoulder.

Mel pulled her closer. "You are beautiful. I don't even know what to do with all your beauty."

Regan drew back with an adoring gaze that soon turned playful. She put a finger to her own lips, rolling her eyes to the ceiling in thought. "How about excusing it from dinner-making responsibilities and agreeing to order in?" she asked. Lowering her eyelids to give Mel a hooded gaze, she added, "*Later.*"

Mel laughed and pushed red hair out of her lover's face. "You're too busy to make dinner, anyway."

Regan giggled. "I am?"

Mel rolled Regan over and pinned her arms above her head with both hands pressed hard against the mattress. She gave Regan a wicked smile. "You are."

REGAN AWOKE ON Friday morning in a completely unfamiliar position. She was wrapped securely in muscular arms and gentle, warm breath blew across the back of her neck. A small sigh of pure bliss escaped her as she pressed her bottom backwards into a firm belly and felt those arms tighten around her. Moments from being lulled into a sense of total peace, an ice-cold foot snaked over to her side of the bed and burrowed itself under her warm leg. Regan yelped in surprise.

"Serves you right," said a drowsy voice next to her ear. "I woke up with my leg sticking out of the blankets and my foot was nearly frozen from the subzero temperature."

Regan opened her eyes and looked at her alarm clock. *5:54 a.m. No wonder I feel so wrecked. All-night lovemaking sessions seemed so much less draining in college. Not that I'm complaining.* She smiled over her shoulder at a drowsy-looking Mel.

"I happen to enjoy abundant air conditioning." Regan lifted her leg just enough to allow Mel to slip her freezing foot between her warm calves. "Is that better?"

"Yes."

"Besides, cold air conditioning makes the sensation of waking up warm in bed just that much more wonderful." Regan extracted herself from their embrace and rolled over to face Mel, who cuddled into her. The position felt so easy and familiar, it was as if they'd lain together like this countless times before.

"That's funny," Mel said. "I was just thinking that Regan O'Riley makes the sensation of waking up warm in bed just that much more wonderful."

Regan's heart fluttered wildly. *Any minute now I'll wake up. I know it.* But she didn't wake up. Instead she laid her head on Mel's shoulder with a sigh of quiet satisfaction. Bringing a hand up to rest on her lover's flat belly, she traced lazy circles over the olive-colored skin with her fingers.

"Can you feel it?" Mel whispered. She stroked Regan's arm as she gazed around at the room. Regan peeked up from Mel's shoulder, joining in the observation. Light shone in from the partially uncovered window and painted the carpeted floor with broad stripes. "Something's different."

Regan cocked her head slightly, brushing her chin against a hard nipple. The shy awe in Mel's voice brought sudden emotion to the front, and she closed her eyes, concentrating on the heartbeat beneath her ear. "Yeah."

Mel lowered her arm to rest on Regan's hip. "I think it's me."

Regan blinked hard. *It's all over. It's only a matter of time before I'm completely, one hundred percent in love with her.* She picked her head up from Mel's chest and gave her a loving smile before capturing her mouth in a deep, soulful kiss. They spent long minutes trading tender kisses and murmurs, and then finally they lay facing one another, sharing a comfortable, peaceful silence.

Minutes passed before Mel spoke. "So we're going to do that road trip, right?" The unguarded enthusiasm in those grey eyes made her look younger than Regan had ever seen her before.

"Right," Regan said.

"You think you'll be able to get the time off from work?"

"Are you kidding me? I have enough comp time to provide

an entire impoverished nation with three-day weekends for a month."

With a laugh, Mel pulled Regan even tighter against her body. "So that's a yes?"

"I'll request it today." Her words felt stuck in her throat, which was suddenly dry. *This is too surreal to be actually happening.* "How about you?"

"I had a good two weeks available before the shooting, and I think Lieutenant Jackson would be more than willing to grant me time off right now."

Regan pressed a kiss into the dark hair that tickled her nose, and inhaled deeply, reveling in her lover's scent. "Everything's going to be okay, you know."

Mel didn't answer for a moment; she kept her face tucked into the space between Regan's shoulder and her neck. Regan shivered when she felt strong fingers tickling a path down her spine, and then over the top of her buttocks. Mel pulled back and gave Regan a shaky smile, her steely eyes shining with emotion.

"I know. I believe you."

"Good. Because I'm right."

Mel blinked and laughed. "So, how about we start working on that road trip after I spend a little quality time working on you?"

Regan groaned as a firm thigh moved between her legs. "Perfect," she said.

And it was.

Chapter
Eight

MEL THREW OPEN her closet door, a cordless phone balanced precariously between her ear and her shoulder. "Jane, you're going to think I'm crazy." She rifled through the row of hangers in front of her. How did one pack for something like this?

"I've known you're crazy for years," Jane said with good humor. "Nothing would shock me at this point."

"Gee, thanks." Mel snatched a long-sleeved Henley from a hanger and tossed it into her open suitcase. "Do you remember the redhead from the bar?"

"The party favor?"

Mel frowned. With her history, she deserved that. But Regan didn't. "Well, we—"

"My God," Jane cut in. "Are you telling me you finally made it to a second date?"

"And then some." A bubble of laughter worked its way up Mel's throat. She didn't even try to stifle it, though she felt her face burn red at the uncharacteristic noise.

Jane made a few sounds that might have been astonishment, or hilarity. Or perhaps dismay. "I guess I am shocked," she finally said.

"I know." Mel grabbed a couple pairs of blue jeans from an open drawer, and then added some cargo pants to her small pile. "The crazy part," she continued, drawing out her confession, "is the fact that I'm packing right now."

"Packing?" Jane choked out a delighted laugh. "Isn't that some kind of lesbian reference?"

"You're such a pervert," Mel said. Chewing on her lip, she crossed over to another dresser drawer and pulled it open. But the reminder was useful.

"I guess that's why you've put up with me for so long."

"I guess so." Mel tucked the harness and dildo she held into her black duffel bag, and then returned to the open drawer for a box of condoms.

"So you're packing," Jane prompted. "And not in a sexual way."

The corner of Mel's mouth lifted into a smile. "I'm packing for a ten-day road trip. With Regan."

"Redheaded Regan?"

"That's the one." Mel sat down on the bed next to her open suitcase. "Crazy, right?"

"Wrong. Where are you going?"

"Southwest," Mel said. "Regan said something about seeing the Painted Desert and Monument Valley. I thought it sounded kind of cool."

"It does sound cool." Jane cleared her throat as if to say something else, but fell silent instead.

"And?" Mel asked. They'd known each other six years and this was the most intimate conversation they'd ever had. She wondered if it felt as weird for Jane as it did for her.

"When do you leave?" Jane asked.

"On Friday, returning a week from Sunday."

"That's a long time. She really must be something."

"She is. But she's not the only reason I'm going. I need to get away — get some distance from work. I have to make some decisions."

"Oh," Jane whispered. "Uh, wow." She sounded afraid to say anything more.

Hardly surprising. Every time her friend tried to have a sensitive conversation, Mel froze her out. When had she become such an asshole? " Jane..." She took a deep breath and forced the words. "I appreciate that you still care for me, after all this time, despite how much I've always tried to keep you at a distance. Thank you."

There was a small, strangled noise, and Mel cringed when she realized that Jane was crying. Straight women, she thought. She was perfectly aware that her derision was nothing but a weak defense mechanism so she wouldn't become emotional as well. "Jane — "

"No," Jane interrupted, not allowing her to hurry past the moment. "That's the nicest thing you've ever said to me."

"Well, that's a pretty sorry track record."

"There's all the time in the world to improve it, though."

"Just be patient with me, okay? It might take a while."

Jane chuckled. "I've been patient with you since we spent half our first night as roommates sitting in that tiny dorm room with nothing to say to each other. If you'd had it your way, we'd never have managed to make it past the most basic of conversations."

"Hang on a second. I was living with a little blonde chatterbox who wouldn't let me brood in peace."

"You looked like you needed a friend," Jane said. "Even if you never seemed to want one, I always thought you needed one."

"I do." It was still hard to say the words. "And you are."

Again, Jane's happiness was clear in her voice. "You are, too." She changed the subject. "You'll be back for my wedding, right?"

Mel's shoulders relaxed. "Wouldn't miss it."

"I *did* address your invitation to Melanie Raines and date," Jane said. "Not that I ever thought you'd bring one."

Mel could not suppress the lovesick grin that captured her mouth. "I'll ask her."

"Good. Well, I should let you get back to packing. I guess I'll see you in a couple weeks."

"Sure," Mel said. "Thanks."

"Hey," Jane said before they could exchange their goodbyes. "Feel free to call me before that, you know...if you want to talk, or whatever."

Mel smiled. A female confidante? Stranger things had happened.

"YOU'RE NUTS." ADAM'S voice sounded almost shrill through the phone. "You're going to drive across the country with a woman you've practically just met. What part of that *isn't* nuts?"

Regan rolled her eyes as she steered her truck through the side streets near Mel's apartment. "How about the part where I'm feeling things I've never felt before." She set her lips into a tense line. "Or the part where I think I'm going to fall in love with her. You know me, Adam. You know this isn't like me."

"That's what I'm saying," her friend protested. "It's insane. I mean, I know you must really believe in this to be doing something so —"

"Impetuous?" Regan suggested, a slight smile tugging at her lips. *Come on, Adam. Be as happy for me as I am.* "I can't explain it." Regan tilted her head to the side, searching for the words. She found them at the same time she found the driveway into Mel's parking lot. "We're just right for one another."

"I guess I can't argue with that." Adam gave in with a resigned mumble. "Just drive carefully, okay?"

"I will," Regan said. She parked her truck in an empty spot

near the stairs that led to Mel's second-floor apartment and tried
to calm her breathing. *This is too much. I think I'm going to throw
up.*

As if Adam sensed her sudden unease, he said, "And don't
be nervous or think too much. She likes you. Trust me. Or she
wouldn't be doing something so, um, impetuous, either."

"Thanks. I know."

"Expect a call from me, okay? You've got to at least let me do
the big brother thing and check up on you once or twice."

Adam's voice was gruff; Regan was well aware that he was
trying to hide his honest concern for her. *Straight guys,* she
thought affectionately. "I always wanted a big brother."

Adam snorted. "And I always wanted a little lesbian."

Regan unfastened her seatbelt. "Later, wonder boy."

"Bye, geek."

She took a deep breath. *Am I ready?* She relaxed her
shoulders, a grin of excitement overpowering her lingering
insecurity. *Hell, yeah.*

Loud rap music thumped through the walls of one of the
apartments near Mel's. Regan had never actually seen Mel's
place, had only dropped her off out in the parking lot. The
building looked kind of run down—appropriate, somehow. She
adjusted the army-green baseball cap that she had pulled
backwards on her head and tucked stray locks behind her ears,
cursing her hair's inability to stay where it was put. Her stomach
twisted with nerves as she knocked.

Fuck, what if she changed her mind? She stuffed her hands
deep into the pockets of her baggy blue jeans. *She would've called
me before I came to pick her up, right?*

The apartment door swung open; a strong hand reached out,
grabbed the front of Regan's T-shirt, and pulled her into the
apartment. Shutting the door behind them, Mel pressed her hard
against the wood surface and captured her lips in a passionate
kiss. Regan moaned and wrapped strong arms around Mel's
neck, returning the kiss with undisguised enthusiasm.

After a few heated moments, Mel drew back slightly. "Do
you try to look even more adorable every time I see you?" She
pressed her lower body against Regan's, still pinning her against
the closed door.

"I didn't even have time to turn on the patented O'Riley
charm."

Mel nipped her lightly on the chin. "The only thing I find
sexier on a woman than a Fraggles T-shirt is a baseball cap.
Backwards, especially."

"Hmm," Regan murmured. "You don't know how grateful I

am that I seem to have good instincts about these things."

"Amazing, isn't it?" Mel released her with obvious reluctance. "Did you get the tent?"

Regan scowled lightly before smiling. "Yeah. I'm warning you, though, be prepared to protect me from wildlife. I am not someone who belongs outside for extended periods of time."

Grateful grey eyes made it all seem worthwhile. "I'll protect you."

"Good," Regan replied. "Tonight. Outside St. Louis, Missouri. I made us a reservation at a gay and lesbian campground."

"Really?" Mel sounded excited. "That's going to be so cool. I appreciate you braving the nature for me."

How could I deny you when you told me that your only camping trip was also your last vacation with your mom, and that it was one of the best times you ever had? "Well, I know camping was a happy memory for you, and I want to help make the happy memories for your future." She blushed at the honest sentiment as it spilled from her lips. *Once again, ladies and gentleman, Regan's heart is on her sleeve. Ta-da!*

"I have to tell you, you've certainly started off with a bang on that front."

Regan attempted a leer. "A bang, huh? Speaking of which—"

"Oh, baby." Mel compressed Regan against the door again, her body so close that Regan could feel hard nipples against her chest. "Is that a euphemism in your pocket or are you just happy to see me?"

Regan laughed hard, right in Mel's face. Mel looked surprised at the unrestrained reaction, but she shot Regan a wide grin then stepped back and picked up a large black duffel bag. She slung it over her shoulder with ease, picked up a pair of sunglasses from a small table, and breezed by Regan to open the door. "Come on," she said, locking the door behind them. "We've got an adventure to begin."

REGAN FINALLY BROACHED the subject about fifteen miles outside of Michigan, on the road to Illinois.

"You know, people quit their jobs all the time," she said. "They change their minds, they figure out that they really want to do something else. There's no shame in that."

Mel crossed one leg over the other, resting her calf on her knee. After a stretch of silence, she said, "I feel like a coward. I think about quitting my job and it feels like running away. I know it's fucked up to feel so guilty about the thought of changing something I hate. But I do."

"Where's the guilt coming from?" Regan took a deep breath and, trusting in their new bond, asked what she really wanted to know. "Is it your dad?"

Mel stiffened noticeably. "My father hasn't really been involved with my life since I left for college. We speak about once or twice a year."

Regan moved a hand from the steering wheel to touch Mel's. "Someone can be a presence in your life even if they're not physically there."

Mel shifted in her seat, her hand sliding away from Regan's. The subject was closed for now, apparently.

With anyone else, Regan might have felt rejected. But this was Mel, and she knew that her reluctance to talk wasn't about them. "Mel, nothing you say is going to change how I feel about you. I know the important stuff already, and you've made the cut. The rest is just detail."

Mel barked out a helpless little laugh. "Goddamn, you're perceptive. Between you and Hansen — "

"Between me and Hansen, we're going to get through to you one of these days. You're worth caring about, even if you don't see it." Regan returned her hand to the wheel as the traffic around them began to pick up. She peeked over at Mel's serious profile when there was no response. "How is Hansen, anyway?"

This raised a slight smile. "I think the nurses are ready to send the grumpy son of a bitch home. He's a junk food addict — thinks a couple weeks without greasy tacos is a fate worse than death." Mel chuckled and looked out at the road again. "He was really excited for me. About this trip, I mean. I think he's pleased that I'm doing something impulsive for a change."

Regan laughed. "He's a bad influence, huh?"

Mel turned and smiled. "He's a good friend."

"I'm glad you're getting so close to him."

"Me, too." Mel was quiet for a moment. "It's all so new, you know, having real friends. You, Hansen...hell, I think Jane and I might even be getting there."

"Do you like it?" Regan asked.

"Yeah." Mel reached out and put her hand on Regan's thigh. "It's been a long time since I've had a real friend. High school, really, and even then I only had one. Her name was Lauren. We met when she moved to Lawton in the sixth grade. I don't know how we got close, because I wasn't close with anyone, but it happened. We were friends until the end of high school. She was the one person who really knew me. We talked, you know."

"Are you still friends?"

Mel's fingers stilled on Regan's thigh for a long moment before resuming their easy motion. "We didn't really speak after we graduated from high school. Typical story—we went to different colleges, you know how it is."

Quiet tension rolled off her. It was not a typical story, Regan suspected. Wanting to put Mel at ease, she shifted focus to her own less-than-typical past. "I didn't have any friends in high school." She blushed, still feeling the embarrassment that had characterized her adolescence.

"None?" Mel asked. "At all?"

"I wasn't very popular." Regan took a deep breath, steeling her nerve. "Actually, I wasn't just unpopular, I was tortured. I was geeky and awkward, and I lived almost entirely in my own head. I didn't have any friends and...well, I guess I made an easy target."

"High school kids are morons."

"Don't I know it." *I always knew it, but it never made it any easier.* "My parents didn't notice or didn't care that I had no friends," she continued. "I spent all my time in my room, playing with my computer. I used to wake up in the morning and just get sick about the idea of going to school, of facing all those kids."

"Kids never bother to look beneath the surface, and that's usually where the most beautiful things are found."

"It would've made a big difference if I'd had even one person I could talk to," Regan conceded, a little embarrassed that she still felt raw when she thought of that time.

"It did for me," Mel said. "Everyone else was just an acquaintance; I guess kind of like everyone has been since then. Well...until now." It was obvious that she wanted to say something more, and Regan guessed what was coming. "Lauren was my first lover."

Regan's stomach churned with conflicted emotion. Mel was opening up to her, and that was good. There had been a high school sweetheart, something she had never considered, and she burned with curiosity, wanting to know more. And she was jealous. The last surprised her with its brief, but intense, flare-up in her belly.

"Wow." Regan snagged a bottle of water from behind her seat.

"It was only during our senior year."

"I can't imagine having found someone back then," Regan said. "As far as I was concerned, I was the only girl who liked other girls at my high school. Hell," she snorted. "I was pretty sure that I was the only lesbian in the entire world."

Mel took the bottle from Regan's lap and opened it for her.

"When was your first time with a woman?"

"My first time with anyone, in any way, was in college." Regan shot Mel a grateful smile as she passed the open water bottle back to her. "With my ex-girlfriend Sarah."

"How long were you two together? And why did she ever let you go?"

Regan grinned at the question. "We were together almost a year. She was a women's studies major, kind of a free spirit, hippy girl. It was a good experience, and she's a really wonderful woman, but we kind of mutually decided that we weren't meant to be. I still talk to her occasionally. She lives in Grand Rapids with her girlfriend and their three cats. I get the impression that they're the very picture of lesbian domestic bliss."

Mel traced her fingers over the bare skin of Regan's neck. "I have to admit, I'm glad she let you get away."

"We were very different people. It would never have lasted."

"Lucky me," Mel said.

They slipped into silence for a time, and Regan concentrated on the merging traffic around a stretch of road works. Her mind kept straying back to the topic Mel had avoided earlier, and she finally decided to risk another question. "Why don't you talk to your father much?"

"He's an asshole." Mel stated it as a simple truth. "I can barely remember a time when he wasn't an asshole."

"I'm sorry." Regan wished she hadn't spoken. In her impatience to know Mel on a deeper level, she was probably opening a wound. "We don't have to talk about it," she added hastily.

"It's okay. You'll know sooner or later." Mel paused, as if gathering her thoughts, then said, "Nothing was ever enough for him. If I got an A, it should have been an A+. If I made the basketball team, I should have been made first-string. It was worse for my brother. Mike didn't have as easy a time with school as I did, and he wasn't into sports like I was. It was really hard after Mom died."

"How old were you?" Regan whispered, sensing her lover's pain and wishing she could find some way to ease it.

"I was eight. She had cancer." Mel turned and looked out the window, at the passing trees and billboards. "It happened fast. One day she was fine, and we were a happy, normal family, and the next, she was just gone. I guess that was a good thing. She didn't have to suffer very long."

Regan swallowed back tears at the catch in Mel's voice. "I can't imagine how hard that would've been. Losing your mom so young."

"It was very hard, for all of us. Especially my dad. The day of her funeral, after we came home — he poured himself a drink, and I don't think he's been without one since."

"So you and your brother lost your mother to cancer and your father to alcoholism. That was very selfish of him."

"I never thought of it like that at the time. He told us how hard we were to deal with, what terrible kids we were, and I guess I believed him. I was sure it was because I never did well enough that he kept drinking." Frustration seeped into her tone. "I just figured that if I could manage to be good, and to make him proud, that we could be happy again. I blamed myself for so much of his misery."

And she'd carried that burden into adult life, Regan realized. It explained a lot. Carefully, she asked, "Was he abusive?"

"Sometimes." Mel exhaled sharply. "He was always emotionally abusive, when he paid attention to us at all. He didn't get physical every day or anything, but it happened." She wrung nervous hands together. "It was pretty bad a few times."

"I'm sorry," Regan said, not really knowing what to say to that. Her heart hurt for Mel, and for everything she carried around with her from her past.

"I feel so stupid for still letting this stuff affect me, you know? I should be smarter than that."

"It has nothing to do with intelligence," Regan responded. "The stuff that happens to us when we're kids, it all shapes us, whether we want it to or not. All of that has helped make you who you are today; of course it's still a factor sometimes." She shot Mel a meaningful sideways look. "And for the record, I really like the person you are today."

"Thank you." Mel's voice shook. "I'm so glad you're with me. It makes everything else seem so much less scary right now."

Hearing her struggle with powerful emotion, Regan decided, *Okay. Pit stop.*

They were approaching a rest area, and she slowed and turned off the highway. Passing a small brick building that housed bathrooms and vending machines, she pulled the truck to a halt in an empty, secluded corner of the parking lot.

"I just needed a hug," she said and unbuckled her seatbelt. Leaning over, she pulled Mel into a tight embrace.

"You needed it, huh?" Mel returned the hug, pressing a string of kisses along Regan's hairline. "Or you thought I needed it?"

"Both."

Mel tightened her arms around Regan, pulling her impossibly closer. "You were right."

Regan curled her hand around the back of Mel's neck and leaned forward to kiss her. "I think you're very brave," she whispered against Mel's lips. "I think you're going to do amazing things with your life."

"You make me believe that." Mel sounded slightly awed, as if the idea was brand new to her.

Regan's chest felt heavy with pleasure. She'd never done that for anyone before. It was the best feeling in the world.

Mel gave her a soft kiss that somehow seemed to acknowledge they were crossing into new territory, then she drew back a little, her expression naked and trusting. "I don't know how to tell you how much this means — being here with you...everything."

Regan cupped a hand to Mel's cheek. "There's nowhere else I'd rather be."

Mel smiled, then, as if making a conscious effort to lighten up, she said, "I promise I'm not always *quite* this dramatic. Sometimes I'm even a fun person to be around."

"Oh, I know that." Regan waggled her eyebrows in lascivious humor. "I've had plenty of fun with you."

Mel allowed a lopsided grin. "You'll have plenty more this week, I promise."

"I'm going to hold you to that." Regan buckled her seatbelt and shifted her truck into reverse, deciding it was probably a good idea to get to St. Louis before dark. "Once we get that tent set up, in fact."

Mel laughed, settling back in her seat as well. "I guess I'd better make camping worthwhile for you in some way, right?"

Regan grinned. "Right."

Chapter
Nine

"I'M GOING TO need a schematic to make heads or tails of this stuff," Regan grumbled, looking down at the pile of material and tent poles at her feet. "I don't understand how we're supposed to produce a tent out of these things."

"Don't look at me." Mel grinned over at her. She inhaled fresh air, gazing around their campsite. Tall trees loomed overhead, and rock formations provided a half-circle enclosure around the area they had staked out. "I've never put a tent together before."

Regan arched an eyebrow. "Funny, I thought you were supposed to be our intrepid guide to the great outdoors."

Mel walked over to stand behind her lover, wrapping strong arms around her middle and pulling the smaller woman against her chest in a relaxed embrace. "I was exempted from tent assembly during my last camping trip, because I was eight years old. I'm sorry."

Regan grumbled a little under her breath. "I forgive you." She tilted her head, providing access to a pale neck, and drew in a quick breath when Mel claimed the proffered skin with gentle teeth.

"We could just stand right here like this," Mel suggested, nuzzling her face into sweet-smelling auburn hair. "Do we really need a tent?"

Regan giggled in her arms, squirming a little but making no real effort to step out of the embrace. "I thought we had plans for that tent."

"We do." Mel splayed her fingers across Regan's slightly rounded belly and surveyed the tent materials. "You should have no problem with this...with your programmer's mind and all."

"I'm pretty sure that logic has nothing to do with tent assembly." Regan freed herself from Mel's arms, picked up a pole, and manipulated it awkwardly.

Mel grinned at the way Regan bit her lip as she puzzled it all out. Shifting on her feet, she also realized just how long it had been since they made love. At least twenty-four hours. Her patience with the tent evaporated. "I could just have you in the bed of your truck," she said, leaning so close her lips brushed against Regan's ear.

Regan groaned and dropped the tent pole she had been holding. "Don't make promises you don't intend to keep."

"Who says I don't intend to keep it?" Mel sauntered over to the green pickup truck that was parked at one end of their campsite and lowered the tailgate. She hopped up to sit on it, and swung her legs back and forth as she beckoned Regan.

Kicking aside the unassembled tent with a careful foot, Regan came willingly. "Why do I have a feeling the tent isn't going up anytime soon?"

"Because we have more important things to attend to at the moment." Mel pulled Regan close and captured her mouth in a hungry kiss. Her lover's body was soft and deliciously curvy, and Mel ran bold hands over every bit of it she could reach.

"I suppose this *is* more fun than struggling with that contraption," Regan mumbled.

Mel made a feral growl and slid her hand under Regan's T-shirt, up over her soft belly to a firm breast. She teased and pinched an erect nipple, then pulled sharply away at the sound of a throat clearing behind them. Two women were staring at them with tentative eyes and sheepish smiles.

"Hey," Mel said.

Regan turned her head in surprise to look at their visitors. When she turned back to Mel, a fierce blush colored her pale skin.

"We're sorry to interrupt," the taller of the pair said. Her companion, a stocky woman with a blonde crew cut, hid a quiet chuckle behind her fist.

"It's okay," Mel grinned. She felt Regan turning around between her legs to face their visitors and wrapped her arms around her lover to give her a gentle squeeze. *Don't be embarrassed,* she telegraphed to Regan. *I'm not.* "Five minutes later and I couldn't have been held responsible for my reaction, but I think you got here just in time."

"Five minutes?" The stocky blonde shot them a suggestive smirk. "I would've given you thirty seconds."

Her brown-haired companion poked her in the side. "We noticed that you seemed to be having some trouble with your tent and thought you might need some help."

"Our saviors," Mel said, scooting herself off the tailgate and standing up with Regan still in her arms. "I'm afraid we're rank amateurs."

The blonde woman stepped forward with an outstretched hand. "I'm Jay and this is my partner, Claire."

Mel shook hands and introduced herself. Hoping she wasn't putting her foot in it, she added, "This is Regan, my girlfriend."

Regan's beaming smile, her expression of pure delight, erased any doubts about that.

"It's good to meet you both." Claire stood over the now neatly unfolded tent, a long tent pole in her hands. "Come on, Jay. The sooner we get this thing together, the sooner we can convince Mel and Regan to let us corrupt them for the evening."

The two women immediately fell into the easy rhythm of experienced tent construction, and, before long the pile of junk that she and Regan had been struggling with started to look suspiciously tent-like.

"How about it?" Jay glanced up at Mel as they worked. "We've got a campfire, plenty of food, and two reasonably civil friends back at our site. We'd love the company."

Mel regarded Regan carefully, suspecting that this was just the kind of social situation that would make her really nervous. "We've been driving all day, so I'm not sure—"

"Thanks." Regan took the responsibility out of her hands. "That sounds nice."

"Voila!" Claire announced as she and Jay secured the last corner of the tent to the ground.

"What do you know?" Mel said. "It really *is* a tent, after all." She nodded at their new friends. "It'll just take us a couple minutes to get our stuff back in the truck, okay?"

"No problem." Jay snaked an arm around Claire's waist. "Take your time."

"You okay with this?" Mel murmured to Regan as she led them to the truck.

"I'll be fine."

Mel touched the small of Regan's back. "I'm appointing myself the ambassador of small talk. Don't sweat it."

"I appreciate that."

JAY AND CLAIRE led them across the road that bisected the campground and along a forest path to their more secluded campsite. Mel kept her hand on the small of Regan's back as they walked, grinning, and breathed in the fresh air. It was a nice change from the sight and smell of Woodward Avenue.

"Gina and Ethan are probably wondering where the hell we are," Claire commented as they made their way over a path almost overgrown with vegetation. "We were on our way back from the bathroom when we saw you guys playing with your tent."

"And each other," Jay supplied.

The comment made Regan's perpetual blush grow deeper. Smitten at the sight of her lover's rosy cheeks, Mel leaned over to plant a chaste kiss on one of them.

"I'm warning you now," Claire said, her voice low and conspiratorial, "Ethan is a shameless flirt, though essentially harmless. I say this because I guarantee that he'll be trying to charm one or both of you all night long."

"Yeah, he'll be thrilled that we managed to find two beautiful women in the middle of the woods." Jay turned to walk backwards in front of them for a moment, and threw Regan a wink.

Mel gave her a wry grin. "Glad to be of service."

They approached an immaculately assembled campsite in a small clearing. The day's dying light cast shadows over the three tents arranged in a semi-circle around an already blazing campfire. An attractive brown-haired woman sat on a canvas travel chair basking in its glow.

"Ethan was ready to send out the dogs," she called out and stood up as they approached, looking both Mel and Regan over with appraising eyes. "I think he'll forgive you when he sees our visitors, though." She offered her hand to Regan. "I'm Gina."

After the introductions, Mel said, "Claire and Jay found us having a little trouble with our tent—"

"And a little fun with each other," Jay quipped.

"God, *enough* already." Claire poked Jay in the side. "Anyway, we asked them to hang out with us for a while."

"Cool," Gina said. "The more, the merrier."

A baseball cap-covered head poked out of the red tent furthest from where they stood. The owner flashed them a sunny smile and swaggered over. He wore a wide, flirtatious grin that was immediately trained on Regan. It wasn't until he strode up to her and offered his hand that Mel noticed the transgender symbol emblazoned in white on his ball cap. He was attractive, and his confident blue eyes shone with that knowledge.

"I'm Ethan," he said, and brought Regan's small hand to his lips for a gentle kiss. "Please don't believe anything these ladies have been telling you about me."

"And if they told us you're charming?" Regan found her voice.

"Then they're absolutely correct and I thank them for the accurate portrayal." He turned to take Mel's hand and gave her a wide smile when she shook his firmly, denying him the chance to repeat his chivalrous gesture.

"I'm Mel and she's Regan," she said. "And for the record, they told us you would *try* to be charming."

"So how am I doing?" He gave Regan a cocky grin.

"Don't give up," Mel advised him, hugging her blushing lover. "The night is still young."

Gina reached out and dragged him over to stand by her. "Come on, Ethan. Give the poor girl a break."

Ethan slid an arm around Gina's waist. "So, uh...do you guys smoke?" He waggled his eyebrows and flashed white teeth.

Clearly, he was not asking about Marlboros. Mel hadn't indulged since joining the force, but she had nothing against it. She gave Regan a sidelong glance, checking her reaction.

"I haven't smoked since college," Regan said. "My first girlfriend was a total pothead, but I never really did it after we broke up."

"I'm up for it if you are," Mel said, thinking maybe it would help her shy lover relax.

Regan gave her a mischievous smile. "Why not?"

The group settled in to sit around the fire. Mel grabbed a spot next to Regan, and Ethan was quick to claim the seat on the other side. Claire sat beside Mel, rolling her eyes at her horny friend as she struggled to light a joint she produced from her pocket.

"So where are you guys from?" Jay asked.

"Michigan," Mel said. "Detroit."

"Yeah? And what do you do in Detroit?"

Claire finally managed to light the joint and took a long drag before offering it to Mel, who looked at it and then Jay with an innocent smile.

"Cop." She smirked at the sudden panic in Jay and Claire's eyes, then snagged the joint to take a calm hit. "But I'm considering a career change." Mel passed Regan the joint, unable to stop her smile when their eyes met.

"How about you, Regan?" Ethan stared at her with unabashed admiration.

Regan's cheeks flushed as she took a long drag and exhaled an impressive cloud of bluish smoke. "I'm a software developer." She was quick to pass the joint to Ethan.

"That's awesome," Ethan said, and gave her an enthusiastic smile. "I work as a computer tech. I swear I hardly ever meet fellow geeks." He cocked an eyebrow at Regan. "And never one so beautiful."

Sensing Regan's discomfort, Mel wrapped her arm around

her waist and gave her a squeeze. "She's a gamer, too. A pretty good one, if I'm not mistaken."

"Yeah?" Ethan cocked his head in sudden, intense interest. "What games do you like?"

It worked like a charm. Regan relaxed beneath her arm as she and Ethan launched into a discussion about computers and video games that went right over Mel's head. She couldn't blame Ethan for flirting, but she was pretty sure Regan would have passed out had she not diverted the conversation to a safer topic.

Mel leaned back and relaxed, occasionally contributing to the conversations around her as she continued to pass the joint around the campfire. Mostly she paid attention to Regan; the way she held herself, or breathed, or a shift in her tone of voice. She thought that she could probably watch her for hours and never get bored. She held Regan's hand as everyone talked and soaked in the pleasure she felt at her lover's every smile, every laugh, and at the glow in warm green eyes.

As one joint somehow became two, Mel noticed that Regan was getting nice and high. Even Ethan's blatant come-ons made her giggle and smile. Mel smiled, too, pleased that he was making Regan feel good. Being jealous never even crossed her mind. As the campfire talk grew increasingly bawdy, Regan seemed to forget her previous nerves completely. She leaned forward and laughed hard as the conversation turned to masturbation.

"Oh, please, Jay," Gina said with a snort. "I think your hand has taken up permanent residence in your pants."

"There's nothing wrong with loving one's self." Jay looked around the circle for support, and Mel guffawed when an enthusiastic Regan nodded in agreement. "Besides," Jay gave Claire a lewd wink, "practice makes perfect. Right, baby?"

"If that's true," Regan said, before Claire had a chance to answer, "I must be fucking amazing at this point."

Jay clapped her hands and laughed in delight at Regan's admission, and Mel raised an eyebrow in her lover's direction. Yeah, she was stoned.

"That's a correct statement," Mel said.

"Really?" Ethan gazed at Mel with beseeching eyes. "Can she keep me?"

Claire sighed in mock exasperation. "Why is it that any given group of adults, if left to their own devices, inevitably talks about nothing but sex?"

"Because it's the one thing any given group of adults has in common with one another," Ethan said. "And it's the only thing on *my* mind tonight."

"As opposed to any other night, when you're pondering the meaning of life and human nature," Gina said.

"And on that enlightened note," Jay got to her feet, "who's up for a midnight swim?"

"Ooh, I could go for a little skinny-dipping right now." Gina grinned at Claire, who nodded her agreement. "Ethan?"

"Sure." He looked over at Regan with an innocent smile. "Make me the luckiest boy in the world and say you'll come, Regan."

"Am I invisible here?" Mel asked.

"Oh, you're more than welcome, too," Ethan said.

"Gee, thanks." Mel gave Regan a gentle nudge and searched her face with cautious eyes. She didn't want to put her on the spot, but she needed to know what Regan wanted to do. Swimming naked couldn't possibly be the easiest prospect for someone as shy as her lover.

Regan gave a nervous little cough and nodded at Mel in acknowledgement. "Skinny-dipping, huh? Do you people get innocent girls high on purpose in an effort to lower their inhibitions?"

"No, but that's a good idea." Gina stood and stretched. "I'm going to get my towel."

Regan grabbed Mel's hand to pull her standing. "Come on. Let's go get ours."

Mel studied Regan as they walked back to their tent, marveling at the way her lover's porcelain skin glowed in the gentle moonlight, almost as if it emanated from within her. She looked ethereal, Mel thought dreamily, almost too beautiful for this world. The day caught up to her as they approached their campsite, and Mel couldn't keep her feelings inside. She pulled Regan into an impromptu embrace.

"You're beautiful," Mel whispered. She snorted laughter when she realized how stoned she was, and how it was loosening her tongue. "No, but I mean...you're really beautiful."

Regan whimpered, then giggled, and leaned up to share in a slow, easy kiss. "You're stoned," she accused when Mel eventually pulled back.

"Maybe. But that doesn't make it any less true." She took Regan's hand and led them closer to their tent. "Are you okay with this swimming thing? Because, you know, we don't have to—"

"I've been having such a good time and I don't want it to end. So I'm trying not to get too nervous about the idea of shedding my clothes in front of a bunch of strangers."

"Especially when one of them has been flirting with you all

night?"

Regan tugged on her earlobe and cast a shy smile down at the ground. "You noticed, huh?"

Mel laughed. "Noticed? Jesus, baby, I thought he was going to hurt himself, trying that hard."

"It didn't bother you, right? Ethan?"

"If someone wants to let you know how attractive you are, as long as it's not bothering you, it's not bothering me. You should hear it as often as possible. You're the loveliest woman I've ever seen."

"No one has ever made me feel that way before," Regan said. "I'm still getting used to it."

Mel was prepared to spend every waking moment convincing her. "You have no reason to worry about skinny-dipping. Unless the thought of making everyone drool over you is somehow scary, I mean."

Regan snorted.

Sensing that she wasn't convinced, Mel kept going. "Honestly. You happen to have what is, in my opinion, the sexiest kind of body a woman can have."

"The sedentary lifestyle kind?"

"I was thinking more along the lines of soft, curvy, warm —"

"Sweet talker," Regan said, but she was smiling. Mission accomplished.

They stopped at the truck and Regan spent long moments in a desperate search for her keys. "C'mon, keys...conspiring against me to make me look like a bumbling idiot in front of this hot babe. Where the hell —" She suddenly pulled them from her pocket and proudly held them aloft in the air. "See? I *am* smooth, after all."

"Why, Regan O'Riley, you get positively goofy when you smoke pot," Mel said, and gave her bottom a light pinch. "I *like* it."

"I like you stoned, too," Regan said, extracting their towels. "In fact, I like you any way I can have you."

"Come on," Mel said, grinning. "Let's go get wet."

REGAN WOKE UP the next morning with a lazy smile already plastered on her face. She felt secure, cradled in muscular arms, and she murmured in pleasure at the feeling of bare skin pressed against her own. She stretched a little within Mel's unconscious embrace, feeling a slight soreness in her body. She wasn't used to skinny-dipping, sleeping on the hard ground, and having sex on a regular basis, and her body was making that known.

Not that she was complaining.

Mel's arms tightened around her and Regan burrowed more deeply into their shared sleeping bag and the warm hug. After a moment, she felt a soft kiss pressed to one shoulder blade.

"Are you awake, sweet girl?"

Regan smiled at the quiet whisper and opened her eyes. Bright blue sunlight filtered through their tent. "Yeah. Just enjoying the nature."

"Nature, huh? Like this rock that's been under my ass all night?" Mel nibbled along Regan's shoulder and neck.

Regan turned to face Mel, grinning at her lover. Peaceful grey eyes stared back at her, conveying the same easy affection that Mel's body did. Mel changed position so their entire lengths were touching.

"Last night was wonderful," Regan said. "Every part of it. I guess camping is a happy memory for me, too, now."

Mel beamed at her, leaning down to kiss her eyebrow. "See?"

"You were right," Regan conceded.

"Just remember that. For future reference, I mean."

Regan gave Mel a playful scowl. "Don't push it."

Mel tickled the small of Regan's back. "So what's the plan for today?" she asked.

Regan considered her mental itinerary. "Oklahoma," she ticked off. She hesitated, unsure of how Mel might react to what she was about to suggest. "We could make some stops there, if you like, or we could try and just drive straight through to Texas tonight."

Mel's body stiffened. She broke their eye contact, staring at Regan's shoulder with a stormy gaze. "Stop there for what?"

Okay, so she doesn't want to see any family or friends. Regan cleared her throat. *Goddamn Oklahoma for lying between Missouri and Texas, anyway.* "I was just saying that we have plenty of time if you did want to stop for any reason, but I'm more than willing to try and drive straight through. It'll be a lot of driving, but that's okay."

"Fine." Mel gave Regan a polite smile. A distant smile. Her grey eyes were impassive. "We'd better get moving, then, if we've got all that driving to do."

"YOU LOOK LIKE you have something on your mind," Regan said. It was an hour after they'd left the campground and they were fast approaching Oklahoma. She was behind the wheel for the first driving shift.

Mel tore her eyes away from the window and stared at her for a moment before dissolving into an embarrassed smile. "I'm sorry. I've been kinda quiet, huh?"

"Kinda." Regan tightened her hands on the steering wheel.

Mel leaned over closer to Regan's body, reaching out and touching her thigh. "I don't mean to be distant."

Regan shot her a careful grin. "I don't mean to be a pest."

"You're not a pest. I'm just not used to having someone want to know how I'm doing. And wanting to tell someone how I'm doing."

"You're getting so good at it, though," Regan murmured.

Mel was silent for a moment, then said, "I was thinking that maybe I should try and see my brother Mike. I haven't been back to Oklahoma since I left for college, so I haven't seen him for about seven years."

Regan made a low whistle at that.

"I know. And we didn't part on the best of terms."

Regan furrowed her eyebrows, doing some quick mental math. "How old is he?"

"He'll be twenty-one now." Sorrow entered Mel's tone. "He was fourteen when I last saw him."

"Do you want to tell me what happened?"

Mel released a mighty sigh. "My father kicked me out of the house when I was seventeen," she said. "Not only did he cast me out, but he turned Mike against me. Christ, I thought the kid hated me until he called me when he was eighteen, after he moved out of dad's house. We've spoken a few times since then, but I haven't actually seen him."

Regan could feel Mel's gaze burning through her cheek. It made her squirm in her seat. "I'm sorry," she said, hoping Mel would continue.

"I never really blamed Mike. When my dad freaked out about my being gay, Mike was just a kid. He wasn't strong enough to think for himself. All he knew was that if he called me a dyke, too, then suddenly dad wasn't focusing on him anymore."

Regan's jaw tensed. "Your dad kicked you out for being a lesbian?"

"More or less," Mel said in a quiet voice. "Anyway, that's all in the past. Hell, we even talk on the phone at this point, you know, on holidays and stuff."

"I bet those are great conversations," Regan muttered. She felt her mood darkening to match Mel's. *That fucking bastard has caused her so much pain.*

Mel gave her a humorless chuckle. "We'll never be friends."

Shrugging, she lifted her hand from Regan's to affect a dismissive wave. "It's not a big deal. I'm used to it. But I don't think Mike's doing very well. The phone number I had for him was disconnected six months ago. I'm not sure why, exactly, but I'm really worried about him."

"Because his number was disconnected, or is there something else?"

"It's just a feeling."

"Then we'll find him," Regan said. "And maybe you can knock some sense into him."

Mel grunted in agreement. "What are big sisters for?"

"I always wished for a brother or sister. That's a special thing to have, a sibling."

"I wish I could find a number for him," Mel said. "I've called information."

"Do you know any of his friends?"

"No." Mel sniffed, then said, "I think I may have to call my father."

Regan said nothing, but reached over to touch Mel's knee. *Sounds like a good reason for a bad mood.*

"I don't want to call my father." Mel shot Regan a petulant look. "Not right now."

"You have a lot going on. I don't blame you."

"But I think maybe I'm *supposed* to do this. See Mike, I mean. I never planned on going back home..."

"I think it's a good idea," Regan said. "And if you want...I mean, if it'd make you feel better—"

"I want you with me." Mel clasped Regan's hand. "Please come with me."

"Of course," she said. "Of course, baby."

There was nothing in the world she wanted more.

Chapter
Ten

"Dad?" Mel's voice shook and that pissed her off. She turned away from Regan's casual gaze to look out the truck window.

"Laney?" His voice was slurred. Mel darted her eyes over to the clock that glowed on the truck's dashboard. It was the middle of the afternoon. "Is that you, Laney?"

Mel sighed. "Yeah, Dad, it's me."

"Laney!" her father cried. "Well, how the hell are ya?"

Mel blinked at the unexpected joviality. "I'm okay. Listen, I was wondering if you knew—"

"How's the beat?" he asked. "They keeping you busy up there in Detroit?"

Mel's mouth opened a bit and she struggled to clear her dry throat. "Uh, yeah, Dad. It's all right."

"I gotta tell you, I don't envy you working in the fucking slums." Her father raised his voice slightly, which only emphasized the unevenness of his words. "Fuckin' trash, living up there in Detroit." Mel heard him take a drink of something. "Course it's no better in Lawton anymore. I tell you that a family of goddamn Arabs moved in down the street?"

Mel stifled a deep sigh. "Detroit's fine, dad. I've met a lot of really wonderful people." *One of whom is going crazy sitting next to me right now, knowing how much I hate talking to you.*

"Take the detective test yet?" The question was loud and brash, and it made Mel cringe.

Her father was the last person she wanted to tell about her recent disillusionment. He would never understand. "Not yet," she answered after a beat.

"Well, what the hell are you waiting for? Goddamn it, Laney, you never did take the initiative on these things. You worried you won't pass?"

"No, dad, I'm not worried. Listen, I actually called for a reason. I was wondering if you have Mike's new phone number."

"Christ, and don't even get me started on that little bastard," her father muttered. "I tell you he's shacked up with some woman now? Doesn't even have a goddamn job."

Mel's heart beat a little faster in her chest. He knew where Mikey was; the phone call was worth something. "Do you have a phone number for him?" she asked again.

"Nah. I don't think he's got a phone in his name, and he never gave me that woman's number."

Stinging tears burned her eyes, and she turned to look out the truck window at the passing landscape. "I've just got an address," her father continued. "I wish I did have his number so you could call him and give him a kick in his worthless ass. He's stopped coming around; I haven't seen him for months. And I've been sick, Laney. I've been real sick."

Mel blinked at the last statement before focusing on the first. "You have an address?" she asked. "Can you give me that?"

"What the hell good is that gonna do you?" He coughed then, a harsh, hacking sound. "It's not like you ever come around, either. Too busy up there in Detroit playing street cop and doing God knows what else."

Mel held her breath, praying that her father wouldn't push this. *I never come around? The last thing he ever said to my face was that I was a goddamn queer who he never wanted in his house again.*

"Are you coming for a visit?" he demanded.

Mel couldn't lie. "I'm driving through Oklahoma. I thought that I might try and see Mikey, since I haven't been able to reach him by phone."

"Were you planning on mentioning this to me?" His voice was softer now, less slurred, and Mel shivered at the familiar anger roiling just below the surface. "What, your old man doesn't rate a visit?"

Mel turned even further in her seat, away from the quick look she got from Regan. She sensed her lover turning her attention back to the road, and she relaxed a little. "I wasn't sure you'd even want to see me. And I'm really just passing through, with a friend—"

"Friend, huh?" Her father's voice rang with disdain. "What kind of friend?"

Mel's throat went dry and she shivered. She had never come close to discussing her sexuality with him since that day when she was seventeen. He had made it pretty clear that he didn't want to know. After a slight hesitation, she said, "The kind I don't think you want to meet."

Her father was silent for countless breaths, and Mel simply sat with the phone to her ear, wishing like hell that she could hang up. When she found Mike, she was going to kick his ass for getting her into this phone call.

She was startled when her father chuckled. "Laney, you don't know what I want. I want to see you, girl! It's been so long."

Mel opened her mouth, but the words caught in her throat. There was so much she wanted to say to him: that he was the one who pushed her away, he was the one who never wanted to deal with her. "Seven years," she said instead, her voice cracking.

"I miss you, Laney, and I'm sick. I told you. Come on, you won't come and see your sick old man?"

"I..." She closed her eyes, her whole body tensing at the idea of seeing her father again. She dimly felt Regan's hand seek her own, but she pulled away on reflex. She didn't know what to make of her father's request. Did he really want to see her? Or was he just old and sick and scared? "I don't know if we'll have time, Dad, but we'll try."

It was like someone else was talking. Self-loathing consumed Mel at her automatic, child-like response to her father's words. All he had to do was pretend to care for her, and she came running.

"Please do try." He spoke to her like she couldn't remember him speaking to her since her mother died, calmly, gently. "I really would like to see you, Laney. I do miss you."

Mel felt tears sting her eyes, and she blinked them back with an angry scowl. She swiped at her face with the back of one hand. "Could I get that address, Dad?" Her voice sounded hoarse to her ears, and she cringed knowing that her father could hear that weakness, too. "I promise I'll try."

He gave her the address without another word, and wished her a cheerful goodbye that made her heart hurt. Mel hung up the cell phone and sat, staring out the passenger-side window with shining eyes.

"Mel?"

Regan's concerned whisper finally loosed the sorrowful tears from Mel's eyes. The outpouring angered her, and she refused to turn to face her lover knowing the evidence of her turmoil was painting her cheeks. It would be so easy to let Regan make her feel better. She could do it with one word, one hug; Mel knew she could.

"Baby, are you...are you all right?"

She was a mess. Ten minutes on the phone with her father and she was a fucking mess. And there was Regan sitting next to her, so beautiful and kind and loving. How could she accept what Regan offered when she was this fucked up? One day, Regan would know exactly how fucked up she really was. And what then?

"Mel?"

With some effort, Mel hardened her heart and stilled her tears. She wiped her face with her hand once more, and turned to give Regan a tight smile. "I got Mike's address. Do you think we could...maybe we could go see him tomorrow?"

"Sure, baby."

Mel blinked at the affection in Regan's voice. Why did she have to be so perfect? Her hands tightened into fists at her sides, and she was immediately filled with self-loathing. She was an asshole to get pissed at her for being someone she was growing to need. "Thanks," she said.

"Are you...are you okay, Mel?"

Regan's obvious hesitation tore further into Mel's heart, and she felt like she would choke on the fear and anger and guilt that swirled around her belly. It had been a really bad day. Not once when she imagined this road trip had she allowed herself to think about the obvious route it would take. She was back in Oklahoma after swearing never to return, and she was confronting things she had never intended to face again. She wanted so badly to let Regan make it all better, but she couldn't expose her need.

"I'm fine," she lied. "I just haven't been to Lawton in a long time. I wonder if it's changed."

"Well, you've changed," Regan said. "So I'm sure you'll find things are different there, too."

The cautious comment unleashed a wave of emotion in Mel, and she squeezed her eyes tightly shut in an effort to stop thinking. Tomorrow they would go to Lawton. Tonight she wanted only to forget. She opened her eyes and glanced at a passing highway sign. "We're almost to Tulsa." She turned to Regan, now under control. "Is it okay if we stop there tonight?"

Regan gave her a cautious smile. "Sure."

"Thanks," Mel said. "What do you think about hitting a bar? I wouldn't mind unwinding a little."

"Um. Do you know of any gay bars in Tulsa?"

"Gay, straight, I just want a drink. We won't stay long." Mel tried hard not to draw the obvious parallel between this escape and the one her father had always chosen to take. Her headache threatened to intensify.

"Well, how about we find a hotel and have a drink there? I mean, I really don't like bars much. Especially straight bars."

Mel suppressed a sigh of frustration and instead gave Regan a wry little smile. "You met *me* in a straight bar, though." She reached over and stroked her fingers across a pale cheek. "And look what that's gotten you — stuck in a truck with a moody bitch for hours."

Regan snorted and shook her head. "You're not a moody bitch."

"Yes, I am," Mel said apologetically. "But I really would like to go get a drink somewhere. I swear we won't stay long."

"No problem." Regan gave a nervous nod. "I know you had a hard day."

Mel immediately felt a pang in her heart. What the hell was wrong with her, manipulating her lover into going to a bar when she obviously didn't want to? Guilt consumed her, and the searing emotion only fueled her anger and inner turmoil. Regan glanced over with such concern that Mel could only look away in discomfort. A warm hand crept over to Mel's lap and captured her fingers. Mel turned her face towards the window and blinked her eyes shut hard, holding back her emotion. *Face it, Laney. You don't deserve her. More importantly, she doesn't deserve you.*

MEL ROLLED THE bottom of her half-empty beer bottle across the sticky tabletop in front of her, staring at the condensation left by the drink she had insisted she needed. Regan sat across from her, but Mel couldn't meet her eyes. She knew her lover was miserable sitting in the seedy country-and-western bar they'd found downtown. She wasn't feeling much better herself. *I guess I forgot that what I always liked about bars was who I could take home with me.*

"I'm sorry," she shouted over the din of the honky-tonk crowd. "This was a mistake. We should go."

Regan blinked at Mel's sudden voice, dragging her gaze from two men arguing by the blaring jukebox. "Are you sure? Do you feel better?"

How could she feel better when she knew that she had dragged Regan to this awful place? If she truly wanted to feel better, Regan was what she needed. Not a drink. "I'll feel better when we get back to the hotel. This sucks."

Regan relaxed into a relieved smile. "This place *does* kinda suck."

Almost as much as me. "I'm sorry I made us come."

"It's okay. You've had a pretty fucked-up last couple weeks."

Mel met Regan's eyes over the table and wondered how much longer it would be before this incredible woman got sick of all this drama. "That doesn't excuse bringing you here for a night at the shallow end of the gene pool."

Regan laughed long and loud at that, giving Mel a fond shake of her head. "How about I hit the bathroom, then we can get out of here?"

Mel gave her a silent nod, and followed her with her eyes as she stood.

Regan bent down, bringing her lips close to Mel's ear. "Why don't you start thinking about what's going to make you feel good tonight? So you can let me know."

"Will do." Mel watched Regan walk to the bathroom with a reluctant smile tugging on her lips. Damn her for being so amazing, anyway.

Mel was deeply involved in her consideration of what exactly she wanted to do to Regan back in their room when a rangy man in a cowboy hat stepped up to her table with a wide smile. He tipped his hat in greeting and gave her a friendly nod. He wore faded Levis and a T-shirt that emphasized his muscular body.

"Interested in a dance, darlin'?" he asked.

Mel gave the cowboy a polite smile. "No, thanks. I'm just leaving when my friend gets back from the bathroom."

The man lifted his eyes from Mel's face to look over her head, and nodded in the direction of the restroom. "You might want to check on your friend, sweetheart. Looks like she's not appreciating the attention she's getting."

Mel stood up so fast that her chair threatened to topple. She pivoted where she stood and saw that Regan was standing next to a table near the ladies room, trying to pull away from a bearded man who was holding her arm. Mel's fists tightened at her sides as she took in the fearful expression on Regan's face, the leering grin on the stranger's, and the tense set of Regan's body as she leaned away from the unwelcome contact. Anger surged through her. That fucking son of a bitch. She was striding across the bar before she had a chance to think about it.

This was her fault. She'd brought Regan here, *and* after being moody and sullen all day. Overcome by rage and deep guilt, Mel reached the table just as the bearded man laughed with his buddies.

"Oh, come on, honey," he slurred. "Sit down with us for a while. I promise you'll have a good time."

Mel stepped to Regan's side and placed a possessive hand on the small of her back. Eyes narrowed, she grabbed the man's wrist and squeezed hard. "Take your fucking hand off my friend," she said, her voice cold and dangerous.

The man let go of Regan slowly before standing up to tower over Mel, reminding her of her father on a bad day. A trace of fear in his eyes vied with the anger directed at her for the interruption. He was begging her to throw a punch, and he had no idea how much she wanted to do just that. Mel knew that if she didn't walk away right now, she was likely heading for a hell of a fight.

Regan slumped against her in relief and grabbed her wrist, trying to pull her away from the confrontation. "Please, Mel," she whispered, tugging her away a couple of steps. "It's not worth it. Let's just go."

"Yeah, listen to your girlfriend," the man taunted, seemingly emboldened by his friends' amusement. "Fuckin' ugly dyke, anyway."

Mel couldn't have stopped herself even if she'd tried. She spun on her heel and swung her fist without thought, connecting solidly with the bearded man's grinning face. He fell backwards against the table, sending glasses and bottles crashing to the floor. His two buddies knocked over their own chairs as they leapt to their feet in shock.

Mel heard Regan gasp her name and she spared a sideways glance at her horrified face. The momentary distraction cost her. A blow caught her across the shoulder and glanced off her jaw, snapping her head back.

With an angry growl, she lunged forward again and her fist connected with the bearded man's face. They landed hard amidst spilled beer and broken glass. White noise pounded through her head, but she could hear Regan screaming. That sound filled her with hot guilt and reinforced her blind wrath against the man who squirmed beneath her body. Flailing fists connected with her chest a couple more times, each blow satisfying in its pain somehow, and she returned the punches eagerly.

All of a sudden Mel felt strong hands grab her arms and shoulders and she was pulled off the man, who immediately scrambled up. His friends restrained him from coming after her, their faces tense with the effort of holding him back. Mel struggled within the grasp of the hands that held her, cold fury still pumping through her veins. The hands that held her tightened until her movement was almost totally restricted, and she released her abating rage in a long, angry breath.

"Calm down, girl!" Someone squeezed her arms painfully. "Calm down before you get yourself in real trouble!"

Mel obeyed the hissed command, willing her body to relax. The moment she let go of her anger, it died a painful death, leaving in its wake sudden shame. Mel turned her head and met horrified green eyes. Oh, God. What had she just done?

Regan's mouth hung open and her eyes were glassy with

fear. She took a nervous step away from the scene, looking like she wanted to disappear.

Mel kept her head down as she was led away from the scene of the fight, her eyes on her own feet and on the feet of her lover walking beside her. Her stomach ached with the sudden, sick knowledge that she had blown it.

Regan didn't speak to her as they returned to their table and gathered their things. The two men who had broken up the fight stayed with Mel until she made it to the front door, casting frequent glances at the angry, drunken shouting that still echoed throughout the bar from the beaten man and his friends. They looked on edge, prepared to break up another struggle at any moment.

Mel could only offer a grateful nod when they held the door open for her and Regan. "Sorry," she said.

"Don't be." One of the men jerked his balding head back towards the drunken man's table. "Asshole got what was coming."

REGAN DIDN'T SPEAK to her until they reached their hotel room. Mel walked in and stood with her back to the door, mourning the loss of what could have been.

"Are you all right?" A hesitant question.

Mel lacked the courage to turn around and look her lover in the eye. "Yeah," she whispered. "I'm sorry."

"Look at me, honey. I need to see if you're okay."

Tears fell from Mel's eyes without warning. "Fuck," she cursed, and swiped at her eyes with the back of her hand. She allowed Regan to turn her around. It took every ounce of her courage to raise her eyes from the ugly blue carpet to her lover's face.

Regan sucked in a harsh breath. "Come on." She took Mel's hand. "Let me get you cleaned up."

Mel followed her to the bathroom, hot with shame over everything: her face, her anger, and her weakness.

Regan soaked a hotel washcloth and pressed the wet towel against Mel's battered face. "Do you want to tell me what that was about?" Her voice was calm and controlled.

Mel dropped her gaze to bruised and bloody hands. "He *touched* you."

"I appreciate that you made him let go of me," Regan said in a careful voice. "But it didn't have to go that far."

"He hurt you," Mel said. "I can't just let someone hurt you."

"And you think seeing you get hurt makes me feel better?

You don't think it hurts me to see you snap like that?"

A choked sob escaped Mel, and she lowered her eyes as her face flushed in horror. She'd never heard Regan so upset before. She couldn't believe what she had caused.

Immediately Regan's arms were around her, holding her close. Mel squirmed within the embrace, so full of self-loathing that she couldn't stand to accept any of the comfort Regan offered so freely. But every time she moved as if to pull away, Regan simply tightened her arms and pulled her deeper and deeper into a desperate hug, until she surrendered with a defeated sigh.

"I'm a moron, Regan," she said. "You deserve so much better than me."

There. It was out in the open now.

"Why would you say something like that?" Regan pulled back and forced Mel's eyes to her own. "You're not responsible for what that guy did. Only for the way you chose to handle it. And as far as that goes, you're human." Regan cradled Mel's bruised face in tender hands. "Deal with it."

Mel shook her head. She refused to let Regan excuse her so easily. "You don't understand, Regan. This is how I am. And you deserve better. I'm weak and I'm fucked-up. I'm just going to hurt you."

"You sound like you're trying pretty hard to convince me. Or yourself." Regan released Mel's face and folded her arms over her chest. "I happen to think you're very good at this. When you're not busy telling yourself that you're not so there's a ready-made excuse to walk away, that is."

Mel snorted and stood up. She took the bloodstained washcloth from Regan's hands and tossed it into the sink with an unceremonious flick of the wrist. She couldn't do this, not right now. Without saying a word, she turned and strode out of the bathroom. She needed space. It was only when she reached the bed that she realized the obvious.

There was nowhere for her to go.

REGAN ROSE FROM where she knelt on the bathroom floor, then dropped down onto the toilet cover with a shaky exhalation.

We've gone from quiet and brooding, to obviously upset, to beating the shit out of some redneck...and now she's ready to end this relationship before it begins. And that's just in one day. This wasn't just about the bar fight. Mel truly thought she wasn't good enough for Regan, and it had all started with Oklahoma and her family. Regan clenched her fists on her lap. *She almost acts like she's trying to beat me to the punch.*

Understanding for the first time how deep Mel's mistrust ran, Regan strode out of the bathroom and halted at the end of the bed. "You know what I always find annoying?" she asked.

The look Mel gave her was so naked that Regan's heartbeat seemed to falter in her chest. "What?"

"In books and movies, when people struggle in their relationships, but can never see what's happening between them because things get left unsaid. Because they don't just talk to one another. You know what I mean?"

"Yeah. I know what you mean."

Regan sat on the bed next to Mel and took her cold hand. "I always get so fucking frustrated by that. It makes me want to scream, just tell her, you moron! Say what you need to say, because that's the only way things are gonna work out!'"

"I don't know if it's that simple."

Regan looked hard into grey eyes and brought Mel's hand to her lips, planting a string of kisses across her knuckles. "It doesn't have to be hard."

Mel's eyes were heavy with pain, regret, and what shone like nervous hope. She looked as if she were right on the verge of taking a big leap from some impossible height, steeling her nerve and praying that she could trust her instincts.

"Let's not do that," Regan murmured. "Let's not leave things unsaid. You can trust me. I promise."

"You make it sound so easy."

"It's not easy. But it's worth it." Regan held her gaze for a long moment of unblinking intensity. "I know it's worth it."

"I'm terrified of how fucked-up I am," Mel said. "I saw it today. I'm scared that you're going to realize how fucked-up I am, and you're going to figure out that I'm not worth the trouble."

"I thought I'd made it obvious that everything about us feels right to me. I've never met someone who makes me feel like you do. Don't you feel it, too?"

"I do. And that's what scares me so much. I'm so terrified about...needing you like this."

"Because you think that, one way or the other, you're gonna lose me eventually?"

"Maybe not tonight, but at some point—"

"Why do you think you're so easy to throw away?" Regan interrupted Mel with a scolding squeeze around the middle. "You're my best friend as well as my lover. You're not going to lose me. No matter what else happens, I'll always want to be your friend."

"You're my best friend, too," Mel murmured.

"So then you have nothing to worry about," Regan said, and pulled back to give Mel a serious look. "I take friendships very seriously. I don't just end them. I don't just leave."

"I guess I just haven't had good luck with caring about people. It's hard to risk that kind of pain again."

"Your mother?"

"That's part of it. My dad, you know, and my brother. Lauren." Mel's voice broke a little on the name.

Regan hesitated, but sensed that this was her chance. *Best friend and first lover...You know you're dying of curiosity. And she actually brought her up.* She caressed Mel's cheek. "Tell me."

Mel met her gaze, grey eyes stormy with her struggle. "I've never talked about this before. With anyone."

"You don't have to talk about it now." Her eyes remained locked with Mel's. "But I'd like it if you did."

"When my dad kicked me out of the house, it was because he caught me with Lauren. It was—" She laughed, a hollow sound. "It was my first time. Both of ours."

"Jesus. I can't imagine, honey. I'm sorry."

"When he walked in on us, he pulled me off of her, screaming at me and calling me names. He started punching me, hitting me...right in front of her." Mel squeezed the back of her neck, obviously struggling with telling her story. "God, she was so scared. So was I. He was so out of control, I thought he was going to kill me."

"God," Regan whispered. She pulled Mel close, pleased when she didn't resist the embrace.

Mel's tears began anew. "I was totally humiliated. Seventeen years old, naked, having just experienced what was, at the time, one of the most intense moments of my life, and I was getting the shit beaten out of me by my alcoholic father who kept screaming at me that I was a dirty queer and a whore."

If I ever see her father, she's going to have to hold me back. Regan kept her eyes calm and reassuring despite the rage that burned through her body. Mel's fears, her fragile confidence, her insecurities...everything made so much more sense to her now.

"Lauren grabbed her clothes and ran out of the house after he started hitting me. The whole thing really upset her," Mel said. "I couldn't blame her. It was devastating."

"And that's when the relationship ended?"

"She was afraid of my dad. And she was afraid of what her parents would think if he outed her to them. She stopped talking to me."

"So in one night, you lost your father, your brother, and your lover," Regan said. "And you feel *bad* about being a little messed up?"

"I'm a lot messed up."

"We're all messed up," Regan said, and kissed the dark hair that tickled her nose. She curled her arm around Mel's tense shoulder, pulling her close. "Nearly everyone I know is messed up in some way or another. The interesting ones, at least. Do you really think I'm not going to want you if you're not a flawless, self-actualized adult human being?"

Mel snuffled quietly, and shook her head. "Not flawless—"

"'Cause if you're expecting perfection, Mel, let me just warn you now. I've got problems, too. I screw up, and things upset me. Silly things. You're not perfect and neither am I. Nobody is." She reached down and captured Mel's chin in her hand, turning her face up until their eyes met. "It's not about being perfect. It's about being perfect for me."

Mel broke their gaze and buried her nose in Regan's chest. "I'm not saying I should be perfect."

"And I think you might be, Mel. I think you could be perfect for me." She felt the body in her arms begin to tremble, and she continued, "I'm not going to suddenly decide I can't handle this. Nothing, nobody, is going to chase me away or convince me otherwise, you hear me? Not even you."

Regan felt the wetness soaking through her T-shirt just as Mel muttered, "Goddamn it."

"I promise, baby," Regan said. Kissing her lover's dark hair, she whispered, "I wish you could see yourself through my eyes, how beautiful you really are."

Mel tightened her arms around Regan's middle. "I've wished the same thing for you, you know."

"See?" Regan murmured, and smiled. "Perfect."

Between the tears and the fists, she looked like hell. And even still, like the most breathtaking person Regan had ever known. "Thank you for making me feel better. Again."

"Thank you for letting me," Regan said. "You feel better?"

"I think you chased it away pretty well this time." Mel drew back and stared into her eyes. "This thing between us. It's moving really fast, isn't it?"

"Yes, it is." Regan found her lips instinctively, meeting Mel halfway as she leaned in for an intimate kiss. The moment of reconnection made Regan's entire body feel warm, and though she felt too exhausted to escalate into passion, she felt her emotion rising. The kiss heightened in intensity until Mel winced and pulled back to touch her cut lip with an apologetic smile.

"Sorry about that," Regan said.

"My fault. I'm the one who decided to throw myself in front of his fist."

As much as she didn't want to encourage her, Regan had to let Mel off the hook just a little bit. "For the record, I kind of liked the whole knight in shining armor thing. Coming to my defense and all." At Mel's gooey grin, she narrowed her eyes and pinned her with a serious look. "Just don't make a habit of it, okay? I don't think my heart can take it."

Mel adjusted her expression to one of suitable gravity. "I promise."

Chapter
Eleven

The address Mel had gotten from her father was a tiny apartment complex with a musty smell in its stairwell. She followed Regan inside on hesitant feet, gazing around at the row of mailboxes on the wall and a recycling bin by the door. These were things that her brother saw every day; the idea was surreal to her. He was a man now, and she barely knew him.

Her heart felt like it would beat out of her chest when Regan started up the steps, so she stopped her with a panicked hand on her arm. "Wait."

Regan turned and gazed down at Mel on the step below her. "Okay?"

With an explosive sigh, Mel turned to sit down on the step where she stood. She dropped her head into her hands and stared at the dirty red carpet beneath her feet. "I feel sick."

It was a moment before Regan dropped down to sit beside her. "It's going to be okay, you know." She reached over and took Mel's hand. "I promise. No matter what happens, it'll be okay."

And it would, because Regan was with her. Mel gave her a sidelong glance and a grateful nod. "I trust you."

"Then come on." Regan stood and offered her hand with a smile. "Let's go do this, baby."

"Right. Okay." Mel allowed Regan to pull her to her feet.

Upstairs, down a dim hallway, they came to a stop in front of a battered door marked with the number 427. "This is it, right?" Regan asked.

Mel pulled a creased piece of paper from her pocket, unfolding it and glancing at the address she already knew by heart. This was where her brother lived, according to her father. She couldn't quite imagine knocking on the door.

"Mikey, get back upstairs!"

Mel looked on in horror as her younger brother walked down the stairs behind her screaming father. He stopped short and stared at her when she yelled up at him, giving her a frightened look.

"Say goodbye to Laney, Mike," her father said as he turned around and grabbed Mike's skinny arm. He dragged him down the last few steps, and then turned to glare at Mel. "Tell her we don't want any fucking queers in this family."

Mike flinched and looked up at Mel with wide eyes. The tears blurred her vision and stung, making the sight of her brother even more painful than the rib she was sure her father had cracked when he'd pulled her off Lauren.

"Mike..." Mel sobbed.

"Or maybe you're just a queer like your bitch sister, huh, Mike?" Her father clapped Mike on the back, drawing a wince from the gangly boy. "Is that it?"

Mike pinned Mel with a terrified look, then dropped his gaze to the carpeted floor. "Nah," he said. His voice, so newly deep, shook. "I hate queers." He raised shining eyes to her face. "They make me sick."

That had been the last time she'd seen her brother. "We were so close once," Mel whispered. "I'm afraid we'll never get that back." She turned to regard Regan, letting her fears take over for a moment. "What if he doesn't want to see me? What if he really does hate me?"

"He doesn't hate you. And if he isn't happy to see you, I'll kick his ass for being an idiot. Okay?" Regan touched Mel's back. "I'm here no matter what happens, got it?"

"Okay." Mel knocked on the door before she could chicken out. "Thank you."

"It felt wonderful holding you this morning," Regan murmured under her breath. She shot Mel a crooked smile.

The quiet comment was just what she needed. She hooked her thumbs into the pockets of her jeans and grinned at the door. "Likewise." After about ten seconds with no answer, she was ready to give up. "He's not home."

"Mel, give it a—" Regan shut up at the sound of locks disengaging and masculine muttering from within the apartment.

"Hold up, one second."

Mel sucked in a quiet breath. *Mike.* Before she had time to process the foreign familiarity of the voice, the door opened and she was face-to-face with a man who looked strangely like the boy she once knew. For a moment he just stared at her, and then his eyes went wide in a look of surprise so comical that she nearly laughed aloud. She saw his mind racing behind intense grey eyes that so resembled her own, and their mother's, and she bit her lip in anticipation.

"Hey, Mikey," she said when he didn't speak. "How's it going?"

"Laney?" His lip trembled for an instant, and his eyes shone with emotion. "Is it...you're here?"

"Um." She spared a quick glance at Regan, who smiled up at her. "We were passing through Oklahoma and I thought I should look you up. Except I couldn't find a phone number, so I hope you don't mind us just dropping in on you."

"You look amazing." Mike relaxed into a dazed grin, stepping forward to pull her into a tight hug. "I can't believe you're here."

Mel blinked at the unfamiliar lean hardness of his body. "I can't believe...Jesus, look at you!" She seized Mike by the shoulders. "You're huge!"

Mike gave her a bashful grin. "Well, I'm definitely not fourteen anymore."

"No, definitely not." She lifted her hand, hesitated, and swept away a lock of hair that had fallen over his eyes. "You look wonderful, Mike. I can't believe this handsome man in front of me."

"And you look just like Mom," he said.

Mel had to bite her lip to keep from sobbing at the softly spoken words. They meant more to her than she ever could have imagined. "Thank you."

"Except for this, of course," Mike added. Smirking, he traced a thumb over the bruise on her cheekbone. "Should I ask how the other guy looks?"

"Worse," Regan supplied.

Mel turned to gaze at Regan with fond eyes. After a silent moment, she wanted to slap herself. "God, I'm so rude. I'm sorry." Mel reached out and took Regan's hand. "This is my girlfriend, Regan."

Regan turned a beaming smile on her brother, offering her free hand. "It's very nice to meet you, Mike."

"It's great to meet you, too."

There was no disgust in his voice, no recrimination. Instead, his words rang with shy pleasure, and his eyes met Mel's in unspoken approval. Mel exhaled, releasing tension she hadn't realized she carried.

"Speaking of rude." Mike took a step back into the apartment and gave them an apologetic smile, gesturing with his arm. "Do you wanna come in?"

"Sure," Mel said. She felt shy, and she looked to Regan for reassurance.

"Sounds great," Regan echoed. As they followed Mike

inside, she whispered, "Laney?"

Mel gave her an admonishing smile. "Don't even think about it."

The small apartment was relatively clean, though it was hard to tell because of the sheer amount of stuff crammed into every available space. Glass figurines, mostly of elephants, littered plain wooden shelves that lined the far wall. They caught Mel's eye because she couldn't imagine her brother was responsible for them.

Mike looked over his shoulder with a raised eyebrow as he led them to a worn couch. "I'm not the collector," he said. "I'm...staying with a friend right now."

Mel chuckled as she sat down, reaching up to tug Regan to the space beside her. "I was wondering." She gave Mike a slow smile. "A girlfriend?"

Mike sank down into an overstuffed easy chair. "Uh, it's not really a girlfriend. It's more like a place to crash."

"Ah." Mel's smile faded. She glanced at Regan, reaching out to rest her hand on her thigh. The joy of connection flared in her belly when green eyes met hers, and she turned back to Mike with a renewed smile.

She could see that Mike's attention was drawn to their point of contact—Mel's hand on Regan's thigh—and she had to fight the urge to squirm in discomfort under his scrutiny. She wondered how weird this was for her brother. Seeing her for the first time in seven years, and she was as gay as the day is long.

Mike lifted curious eyes to her face. "I didn't realize you'd found someone special, Laney."

"Mel," she corrected her brother. At his curious look, she explained, "I go by Mel now." He shot her an apologetic grin. "I haven't known Regan very long, but you're right. She is very special."

"Well, I'm really glad for you," Mike said. He dropped his eyes, raking his hand through his hair. "I really am."

"Thanks." And like that, the dense ball of fear in her stomach began to dissipate. He wasn't fourteen anymore. He didn't hate her. She blinked as she remembered why she had come. "It's been a while since you've called."

Mike gave her an embarrassed shrug. "I know. I'm sorry."

"When I realized that your number was disconnected, I was hoping you'd call and give me a new one," Mel said. She kept her voice low, non-threatening, but she knew Mike could read the anxiety in her tone when his eyes filled with self-criticism and he twisted his hands in his lap. She flinched at the sight of familiar emotion flashing in her brother's eyes.

"I really am sorry, Laney. It was a shitty thing to do." Mike raised his hand to hold off her protest. "For a while I was moving around a lot, then when I moved in with Dani, I kept meaning to call you, but..."

She gave him an encouraging nod. "But what?"

Mike looked uncomfortable. "But the truth is that I didn't know what to say to you. I don't want you to be disappointed in me."

"Disappointed in you? Why? What's going on?"

Mike shrugged before answering. "Not much."

Mel felt her stomach flip-flop at the vague answer. "What does that mean?"

Mike shot Regan a self-conscious look. "I, uh...I quit going to school."

"Oh, Mike," Mel murmured. Her disappointment rang clear and her brother tensed when he heard it.

"Yeah, well, I never was any good at school, you know that." He looked down at his hands, picking at his cuticles nervously. "I was sick of it. I'm not like you."

Mel fought to maintain a placid expression even as her heart was breaking. How many times had she watched as their father made him feel like he was good for nothing? And now he believed it. She leaned over and touched Mike's knee, weighing her response. The last thing he needed was her anger. "School isn't for everyone, I guess. So what are you doing now?"

"I dunno," Mike said. "Different things. I'm supposed to start helping a guy I know do some roofing. Sometimes I get work painting." He shrugged again and looked up at Mel with a small smile. "How's the cop business?"

Mel's shrug mirrored her brother's. "Actually, I'm thinking of quitting, too."

"What?" He looked shocked. "Are you kidding me?"

"No."

"Wow." Mike shook his head, a dazed expression on his face. "I can't believe it. That's all you ever talked about when we were growing up."

"Yeah, well," Mel said, and gave Regan a quick glance to find support shining in green eyes. "I realized that I'm not doing it for me. I hate it."

"I understand," Mike said. After a moment of awkward silence he added, "I really am sorry about not calling. I missed talking to you."

She couldn't let him think it was all his fault. "I could've called Dad before now to ask where you were living, so please don't worry about it. Okay?"

"You talked to him?"

"For a few minutes." And she was still paying for it.

"Was he an asshole?"

"Not so much," Mel said. "He was Dad, you know, but he asked me to come and see him. He said he's sick. He actually tried to be nice...for a moment."

She watched Mike's jaw tighten. "What's that like?"

"Unpleasant," Mel said. "To be honest. Even though I know it's all bullshit, that he's still the same guy...as much as I hate to admit it, I still find myself wishing—"

"I know." Mike shot Regan a self-conscious look. "I'm sure that's why I still call him from time to time. Wishing."

Mel felt Regan's hand land on her knee. Just like she'd predicted, the words came without struggle. "No reason for us not to be a family, though. You and me."

Mike closed his eyes and turned away, obviously fighting to keep control. His jaw muscles bunched and tensed as his breathing grew louder. Then, "No reason except that I'm the kind of fucking weakling who would call my sister a goddamn queer because I was scared to go against him. You were my hero. You always looked out for me. And I failed you."

Mel's heartbeat stuttered for a moment, then continued on double-time. This was the first time they had ever spoken about that day. What could she say? "I understood that you were scared of him. I understand. I...hoped you didn't really feel that way." She lifted her eyes to her brother's face. "I'm glad that you don't."

"I'm sorry I never told you before." Mike brought his hand to his face and covered his eyes, voice cracking. "I'm sorry for everything. I've hated myself since that day. I fucking *hate* myself for what I did to you."

Mel moved forward off the couch, kneeling on the floor in front of Mike. "I'm not mad at you," she murmured, and laid a calming hand on his thigh. "I was never mad at you, Mikey."

"I hurt you," Mike said. When he dropped his hands to his lap, Mel grabbed one and squeezed it tight. He tried to pull away, but she refused to let him go. "I know I hurt you. I saw it in your eyes even as I was doing it."

"I got hurt, Mike, but I was never mad at you. You were just a little kid, and honestly, I felt bad leaving you behind."

"How can you think like that?" Mike said in a hoarse voice. "After the way I failed to protect you like you used to protect me. I can't believe you're even wasting your time with me."

Mel rose up onto her knees, reaching out to put a hand on Mike's slumped shoulder. "You're not a waste of time. I'm so happy about the idea of being closer with you." She gave his shoulder a firm squeeze. "You're my brother."

Mike dissolved into silent, racking sobs. He folded his arms over his stomach, leaning forward on the couch. Mel grabbed him in her arms and held him tight against her body.

"I'm sorry." Mike stayed tense in her arms. "I'm so fucking sorry."

"I forgive you," Mel whispered into his ear. "Now I want you to forgive yourself."

Mike's arms came up to cradle her then, holding her close. Mel's world stilled for a moment before resuming its forward motion. She had a family again. It took some time before they pulled apart. Mike drew back first, swiping at red-rimmed eyes with his hand.

Casting an embarrassed look over Mel's shoulder, he said, "I apologize. I swear I'm not usually like this."

Regan shook her head, one hand pressed to her lips. Her eyes were shining.

Mel touched Mike's stubbled cheek, drawing his attention back to her. "Mikey. All of this bullshit—thinking you're nothing, hating yourself—you know that's all Dad, right? That's what *he* was always telling us. You've got to let it go and make your own path."

Mike gave her a sad smile. "He is sick, you know."

"Dad?" Mel returned to Regan's side on the sofa. A warm hand found the small of her back.

"Yeah," Mike said. "I actually called him a few weeks ago. Don't know why, 'cause it sucked. But he told me he's sick. His liver, he just found out."

"What a surprise," Mel muttered. "It's serious?"

"The doctor told him to stop drinking or it'll kill him." Mike snorted in disgust. "The day that bastard gives up booze is the day I start training for the priesthood."

"I guess he's not listening to his doctors," she said. "He was slurring his words when I spoke to him this afternoon."

"No. He's still drinking, as far as I can tell." Her brother clenched his fists in his lap, his eyes flashing with anger. "He told me you'd take care of him. How glad he was that Laney had turned out so well, because he couldn't count on a loser like me to help him when he's sick."

Mel huffed in disbelief. Regan began rubbing small circles over the tense muscles of her lower back, soothing her with startling ease. "I turned out well? Now that's a shock, coming from him."

"Better than me," Mike said.

"That's what I mean!" Mel exploded. "Right there, that's Dad talking and you know it. Don't do that to yourself."

Mike turned away with a scowl. "It's true, though. I'm fucking up." He shot Regan an uncomfortable look, an apologetic smile. "I just...don't know how to be better than I am."

Their handful of phone conversations had never come close to revealing the depth of Mike's insecurities. There was so much to say, but she wasn't sure she knew how to ease his pain. But she would try.

"Listen to me. You're not the only one who feels fucked-up because of him. Doubting yourself, thinking you're not good enough, that you're only going to disappoint people. Until I met Regan, I..." Mel reached over and wrapped her arm around Regan's waist, pulling her close. "So it affects us, Mikey, but we need to forgive ourselves that. I spent so much time hating myself for letting him get to me, and for still wanting his approval, that I never let myself move past it. There's no shame in being affected, but we've got to start living for ourselves now."

"That's why you're quitting?" Mike asked. "Being a cop, I mean?"

"I guess so, yeah," Mel said. "Making my own decisions for once. I just want to be happy."

"What do you think you'll do?"

Mel started to give him an embarrassed shrug, but Regan was quick to answer. "I suggested that she look into graphic design and digital art. Mel told me she likes to draw."

Mike's eyes lit up. "You still draw?"

"Sometimes," Mel muttered. Her cheeks burned red. "Not lately, but—"

"Have you seen any of her work yet?" Mike interrupted, shooting Regan an enthusiastic grin.

"No." Regan glanced at Mel with an upraised eyebrow. "Not yet."

"Oh, man, you know that'd be perfect for you," Mike said. Nodding to Regan, he added, "She's awesome. She used to bribe me when I was a kid and refused to go to bed by telling me that she'd draw a picture for me to have when I woke up."

"Oldest babysitting trick in the book," Mel said, offering her little brother a smile.

"For real, though," Mike continued. "She could draw anything. Some of her pictures were like whole stories in themselves—"

"Jesus, Mike," Mel interrupted with a nervous chuckle. "Try not to talk me up too much. I'd hate to disappoint."

"I doubt that'll be a problem," Regan said.

"So, do you want to go out and get some lunch or something?" Mel asked. Regan snickered, she presumed at her obvious attempt to divert attention away from the subject of her art, and Mel wrinkled a playful nose at her lover.

"Oh." Mike offered them an embarrassed smile. "Actually, I'm supposed to be waiting for the guy from the cable company. Dani asked me to. You know, because she works and, uh —"

And he doesn't. "That's cool," Mel said. "Want to order a pizza or something? I mean, if you don't mind the company."

Mike leaned forward on the couch, hands on his knees. He gave her a wide, excited grin. "No! No, I don't mind at all. I'd love it if you guys could hang out for a little while."

"Hey, Mike?" Regan asked. "Is that your Playstation 2?" She pointed over to a black object near the television, an innocent smile on her face.

Mike beamed at her. "My prized possession. Are you a gamer?"

"Am I a gamer?" Regan scoffed. "Pick a game and I'll show you."

Mel chuckled at Regan's bravado. In this, the woman wasn't shy. "Be careful, Mike. As far as I can tell, she's pretty much great at everything she does." A quick leer at Regan left both her lover and her brother blushing.

"Uh," Mike fumbled. "Even Tony Hawk?"

Regan managed a cocky grin. "*Especially* Tony Hawk. Bring it on."

"This should be good," Mel said, and rubbed her hands together with a grin.

"You're gonna root for me, right?" Regan asked.

"Hey, I'm *blood*," Mike protested. "You can't boo me or anything."

Mel shook her head. "For the record, I'll be an impartial observer. No booing or cheering, just observing events as they unfold."

"Cop out," Regan muttered beside her.

"For sure," Mike agreed.

Mel grinned at the teasing, feeling at once overwhelmingly loved. This was how family should feel.

MEL STOOD AT the apartment door with her brother while Regan made a last-minute trip to the bathroom. They would be leaving in a couple minutes, and she felt an opportunity slipping away.

When would she have another chance like this? Mel bit the bullet. "You ever think of leaving Lawton?"

Mike folded his arms over his chest and leaned on his shoulder against the door. "And go where?"

"Anywhere," she said with a shrug. "You could come to Michigan."

Mike shook his head. "I don't know about that, Laney."

Mel didn't bother to correct him. *Laney it is.* "You said you don't know how to be any better than you are, right?" At his reluctant nod, she said, "Maybe you need to get out of here, kiddo. Start fresh. And you know, I'd love to have you in my life again."

"Start fresh? Doing what?"

"Doing whatever. What are you doing here?"

Mike shrugged. "Nothing, but—"

"You said the girl, Dani, that's not serious, right?"

"No, it's not serious, it's just..." Mike looked her in the eyes. "I guess I just don't see the point of being a loser in Michigan when I can stay here in Lawton and at least be a loser with friends."

"You don't have to be a loser, Mike. It's your life, your decision." She so wanted him to yearn for something more than this. "Leaving Lawton was the best thing that ever happened to me. I'm not sure I would have ever been able to find my own way if I'd stayed here and lived in his shadow."

Mike was careful to avoid her eyes. He didn't respond, just shuffled his feet.

"These are the drinking buddies?" she finally asked. "Your friends?"

Mike met her gaze with a defensive scowl. "They're all right. We have a good time."

She knew she couldn't tell him to live his own life in one breath and dictate his future in the next. Sighing, she let it go. "It's cool, Mike. You're an adult. I trust you to make the right decisions. I just want you to know that if you ever need a change, well—"

"Thanks, sis." Mike darted his eyes down the hall when the toilet flushed. "Speaking of right decisions, I hope you're planning on doing everything you can to keep Regan. She's awesome."

Mel couldn't suppress her grin as she basked in the glow of her brother's approval. "I know she is. And I have no intention of letting her go."

"Even if the victory dance *was* a little obnoxious," Mike added with a laugh.

"You're just a sore loser."

"Is he?" Regan asked as she emerged from the bathroom. "Didn't like the victory dance?"

Mike snorted laughter. "No, no. That was fine. I'm just not used to seeing that kind of display. I usually win, and I've never really felt the urge to dance about it."

Regan raised her eyebrows in disbelief. "You should try it sometime. That's one of the best parts." Then she extended her hand. "Really, though, it was very nice meeting you and playing with you. It was fun."

"Yeah." Mike took her hand and pulled her into a quick hug. "It was."

"Looking forward to a rematch," Regan said. Her cheeks flushed pink as she stepped back from their embrace.

Mike relaxed into a cocky, too-wide grin at that. "I'll practice my victory dance."

"Do that."

He turned to Mel and pulled her into a bear hug. "Thank you for stopping by, sis. It was really cool to see you again."

"It was cool to see you, too," Mel murmured into his neck. She brought her lips to his ear and whispered, "Remember what I said, okay? Please?"

"I'll remember." He stepped to the door. "I'm going to get a cell phone in a couple weeks and I promise I'll call you and give you the number, okay?"

"You'd better," Mel said.

He let them into the hallway, but leaned against the doorway as Regan began to walk down the hall. "Hey, sis?"

"Yeah?" Mel asked, turning around to smile at her brother.

"Thanks again for coming to see me." He looked like he wanted to say something else. She waited for it, and he cleared his throat and added, "Love you."

Mel felt her throat catch, and she held the inside of her lower lip between her teeth to stop her own eyes from tearing. After a breathless moment, she responded, "I love you, too, Mikey."

Mel wore a smile all the way down the dingy, red-carpeted steps. When they reached the bottom, she turned to a silent Regan and said, "Even though he didn't appreciate the victory dance, I'd be lying if I said it wasn't the cutest thing *I've* ever seen."

Regan hopped forward to hold the door open for Mel with a cheerful grin. Happiness shone in her eyes, both echoing and enhancing Mel's joy. "I'll have you know that the patented Regan victory dance is an important part of any trouncing. The fact that you think it's cute is mere icing on the cake."

Mel laughed and grabbed Regan's hand as they emerged into the parking lot. The sun shone down upon her face, and she smiled up at the sky as she led them to the truck.

"Feeling better now?" Regan asked.

Mel gave a relieved nod. "Yeah. Thank you."

"Hey, I didn't do it." Regan dug her keys out of her pocket and dangled them in front of Mel. "You want to drive or should I?"

"I'll drive." Mel snatched the keys out of Regan's hand. She waited until Regan was settled in the passenger seat before reaching out and taking her lover's hand. "Regan?"

Tender green eyes stared back up at her and stole her breath. "Yeah, baby?"

"I mean it, thank you. You say you didn't do it, but you did. Being here for me, during all of this, you make me feel strong. You make me feel like I can do anything."

Regan squeezed her hand. "I'm just glad I can be here for you. Making you happy matters so much."

Despite all her peace at seeing Mike again, a feeling of quiet anxiety tugged at Mel's belly. One niggling detail wouldn't let go of her brain. Even though she didn't want to admit it, she knew what she had to do. And though it scared her to death, she found courage when she looked into Regan's eyes.

"I think I need to go see my father," Mel said. She concentrated on keeping her voice steady; she was unwilling to let the very idea of him make it falter. "It occurred to me when I was telling Mike to forgive himself for everything and to take control of his own life, well, I was being a hypocrite."

"What are you talking about?" Regan said. "You've been amazing. You've really started to talk to me, to trust people, and you're doing brave things, Mel, and—"

Mel leaned over and kissed Regan's still moving lips, quieting her and thanking her for the impassioned defense in the same action. When she pulled back, Regan wore a crooked smile.

Mel looked at her with serious eyes. "Yesterday, talking to my dad for *ten* minutes got me so upset that I ended up making a complete ass out of myself in front of you. I ended up hurting you." God, it was embarrassing. "That's not exactly letting go of my past and moving on. And I want to do that. But I think, to do that, I need to do this."

"I just don't want you to get hurt," Regan whispered. Worried green eyes searched Mel's face.

"Neither do I. But I think that right now I need to be really brave," she said. She put her hands on the steering wheel. "I need to see him as an adult. I need to face him as someone who doesn't need him anymore. So I can start over." Lowering her eyes, she murmured, "With you."

Regan touched her thigh, and pressed a light kiss to her cheek. "Are you sure you're up for this, baby? It's been a hell of a last few weeks."

"I think I have to be up for this," Mel said, and gave Regan a brave smile.

Regan brushed dark hair away from Mel's face. "Maybe that's why we ended up on this trip, in Oklahoma."

"Maybe," Mel agreed. She hoped so.

"Where does he live?"

"Only a couple of miles from here." She shifted the truck into reverse, keeping her foot on the brake. "Look, I don't expect you to go with me, don't worry. You can stay in a hotel room or something, or drop me off."

"Would you rather I not go?" Regan asked. "Because I'd like to be there for you, if you'll let me."

Mel felt a cold clutch of fear in her gut at the suggestion, even as she was warmed by the fierce loyalty in Regan's eyes. She wanted Regan to stay with her so badly, but the thought of taking her home to her father was absolutely terrifying. She couldn't predict how he would react.

Or how Regan would react.

"I'm not Mike, baby," Regan said, as if she could read her thoughts. "Or Lauren. He can't scare me away. I promise."

Mel stared at Regan, thinking about every conversation they'd had, every time they'd made love, every moment spent studying her, unnoticed, with adoring eyes. And she believed her.

In that instant she knew. "I trust you." *And I think I love you.*

"Thank you," Regan said. "I won't let you down."

"Even if he's the biggest asshole you've ever met?" Mel asked with a nervous chuckle. She wiped the back of her hand over her eyes, then shifted the truck into reverse.

"Bring him on. Let him do his worst."

Mel pulled out on to the street, sparing Regan a sad smile. "You don't want to see him at his worst, baby. Trust me."

Regan was quiet for a moment, then said, "Tell me about his worst?"

Breathe in, breathe out, turn left on Maple Road. "You don't want to hear about that."

"I do if you want to talk about it."

The last time she'd spoken about the abuse, she was lying on her bed with Lauren. She was seventeen then, and it had been one of the hardest things she'd ever done.

It shocked her, how easily the words came now.

"Like dinner, you know? We were supposed to have dinner on the table when he got home from work." Mel flexed her fingers on the steering wheel as she spoke. "I remember always listening for the sound of his car pulling in the driveway after school. God, that sound terrified me. My heart would start pounding until I'd want to throw up. And that was even when we had dinner ready. Those few times we didn't were the worst, but even if we did, if he didn't like it or something—"

"It must have been terrible," Regan said.

"One time when I was fourteen, I got held up after school tutoring a kid for a math test. Mikey was ten then, and when he realized I was late coming home, he panicked because he was afraid dinner wouldn't be ready for Dad." Her voice was calmer than she would have expected. "Mike wasn't much of a cook, so he was freaking out. Anyway, by the time I got home the food was burnt and he'd made this huge mess in the kitchen."

"Shit."

"I remember standing there in the kitchen, just frozen, when we heard Dad's car pull into the driveway." She felt the fear lance through her belly, just as it had that day. Remembering was tough.

Regan rested a warm hand on her thigh.

"God, we freaked out. I grabbed Mikey's hand and just started running. I dragged him upstairs with me until I got him to his bedroom." Mel turned and gave Regan a sad smile. "It was my fault, you know, for not watching the clock. I was older. I knew better."

"So you went back downstairs," Regan said.

Mel nodded. "He was in the kitchen. I could see right away that he'd had a bad day, and he was already pulling his belt off and winding it around his fist."

"I have to admit, I'm going to have a hard time looking that bastard in the face," Regan said. She gave Mel's thigh a gentle squeeze.

"That's okay. So will I."

"No, you won't. You'll walk in there and you'll look at him and you'll see that you deserve to be happy. You'll see that he has no power over you now."

Determined, Mel nodded in agreement. "We're almost there." After a silent moment, she gave Regan a sidelong glance. "You know the scar below my collarbone?" she asked, and traced her finger over the area in question. "Right here?"

"Yeah."

"Burned food and dirty pans." A humorless chuckle died in her throat as they approached a familiar street. "Here we are."

Regan reached out and covered the scar Mel had pointed out with the palm of her hand. "I'll do anything to make sure he never hurts you again."

"Just be with me," Mel said. She pulled up to the curb outside her childhood home and parked the truck. "That's all I need."

"You got it," Regan said. She followed Mel's gaze over to the small house. "Are you ready?"

Mel's lips stretched into a pained grimace. "I'm trying not to throw up," she admitted. "I never thought I'd be back here again."

"Tell you what," Regan said, giving Mel's earlobe a gentle tug. "The sooner we get through this part, the sooner we can go on to the rest of this trip. We have so much ahead of us, no matter what happens tonight."

Maybe it was that simple. After all, she'd been on her own for years now, and she had people she cared about who had nothing to do with her father. She could walk away from today and still have someplace to go.

Mel curled her fingers around the back of Regan's neck and pulled her into a gentle kiss. "You're right. Let's go."

Chapter
Twelve

MEL PLODDED UP the old concrete walkway that led to her father's house, eyes glued to her feet. She took deliberate steps, trying to slow her journey to the front door. *Step on a crack, and you'll break your mother's back.* This very walkway had inspired her to that sing-song rhyme many times in childhood, up until the day her mother passed away.

Regan matched her slow pace, offering quiet support beside her. "Just remember," she said in a low voice, "you're an adult now. He can't hurt you. And I'm here with you, okay? We can leave whenever you want."

Mel nodded and looked up at her father's house. It was just as she remembered it: ugly red brick, heavy wooden door, crumbling front porch surrounded by a rusted black metal railing. The path beneath her feet was overgrown with weeds. She reached the porch steps, then, before she could hesitate, found herself at the front door.

She knocked hard three times. It was automatic, just like going to a domestic. She bit back a nervous grin at the memory of Hansen's "three-knock theory" for potentially dangerous situations. *Three knocks, I'm telling you, Raines. One knock, maybe you slipped or something. Two, sounds like you don't have the balls to make a point. Four? Overanxious. Three knocks. Three knocks shows you mean business.*

Her grim amusement quickly turned to nausea as she realized what she was doing. The urge to turn and flee was strong, and she peered in the front window, hoping for a reason to turn away. The curtains were drawn, no lights. Either he wasn't home or he was passed out already.

She turned to voice her hopes to Regan. But before she could utter a word, a light flicked on inside the house and footfalls approached. Her heart sped up as she heard the clumsy racket of locks being disengaged.

I never want you to come back here again. Mel remembered his face, contorted as he shouted at her. He had been standing on the same crumbling front porch. *Disgusting queer bitch.*

She flinched when the door opened, and took an involuntary step backwards at the sight of her father. She zeroed in on his eyes first; cold steel blue, the same eyes that had narrowed at her countless times, icy in their anger. She felt hyper-aware, inhaling in acute fear when she saw his pupils dilate as he looked upon her.

"Hell, Laney." His voice was soft and a little awed, but she could hear in his deep timbre the angry refrains of her childhood. The smell of alcohol on his breath sent a shudder through her body, and for a moment she felt like she might pass out. But the discreet presence of Regan's small hand pressing against her lower back seemed to anchor her to the self that had threatened to slip away the moment she saw her dad. At once she no longer felt like a child, but like the woman she had become.

"Dad," she greeted. Looking at him with calmer eyes, she was shocked by what she saw. Jesus, he was an old man.

That towering, menacing specter from her childhood now stood before her, looking every one of his fifty-odd years. He studied her in shocked silence. Although he still stood several inches taller than she, his once-broad shoulders were slumped and he looked weary with age and sickness. His eyes, once cold and hard, were dull and lifeless, and his face was rough with overgrown stubble. He looked sallow and drained and, most of all, entirely unthreatening.

"Christ, Laney." A trembling hand reached for her cheek, and Mel moved back to avoid his touch. "You look just like her."

Tears stung her eyes unbidden, and Mel fought for control with a will summoned from the bottom of her soul. She would never let him see her cry again. "It's been a long time," she said.

He stared at her for a moment, and then he reached out and grabbed her arms, pulling her tightly against him. "Give your old man a hug, girl. It's good to see you."

Mel stiffened in his embrace, hot anger surging through her veins. He was acting like nothing had ever happened. She stepped back, and his hands dropped to his sides.

"We can't stay long," she told him. "We're supposed to be in New Mexico tomorrow."

Martin Raines looked over and took in Regan with a dismissive gaze. "We, huh?" His voice took on a definite chill, giving Mel her first glimpse at the hateful man she remembered.

"This is my girlfriend, Regan."

The shock on her father's face at the introduction was only slightly surpassed by Mel's own surprise at having made it. She reached out and wrapped an arm around Regan's waist, pulling her close. *This is my life, Dad. Fuck you.*

"I see," he said in a flat voice. He stared at the two of them for a moment before visibly relaxing, a wide smile overtaking his face. "Well, come on in. You might as well have something to drink before you have to leave."

He turned and walked inside, leaving Mel and Regan to follow behind. Mel turned to Regan, expecting to see her lover freaked out over meeting someone like him.

Amazingly, Regan seemed at ease. With a warm smile and a tender gaze, she mouthed, *You okay?*

Mel thought for a moment. *He's an old man now. He can't hurt me...and I can do this.* She flashed Regan a confident grin and mouthed, *Yeah.*

"Beer, Laney?" her father asked from the kitchen doorway.

"No, thanks. I'm not much of a drinker."

"How about your little friend?"

Mel glared at him. *Rude bastard.*

"No thanks, Mr. Raines," Regan answered. "I don't drink, either."

"Not water or anything, huh?" he snapped.

Mel turned and fixed her father with hard eyes. "We're fine."

At that he turned away with a shrug, disappearing into the kitchen and leaving them alone for a moment. Mel looked around at the faded fabric couches she remembered so well from when she was a child. She shook her head at the rifles mounted on display at one end of the room.

"This place looks exactly the same as it did when I left," she murmured. Everywhere she looked triggered flashes of memory.

She dropped her eyes to the threadbare brown carpeting, and ran a distracted hand over the worn arm of the couch, the site of one of the most humiliating experiences of her young life. She was twelve years old and she'd received the brutal spanking without shedding a tear, though she'd bit her lower lip so hard that warm blood ran down her chin. "I don't think he's changed a thing," she said in a quiet voice.

"You sure you're okay?" Regan stood so close that Mel could feel the heat from her body.

Mel straightened up, taking a deep breath. He was old now, and she wasn't scared of him anymore. She started to smile at Regan, but faltered when she spotted an old patchwork quilt folded at one end of the couch.

"You ready to hide with me, Melly-belly?"

Mel looked up into her mother's laughing grey eyes, giving her a too-wide grin. "It's dark under there," she said, pointing at the quilt her mother had draped over her head.

Elizabeth Raines chuckled at the four-year-old, pulling the quilt up and over both of them. Mel crawled into her mother's lap, giggling at the silly game, and burrowed into a warm embrace.

"Yeah, but you're my brave girl, aren't you?"

"I'm fine," Mel said. It was the truth. She gazed around for another moment and then tugged Regan down to sit on the couch beside her. From the kitchen she heard the telltale sounds of glass and bottle clinking together; her father was fixing a drink. "Great," she muttered in a soft voice. "Prepare for him to turn up the charm."

"Super," Regan whispered. "I don't think he likes me very much."

"I'm finding that I don't much care about what he likes and doesn't like," Mel said. "He's...God, it doesn't matter now, you know?"

"See?" Regan murmured, smiling. "I knew you could do this."

Mel was grinning at that when her father returned to the living room, a glass of amber liquid in his right hand.

"How've you been?" he asked, settling in his favorite chair with a low groan. "I was hoping you would come by, but I figured you'd be too busy to see your old man."

"I thought the doctors told you to stop drinking, Dad." Mel blinked in surprise at her own bold words.

His response was to glower in her direction, which sent a brief ripple of fear through her body at the familiarity of it all. "Who told you that?"

The fear vanished when her father took a defiant sip of his drink, smacking his lips for emphasis. *He really is pathetic.* For Mel the realization was sudden and complete, and it altered her in ways she couldn't yet define. *Why have I let him make me so miserable for so long?*

"I saw Mike today," she told him. "He mentioned that you'd been diagnosed with liver disease."

"Kid should worry about his own life and keep out of mine." He took a deep, rasping breath. "Don't you worry about me, young lady... Besides, it's a special occasion. My beautiful daughter home again after all these years."

Who was he channeling? Mel tried to keep her voice steady. "I am worried about Mike."

"He's not doing shit with his life. Fucking shame."

"And what a surprise, too." Mel avoided looking at her

father with the fury she knew was in her eyes.

"You, on the other hand..." He gave her a leering smile and raised his glass in a mock toast. "Looks like you're doing well for yourself."

Mel's eyes were cold. "We're talking about Mike right now, Dad," she said. "Aren't you concerned about him? Or have you been as supportive of him as you were of me?"

They seemed to share a moment of shocked silence at her naked sarcasm. Her father recovered first, giving her a blank look. "What are you trying to say? I've done everything I could for that boy."

"Except believe in him," Mel said. "Dad, you know you've never made him feel like he was worth a damn. Maybe if he didn't think he was such a hopeless loser, he'd have the will to turn his life around." It was something she'd wanted to say to her father for years, and she felt a great weight lifted from her soul as the words left her mouth.

"You don't know what you're talking about." Her father took an absent-minded swig of his drink. "Mike wouldn't have problems if he'd been more like you — motivated, always working towards your goals..."

Mel worked her jaw in silence. Was he really this stupid? Did he think she wouldn't remember how it was? "I find it hard to believe that you have much idea about how I've really turned out."

"You're on the beat," her father said, raising his glass again. "I know that much."

"I'm quitting," Mel said. She suppressed a smirk at the mute shock in his eyes. "I'm actually going to hand in my resignation when I get home from this trip."

Blue eyes grew cold and angry. His expression mingled disapproval and disbelief, and it was almost comical in its exaggeration. "What?"

She gave him a calm smile. "I don't want to be a cop anymore."

"What the hell is wrong with you?" her father snarled. "What do you think you're going to do now?"

"I haven't exactly decided yet," Mel answered. She flicked a small sideways smile at Regan. "Maybe something in art."

Her father dropped his face into one hand and shook his head. "Both of my kids are fucking idiots." When he looked up at her again, his eyes were full of dark challenge. "That's the dumbest thing I've ever heard."

You're a stupid little girl for wasting your time with this bullshit. She had been fourteen years old when her father destroyed most of her drawings and supplies in a drunken rage. His anger and disdain had banished art to a very private and personal corner of her mind, never shared with anyone again. Now she wanted it back.

Mel shrugged. "Maybe. But it's my dumb thing."

"How are you going to take care of yourself? You have responsibilities."

"What responsibilities?" Mel could see where this was going.

"Don't you understand, Laney? I'm sick. One faggot doctor tells me—" Her father stopped speaking, hissed out a breath through clenched teeth, then set his glass down on the coffee table. He pinned her with pleading eyes. "Listen, I can't depend on Mike. I'm counting on you to help me out."

Mel stared at him, incredulous. "Are you kidding me? You expect me to help you when you never bothered to help Mike and me when we were kids? You want me to support you now that you're sick? Where was my support? Or Mike's?" Mel's voice trembled a little with her anger, the hint of weakness further fueling her rage. "Do you even realize how ridiculous you are? You won't even help yourself. Are you going to stop drinking?"

"I think you'd better be very careful about the way you talk to me, girl. Do you think you're too old—"

"Yes," she answered his unfinished question in a controlled voice. "I *am* too old. I'm too old for you to talk to me like this, too old for your intimidation, and I'm too goddamn old for you to try and make me feel guilty anymore." Her voice was full of venom and he flinched at her angry words.

Blue eyes flashed and Mel tensed her body in anticipation of a violent reaction from the man across from her. She shifted closer to Regan on the couch. *Fuck, I'm pushing this. The minute he explodes, we're outta here.*

Martin Raines didn't explode. His voice was cold now, his eyes hard and glittering. "I have always supported you. I gave you a roof over your head and food to eat. I encouraged you to work hard because I cared about you, about how you'd turn out. I'm proud of you, Laney."

"Don't lie!" Mel's voice rose for the first time. "You've never been proud of me. Not one day. I spent the first eighteen years of my life trying to be the best at everything I did, just to make you happy. All I ever wanted was to hear you say you were proud of me, so why am I hearing it now for the first time?"

"Laney, I—"

Mel didn't let him finish. "Though I guess in a way I should be thanking you for how I turned out, right? I mean, with all your *support* and everything, you have been quite the influence in my life. So many miserable things about me I owe to you."

That was it. He exploded. "Listen, you little bitch!" He pitched forward in his chair to lean his elbows against his knees, breathing hard, before pushing himself up to tower over her and Regan. "Who the hell do you think you are, talking to me like that? I'm making an effort here, welcoming you back into my home, ignoring the fact that you're flaunting your disgusting lifestyle in my face." He glared over at Regan, hate darkening his eyes.

Mel rose from the couch without hesitation, getting right into her father's face. She gave him a cold smile when he looked away from her silent lover on the couch. "There, that's more like it. This is what I remember. Keep going, Dad." She folded her arms in front of her chest, refusing to break their gaze.

I fucking dare you to try something. I'm not a kid anymore and you can't hurt me.

"You've never failed to disappoint me, Laney." His voice grew chilly. "The one good thing you ever accomplished, becoming a cop, and you managed to screw that one up, too."

Disgust colored his face and Mel waited to feel the internal blow of his disapproval. It didn't come. Instead, she felt tired. Damn tired of this all. "I don't need you anymore, Dad. I especially don't need your approval. I like who I am...who I'm becoming, for the first time in my life. That's what matters. Not you."

Her father shook with rage. For a moment he sputtered wordlessly, as if unable to form a coherent thought, before he growled a choked, "Get the fuck out of my house, you ungrateful little cunt. Take your dyke friend with you. Don't give me a reason to beat your queer ass again."

Mel held her father's gaze for a moment, then dropped her eyes to Regan. Her lover's outward demeanor was calm, placid, despite the muted fear Mel could see in her green eyes. Mel offered her a hand and Regan accepted it gracefully, allowing Mel to pull her to her feet. They stood side by side as Mel answered his threat in a quiet voice. "Goodbye, Dad."

Her entire body shook with adrenaline but she turned her back to him, something she never would have done as a child. Guiding Regan in front of her, keeping her own body between her father and her lover, Mel headed for the front door.

They stepped outside without a word, neither turning their head at the sound of the angry voice behind them. "Don't come back here, Laney. Ever. Not ever again."

Mel gave a silent nod. She didn't even spare a glance backwards as she walked away.

"YOU KNOW, I think my mom would be proud of me."

"I think so, too," Regan agreed. *I know I am.*

She could feel the nervous energy rolling off Mel in waves, and she felt an answering thrum in her own body. The quiet they shared as they drove away from Mel's childhood home was comfortable, an acknowledgement that no words were needed, but the atmosphere was electric. Something had changed and they both seemed to know it.

Regan stopped in front of a park, killing the engine without a word. She and Mel both opened their doors and hopped out of the truck, walking around to meet in front of it in a fierce embrace.

"Mel, you were incredible," Regan whispered. "Are you okay?"

"I'm more than okay. I'm happy," Mel affirmed. "So happy. Thank you."

"I didn't do anything."

"Yes, you did. You believed in me. You stood by me. You'll never know how much that means to me." She cupped Regan's face in both hands, holding her gaze with serious eyes. "You mean the world to me, Regan O'Riley."

Mel swallowed Regan's small cry at the declaration, leaning forward and taking her mouth in a passionate kiss. Regan groaned low in her throat. The kiss told her a million things Mel hadn't yet spoken aloud, and it invited her to feel completely safe and loved. She was panting when they broke apart, leaning her forehead against Mel's, overcome by bliss.

"Thank you for trusting me." Regan paused, considering. "I...you mean the world to me, too, Mel. I always want to be there for you."

Mel took Regan by the hand and led them around a chain-link fence that separated the park from the street, then to a playground that adjoined a small elementary school. A large swing-set sat abandoned and still in the moonlight, its row of plastic swings suspended by glinting silver chains. Mel released Regan's hand and claimed the end swing, plopping down with a grin before wrapping her hands around the metallic links that framed her body.

Regan sat down on the swing to Mel's left, pushing off with her feet to sway back and forth. For a moment the only sound was the gentle creaking of the swing and the scraping of her Doc Martens in the soft dirt beneath their feet.

"He really is an asshole, isn't he?" Mel asked after a moment.

Regan gave Mel a sympathetic nod. "Yes."

"When I saw him, I don't know..." Mel pushed her own

swing into gentle motion. "I can't believe I gave him so much power over me."

"He's your father," Regan said. "That's why he had that kind of power."

"I know," Mel acknowledged. "I know that being hurt by what he did is natural. I was a defenseless kid. But it's over now. If I let him continue hurting me as an adult, that's my fault. So I won't. Not anymore."

Regan gave her a tender smile. After a moment, she said, "I have to admit that I was a little scared. He really hated seeing me, huh?"

"You were scared? I thought I was going pass out. I don't know if I could have done what I just did if you hadn't been there."

Regan snapped her head up to catch Mel's eyes. "You could have. You would have."

Mel reached up and grabbed the chains of Regan's swing, arresting it so they could face one another. Leaning forward, she brought her mouth to Regan's. "Don't argue with me," she whispered against Regan's lips. "Feeling you there...it was like everything became clear. I really looked at him. And he was just a sick, pathetic old man and not a terrifying monster, the one from when I was a kid." Mel flashed her a shy grin. "You saved me."

Regan leaned forward to deepen the kiss, tracing the outline of Mel's mouth before dipping inside. Their kiss was slow and unhurried, a gentle exploration that felt so much like the first time it set Regan's heart racing. She tangled one hand in Mel's dark hair and slid the other to the back of her neck, caressing gently. When she finally broke away for a lungful of air, she looked around at their surroundings with a dreamy smile. Empty playing fields and a paved blacktop with basketball hoops rounded out the school's lot. "So this is where little Mel went to elementary school?"

"Indeed it is." Mel turned her head and pointed to a spot next to the squat brown building beside them. "In fact, I believe it was right there that I gave Jimmy Duncan a bloody nose."

"And what did poor Jimmy do to deserve that?"

"I let him kiss me, and then I punched him when he tried to feel me up."

"Did you even have anything to feel up?" Regan asked, smirking at Mel's chest.

"Well, that was about fifth grade, so I had enough to be enticing, I guess."

"I can't say I blame him," Regan said. "I guess I'm just lucky

I didn't end up with a bloody nose the first time I tried to get to second base."

"Baby, I was dusting off home plate for you the moment I saw you across the room."

Regan's laughter mingled with Mel's, filling the quiet night with the sound of their shared joy.

"Mom would pack the biggest picnic lunches for our days at the park," Mel said with a wistful sigh. "I remember her applesauce the most. God, that was a treat." She indicated the grassy field that separated them from the baseball diamond. "That's where she brought us to tell us she was sick. I got so mad at her at first. I just didn't understand why she'd want to leave us."

"That must have been so hard for her," Regan murmured. "For everyone."

"I came here after she died, too. When I needed to cry." Mel shrugged one shoulder. "When I still cried, I mean." At Regan's questioning look, she said, "My father didn't believe in crying. Some of my worst beatings were for crying."

Tears fell from Regan's eyes then, an unstoppable release of the anguish she felt at what Mel had endured. Mel cried too, and they held one another until the weeping abated. It was Mel who first drew back with an embarrassed smile. I'm sorry. I think the day just caught up with me."

"I think more than a few years just caught up with you," Regan acknowledged with a half-smile. "I'm in awe of your strength, baby. The more I learn about you, the more amazing you are to me."

"It's mutual," Mel said. "God, I feel so free with you. No matter how fucked-up I feel inside, you just...get me. I feel like I can tell you everything."

"That's because you can." Regan traced over Mel's lower lip with her thumb. "And after tonight, I'd say you're wholly and completely free."

Mel tipped her head back to gaze up at the night sky and Regan followed suit, searching for the Big Dipper while she waited for Mel to respond.

"It's incredible," Mel finally murmured. "The one thing I do know about my future, Regan, is that I want you in it. I mean, if you still want to hang around with an emotional wreck."

"Of course I do."

Mel chuckled, relaxing into a smile. "I don't know why you've put up with me this far. Or how." She reached out and cupped Regan's chin in her hand. "I just know that I'm very, very glad you have."

No thought preceded Regan's next words. "I 'put up' with you, Mel, because I love you."

Mel was silent for a long time. There was almost no perceptible reaction at first, merely a slight widening of her eyes.

I really said that, didn't I? Regan kept her eyes on Mel's face, straining to read her reaction. *I meant it, though. It can't have been wrong to say it when I mean it so much.*

Mel couldn't quite meet her eyes, staring past Regan and then down to the ground in embarrassed silence.

God, you've overwhelmed her. Regan bit back a smile, warm sympathy flooding her body at Mel's flustered response. *This really isn't the time to tell her how cute she looks.*

Mel looked up. "Regan, I — "

"Don't," Regan whispered. "Don't say anything right now."

"But — "

"This has been a hell of a day for you and I think I just ambushed you a little. I didn't tell you because I wanted a response. I told you because I want you to know. I love you. With all my heart." She punctuated her words with a passionate kiss.

The kiss Mel gave her in return told Regan everything she needed to know. *What she can't say with words, God...*

Mel's tongue stroked Regan's, then retreated to allow Regan to explore. *I want you, Regan.* Mel wrapped her in a tight embrace and pulled her, swing and all, close against her. *I need you, Regan.* Strong hands moved over Regan's body, caressing her back, chest, and abdomen. *I love you, Regan.*

They ended up in a tight hug that lasted long after Mel's kisses ceased. Mel pulled back to look at Regan and they shared a warm smile.

"Thank you for telling me," Mel whispered.

"Thank you," Regan said. *For showing me.*

Chapter
Thirteen

MEL WOKE UP in Amarillo, Texas with a smile on her face. *And why not?* Her lips twitched with sleepy bliss. *She loves me.*

She could feel the heat emanating from Regan's body before she opened her eyes. Auburn hair lay across her shoulder and tickled her nose and cheek, turning her smile into a full-fledged grin. Mel beamed at the woman sleeping next to her, and then reached over to trace her thumb along one perfect eyebrow. Driving all the way to Texas overnight hadn't even been a challenge, as wired as the whole day left her. Even when Regan surrendered to sleep for the last hour of the jaunt, Mel was content to drive in peaceful silence, stealing occasional glances at her dozing lover.

That she was free, and that she still had Regan beside her, left her fundamentally changed. It felt like some part of her she'd thought long dead was being slowly restored. Mel released a contented sigh and gazed over at Regan's face, peaceful and relaxed as she slept.

I feel like drawing.

She blinked in surprise at the sudden flood of inspiration. After only a moment's hesitation, she climbed out of bed, eliciting a sleepy grumble from Regan. She walked over to the large duffel bag she'd dumped by the door the night before and dug through it until she located her long-abandoned drawing pad and the small case containing her pencils. She ran her hands reverently over the polished wood case, unused for years, then tiptoed over to the chair next to Regan's side of the bed. Grinning, she sat cross-legged and gazed at the sleeping woman. Pale skin, smattered with freckles, auburn curls fanned out across a pristine white pillow—she had a perfect view.

Eyes glued to her lover, she opened her drawing pad and took out a pencil. As she waited for that inspiration to start moving her hand, she tried to burn the memory of Regan like this into her brain. But she didn't want to draw her sleeping. She closed her eyes and brought her pencil just centimeters above her drawing surface. She wanted to capture Regan unguarded like this, but smiling. It came to her in an instant, and she opened her eyes to begin sketching with bold and confident lines.

From the loving strokes emerged a gradual outline of Regan's face, which Mel filled in from memory. Slowly, her eyes took shape, a fine nose, and full lips that stretched into a tender smile. On occasion Mel would glance up and gaze at Regan; not because she needed a reminder, but because it made her feel good.

After a while, she became lost in her work and even her infrequent glances at Regan ceased. She stared at the drawing with a critical eye, reaching down now and again to add some shading or detail. When she finally finished, she grinned and lifted her eyes to take in her subject.

Sleepy green eyes peered back at her.

"How long have you been awake?" Mel asked.

"I dunno." Regan reached her hands above her head and stretched like a lazy cat. "I was afraid to move around too much. I didn't want you to stop."

"I was pretty deep into that place where you probably wouldn't have been able to distract me even if you'd tried." Massaging the back of her neck, she shot Regan a smile. "Good morning."

"Yes, it is." After a moment of shared silence, Regan asked, "Are you going to let me see what you were working on?"

Mel knew that Regan had seen her at her worst, and wouldn't make her feel funny about this. But that didn't make it any less nerve-wracking. Bashfully, she said, "I haven't drawn in a while, but I woke up this morning and looked at you sleeping and I guess I felt inspired."

"You didn't draw me, did you?" Regan ran a self-conscious hand over her face, and groaned. "I can't imagine I make a very compelling subject, especially dead to the world."

"You looked like an angel." Blushing at her own words, Mel turned playful. "Don't worry, I didn't include the drool spot in the picture."

Regan's eyes widened with alarm and she swiped the back of her hand over her face. When her fingers came away dry, she shot Mel a dirty look. "Jerk," she muttered with an adoring gaze, then stretched again, causing her blanket to slip down and expose her breasts to Mel's hungry eyes.

"I find your drooling endearing," Mel teased, then pointedly dropped her eyes to enjoy the sight of erect nipples against pale flesh. "And those work for me, too."

Regan met Mel's gaze, one corner of her mouth lifting in a patient smile. "Please show me what you were working on."

Mel steeled her nerve, and handed the drawing to Regan.

A pale hand immediately flew up to cover her lover's open mouth, muffling a gasp. "Mel." She shook her head, speechless.

Mel joined Regan in her close study of the drawing. It was Regan as she'd looked at the campground outside St. Louis, moonlight playing upon her skin, wearing a contented half-smile like she held some incredible secret. She glanced up at her lover, looking for her reaction.

Finally, she had to ask. "What do you think?"

She wasn't expecting the tears that fell from Regan's eyes, or the slim hand that trembled as it wiped at the wetness on her cheeks. Regan caught Mel's gaze, opening and closing her mouth in silence.

She likes it. Mel shifted in her chair, awkward, and cleared her throat. She wasn't sure how to deal with this kind of reception to her work. "It's not that bad, is it?" she joked in a weak voice. Lame, but she didn't know what else to say.

"Mel, you're amazing."

"Be quiet."

"You are." Regan dropped her eyes to the drawing again. "This is amazing. Too amazing, probably. This is much too beautiful to be me."

"No, it's not. You're the most beautiful woman I've ever seen." When Regan averted her eyes, Mel softened her tone. "Are you saying it's a bad likeness?"

"No," Regan said. "I just—" She stopped speaking, looking back down at the portrait, then lifted awed eyes to Mel's face. "Is this how you see me?"

"It's how you are. And I'm gonna keep telling you until you believe me."

"Thank you," Regan whispered. "You make me feel this beautiful."

"Good." Mel slid off the chair to kneel on the floor beside the bed, tracing the back of her knuckles over Regan's still damp cheek. Regan turned a watery grin her direction, and Mel leaned forward to press a soft kiss against her forehead.

"You coming back to bed?" Regan asked, turning down the blanket that covered her.

"Yeah." Mel placed the drawing pad on a chair before lowering herself on top of Regan's naked body with a contented moan. She slipped one leg between Regan's thighs, then planted her elbows on either side of her lover's head.

Over twelve hours, and it still didn't seem real. Regan loved her. Mel cleared her throat. "Fifteen beautiful things about Regan O'Riley," she announced, and paused for dramatic effect. "By Mel Raines."

"Mel—"

Mel stopped the protest with a finger pressed against Regan's lips. "Number one, her gorgeous green eyes." When Regan closed them in response, Mel planted a gentle kiss on each eyelid. "Open them for me, baby. I want to see them."

Regan looked up at Mel with a fierce blush on her face. "You're incredibly sweet."

"Hush. This is about your beauty, not my sweetness."

"Sorry."

"Number two," Mel continued. "Her left breast." Wolfish smile on her face, she bent her head down to kiss a soft pink nipple, then teased it with her tongue until it stiffened. "Three," she whispered against the turgid flesh. "Her right breast." She moved over to give the other nipple the same treatment.

"Okay, I like this list," Regan panted.

Mel pulled her mouth away with some reluctance. "Number four, her beautiful red hair." Reaching a hand between them, she cupped Regan between the legs and drawled, "*Everywhere.*"

Regan giggled and thrust her hips into Mel's touch. Mel drew away, clicking her tongue in disapproval. "Number five. The way she keeps me safe when I'm hurting and gives me strength when I'm weak."

Regan opened and closed her mouth without a sound, her eyes bright with emotion.

"You weren't expecting that one, huh?" Mel gave her a half-smile. Sometimes she even surprised herself.

"Nuh-uh. But I liked it."

"Six. The way she looks when she comes." Mel leered and Regan let go a short bark of laughter. "Seven, the way she *sounds* when she comes." This drew a soft murmur from Regan, then an unthinking answering moan from Mel.

"You're easy," Regan said.

"Eight, her intelligence and strength." Mel paused. This was almost too easy. How was she going to stop at only fifteen? "Nine. Her courage and determination, and all those other things that make me look up to her, and that I hope to achieve for myself one day."

"Oh, Mel." Regan laid the palm of her hand against Mel's cheek.

Mel fought back the emotion that threatened to overwhelm her. Time for some levity. "Number ten is that cute little mole on her butt."

"What?" Regan exclaimed, laughing. "What mole?"

"You have this adorable little mole," Mel said, rolling off her lover and then coaxing her to turn onto her side. "Right..." She traced delicate patterns over the smooth skin of Regan's bottom before stopping to rest on a spot near the hip. "Here." She bent down and planted a kiss on the spot. "And it's beautiful."

Regan giggled and squirmed away from her lips. She rolled over and waved Mel back on top of her. "You're so biased."

"Number eleven. Her sexy computer skills and all the other things she thinks make her a geek, but really just make her incredibly attractive. Including, but not limited to, that cute Atari shirt she was wearing when I met her." Regan's blush seemed to deepen. Moving on, Mel said, "Twelve. Her freckles."

"My freckles?"

"Yes." She kissed the light smattering on Regan's nose. "All of them."

"My grandma used to say that freckles are the footprints of angels."

"I like that. A lot." Mel traced her fingers over the freckles covering Regan's face, arms, and shoulders. "It means that you're an angel's playground."

Regan directed a bashful grin down at where their chests pressed together. "What's number thirteen?"

"Thirteen is her beautiful body." Mel shifted and ran an admiring hand over soft curves and gentle dips. Her gaze chased her fingertips across Regan's pale skin. "Perfect."

Regan closed her eyes.

"Number fourteen is the way she stands by me, even when she's afraid, and the way she believes in me." Mel kissed Regan's eyelid, then the corner of her mouth. "That means more to me than anything ever has."

"Always." Regan turned her head to capture Mel's lips in a sweet kiss.

Mel broke their kiss with a regretful groan. She had something else to say. "I have to finish."

"Finish?" Regan breathed, opening dazed eyes.

"Number fifteen." Mel hesitated only a moment. "The fifteenth beautiful thing about Regan O'Riley is the look on her face when I tell her how much I love her." It only took Regan a moment to react, and it was every bit as amazing as she'd anticipated. Green eyes shone with unveiled adoration, and she wore a breathtaking grin. "I love you, Regan. With all my heart."

Mel surrendered to Regan's fierce embrace with a grateful whimper, burying her face in the smaller woman's neck and wrapping her arms around her warm body. She pressed gentle kisses over Regan's throat, and smiled against the pale skin. *I said it.* Mel groaned when Regan's hand found the back of her neck and guided her face to warm lips. They traded slow, wet kisses, murmuring soft words into one another's mouths. Her entire body was trembling; she'd just told Regan what she never thought she would be able to say to anyone.

Mel had never felt such simple, overwhelming joy in her entire life. Everything about Regan made her feel alive. Words that had once seemed so scary now felt vital, and she wasn't sure she would ever be able to stop saying them.

She drew back, moaning when Regan's lips continued to kiss and suck her face and neck. "There are a lot more than fifteen beautiful things, by the way." She dropped a kiss on Regan's shoulder. "I just figured I should save some, you know, for later."

Regan's smile was as brilliant as anything she'd ever seen hanging in a museum, soul-stirring and perfect. "I love you, too, Mel."

"I love you," Mel said again, then proceeded to show Regan just how much.

"FOR REAL. THE Star Wars mythology has been completely ruined by the prequels."

"If this is another Jar-Jar rant, you can save it," Mel said in a light voice. She glanced away from the road and raised an eyebrow at Regan. "Yeah, he's annoying, but you can't condemn one of the greatest film series of all time just because of an obnoxious computer-generated alien."

Regan cast a stern glance at Mel over the top of her glasses. "No, it's far more insidious than some stupid floppy-eared creature. I mean, I suffered through and accepted those Muppets in *Return of the Jedi*, so I can get over Jar-Jar."

"Muppets?" Mel took a hand off the steering wheel and reached over to tousle Regan's hair. "Come on, the Ewoks aren't *that* bad."

"Yes they were, but that's beside the point," Regan said. "*My* problem with the prequels is that George Lucas changed the entire meaning of the Force, and therefore diluted one of his most powerful metaphors."

"Go on," Mel said with a smirk. "I'm intrigued."

Holy shit, Regan thought with some shock. *I can't believe I'm debating the philosophy of the Holy Trilogy with the most beautiful woman I've ever seen. And she loves me.* She took a calming breath and gathered her thoughts.

"Well, what does Obi-Wan Kenobi tell Luke about the Force in the original *Star Wars*?"

Mel raised an eyebrow in anticipation.

Excited, Regan said, "He tells Luke that the Force is what gives a Jedi his power. It's an energy field created by all living things. It surrounds and penetrates everyone, and it binds the galaxy together."

"Whoa. I can already see that I'm in over my head here."

Regan gave Mel a sheepish grin. "So I'm well-versed in the Force debate. I inhabit geek culture. It's unavoidable."

Mel covered her mouth with her hand, coughing before she returned it to the steering wheel. "Go on."

"*Anyway*," Regan obliged. "The Force flows through a Jedi. Luke asks Obi-Wan if it controls one's actions, and Obi-Wan tells him that it does, partially, but it also obeys your commands." Regan paused to let that point sink in. "So at first, the Force was a metaphor for inner strength and for realizing your own potential."

"I thought the Force was really like a universal deity," Mel said. "Not God, per se, but something through which, with faith and belief, one can attain some higher spiritual understanding and communion with the world around him."

Regan swiveled her head around to stare at Mel in shock. *No fucking way.* "You're the perfect woman."

Mel squirmed beneath Regan's scrutiny. "Does that mean I win that point?"

"No." Regan smiled. "Maybe it's some kind of agnostic bias, but I think the Force is about looking inside yourself, realizing your own potential, and facing challenges in your life. When Yoda is trying to teach Luke to levitate the X-Wing out of the swamp on Degobah, Luke fails when he doesn't have faith in himself and his ability to do it."

"But who's to say that he didn't fail because he didn't have faith in the Force? I mean, think of the language used in reference to the Force. *May the Force be with you* sounds a lot like May God, or whatever, be with you. Or *Trust in the Force*...trust in this deity. Have faith in something higher than you." Mel gave Regan a serious look. "You think?"

I think she's making me wet. Regan cleared her throat and shifted in her seat. "If you're gonna play word games, let's look at *Use the Force, Luke.* To use something is to have control over it, just like Obi-Wan told Luke that the Force would obey his commands. You can't control God."

Mel seemed to be giving her words a great deal of thought. "I guess I can accept that," she finally said. "But you've got to admit that the Force is a potent metaphor for spiritual guidance and faith in some kind of higher power."

"I can accept that, as well," Regan said. "Regardless, the prequels totally ruin the entire idea of the Force."

"What do you mean?"

Emboldened by Mel's interest, Regan explained, "In Episode One we suddenly hear all this crap about midi-chlorians. Qui-Gon tells Anakin that midi-chlorians are these microbes that inhabit all living cells and communicate with the Force. There's a symbiotic relationship with midi-chlorians that reveals to living beings the existence of the Force, and even imparts upon them the will of the Force. First of all, since when did the Force have a will of its own? I have a big problem with this sudden sentient, biological component to what was supposed to be a metaphor for self-belief."

"Or even a universal deity," Mel interjected with a grin, but gave Regan a serious nod. "I remember thinking it was a little strange, too. Especially since we'd never heard about these microbes before."

"Exactly. It was bad enough when they decided that being strong with the Force was hereditary in *Return of the Jedi*, because that already weakened the metaphor, but the prequel midi-chlorian bullshit flew in the face of everything we'd already learned in the original trilogy. It wasn't even mentioned then, so how can we reconcile that? Plus, it doesn't make sense."

"Give me some examples."

Regan grinned. "Qui-Gon tells Anakin that life wouldn't exist without midi-chlorians, right? If life couldn't exist without them, then where did midi-chlorians come from? How did they become a part of all cells? And think about it, in the Star Wars universe life exists across the galaxy on millions of worlds. I guess all of this life possesses midi-chlorians, but how the hell did it arise spontaneously on all worlds, in such radically different life forms? It's ridiculous."

Regan paused to take a breath, almost expecting that Mel would've lost interest in this conversation by now. To her surprise, Mel was staring at the traffic in front of them in thoughtful concentration. Regan was pleased when Mel gave her an expectant look. *Well, shit. I might as well go for broke.*

"And then there's the whole virgin birth of Anakin thing, and the theory that he was actually conceived by these midi-chlorians, somehow, which explains his unusually high concentration of them. I mean, is George Lucas out of his mind?"

"So your grudge is that the Force was changed from a metaphor, in your opinion, or a mythological concept, to something not only biological, but quantifiable and measurable?"

"Well, yeah," Regan said. "I mean, we go from the idea of belief in one's self to these crazy little microbes that can initiate an immaculate conception and bring about a *Chosen One* to restore balance to the Force. The Force used to represent something anyone could strive towards; faith and belief in yourself, the ability to overcome life's obstacles. Now it's a biological phenomenon that apparently fosters the birth of a messiah. The whole thing de-mythologizes *Star Wars*."

Mel looked deep in thought for some time, then finally said, "You're right. I mean, if the Force is this universal deity, and midi-chlorians are needed to channel the Force, then just what the hell *are* midi-chlorians?"

Regan looked at Mel in wonder. "The fact that you're taking this conversation seriously means a lot to me."

Shrugging, Mel said, "It's interesting."

Regan took Mel's hand and entwined their fingers. "I've never been with a woman who didn't make me feel like a total geek or an insufferable bore when I'd talk about stuff like this. It's cool. Thank you."

Mel gave her hand a gentle squeeze. "I love you. Everything about you."

"I never thought I would ever feel so comfortable with someone, you know?" Regan said, beaming. "All my life, I've felt so different from everyone else, so separate. I felt like nobody ever really knew me and like nobody ever would. I feel safe letting you really know me."

"I understand," Mel said. "I've always had people around me, but I felt apart from everyone else, even if it's seemed to them like I'm right there."

Regan stared at Mel's profile, awed that she truly did understand. "Except I was never able to fake it, you know? It always seemed so obvious that I was different."

"You were pretty lonely, huh?"

Regan steeled herself against the hot wave of shame this topic always seemed to elicit. "I couldn't believe it when you asked me to dance, you know." She kept her voice light, as casual as she could. "I'm so used to...Well, I honestly don't expect something like that."

"I don't know why not. You're quite the catch."

"Oh, yeah," Regan said, and straightened her glasses. "Chicks dig painfully shy computer nerds."

"I guess I'm just lucky you felt so comfortable around me, right?"

I'm the lucky one. Regan's cheeks flushed with heat. "You don't make me feel bad about being...this way."

"About being you?"

"Yeah," Regan said. "Other people—like my ex-girlfriend—have made me feel, well, guilty and a little silly about my anxieties, you know? You don't make me feel that way. And honestly, the way you make me feel, it almost makes me wonder why I have these insecurities at all."

Mel smiled, her eyes on the road. "I wonder, too."

"I've never really told anyone about this stuff before."

"It means a lot that you trust me."

"When I was in high school, boys used to ask me out as a joke." Regan swallowed, face burning. "Lots of boys, all the time. Some thought it was funnier just to make fun of me to my face, you know, but I did get a lot of fake propositions. So many, really, that I still get that moment of fear when someone expresses an interest in me, like I'm just sure they're going to start laughing. I know it's really fucking dumb."

"No, it's not. That's horrible."

"The worst thing was that I really started to feel like they were right, you know? I was always so awkward with other kids...the only thing I wanted to do was play with my computer, or read, or watch movies. I mean, I had friends in elementary school. Not many, but some. It was like the minute we got into junior high, everyone else just changed in a way that I didn't." Regan picked at her blue jeans, surprised at how easy it was to put words to something she had never spoken aloud. "I didn't have the same interests they did, and I didn't know how to interact with them like they did with each other."

"Let me guess," Mel said with a wry smile. "Puberty struck."

"I guess so. Something struck. All of a sudden I felt like a total freak around my peers. It didn't help that I was becoming aware that I seemed to like girls instead of boys."

Mel gave her a brief sidelong glance. "When did you know?"

"Oh, I always knew I didn't like boys in that way. I liked girls for a long time before I really named what I was feeling and accepted it as reality." Regan glanced over at Mel, then back to her lap with a half-smile. "I don't think I came out to myself until I was about fifteen, but I had been lusting after women ever since I first saw Jo on *The Facts of Life.*"

"Amen."

"Yeah, so that naturally made me feel like even more of a freak. And kids are perceptive, you know? Girls were never really mean to me in school until everyone decided to start calling me a dyke, but they were some of the worst then. It got a lot better in college, really, and I found other people like me and made friends, but I've never really been able to forget how it all felt." Regan glanced out the window at the brown-red desert landscape of New Mexico.

"You shouldn't feel embarrassed about that, baby," Mel murmured. "That must have been really hard."

She gave Mel a meaningful look. "I know that there have been times when you've felt weak for letting all the hurt and disappointment of your childhood affect you as an adult. But I do understand, I really do, because every time I walk into a social situation I get short of breath, and every time I meet a new person I pray that I'll be able to find my voice and not make a fool of myself."

Mel glanced over at her with sad, tender eyes. Without a word, she flipped the turn signal and steered the truck onto the shoulder of the road. Regan looked behind them as they slowed to a stop, then out the front windshield.

They were roughly two hours outside of Amarillo, heading towards Santa Fe, and the dry, desolate landscape was just beginning to show signs of the mountainous regions that lay ahead. The highway was nearly abandoned; a car a quarter of a mile ahead of them disappeared into a hazy cloud of dust, leaving them alone on the side of the road.

Mel leaned over and pulled Regan into her arms. The embrace filled Regan with strength, a wordless reassurance that centered her and erased any lingering fear of talking about who she was.

"I love you," Mel murmured. "I wish I had known you then. I think we could have been very good for each other."

"We are good for one another. And I love you, too."

Strong arms tightened around Regan and she murmured happily, sliding a hand up to tangle in dark hair. Mel's heart pounded against her chest and her own heart beat in rhythm with it, hard in her breast as if straining to reach its twin.

"I never imagined finding someone like you," Regan said. "Even if I had nothing else, you would be enough."

Mel's mouth hung open and she shook her head as if dazed. "There are no words..." She faltered, her voice cracking with emotion. "I don't know how —"

"Just kiss me."

Mel leaned in and obeyed the whispered command without hesitation. Their kiss was unhurried and gentle, and Regan poured of every ounce of feeling she had into their joining. She couldn't bear to break their contact even when she needed air, and so she pulled back a fraction of an inch to inhale, then closed the distance between them again.

We're on the side of the highway. I really should stop.

She pulled back with a small sigh of regret. For a moment Mel remained as she had been during their kiss, eyes closed, panting, before she blinked and fixed Regan with intense grey eyes.

"How do you do that?" Mel whispered.

"Do what?"

"You always know exactly what to say, and what to do, to make me feel incredible. It's...well, it's amazing, really."

"I could say the same of you," Regan said. One hand remained tangled in Mel's hair, while the other mapped the contours of her face.

"You know," Mel said, and kissed Regan's hand, "no matter how awkward you may feel with other people, you're really fucking good at this relationship stuff. You're just so open, so brave."

Regan smiled, nose crinkling. "I think I'm pretty good with people once I know them and trust them."

"Well, you're pretty good with me."

"And just imagine how good I'll be with a few months under our belts."

Mel gave her a smile that told her that she enjoyed imagining a future together just as much as she did. "Who knows? Maybe I'll even develop some new skills."

Regan patted her knee. "Darling, I'm not sure I can handle any new skills from you. I almost passed out the other night with that little tongue trick you pulled."

With a chuckle, Mel drew back and glanced in the rearview mirror. "I'd better start driving, huh?"

"I guess so, yeah." Regan glanced out the side window at a small group of cows grazing nearby. "Or else the cattle will start wondering what the hell we're doing just sitting here."

Mel snickered as she pulled back onto the road. "Right. That's just what I was worried about, too."

"Shaddup."

Mel made a show of zipping her lips closed and throwing away an imaginary key. She glanced over at Regan with upraised eyebrows, then turned to study the road with feigned obedience. Regan settled back in her seat to enjoy the show, a distracted grin on her face. About a mile down the road, she said, "I'm just waiting for your illusions about me to be shattered. It'll happen eventually, you know."

"Oh, yeah? So what about you is so terrible?"

"Hey," Regan protested. "I'm not saying I'm *terrible*, just that

I can be...unpleasant, and I don't want you to be surprised."

"Hit me with the worst you've got," Mel said. Challenge rang clear in her voice.

"Okay. You haven't seen me in the throes of PMS yet. Then you'll wonder how you got so lucky."

"Nah." Mel chuckled. "I'm sure I can handle it. You're probably just all cute when you're grumpy. I'm not too worried."

"Grumpy, whiney, bloated," Regan recited in a serious voice. "The list goes on."

"I think I can handle it. I give excellent back and belly rubs, by the way."

"You'd better," Regan purred. "It'll help get you through it in one piece, that's for sure."

"So is that all you got? PMS? You'll have to do better than that if you want to convince me that you're not as amazing as I think you are."

"I can be kind of solitary sometimes," Regan said. "Sometimes I just like to be alone with my code, you know?"

"I respect that," Mel said with a serious nod. "I need my alone time, too. I'm relieved you'll understand."

"Oh, thank God." Regan slumped back in her seat at the magnitude of this revelation. "Nobody understands alone time. Sarah always got offended, like it reflected on her."

Mel wore a smug smile. "See? You're not horrible at all."

Time for the trump card, Regan decided. "I'm a criminal."

Mel laughed out loud. "Oh? And what terrible acts have you committed?"

"A little high school hacking to change grades for some of the kids who were assholes to me," Regan said. "And when I was seventeen, I decided to fuck with some display computers in a department store and brought the entire store's network down for the day." She flashed Mel a wicked grin. "I made the paper and everything."

"A teenage hacker, huh?" Mel gave a soft snort. "We're not going to get chased through the desert by a fleet of squad cars, are we, Thelma?"

"Don't worry, Louise," Regan replied, deadpan. "As long as you don't turn me in, I think I covered my tracks."

"Good to know."

"And how about you, Officer Raines? Have you ever dallied on the other side of the law? And smoking a little weed doesn't count."

"Beyond committing various acts of sodomy — including some very pleasant ones this morning — no. I really am a saint." Mel sat back in her seat with a self-satisfied smile.

"Oh, but remember honey, the Supreme Court says we're allowed to have sex now."

"Generous of them." Mel rolled her eyes heavenward.

"Well, I appreciate it. You have a magnificent tongue that should never be legislated."

Mel laughed long and loud. "Have I mentioned that I love your comfort with your sexuality? You're so confident about sex. I have to admit that it surprised me, but I love it."

"I've never worried about sex," Regan said. "I've had lots of time to think about it. And engage in self-directed training."

"Oh, yeah," Mel drawled. "I remember hearing something about that around the campfire."

Jesus, I was stoned. What the hell did I say? Regan thought for a moment. "I told you I practiced a lot, right?"

"Baby, you told *everyone* you practiced a lot."

"Yeah, well, I do. I even lettered in masturbation, back in high school."

Mel guffawed. "Do they have varsity jackets for that?"

"Damn it, they should."

"So, is that considered a spectator sport?"

Mel's low voice sent a jolt of excitement through Regan's body. She squeezed her thighs together as if to stave off the flow of wetness their conversation was creating. "That depends." She watched Mel's throat work for a moment at the sultry tone of the reply. *You turned me into an oversexed pervert, now deal with the consequences.*

"On?" Mel rested her hand high on Regan's upper thigh, but kept her eyes locked on the road.

"On how nicely you ask?" Not that it would take much to convince her at this point.

"Please?" Her voice was so sweet Regan didn't even consider refusing.

"Yeah, that was pretty nice." When Mel didn't respond, but instead slid bold fingers down along her inner thigh, Regan blinked. "Wait, right now?"

"Right now." Mel's voice was rough with passion.

Regan looked around at the road. *I don't want more spectators than I bargained for.* An ancient pickup truck trailed far behind them and the road ahead was clear.

"Here?" She waved her hand in the air, indicating the interior of the truck.

"Right here. Sitting next to me where I can watch. And listen."

Being shy didn't even occur to her. "Okay," Regan agreed, and proceeded to surprise her lover once again.

Chapter
Fourteen

"HELLO?"

MEL FOUGHT a brief moment of anxiety at the sound of Hansen's voice even as she marveled at how much stronger he sounded. She threw her shoulders back, holding her cell phone tight against her ear.

"Hey there, partner." She watched a young couple across the street barter with a Native American vendor whose table was loaded with handcrafted jewelry and blankets. "Jesus, you sound great."

"What the hell are you doing calling me? You're supposed to be having a good time with your girl."

She could hear Hansen's smile and succumbed to a blush of sheer pleasure. "Oh, I am. But my girl's busy poring over a bin of used video games in a store down the street. She's dead to the world until she looks through every last one of them, so I thought I'd step outside and give you a call...see how you're doing."

"Better. We're all doing better, thank you. And the deck looks fantastic, by the way."

She soaked up Hansen's praise. "So does that mean you're up and around?"

"I'm not running any marathons, but I don't feel quite as useless as I did a few days ago." Hansen chuckled. "The grub's not as good as it was in the hospital, though. Annie's insisting I eat the rabbit food she keeps cooking for me."

"Well, that's because she loves you," Mel said. "I'm afraid I have to take her side on that issue."

"Hey, you're the one who smuggled a cheeseburger into the hospital for me."

"And if you ever tell anyone—"

"Yeah, yeah," Hansen grumbled.

Mel started walking briskly as two women leading a large group of small children headed straight for her. "Scary," she muttered.

"What's scary?" Hansen asked. "Being in love?"

Mel stopped in her tracks directly in front of a jewelry store that had an outside display table lined with glass cases. "What—"

"You're really going to waste your breath denying it?" A quiet chuckle floated into her ear. "Christ, Raines. I can hear it in your voice."

"I—"

"Have you told her yet?" Hansen interrupted. "And where are you, anyway?"

"Whoa, there. Give me a minute." Mel turned her face away from the bright sun, looking down at the jewelry on display in front of her. "We're in Santa Fe, New Mexico. And, yeah. I told her."

"Good for you." The quiet seriousness of his voice surprised Mel. "I mean it. I'm proud of you. It takes courage to give your heart to someone. But it's worth it."

"Yeah, well, I don't know that I had a choice. Regan pretty much stole my heart without my knowledge or consent."

"You want that I should arrest her, partner? Sounds pretty dangerous to me."

"I think I can handle her." Mel took a closer look at several rows of gold rings. One particularly attractive design caught her eye. It was a small gold Claddagh with a slim, feminine band.

"So, Santa Fe, huh? You two are making good time," Hansen remarked. "Which route did you take?"

"Missouri...Oklahoma...Texas." Mel answered vaguely, studying the Claddagh ring.

Hansen didn't miss a beat. "Do anything fun in Oklahoma?"

Why hide it? "I saw my father. I hadn't seen him since I left for college."

"Rough visit?" He radiated quiet empathy.

"A little rough. But good. Regan was there with me, and I said some things I've always wanted to say." Mel's words died in her throat when she realized how much she was talking, and how easy it felt.

"Like I said. I'm proud of you."

"That means a lot, Hansen. Thank you."

They shared a comfortable silence, then Hansen said, "You're going to bring Regan to meet me when you get home?"

Mel exhaled, a calming breath. "I guess I will, yeah."

"You'd better," Hansen said. "After all, if you're thinking of *marrying* this girl—"

Mel straightened up in alarm at Hansen's light comment. "Marry...what—"

"It's nice to hear that I can still get you all flustered."

"You know that's not exactly legal in Michigan, right?" Mel knew that was lame, but she couldn't quite believe that she was even talking about this level of commitment with a woman. Out loud. No matter how right it felt inside.

"I'm not talking about the law," Hansen said. "I'm talking about sharing your life with someone."

"Tell me something," Mel voiced a concern she'd always had when it came to the idea of *forever*. "How did you know Annie was the one?"

Silence stretched out between them for long moments, and Hansen seemed to give her question a great deal of thought. "Because I couldn't bear to think that she wasn't. I didn't want to imagine not having her in my life."

Mel closed her eyes, and swallowed. When she opened them again, it was to gaze upon the Claddagh ring. "I think she's the one."

"Then don't wait too long to tell her," Hansen said. "And say hello to her from me."

"Will do. Take care of yourself, okay? Enjoy that home cooking." Mel wanted to say something more meaningful, to let him know how much it meant that they could talk this way. But she knew Hansen got it. He said goodbye with a gruff tenderness that made her feel like the beloved daughter of a proud father.

Touched, Mel flipped her cell phone closed and met the eyes of the young woman who watched over the jewelry display. Pointing down at the delicate Claddagh ring, she said, "I'd like to see this one, please."

REGAN'S STOMACH WAS mercifully calm when she drifted into consciousness the morning after their arrival in Santa Fe. It was the first thing she noticed and she breathed a sigh of relief.

Does this mean I'm acclimatized now?

Regan's first bout with altitude sickness had been unpleasant, and especially disappointing because it sent her to bed early, unable to appreciate the atmosphere of the lesbian bed and breakfast she'd booked online. She opened her eyes and looked around now, smiling at what she'd been too ill to appreciate last night.

Their room was cozy, decorated with numerous pictures and trinkets that created a decidedly woman-centered atmosphere. Two older grey-haired women, arms around one another, grinned back at her from a large framed picture across the room. A small poster of Rosie the Riveter was mounted next to it.

Regan yawned and burrowed even deeper into the comfortable queen-sized bed where they lay. A handmade quilt pooled around her feet, pushed away during the night to leave both her and Mel covered in only a white sheet. *Too bad I didn't plan for the altitude like I planned for romance.* She sighed quietly. *Mel was pretty cute when she got all butch on me, though. Sweeping me into her arms and carrying me up to the room was a nice touch.*

Next to her, Mel was unconscious, stretched out on her stomach with one leg bent towards Regan at the knee. A possessive arm curled over Regan's belly and a slight smile played upon full lips. *I've never seen her so relaxed. Or so beautiful.* Regan stroked her fingers over her lover's bare shoulder, all the way down to one supple hip. Mel didn't even stir. Regan's other hand traveled down her own stomach, skimming over the top of Mel's arm on her way to the curly hair between her legs. She found her wetness with sure fingers, unsurprised.

*I'm in constant heat these days, aren't I? Now should I take care of myself and let her sleep, or...*Regan bit at her lower lip, casting an apologetic look at the vision of perfect serenity beside her. *Sorry, baby. It's really no contest.*

She slid the sheet down to Mel's calves, exposing her coppery skin with a careful hand. Mel didn't move a muscle when Regan pulled out of her lazy grasp, and her breathing remained steady when Regan propped herself up on an elbow to give her powerful frame an appreciative stare. She worshipped Mel's body with gentle touches and tender caresses. Even as she treated the familiar solid frame like something that might shatter beneath her fingers, she wondered at the strength of her lover's lines.

And wondered how much Mel could sleep through.

Her touches became firmer, more deliberate, and she covered the expanse of Mel's back with loving strokes. She wanted Mel awake. Now.

Mel's bent knee exposed her to Regan's exploring touch. She moved her hand from her lover's lower back to her ass, trailing her fingers down until she found her slick center and already abundant wetness.

Looks like someone's a little awake already.

Regan teased swollen flesh with tentative fingertips, grinning when she heard a shaky intake of breath and felt the gentle rolling of hips beneath her hand. She dragged her attention away from her hand working between Mel's legs, and looked into grey eyes, open and intense beside her. Face turned to the side, Mel's gaze was stormy with desire and raw in her newly awakened state.

Neither of them said a word. Regan continued to explore her while Mel's breathing grew loud and ragged. She pressed her fingers downwards until she found Mel's clit and circled it with teasing strokes, too light to do more than increase the flood of wetness that coated her fingers. She kept her eyes locked on Mel's.

Slowing her motions, she pinched swollen tissue with exquisite tenderness until her lover gasped. Regan claimed Mel's body with a firm touch, holding her in the palm of her hand. She let her eyes tell Mel exactly how badly she wanted her.

Still sprawled out on her stomach, Mel whimpered and nodded in wordless agreement. The sound lanced through Regan, breaking her focus and sending her fingers from Mel's clit up to tease at her opening. She sat up and put her left hand on a moving hip, then leaned over to stare at her right hand stroking between Mel's thighs. Her fingers were wet and Mel ground against them with immodest pleasure.

Regan pressed two fingertips just inside of Mel, felt eager hips buck backwards against the pressure, and pulled out again. She returned to wet heat with noncommittal strokes. A frustrated growl tore Regan's eyes from Mel's arousal to stormy grey eyes that shone with need.

Regan pressed two fingers inside, stopping at the first knuckle. Mel met her gaze, unblinking, and pushed backwards against her hand. Regan allowed her fingers to be drawn inside another half inch by the motion.

At that Mel groaned long and low, and let her eyes slip shut. A flush arose on her face. Her brow furrowed in concentration. Regan watched her lover's shoulders tense, and gasped when Mel opened her eyes to reveal her naked soul.

She answered the unspoken plea and pressed deeper inside, sliding into tight, wet warmth with a throaty moan. Mel echoed her moan, a breathy sound that was followed by gentle tremors that momentarily wracked her strong frame. Regan stilled her arm, letting Mel adjust, and enjoying how her fingers and wrist were slick from her lover's arousal. The air smelled of Mel.

Mel dropped her face into her pillow with a whimper, and rotated her hips against Regan's touch. Regan withdrew her fingers, waited only seconds, and then thrust back inside. Mel pushed back into the contact, turning her head and gasping, and Regan got on her knees to lean over her lover's back. She panted as she fucked Mel with slow thrusts, knees weak and breathing erratic.

Only moments into their rhythm, Mel's body froze and tensed beneath and around Regan, and her shameless motion ceased. Regan stilled her fingers and cocked her head in question.

"What's wrong?" Regan asked. Her voice was still slightly rough from sleep. "Did I hurt you?"

Mel hesitated. "I guess I just realized how I was...acting."

Regan leaned over Mel so that her breasts pressed against her warm back and her lips brushed against her ear. "How were you acting?"

"I don't know. Just so—" She dropped her flushed face onto her arm. "Submissive."

Regan felt a rush of concern. Obviously she had crossed a line she hadn't known existed. "I'm going to pull out now."

"Regan, you don't have—"

"Let's just talk for a minute, okay?" She withdrew her fingers from Mel completely and rolled back over on to her side, keeping a soothing hand pressed against Mel's bottom.

"I'm sorry," Mel mumbled into her pillow. "I guess it just freaked me out a little bit."

Regan searched for the right words. "You know we don't have to do it like this, right? Why don't you turn over and let me touch you?"

Mel shook her head. "No, it's not that. I mean, I can't say that I've never fantasized about—"

"Being taken like that?" Regan stroked her fingertips along the crease where Mel's thigh met her left buttock.

"Yeah." Mel finally met her eyes. "I've just never felt—"

"Comfortable?"

"Yeah."

"And right now?" Regan whispered. "I'll follow your lead on this one, baby."

Mel released a shuddering breath. "God, it's turning me on. And I trust you, I really do. It was just a little overwhelming for a minute, you know?"

"I understand."

"But I'd really like to—" Mel dissolved into an embarrassed grin. "I mean, can we try again?" She sounded uncharacteristically timid.

"I'd like that," Regan admitted. She slid her fingers down the cleft of Mel's buttocks, stopping when she found her hot center. "I'm really turned on, too."

Mel stretched her arms above her head, exhaling, then brought her knees up under her body to raise her hips slightly higher off the bed. Eyes on her pillow, she presented Regan with an image of perfect surrender. "Then touch me."

Regan exhaled shakily as Mel's position exposed both her

trust and her obvious arousal. Her hand trembled as she lowered it between Mel's legs. Regan got to her knees and crawled to kneel behind her prone body.

"Do you know how much I want you?" Regan kept her voice quiet and steady.

Mel growled in frustration, looking back over her shoulder. "As much as I want you?"

Regan's nostrils flared at Mel's darkened gaze. "More." She licked her lips, then leaned forward to bring her mouth within inches of Mel's center. "I think you're so fucking sexy." Her hot breath blew across wet, swollen flesh and she grinned at tan thighs quivering inches from her arms.

"You're killing me, baby." Mel's throaty voice shook with desire. She arched back until she nearly found contact with Regan's mouth, and groaned when Regan retreated with a soft chuckle. "Please, Regan. Please, just...Please."

Regan moved forward so that her lips just barely brushed against Mel's skin. "I like hearing you beg." She pressed her face to nuzzle against Mel's wetness. "It gets me so hot."

"Then please, Regan," Mel said. Regan dragged the tip of her tongue up along the length of Mel's sex. "Oh, God, please."

Regan moaned in pleasure at Mel's flavor and pushed her tongue deeper inside. She closed her eyes, inhaling sharply, and savored the delicious teasing. "You taste so good," she mumbled into Mel.

Mel jerked at the contact, and let out a frantic moan. "Jesus, Regan, God..."

Regan impaled her with a stiff tongue, thrusting in and out of Mel with deliberate strokes. After a moment she pulled back with a final swipe of her tongue across slick skin.

"You're putting me in some pretty lofty company there." She kept her mouth close to Mel, grinning when she heard the quiet whimper her warm breath elicited.

"You're mean," Mel complained in a petulant voice.

"Should I stop teasing you?" Regan sat back on her heels behind Mel, bringing one hand forward to press her fingers where her mouth had been. A cry of relief met her gentle touch. She moved up on her knees to bring her other hand down and around to Mel's breast.

"I think you should," Mel said. She growled again in frustration.

"I think you're right," Regan said. She bit her lip, hesitating for only a moment. Gathering her nerve, she made a request. "Will you get up on your knees further for me, baby?"

Mel's compliance was immediate and unselfconscious. She

got up onto her knees, leaned forward on her forearms, and stared back at Regan with desire-darkened eyes. "Just fuck me. Please."

Gone was Mel's shy reluctance and in its place shone a self-assurance that set Regan's heart pounding. "You want me to fuck you?"

"I want your fingers inside me." Mel flexed her own fingers on the pillow and groaned. "So bad, baby."

It was all over when she arched her back, openinand g herself completely. Regan sank her fingers into Mel's depths, her lover's languid moan became louder, more intense.

"You feel so good," Regan murmured, moving her other hand to pinch and tug an erect nipple. She leaned forward and sank gentle teeth into Mel's shoulder, tasting salty flesh with her tongue.

"I love this," Mel gasped out, meeting Regan's steady thrusts with her hips. "You taking me like this." Her confession was breathless, made through the hair that curtained her downcast face.

"I love it, too, baby." Regan moved her free hand from Mel's nipple to her hip, giving her an affectionate squeeze. "I love you."

"God, me too, Regan," Mel cried out. Small noises continued to fall from her lips, meaningless syllables and soft cries. Her head hung until her hair brushed against the pillow.

Regan was hungry for her, thirsty for her, totally beside herself with wanting. Her free hand blazed an almost frantic trail over Mel's skin, savoring the damp softness of it. She couldn't get enough, and verbalized a silent desire without thinking. "Times like this, I wish I had an extra hand."

Mel threw her head back, and her moan quickly turned into a laugh at Regan's frustration. Regan reached beneath her and brushed searching fingertips across her abdomen, then lower to part wet curls and tease her clit. Mel's laugh turned back into a moan.

"Regan." Mel stilled the motion of her body, panting with effort.

Regan continued to slide her fingers in and out of Mel, but looked up when she realized that the backwards thrusts had stopped.

"There's...uh...there's..."

Regan drew her brows together in confusion and she stilled her hand. "What, baby?"

Mel bowed her head, causing her shoulder muscles to stand out in stark relief. "In my bag," she managed. "I have something in my bag. And condoms."

Regan's knees shook with arousal as she straightened up behind Mel. *She has something? In her bag?* Without a word, she removed her fingers, drawing a pathetic whimper and a weak mewl of protest from her prone lover. Bending down, she pressed a kiss to Mel's damp temple. "I'll be right back. Don't move."

Entranced by the lustful look on Mel's face, she half-stumbled towards the black duffel bag that sat near the door and unzipped it with shaking hands. "Where?"

"In the side pocket." Mel moaned a little and Regan turned to look at her, impatient to return. "Hurry. I can't wait to feel you inside of me."

Regan grinned as she found Mel's surprise: a sturdily constructed leather harness, a smooth black dildo, and an unopened box of condoms.

"When was I going to hear about these, honey?" she asked, smirking at Mel's abashed expression.

"Just waiting for the right time." Mel produced an innocent smile.

Regan fastened the harness around her hips, her hands trembling as she struggled with the straps. *I just need to hold it together. If I come while I'm standing over here, I'll die of shame.*

"You know you never have to hesitate to approach me," Regan said, keeping her voice even as she prepared herself. "With things you want to do, or try. I'm easy."

"So to speak."

Regan unwrapped the condom and slipped it on the dildo, with a nod of approval. "Nice. No frantic trips to the sink to wash this thing."

"What can I say? I believe in coming prepared."

"So to speak." Regan gave Mel a pointed look.

Mel dropped her gaze to take in the harness and dildo that were now securely fastened to Regan's pale hips. "Get over here," she commanded in a soft voice.

Regan walked to the bed, helpless in her obedience, and climbed behind where Mel rested on her stomach. Taking Mel's hips with firm hands, she pulled her back and up onto her knees.

"You're beautiful," Regan whispered in reverence. She drew her fingertips down Mel's spine.

"And you're driving me crazy." Mel reached back and put a hand on Regan's thigh. "Just fuck me, baby."

Regan's head swam at the quiet plea. "You want me to fuck you?" She wrapped her hand around the dildo and pressed its head against Mel's wetness, sliding it back and forth over shiny pink skin.

Mel moaned and shook. "Yes. God, please, just do it."

Regan pressed her hips forward to push the dildo into Mel, slow and steady. She resisted the urge to thrust her way inside, allowing Mel to push backwards and take in more of its length. Regan rested a hand on Mel's shoulder, keeping still, and exhaled. "Feel good?" she asked. "Is this what you wanted?"

Mel nodded and ground back against Regan's hips. She gasped into the pillow, bringing one arm up under her face and muffling the sound.

She squeezed Mel's shoulder, then leaned over until her breasts brushed against her bare back. Regan drew her hips back before bringing them forward again, thrusting into Mel at the same time she bent to lick and bite at her shoulder blade. "Do you like being fucked like this?"

Mel's first response was a strangled groan, which rose in volume as Regan continued the motion of her hips.

"Does this feel good?" Regan asked again. "I hope this feels as good for you as it does for me."

"It feels so good, baby." Quiet whimpers escaped Mel's mouth in an unashamed incantation of pleasure. "God, I love you."

"I love you, too." Regan continued to thrust, running her hands up her lover's firm sides, down her back, over her flanks. Her eyes were glued to the sight of Mel's moving body, of the dildo disappearing again and again inside of her. Her ears were filled with the sound of Mel's excited moans and whimpers, of flesh slapping against flesh. Her nose was alive with the smell of their combined arousal.

She felt herself getting close to release, and sensed that Mel wasn't far behind. She reached around Mel's body and found her engorged clit with her fingers.

"Are you going to come for me?" Regan grunted a little, increasing the speed of her thrusts. "I want to feel you come around me."

"So close," Mel whimpered.

Regan gathered slippery wetness, swirling her fingers around Mel's entrance. She circled the dildo that disappeared into her depths, then moved up to tease her clit with a fleeting touch. Mel cried out sharply at the contact but Regan withdrew her hand after just a moment, sliding her fingers up until she encountered puckered flesh. She didn't try to penetrate Mel, but applied light pressure to the tight ring of muscle, probing and pushing and then withdrawing.

I wonder how she feels about this.

Mel moaned into her arm, a loud, explosive noise, and arched her back. The motion opened her further to Regan's exploration.

I think she likes it.

Emboldened, she pressed a fingertip just barely inside of Mel. Her lover's anus relaxed to accommodate the invasion even as her body tensed in anticipation. "Do you like that?" Regan murmured, and pounded a little harder into Mel with the dildo in a desperate bid for sweet pressure against her own clit. She gave herself another thirty seconds before she totally lost it.

Mel nodded and pushed herself back onto Regan's finger. She took in the whole length of it with a low moan. A trickle of sweat gleamed at the side of her neck. She turned her face to the side, squeezing her eyes shut. "Yes. Fuck my ass, baby."

Ten seconds, tops.

Regan worked her finger in and out of Mel's anus, letting the frantic thrusting of her lover's hips dictate the motion of her hand. Mel was hot and tight around her finger, throbbing and pulsing and incoherent with pleasure.

"Regan, I'm gonna—" Mel's words turned into a loud cry and her body stiffened and stilled and quaked with the force of her sudden orgasm.

Regan ground herself against Mel's bottom once, twice more, and then she too was falling, crying out, the sounds of her pleasure mingling with those of her lover. She followed Mel down when she collapsed onto the bed, reveling in the feeling of her breasts pressed against Mel's damp back.

For a few moments, they simply trembled and panted together, lying in a tangled heap on top of the sheets. When Regan could move, she slowly withdrew her finger, kissing Mel's neck when the action elicited a plaintive whimper. She brought both arms up to wrap around Mel, kissing and licking between her shoulders.

"I love you, Mel. Thank you."

Mel turned her head and Regan bent down to claim smiling lips with her own. When they broke apart from their wet kiss, breathless, Mel murmured, "Love you."

Pulling back, Regan whispered, "I'm sorry for this." Then she withdrew.

Mel moaned again, shivered, and then rolled over beneath Regan to stare up at her with grey eyes filled at first with dazed satisfaction, then suddenly with raw need. She brought her hands to Regan's hips and began unbuckling the leather straps in wordless urgency. Sweating beneath the heat of Mel's gaze, Regan rushed to help her with the task.

When they succeeded in removing the harness, Mel tossed both it and the dildo to the carpet. She brought her hands back to Regan's hips, squeezing them, and moved around to knead her buttocks firmly.

Regan felt dizzy from the wave of renewed arousal Mel's hands created. *But what a way to go.*

"Come up here." Mel flashed Regan a feral grin and tugged on her hips. "Over my face, baby."

Regan crawled up Mel's length without protest, straddling her face with one knee planted on either side of her broad shoulders.

"May I taste you?" Mel whispered

Regan shivered when Mel's warm breath blew over her center. "Yes." She groaned when Mel's firm tongue swiped across her inner thigh.

"You want me to eat you?" Mel wrapped her arms around Regan's thighs, pulling her close.

"Please." Regan stared down into Mel's eyes, allowing her own to plead. "I wasn't *that* mean to you."

"Are you wet for me?" Mel said. She grinned up at Regan from between her legs. "Show me how wet you are."

A whisper of shyness invaded Regan's consciousness for maybe a second before it was replaced by a powerful wave of confidence. *I trust her.* Regan spread herself open with her fingers, exposing her wetness to Mel's lustful eyes. She watched Mel's reaction, grinning at the desire she saw.

Mel's breathing hitched. "Touch yourself."

Regan moved one hand between her legs and began rubbing her clit with slow, firm strokes. She kept her touch light, unwilling to make herself come before Mel could do it for her.

Mel's control snapped only seconds after Regan began pleasuring herself. With a small cry, she pulled down on Regan's hips and lifted her head from the pillow, covering swollen folds and slick fingers with the wet heat of her mouth. Gasping, Regan removed her hand to give her better access.

Mel mumbled into Regan's center, letting her head fall back to the pillow and pulling Regan with her. Regan grabbed hold of the headboard with two hands and rode Mel's face in the mindless pursuit of pleasure. Noises poured from her mouth in a stream of nonsense sound, increasing the speed of Mel's lapping and the suction of her lips. Regan ground down as a tongue pressed deep inside her, then pulled out again to move up and circle her throbbing clit. "Just like that," she hissed.

She could feel the wave of sensation building again, and knew that she was near the edge. Her fingers tightened on the headboard as Mel's fingers tightened on her buttocks. Mel pulled back a fraction of an inch and for a moment Regan felt empty and distressed by the loss of contact.

"I want you to come on my face, Regan." Another command, then Mel's mouth was back on her, sucking at her, nibbling, lapping at her engorged flesh, and she was helpless to do anything but obey.

Chapter
Fifteen

MEL LAUGHED WITH joy and tightened her arms around Regan, who was still panting on top of her.

"What's so funny?" Regan asked, wearing a satisfied smile that mirrored the one Mel knew was plastered on her own face.

"Sex is just so intense with all these emotions, you know?" Mel said, awed by the discovery. For all of her past experience, she'd never felt anything like that.

"I know."

"And that was just..." Mel stopped, struggling for a way to verbalize the elation that pumped through her veins.

"Fun," Regan supplied.

"Yeah. That was so much fun." She gave Regan an adoring look. "You're the most amazing lover I've ever had. Oh, God, I've never felt this way before in my life."

A goofy grin briefly overtook Regan's face, then she grew more serious. "Me, neither."

Mel swallowed at the look Regan gave her, which conveyed things she never dreamed she'd see directed at her. At once sober, almost overcome, she whispered, "How is it that I feel like I've known you forever? It's like I can't remember ever not being with you, but at the same time—"

"At the same time, it's all so new and exciting that it scares you? Like it just doesn't seem real yet?"

Mel nodded. Her emotions swung wildly in the other direction and she was overwhelmed with a strange kind of melancholy and longing. "I want this to be real." Her voice broke on the words. "I don't want this to ever go away."

"I'm not going anywhere. I promise."

Mel managed a weak grin at the seriousness with which Regan treated her fears. Her spirits lifted when Regan leaned down and kissed her sweetly, which led to a number of sweet kisses, and eventually into a breathless mutual worship that ended when Regan pulled away with a small gasp.

Mel grinned up at the beautiful redhead who loved her, and

who was again panting on top of her. "Pity we have to breathe."

"Only momentarily." Eyes sparkling, Regan asked, "So what we did, you liked it?"

Mel ran her fingertips down a smooth back, damp with sweat, and settled her hands on Regan's bottom. "More than I ever imagined I would. You couldn't tell?"

"Well, I thought so." Regan wiggled her hips. "I was just making sure. I thought it was amazing."

Mel suppressed a groan at Regan's wanton movements, but a whisper of doubt invaded her afterglow. "You sure it's not ruining that whole tough cop image that attracted you in the first place?"

"Do you think being submissive sexually is being weak, Mel?" Regan's green eyes narrowed in concern.

"Maybe not weak, but—"

"Did you feel weak just now?"

Mel's lip twitched at the question. "Actually, no. I felt kind of...powerful." She traced her fingers up Regan's back until she reached her shoulder blades, then down again to her hips. After some consideration, she murmured, "I thought I had to be in control to feel powerful, but I didn't."

Empathy shining in her gaze, Regan asked, "What made you feel powerful?"

"Well, like seeing what it was doing to you. How my giving up control was turning you on." Mel felt a twinge of surprise when she reflected on how it had been to give herself to Regan. She wasn't sure she'd ever been so excited by something in her entire life. "I felt in control of your pleasure."

"Oh, trust me, baby. You were."

Emboldened, Mel went on. "And, uh, it was my choice to give myself to you. I had that power."

"You did," Regan said, and bent to whisper against Mel's mouth. "And I'm glad you understand."

"Trusting you, knowing you trust me, is the most amazing high I've ever felt." Mel stared up at Regan, aware of how much she was revealing, but strangely untroubled. "It's really cool, you know."

"What is?" Regan wiggled her hips again to grind her sweaty lower body against Mel's. "This?"

Mel lifted her head to give Regan's nose a playful nip. "That, too. But I meant that it's really cool that I feel like I can talk with you about anything. I feel so comfortable with you, and I've never felt that way before. Not once in my life." Never had she imagined that someone would care about her like Regan did. It brought her a peace unlike anything she'd ever known before.

"Thank you." Regan laid her head down on Mel's chest, releasing her from their intense shared gaze. "Your trust, it means everything to me."

Mel wrapped her arms around Regan and gave her a full hug, squeezing as tight as she dared. Then she turned and deposited Regan on the mattress beside her. Never breaking their embrace, she pulled Regan close and threw one leg over her hip.

She wondered if Hansen knew the best way to give a woman a ring. She really should have asked him. Stroking lazy fingers over Regan's back, she pondered that, and idly wondered if this was all as mind-blowing for Regan as it was for her.

"What are you thinking about?" Regan whispered.

Busted. Mel smiled at her lover's easy perception. "I was wondering if it was like this for you with Sarah."

Regan snorted softly. "Sarah and I had a nice relationship, but that was all. We had fun together. We liked having sex. But she never got inside of me like you have."

"So—"

"To speak." Regan chuckled. "I know." Warm breath blew across Mel's neck when Regan sighed, then, "No, it's never been like this before."

Mel rested her cheek against Regan's, grinning over at the wall. A framed vintage photograph of a woman in some kind of military uniform stared back at her. "I hope you understand what I mean when I say this—"

"What?"

Mel gripped Regan's bottom and pulled her even closer. "I hate knowing that you've been lonely, but I love that I'm the first one to make you feel this way."

"I completely understand," Regan said. She pulled back to beam at Mel. "I love you."

"I love you, too."

Regan hummed in pleasure, then groaned with feigned despair. "We should really go shower."

Mel wrinkled up her nose, sniffing the air, and picked up Regan's arm to sniff underneath. "You're right." She didn't even attempt to dodge the playful swat she received. "We worked up a nice sweat, I think."

"That was your fault." Regan rolled out of bed, and Mel was instantly cold from her absence.

"My fault? I was sleeping when I was *attacked* by this crazed—"

"Crazed?" Regan interrupted with a bark of laughter. "Hey, you didn't put up much of a protest."

"I was *unconscious*," Mel said, and folded her arms over her bare chest. Despite her best efforts, she was having a hell of a time not staring at Regan's pink nipples. "Innocent and defenseless."

Regan laughed harder, and gave Mel a pointed look. "You can't even stop leering at me for a second." Lustful eyes watched Mel as she stood up and stretched. "And besides, if you weren't so fucking gorgeous and sexy, you wouldn't have to worry about me."

"I'm allowed to leer at you." Mel grabbed Regan's hand and led her to the bathroom. "It's my job." With her free hand, she gave Regan's bottom a light pinch.

Giggling, Regan jumped and looked over her shoulder.

"Sorry," Mel said with a shrug. "If you weren't so fucking gorgeous and sexy..."

"Touché."

STEERING WHEEL IN her hand, Regan sang along with the fast hip-hop song that pounded through the truck's speakers and danced in her seat with carefree abandon. She saw Mel's amused grin, but she was beyond caring, feeling entirely comfortable around her lover now. *I love this song, goddamn it.* She launched into rapid-fire rapping, raunchy lyrics and obscenities spilling from her lips. *And I feel too good not to sing along.* "Put the needle ..."

Mel reached out and turned down the stereo. "So, I've got a question."

Regan glanced over, warming at the crooked smile on Mel's face. "Yeah?"

"How many people get to see you like this?"

Regan fought an instinctive blush. "This?"

"So unbelievably freaking adorable it makes my hair hurt," Mel elaborated.

Laughing, Regan said, "I guess I'll take that as a compliment."

"Damn right, it's a compliment. You know, when we started this trip you'd barely tap your foot along with the music. Then you started humming, and then that quiet singing. And now you're singing and rapping like nobody's business." Mel took hold of a lock of her hair and gave it an affectionate tug. "You've got a lot of layers, baby, and I have a feeling not many people see past the first few."

"Adam," Regan said. At Mel's questioning look, she said, "My friend Adam is the only other one, right now, that I'm really comfortable around. And Dan, a little, but not quite as much. I show you more than I show Adam, though."

"Well, I certainly hope so," Mel said with a suggestive leer.

Regan opened her mouth to respond, then stopped, looking out the window past Mel at the landscape she was just noticing for the first time. "My God, Mel, look," she breathed. Her mouth hung stubbornly open at the sight for a few moments until she had to turn her eyes back to the road.

During their brief conversation and the singing jag before that, the scenery had undergone a dramatic change. What had been impressive mountains and arid brown-red desert in New Mexico was now bright red dirt and rolling hills layered in color. Enhancing the magnificence of the scene was the brilliance of clear blue sky littered with fluffy white clouds, in total contrast to the red and purple desert below.

"Holy shit." There was an audible wince, and Mel said, "I mean—"

"No." Regan shook her head, eyes scanning the surreal rock and earth around them. "Holy shit is right."

Mel's hand crept over and found Regan's thigh. "I mean...just...I had no idea."

"Neither did I," Regan whispered. She dragged her eyes away from the beauty around them to glance at the beauty sitting beside her. "I've seen pictures, but I guess I never realized how real," she turned her attention back to the road, "and how *unreal* this would all look."

"So this is the Painted Desert?" Mel's voice was quiet, as if speaking out loud would shatter the absolute serenity of the scene around them.

"Yeah," Regan said, equally as hushed and reverent. "We're going to take 190 North through the Navajo Reservation, then catch 163 West shortly after we hit the Utah border. That takes us through the Painted Desert and then on to Monument Valley." She exhaled, overwhelmed. "I've gotta tell you, I thought I was most looking forward to Monument Valley, but I'm not sure that anything is going to be as breathtaking as this."

"I've never felt so affected by nature in my entire life," Mel murmured. "How perfect that I'm sharing this with you."

Regan's face almost hurt from the grin that stretched her lips. "I was just thinking the same thing."

"Thank you for being here with me," Mel said. Emotion rang clear in her husky voice.

"There's nobody I'd rather share this with," Regan said. "So thank *you*. For coming along on this crazy trip, and for being as excited about this as I am."

"I am," Mel said. "I wish I had the words to even describe—"

"It's clarifying." Regan steered the truck along the winding road, awed by the red rock that jutted out from the cliffs they drove between. "It just makes so many things seem so—"

"Insignificant," Mel said, and met Regan's sidelong gaze. "It is clarifying, just like meeting you. It feels like a turning point, like you did. It's like I've finally reached an impasse in my life, the way things were, and I can see so clearly that there's more out there than I thought there was."

"Well, that's what this trip was supposed to be all about, right? Reexamining. Reevaluating. Exploring life's possibilities."

"Who knew it would work?" Mel sighed deeply. "I was so unhappy before. I used to feel so old. Nothing makes you feel older than knowing that nothing will ever change—nothing important, I mean."

That was something Regan understood intimately. "Talk to me, baby."

"I was lonely," Mel said. "I went through my life with my eyes closed, you know? Get up, work out, do my job, come home, go out to the bar. I was so numb I couldn't even put a name on it. Until I met you." She paused. "I never want to feel that way again."

"You won't," Regan reached for Mel's hand and pressed a gentle kiss on her lover's knuckles. "Not if I have anything to do with it."

"Somehow, I don't think it's going to be a problem. Being with you makes me feel so alive that I can't ignore how dead I used to feel inside. And I'm never going back."

"I'm proud of you," Regan said. It was the honest truth.

Mel chuckled. "You know, you're the second person this week to say that to me, and mean it. I'm still trying to get used to it."

"Hansen?"

"Yeah." Mel's voice was full of embarrassed pleasure. "I talked to him the other day."

"Well, I'm glad there's someone else who's telling you they're proud of you. You deserve to hear it." Regan smiled at the road ahead. "I like Hansen."

"So do I," Mel said. "And somehow, I think he likes you, too. He wants me to bring you to meet him when we get home."

Regan whistled under her breath, low and nervous. "Sure." *That doesn't sound terrifying or anything.*

"I don't want you to feel freaked out about it—"

"No, it's just—" Mel's sensitivity helped ground her, and allowed her to focus. "It's a lot like meeting your parents, you know? Meeting someone so important to you."

"Like I said, he already likes you. And so do I," Mel said. "In fact, I love you."

"That's all that matters, then," Regan said, and managed a confident smile. "And for the record, you're incredibly sweet. I thought you weren't any good at this talking stuff. And feelings stuff."

"Yeah, well." Mel shifted in her seat, then fiddled with a bottle of water that sat in the center console. "Whatever. Just drive."

Regan snickered and put both hands on the steering wheel. The road was becoming increasingly curvy, winding in and out of mountains and along the edges of cliffs. Regan raised an amused eyebrow without taking her eyes away from the challenging landscape. "Tough guy, right?"

"Bad-ass and aloof," Mel confirmed with a nod. With a growl, she added, "And don't you never say nothing to the contrary."

"Or what?"

"You're not the only one who can reveal dirty little secrets, my darling." Mel sounded smug. "For example, who would guess that you're an animal in bed? I don't think anybody knows that from looking at you."

Regan blushed at the very idea. "All right, already. I give. Your secret's safe with me, and you can just keep the fact that I'm insatiable to yourself."

"Yes, I think I'll *definitely* be keeping your insatiability to myself, thanks." Mel's throaty laugh sent shivers down Regan's spine.

"Trust me, baby, there is nobody with whom I'd rather be insatiable."

"And there you have it, ladies and gentlemen. From zero to monogamy in five seconds."

"Is that a good thing or a bad thing?"

"A good thing," Mel answered without hesitation. "A new thing, but I wouldn't want it any other way."

"Will people be shocked?"

"Most certainly," Mel said. "Congratulations, you've tamed me."

Regan took one hand from the wheel, blowing on her fingernails and buffing them across her T-shirt. "Wasn't so hard."

Mel's laughter filled Regan with delight and she spent the next stage of their journey in a pleasant haze, juggling driving and awestruck observation. The land kept changing, shifting, and just when she thought she couldn't see anything more

beautiful than what was in front of her, she would find
something even more breathtaking around the next bend.

The desert became less cream-purple, growing red, and they
saw the first monument just as Regan's stomach rumbled in
protest.

Mel chuckled and reached out to rub her T-shirt covered
belly. "How can something so cute and soft make such a big,
scary noise?"

Regan wrinkled her nose. "I'm ready for something to eat.
How about you?"

"We could pull over and have a sandwich. Enjoy the scenery
for a while."

"Sounds fantastic." Regan rolled her stiff shoulders,
grimacing at the tightness in her muscles. "I could use a break."

"I'll take the next driving shift," Mel said. "After we eat."

"You're on."

REGAN GOT OUT of the truck and, with a blissful groan,
stretched her stiff back and legs. On the passenger side, Mel
mirrored her action. Catching her lover's gaze, Regan wondered
once again how she'd gotten so lucky. *How did someone like her
ever fall for someone like me?* She watched Mel lean into the truck,
hefting the cooler out from behind the passenger seat. *And how
the hell does she think I'm so wise and together when I always feel like
such a bumbling geek?*

Her smile faded, and she drew her eyebrows together in
quiet thought as she made her way to the bed of the truck and
climbed up.

Mel crawled over to Regan on her knees, offering her a
sandwich in one outstretched hand. Her eyebrows were drawn in
mild concern.

"Yeah, baby?" Regan took the sandwich with a grateful nod,
sitting cross-legged with her back against the cab of her truck.

"Do you want to talk about it?" Mel asked. "You don't have
to, but I just figured if you wanted to, then...I want to listen."
Quiet and tentative, she took a nervous bite of her sandwich
after she stopped speaking.

"Why do you think something's wrong?"

"You looked sad just then," Mel said. "I hate seeing you sad.
What're you thinking about?"

With a shrug, Regan swallowed a bite of her sandwich. "Just
feeling like a hypocrite, I guess."

"Why?"

"It's just that I feel like I've talked a big game about making changes, about moving past things, but there's plenty in my life that needs changing and I just don't know how to do it." Almost immediately, she felt the relief of having just said the words. "I mean, you want to talk about issues. God, have I got issues. And I don't have any idea how to overcome them. So the fact that you've been giving me so much credit for helping you these last few weeks, well, it makes me feel like a fraud."

"You're talking about being shy? The social anxiety?"

"Yeah," Regan whispered. "Basically." *Does talking about this make it real?* "I've never really talked about this like it was something that I could overcome. I want to feel comfortable meeting new people. I want to be able to go into situations without feeling sick to my stomach. But what if I—what if I can't? I don't even know how to fix it." Regan slumped her shoulders in defeat, finishing off her sandwich with a listless bite.

"Have you ever thought about seeing someone?" Mel asked in a gentle voice. "Talking about it? Or maybe even looking into medication to help control it?"

It was getting more difficult to meet Mel's gaze. "I've thought about it. I guess I'm scared. Kind of ironic, really. Too scared to see a therapist to talk about my anxiety."

"I'd go with you, if you want," Mel offered, finishing her own sandwich. "When we get home."

The cautious offer brought a genuine grin to Regan's face. "I really appreciate that. I'll think about it."

Mel kissed Regan's hair, then pulled her down so that her head rested against her chest. Regan sighed, staring up at the impossibly blue sky and the red rock formations that littered the desert. No words passed between them for a while, until Mel cleared her throat.

"You shouldn't be so hard on yourself. Aren't you the one who told me that you didn't expect me to be perfect? That it's never too late to change?" The hand that curled around Regan's shoulders moved lower, stroking over the side of her breast. "Please don't feel like a hypocrite just because you're not where you want to be yet. It just means that we're both works in progress."

Regan smirked. "You're getting very good at this *tossing my own words back in my face to prove a point* thing."

"What can I say?" Mel drawled. "I learned from the best."

"Indeed you did."

Mel hesitated a moment, then murmured, "Just promise you'll let me help you when you need it, okay?"

"You help me, I help you?"

"I guess that's the point, isn't it? Of this — of being *us*."

"Yes." Regan leaned up and pressed her lips to the corner of Mel's mouth. "It is." She looked down the long road behind them, lonely and shimmering in the desert heat.

"Hey, Regan?"

"Yeah?"

"You know that all this stuff, the shyness, the social anxiety — well, you know it doesn't matter to me, right?"

She knew that Mel truly believed that, but she couldn't help worrying about how long it would last.

"What's that?" Mel asked. "What were you just thinking?"

Am I that obviously insecure? "What do you mean?"

"I saw something in your eyes. Do you not believe me? Have I ever made you feel like those things matter to me?"

Regan flinched at the plain hurt in Mel's voice. "No. Not at all. I believe you that it doesn't matter to you. I just —" She struggled for a way to articulate her deepest fears. "Sometimes people think it doesn't matter, but after a while it gets old, you know? It's frustrating for people, that I don't enjoy going out a lot, and that I get so nervous about stuff —"

"Who are these people you're talking about?" Mel asked. "I'm not going to get frustrated with you." At Regan's shrug, she tightened their embrace. "Listen to me."

Regan lifted her gaze to meet Mel's. "I'm listening."

"The only thing that matters to me is what's happening between us, you and me. Other people have nothing to do with what we have, okay?" Insistent grey eyes searched out Regan's face. "You think I'm all that anxious to share you with the general public, anyway? I like keeping you to myself."

Regan felt the hot burn of tears in her eyes and brought a shaky hand up to wipe across her face. "Thanks."

"I just want you to be happy, baby." Strong fingers reached over and traced a pattern over her damp cheek, a thumb brushed an errant tear from her face. "The only thing that upsets me about your feelings is that they're so painful for you, and I promise to give you whatever you need to help you deal with them."

"I'm not sure how I ever found you. I never thought I would get this lucky. Never." As soon as she said the words, her fears almost overwhelmed her.

Losing her relationship with Sarah, even knowing that some of it had to do with her shyness, hadn't been terribly painful. But it would surely kill her with Mel. She glanced sideways at her lover. Mel might think they could spend the rest of their lives in a happy bubble built for two, but no one could do that. She watched her lover's expression change to one of unease.

"You think I'm going to get bored and go back to my old habits?" Mel asked with an edge of disappointment.

"I think you're only human. And I think I would get frustrating after a while."

"You need to understand something. Yes, I went to bars. It wasn't because I really enjoyed it. I've been with a lot of women. It wasn't because they were my friends or because I loved them. I don't want that anymore." Mel pulled her into a desperate hug. "You *are* enough for me, Regan. You fill me up. I don't need anything else. Just you. Whatever you can give me and what I can give you. Please believe me."

Incredibly, the knot of tension in Regan's stomach began to ease. "I do believe you," she whispered, startled to find it was the absolute truth. "I trust you."

"Just like I trust you," Mel said. "Isn't it cool how that works out?"

"It really is."

Mel gave Regan a blinding, open look of utter joy and pleasure that left her gasping at its brilliance. "This has probably been the best day of my life. And it even started with incredibly hot sex!"

Regan arched an eyebrow in amusement. "Can't keep your mind out of the gutter for even a minute."

"And you're any better? Besides, you love it. I know you do."

"Prove it," Regan said, relaxing into their familiar banter.

"Prove that you love it?" Mel snickered. "Trust me, I have plenty of ways I can prove it. And you'd *definitely* enjoy them all."

"And if I did?"

"Then I guess I'll have proven it, won't I?"

"You know what?" Regan said. "Forget all this 'proving it' shit. Let's just fuck instead."

Mel tipped her head back and laughed, a deep, sonorous sound that rumbled up from her belly and exploded out her mouth. She shook with loud guffaws for a good minute, during which time Regan simply sat back and watched with a delighted grin. Finally, wiping tears from her eyes with the back of her hand, she regained control and leaned back with a happy sigh. "I really like you, O'Riley."

"You're not so bad yourself, Raines."

"Come here," Mel said, and encouraged Regan to crawl between outspread legs. She settled down with her back against Mel's chest, grinning as strong arms came around her middle.

"We'll keep driving in a couple minutes, okay? I just want a little more of this moment with you."

"So do I," Regan murmured. "Being here with you is really making me look at everything through different eyes."

At Mel's hum of agreement, Regan opened her mouth to share a sudden, perhaps slightly silly, epiphany. It struck her how nerdy she was going to sound, and she hesitated while she struggled with whether to say anything at all.

"What?" Mel asked lazily. "Tell me."

"Am I a complete geek if I've found a programming analogy in all this? In what we've been talking about with, you know, making changes and growing?"

Mel chuckled, kissing Regan's temple and nuzzling auburn hair with her nose. "You do realize that you're adorable, right?"

"As opposed to a complete geek?"

"Hush," Mel said. "I'm interested to hear this. What's the analogy?"

"Well, I don't know how much you know about programming, or what you remember from your college class, so this may be totally worthless to you. Hell, it may be totally worthless in any event, but—"

"Tell me," Mel commanded.

"Do you know what an infinite loop is?"

The way Mel's body trembled in response startled Regan and she sat there, half in shock, as a wild burst of laughter escaped from Mel's mouth. "That wasn't even the really geeky part," she pointed out.

"Oh, baby, I'm not laughing at you." Mel stifled her laughter with obvious effort, wiping away the tears that had leaked from the corners of her eyes. "You just happened to bring up the one programming concept I'll never forget, because it's the reason I got a C- on my final exam."

Regan grinned in sympathy. "Trust me, I had my share of infinite loops back in the day."

Mel scrunched up her face in playful self-disgust. "I was so proud of that answer, but I didn't have a chance to test it before our time was up. I was supposed to keep doing whatever it was that I was doing— incrementing a timer, I think—until X was equal to twenty. Of course I forgot to increase the value of X at the end of my loop, so X never stopped equaling 1. The professor came over to check my work and my program just kept running...and running..."

"That sucks," Regan said, wholly empathetic. "When you're dealing with records in a database, you do something similar. Maybe you want to do something with each one of a bunch of records you retrieve until you reach the end of the records. At the end of your loop, you'd tell the recordset to move to the next record, and to do what it's doing while there are still records left. But if you forget to move to the next record, you'll never get past the first record, and you'll never get to the end of the records—"

"And you'll be stuck in an infinite loop."

"Exactly. So I was thinking that people can kind of get themselves into infinite loops, too."

"Yeah?" Mel murmured. "Like me?"

"Well, yeah," Regan said. "And me. Things happen that get us into habits, bad habits, and we get stuck in this endless pattern of behavior, accomplishing nothing. Like we forget the move next command. You said you felt old because nothing was changing, right? I think that's it exactly. Fear keeps people doing the same old thing, no matter how miserable it makes them. It's unhealthy, and pointless."

"You're absolutely right."

"People are like that, though. Doing the same stupid shit every day, making the same mistakes."

Mel smiled. "Why do you worry so much about telling me what you're thinking? This makes sense."

Regan's cheeks warmed at the compliment. "So you know what happens to a program stuck in an infinite loop, right?"

"It crashes."

Regan nodded and turned her face to press a kiss against Mel's throat. "So I'm glad we've decided to get out of our infinite loops. And I'm really glad I can share nerdy shit like that with you."

"I like hearing how your mind works. And honestly, something about nerd-speak turns me on beyond all reason."

"Then I really am the luckiest girl in the world, aren't I?" Regan beamed up at the blue sky. "Because, honey, I am all kinds of bursting with nerd-speak."

Mel grimaced. "Sounds like a personal problem. And painful, too."

Regan pinched at the tan arm that lay across her belly. "I'll give you painful if you're not careful, darling."

"Promise?"

"I promise," Regan said. "Plenty of pain. Maybe even the good kind, if you ask nicely enough."

Mel sat up a little, still holding on to Regan. "Oh! Speaking of pain—"

"Always a sign of a cheerful topic change."

"Be quiet," Mel laughed. "I just wanted to tell you that I decided how I always want to remember this day. This whole trip, really. This has all been so important to me."

"Me, too," Regan said. "But what does how you want to remember all of this have to do with pain?"

"Because I'm going to get a tattoo," Mel said. Her voice was light, happy, and it made Regan shiver with pure bliss. "To commemorate this trip, and meeting you, and everything."

"A tattoo?"

"Yeah. I've thought about getting one before, but if I mark myself I want it to be something really important to me. Nothing was ever important enough before now. But I think this is perfect, don't you?"

Regan licked her lips at a fantasy image of Mel wearing some ink. "Perfect. I think it's a great idea, actually. I've thought about getting a tattoo before. But frankly, I'm chicken."

"About the pain?"

"Pretty much, yeah," Regan said. "You know, my parents used to always tell me that they'd disown me if I came home with a tattoo or piercing. They weren't completely serious, of course, but I know they'd freak out. They're pretty conservative."

"And they raised you?" Mel joked. Regan shrugged, and Mel said, "So you're chicken about the pain and the disownment?"

"Oh, no. The *freaking the parents out* factor is actually a plus. Little did they know that it was the pain and not their threats that kept me from doing it," Regan said. "I take secret delight in confounding them. I think it's an unconscious reaction to feeling like they don't know me at all. Sometimes it's just fun to prove it."

"We could get tattoos together," Mel suggested. Kissing Regan's neck, she mumbled, "I think it'd be an incredible bonding experience."

"Um," Regan said, and tilted her head to bare her throat for Mel's mouth. "Remember that whole pain thing?"

"It's your decision, baby, but you shouldn't let a little pain stop you. I've heard it's not that bad." She scraped her teeth along Regan's neck, then sucked on pale flesh. "And I'll hold your hand. And tell you how sexy you are."

Be brave, Regan. She shifted in Mel's lap, sighing at the attention being lavished on her by her lover. *Isn't that what you've decided today? That you should start being brave?*

"You think it'd be sexy?"

Mel grinned hard against her neck. "And how."

Chapter
Sixteen

"DAVE AND BUSTER'S?" REGAN squeaked. "You're taking me to Dave and Buster's?"

Mel pulled into an empty spot at the rear of the parking lot. "Yes, ma'am."

"Mel, I've never even met a woman who wanted me to *talk* about video games, let alone take me to a restaurant specializing in them." Regan could hear the unreserved excitement in her own voice and almost laughed at herself. There was no way to explain what it meant to her that Mel was doing this just for her. Instead, she unbuckled her seatbelt and launched her body into Mel's arms. "This is awesome, baby. The second you mentioned playing Shamus on Atari, of all things, I *knew* that you were the perfect woman. You just keep proving it over and over again."

Mel grinned widely. "See, it was meant to be." She swung open her door, obviously pleased with herself, and said, "Let's go play some games."

IT WAS LIKE heaven. There were arcade games as far as the eye could see. Despite the bustling throngs of people that made Regan slightly uneasy, she was enthralled by the incredible array of digital and interactive entertainment that surrounded them. Most of the restaurant's occupants were male, but Regan was in her element. Mel seemed eager to play, and by the time she settled into a Skee-Ball winning streak, Regan knew she'd found a formidable opponent.

"In your face!" Mel hooted. She raised her arms in victory, pumping one fist into the air.

"Whatever," Regan said when she could affect an unimpressed air. "So you're good at rolling balls up a ramp. Do you want a medal or something?"

In truth, though, Regan loved that Mel cared who won. She loved the way Mel was losing herself in the moment, switching off her anxieties and reserve. This was so much better than trying to invent things to have in common with girlfriends who couldn't relate to her except in bed.

"You're just upset because I already kicked your ass in Tetris, just like I said I would," Mel said, smirking hard. She stepped away from the Skee-Ball machine, heading into the crowd of game players and calling back to Regan over her shoulder. "And I *almost* beat your Galaga score."

"At least I won the important games." Regan trotted to Mel's side, dodging a nudge of mock outrage. "The ones that require real skill."

"Yeah, making your little digital woman kick my little digital man's ass was a really important moment." Mel grabbed Regan's hand, bringing it to her lips for a quick kiss.

"Damn right. It may just look like mindless button mashing to you, but it's a carefully orchestrated symphony of ass-kicking."

"Uh huh. Sure." Mel tugged Regan towards a row of elaborate video games. "How about you find a game you think is important...one where I can kick your ass? Something that requires skill."

Regan released a dramatic sigh. "That's a pretty tall order." She scanned the crowded room, and then changed their direction mid-step when she spotted a familiar-looking game.

"House of the Dead 3?" Mel read the title dubiously and her eyes dropped to take in the two plastic guns holstered at the front of the machine.

Immediately Regan realized her insensitive mistake. "Oh, no, I-I mean...Fuck, I'm sorry, Mel. Forget it. That was a stupid idea."

She watched Mel's eyes swim with something unreadable and reached for her hand, intending to walk her away from the game. "Wait." Mel's voice was soft, but Regan heard it over the cacophony of sound around them: bass-heavy music, various beeps and whistles, excited conversation and cheers. "It's okay." She gave Regan a careful smile. "It really is."

"No, it isn't. I'm sure the last thing you want to do is pick up a gun. Come on, I can humiliate you at some other game."

Mel touched Regan's face. "It's just a video game." She grabbed the large plastic gun on the right and nodded at Regan to take the other weapon. "I want to play this, honestly. It looks like fun."

"But—"

"They're zombies, honey." Mel pushed dark hair away from her face. "I just drifted away there for a second, I promise. This isn't a big deal. Plus..." Mel lifted the gun, set her feet apart to take a predatory stance, and squinted at the screen through the sight. "I bet I can kick your ass at this game. I'm an excellent shot."

"If you're sure..."

"Just set us up, sweetheart."

Regan slid her plastic card through the reader then picked up the gun on the left and took careful aim. She heard Mel exhale as a group of zombies burst out of their hiding place and rushed towards them.

Regan took a shot and hit one of the undead, then followed up with two more quick shots to bring him down and score a number of points.

Mel hesitated briefly, then muttered, "Fuckin' zombies," and unloaded her gun into a snarling digital monster's head.

Her aim was impeccable and Regan soon found herself struggling to keep up with the accuracy and speed of her lover's shots. Mel's greater skill was confirmed as she defended herself against the onslaught of creatures and weapons, taking down nearly every monster in her path. Regan wasn't bad, but her score was nowhere as high as Mel's, and twice she was forced to bend to the card reader to restart her life while Mel still worked on her original turn.

When Mel's turn finally ended, they both set down their guns in unspoken agreement and turned to one another. "I knew all that time I spent at the shooting range would come in handy." Mel's expression radiated pride.

"Wow." Regan raised sparkling eyes to her lover, awestruck. "That was sexually arousing, even."

The corner of Mel's mouth twitched in amusement, and then she leaned over to brush her lips against Regan's ear. "God, you're easy." Her tongue snaked out to trace the lobe. "Have I mentioned how attractive I find that quality in a woman?"

"I believe you may have said something to that effect." Regan glanced around at the people walking by them, fighting back a giggle. "Once or twice."

Mel's breathing hitched and she took a step to angle her body in such a way as to provide a shield between Regan and the people around them. She reached down and captured the hand that still rested against her hip, sliding Regan's palm over to press against her inner thigh.

Regan gasped, turning her face away from the passing crowd.

"So I've taken you out video-gaming," Mel whispered into her ear. Her throaty voice sent a shiver through Regan's body.

"We've had a nice dinner. And now all I want to do is take you back to the room to taste you...and touch you...all night long." She gave Regan an innocent smile. "How does that sound?"

"Sounds like a plan to me." Regan's voice shook with her desire.

"Tell you what. I'm going to hit the bathroom before we go. Why don't you stay here and spend the last of the video game fund?" She leaned forward as if to whisper into Regan's ear again, but instead gave her a gentle nip at her neck before pulling back again. "And when I get back, I'll start seeing about making you scream."

Regan stared at Mel with her mouth agape. "Go." She pushed against Mel's chest to urge her towards the restrooms. "Hurry back."

Mel grinned and took a step backwards, then winked before turning to disappear into the crowd. Regan watched her leave, strangely fascinated by her every movement, the spell broken only when her lover's dark head vanished in the sea of gamers. Feeling lost, she blinked and felt around for the plastic card in her pocket.

Right. Time to drain the video game fund.

Regan gazed around, looking for something fast. She smiled in satisfaction when she spotted a large Soul Caliber 2 machine.

Awesome. A mindless fighting game. The perfect prelude to a night of sexual frenzy.

Regan claimed the machine and bent to reach the card reader when the sound of a hand slapping on the console above her stopped her cold. She straightened to face a group of three smirking young men and, for a moment, she forgot that she was no longer a scared teenager.

Regan's heart started to pound.

"How does it feel to have no friends, geek?"

She kept walking through the groups of classmates crowding the hallway, willing her shoulders not to tense at the attack from behind her.

For a moment, it was like nothing had changed. Like she hadn't changed. Her breathing caught and her throat felt so dry she was unable to speak.

It was a stroke of bad luck that had her sitting in the back row of her eleventh grade chemistry class. David Somers sat at the desk to her left and every day was a new torment, out of her teacher's earshot.

"If a guy asks an ugly girl to prom, will she be so thankful that she'll put out?" David asked his friend Mark, who sat in front of him.

"I don't know," Mark said, and tossed a smirk over to Regan. "Ask O'Riley and find out."

She was an adult now. Regan clenched her fingers into tight fists at her sides and willed herself not to panic.

"Outta my way, loser."

Regan never saw who shoved her as she entered the school cafeteria. She kept her face down, eyes locked to the floor, and tried to puzzle out the complex Perl script she was writing at home.

Regan looked one of the cocky-looking young men in the face. He had shaggy brown hair and a condescending grin. "Sorry, honey. We were just going to play this game."

His two friends backed him up with smug smiles. Regan's face turned hot and her feet itched with the familiar urge to bolt.

She forced herself to stand her ground. *Come on, don't be a complete wimp. You're an adult now. These guys look like kids. What does it matter what they think?*

"Actually, I was here first. I had my card in my hand."

A second boy, blond and wearing a tattered baseball cap, lifted an amused eyebrow and jerked a thumb over his shoulder. "I think there may be a Pokemon game or something over there. Why don't you leave this game to guys who can actually play it?"

Regan's shyness receded under a sudden wave of righteous fury. *Oh, no, he didn't. He did not just insinuate that girls don't know how to play video games.* She folded her arms over her chest in cool defiance. *You just found my pet peeve, lugnut. Others have questioned my prowess in the past and all lived to regret it.*

"Guys who can actually play it?" Regan repeated. "Like you?"

"Yeah, sweetheart, like me. Or like just about anyone except you. And my mom and grandma."

The shaggy-haired boy laughed and took a step towards the video game, attempting to shoulder past Regan. She held out a hand and stopped his progress with a cold glare.

"Which one of you is the best?"

The three of them looked around at one another before seeming to come to a silent agreement.

"We're all pretty good," the young man who hadn't yet spoken said. He had dark hair and kinder eyes than his friends, and she suspected that he was a couple years older than his companions. "But Kyle rarely loses." At that, the guy in the baseball cap raised an eyebrow at Regan in silent challenge.

Regan weighed her options. *What are the chances that the kid is an absolute prodigy at this game?* Studying the brightly colored buttons on the arcade game, she ran through some moves in her head. *Maybe I could win. I know I'm good.* With a mental shrug, she decided to take a chance. *Worst-case scenario...I lose, they laugh, and I still go home to bed with the most beautiful woman I've ever seen.*

"Kyle," she said in a bold voice. "I'm Regan. Would you like me to show you how a girl can play this game just as well — oh, hell — *even better* than you can?" She mustered a calm smile for maximum effect.

Kyle stood for a moment in silence, obviously surprised. His buddies burst out laughing, and they both clapped him on the back in encouragement.

"Come on, man!" the shaggy-haired kid giggled. "This should be good."

"Yeah," the other one said, and shot Regan what almost looked like a smile of respect. "The least you can do is put your money where your mouth is."

Kyle snorted but said nothing. She could see that her confidence had caught him off-guard and she smiled wider at the knowledge that she had unnerved him.

"Unless you're nervous, Kyle." Regan unfolded her arms and hooked her thumbs in the pockets of her jeans. "I don't want to embarrass you or anything."

He glared at her with cold brown eyes. "I'm not worried about being embarrassed, *Regan*," he said, and looked her up and down with a cruel smile. "I'm just wondering what you could possibly have to offer me when I win."

Regan fought the urge to blush at his words, forcing a smile on her face instead. Inside, she grew even angrier. *I need to school this guy for geeky girls everywhere.*

"I might worry about the same thing, *Kyle*, but I think all I'll want from you is acknowledgement that a girl kicked your ass. And that you're a cocky asshole who really shouldn't make assumptions based on stupid, sexist stereotypes."

"Oh, holy shit." The shaggy-haired boy tracked something over her shoulder with lustful eyes. "Why don't we ask *her* to reward the winner?"

Stupid, ogling — Regan blinked, then turned to look where all three boys were staring. *Oh, they're asking for it now.*

Mel approached with a vague smile on her face. From a distance, grey eyes caught hers and asked a silent question. *Are you all right?*

Regan gave Mel a subtle nod. *These guys are assholes, but I'm okay.*

"Oh, my God, is she coming over — "

"Damn. I'd take her as first prize."

Regan wrinkled her nose in disgust and turned to glare at the distracted young men. She opened her mouth to continue their conversation, but snapped it shut as the shaggy-haired guy called out to her lover.

"Excuse me, miss?" He nodded and grinned, flashing white teeth and twin dimples. "Yeah, you."

Oh, please. Regan coughed into her hand, which drew an annoyed glance from Mr. Smooth. *Like she'd go for that.*

"What's going on, boys?"

Regan felt Mel step close behind her and graze her arm with inconspicuous fingertips. Mel joined the group with a little smile meant for Regan's eyes only, then a brighter smile trained on the three guys. What remained of Regan's nervousness dissipated.

"Actually, we were just about to have a little contest," Kyle said, then laughed. "Well, no contest, really."

Regan scowled over at him as Mel nodded with polite interest.

"Oh, yeah?" Mel said.

"Yeah. This young lady here just challenged me to a game, and we were just agreeing that any good contest needs a beautiful woman to officiate." Kyle grinned, eyes flashing. "An impartial observer, if you will, and as luck would have it, the most beautiful woman in the place comes walking up behind us."

Regan rolled her eyes and heaved a long-suffering sigh. She could hear Mel's soft snicker but it seemed to escape the young males.

"Really?" Mel raised a skeptical eyebrow. "An impartial observer is that important in a game where scores are kept?"

The shaggy-haired guy waggled his eyebrows and leered. "Well, we wouldn't complain if you also offered to donate sexual favors to the winner. And/or his circle of friends."

Kyle smacked his friend's arm, giving him a dirty look. At his other side, the dark-haired kid actually blushed and elbowed his buddy in the ribs.

"Jesus, Paul," the dark-haired boy said. "Don't be an asshole."

Regan glared at the shaggy-haired kid, Paul, then at Kyle, who was now trying to suppress a laugh.

"Well, you're not shy, are you?" Mel folded her arms over her chest, looked at all three boys, then glanced over to Regan. Her eyes twinkled with something subtle that made Regan lean forward in anticipation.

"Nope," Paul said with a proud grin. "Not when I see something I want."

This kid really doesn't get women, does he? Regan watched Mel for a reaction.

"Okay," Mel said, and Regan blinked in surprise. "I'll officiate. As for the rest, I don't know. Let's see what happens.

Maybe something can be arranged." At the look of shock on all three male faces, she smiled and said, "So, are you going to play?"

"I'm ready." Regan raised a tentative hand into the air and showed Mel her card. *God, I hope I can win this thing.*

Kyle held Mel's gaze for a beat, then turned to bend down to the card reader. "Then let's go."

Regan stooped to slide her card, and when she arose Mel was standing at her side. Her opponent's friends stood on his other side, engaging in a quick pep talk as he and Regan chose their players. Mel leaned over and whispered to Regan in a voice so soft she knew the guys wouldn't be able to hear.

"You seemed pretty fucking good at this game earlier," she breathed. "You think you can beat him?"

Regan chose a female fighter purely out of principle, and gave Mel a subtle grin of feral confidence. She looked back at the screen after just a second, suppressing her amusement at the throaty chuckle beside her. *They don't need to know that she's with me. Yet.*

Kyle decided to play with a muscle-bound giant who oozed digital testosterone. Regan snorted at his choice. *Typical.*

When the match began, Regan allowed everything around her to disappear except the screen in front of her and the almost mechanical motion of her hands and fingers on the buttons and joystick below.

A game consisted of three matches, and they had only traded a few blows in the first one when Regan felt her confidence surge. *He's good, sure, but he's not better than me. Actually, I think Adam might even be better than this guy.* She blocked a kick, smiling at the screen. *I can do this.*

Regan executed a combination move that sent Kyle's character flying backwards and crashing to the ground. Another quick kick when he attempted to stand and she was declared the winner of round one.

Kyle's dark-haired friend raised his eyebrows and looked at Regan with newfound respect. "Wow."

"Fuck," Paul muttered. "She really can play."

"No shit, asshole." Righteous indignation flowed through Regan's veins. She felt Mel convulse with silent laughter beside her, and a carefully hidden hand gave her side a soothing caress. Regan met Kyle's glare with a confident smile. "Ready for round two?"

"Don't get cocky, bitch," Kyle snapped. He turned to blink at the screen, obviously flustered.

"Hey—" Mel protested.

Regan cut her off with a small smile. *It just means he's frustrated, baby. I can take a little trash talking.*

"Look where being cocky got you, right?" Regan shot back. She gave herself an internal high-five when she saw the scowl appear on Kyle's face, and the way his friends hid their laughter behind their hands.

Kyle opened his mouth to answer, then closed it as loud music announced the start of the second match. They both turned their attention back to the game and resumed their fierce battle.

Kyle's anger was palpable in his play. He flew into the round with reckless abandon, pummeling Regan's buff chick with a series of punches, kicks, and fancy combinations. Still, Regan fought back, and it was only by one or two lucky moves that Kyle won the match.

Paul clapped Kyle on the back with a triumphant hoot, and the third dark-haired boy merely folded his arms and raised an expectant eyebrow at Regan.

Damn, Regan thought. *I would've liked to end it in two rounds.*

Kyle looked past Regan to Mel. "So do you think I can buy you a drink or something after our game? I really would like to get to know you better."

Mel gave the boy a calm wink. "How about we just worry about the game for now, okay?"

Regan glowered at the confident grin on Kyle's face, and narrowed her eyes at him when he turned it on her. *Oh, yeah. Two rounds would have been ideal, but I'll settle for three.*

"Let's finish this, Kyle."

Kyle smirked at her words. "With pleasure." He shot one last wink at Mel.

Mel let out a near-silent strangled whimper as she turned back to the screen where the third match was about to begin. Regan could feel her lover's body shaking as she struggled not to break into guffaws.

Regan turned her attention back to the game, flexing her fingers in cold determination. *Assholes. If someone's going to treat Mel like a sex object, it'll be me!*

Regan came into round three with her figurative guns blazing, unleashing a series of punches and kicks that Kyle was unable to block to gain an early advantage. Kyle's muscle-bound thug leapt up from his position on the ground into a powerful combo that likewise knocked her character flat on her ass. Regan grumbled and concentrated harder.

I know I can beat this moron. Come on!

Silent encouragement flowed from Mel in waves. Regan was

aware of soft breasts pressing into her upper arm, reminding her of what was waiting for her back at their hotel room.

So what the hell am I doing here playing video games with a bunch of punk kids?

With a triumphant little cry, Regan executed a complex combination move that sent Kyle's man flying and drained the rest of his life meter. Flashing text announced her as the winner amidst digital cheering, and Regan stepped back from the game wearing a very satisfied smile on her face.

"Holy shit, Kyle." Paul gaped at the blond, who wore a look of supreme embarrassment and frustration. "She kicked your ass, man."

"Good game," the dark-haired guy offered, and Regan gave him a shy nod. "Come on, guys. Let's stop bothering her and go find another game."

Kyle turned cold eyes to Regan and she stared back with as steady a glare as she could muster.

"I'm playing like shit tonight," Kyle stated.

"I thought that was supposed to go, 'A girl kicked my ass and in the future I won't be such a cocky asshole who's so quick to make assumptions based on stupid, sexist stereotypes'." Regan folded her arms over her chest and arched her eyebrow. "That's all I wanted for my win."

"Whatever," Kyle said in a dismissive voice. "You're not that shitty, for a girl."

"Gee, thanks," Regan said with a snort of disgust. *That's the best I'll get out of him, I think.* "So big of you to say it."

Kyle dismissed her with a careless shrug. Looking at Mel, he managed to regain a confident smile. "So what do you say? Do you want to come have a drink with my friends and me?"

"I'm sorry, Kyle," Mel said, though her voice was decidedly unapologetic. "But I'm going to be busy rewarding the winner."

"Excuse me?"

The high-pitched incredulity of Paul's voice wrenched an involuntary giggle from Regan. Her laughter stopped short when Mel stepped in front of her and raised a hand to caress her cheek. Regan leaned into the touch, looking straight into amused grey eyes.

"Wasn't the deal that the winner gets sexual favors from me?"

The low timbre of Mel's voice sent uncontrolled shivers down Regan's spine. She blushed with pleasure at the way the three boys stood and gawped as if unable to believe what they were seeing. "Someone did mention something about that, yeah," Regan said.

Mel traced her fingers down to the soft skin of her neck, slid them over her shoulder, then boldly grazed the side of her breast. She let her hand come to rest on Regan's hip. Regan smiled, thoroughly enjoying the tease.

"And are you interested in collecting?" Mel murmured.

Regan ran appreciative eyes up and down Mel's strong body. "Very interested, yes."

Mel's eyes flashed with suppressed laughter and unchecked arousal. "Good. Because I think you're beautiful and I'd like nothing more than to take you back to my hotel room right now."

"Let's go," Regan breathed, by this point oblivious to her surroundings.

"Maybe we'll see you around sometime, boys," Mel drawled, and grabbed Regan's hand. She walked them towards the exit with purposeful strides, leaving Regan's three foes with looks of shock, arousal, and blatant jealousy.

Regan glanced over her shoulder and tossed the young men a beaming grin. *Okay, one last jibe. I earned it.*

"Oh, you guys can have that game now," she called out. "I've got something better to do."

Chapter
Seventeen

"SO SHE DIDN'T turn out to be some kind of super-hot psychopath, right? You're alive and well?"

"Alive and very well." Regan glanced over at Mel, who was sitting in the passenger seat trying not to pay attention to her cell phone conversation. "While she is most certainly super-hot, she's not a psychopath."

Mel's head snapped up at the comment and Regan winked at her.

"Okay," Adam said. "I just thought I should check up on you, you know...do the whole big brother thing."

Regan dissolved into a warm smile. *I may not have a ton of friends, but the ones I do have are quality.* "I know. I appreciate that you're looking out for me. Really."

"Yeah, well." Adam's voice was a little gruff, as if he were all of a sudden uncomfortable with the sensitive turn their conversation had taken. "I also wanted to ask if any illicit lesbian sex was had in my tent."

Regan barked with laughter and blushed at the flash of memory from their night at the campground in St. Louis. "Wouldn't you like to know?"

Mel's lip twitched in quiet humor. The subject of their talk must have been clear from the redness of Regan's face.

"I knew it," Adam replied in a smug voice. "Somehow that makes me very happy."

"Yeah, well...just keep that happiness to yourself, will you?"

Adam chuckled, then sighed. "I'm glad you're having a good time, but I miss you. It sucks playing Halo without the other half of my two-solider army."

"Did I tell you that Mel plays video games? She took me to Dave and Buster's last night."

"For real?" Adam sounded impressed. "Where the hell are the straight women who'll take me to Dave and Buster's?"

"I know. I'm lucky." Regan met Mel's eyes before turning

back to the road. Traffic was light and they were moving into increasingly desolate country.

"So am I going to get a thank you for dragging you to that bar now?" Adam asked.

Regan could hear a certain smug satisfaction in his voice, though she couldn't even bring herself to care. "Thank you."

"You're welcome. Now I'll let you get back to your hot lesbian stuff, and I'll get back to my boring old code."

"Have fun!" Regan teased. "I'll call you when I get home."

"You'd better," he said. "And I want to meet Ms. Right again sometime, okay?"

"Of course," Regan answered. "I don't think that'll be a problem." *Since I hope to be spending a lot of time with her from now on.*

After their goodbyes, Regan turned off her cell phone and slipped it back into the cup holder in the center console. "Adam was a little nervous about the idea of me running off to drive across the country with someone he barely knew."

Mel cast her a quick smile. "I guess I can't blame him. I'm glad you've got someone who cares about you like that."

"Me, too." Regan squinted up at the blue sky above them, watching fluffy white clouds through the front windshield. "He's a good guy. Our friendship usually doesn't go much deeper than talking code, lusting after women, and playing video games, but I know he loves me like a sister. And he's the closest thing I've ever had to a brother."

"Did you meet him on the job?"

"No, I knew him in college. He got me an interview with his company a couple years after we graduated and we've been working together since." Regan looked over to Mel with tentative eyes. "He wants to get to know you better. I'd like that, too, if you're up to it."

"Of course I am. He's an important part of your life."

She's willing to bridge the gap between lesbian and geek? Regan beamed out at the road, taking one hand off the steering wheel and resting it on Mel's thigh. *I really think this is going to work.*

Mel entangled her fingers with Regan's, pulling their hands towards her stomach. "So..." she said after a moment. "Last night. I didn't embarrass you, did I? Or go too far? With those guys, I mean."

"Are you kidding me?" Her smile became a full-fledged grin at the memory of the looks on those cocky young faces. "God, you don't know how many times I would have killed for something like that to happen to me in high school."

"I have to admit that I enjoyed it, too," Mel said, giving her a mischievous smile. "I just wanted to make sure that it didn't make you uncomfortable."

"Oh, yeah. I was so terribly uncomfortable that the woman they all wanted to take home ended up coming home with *me*." Regan winked, squeezing Mel's hand. "Last night was wonderful, Mel, all of it. Thank you."

"You're welcome," Mel said. She beamed over at Regan. "It was selfish, though. I just love making you smile."

"You're good at it." Regan leaned back in her seat a little, glancing around at the farmland that surrounded them. "Could you take a look at the map and try to get an idea of where we're at?"

Mel let go of Regan's hand to bend down and fish around under the seat, pulling out a state map of Kansas with a triumphant flourish. She unfolded it, and studied it for a moment, then said, "I think we're about thirty miles past Hays, still a little way from Missouri. Maybe another five or six hours?"

Regan scanned green prairies, blue sky, and fluffy white clouds. "It's pretty here, too. Not like Arizona and Utah, but really peaceful."

"Yeah, it is." Mel folded the map up, tucking it beside the seat. "When do you want to stop for lunch?"

Regan remembered the cooler sitting in the bed of her truck. "Right now?"

Mel made a show of looking around at the abundant farms, fields, and trees, and nary a restaurant in sight. "If you say so. I'm not sure we're going to have many choices, though."

"We've still got some turkey and tomato, right? And those flatbread wraps?"

"Yeah." Mel reached over and fingered a lock of Regan's hair. "Thinking about a picnic?"

"Thinking about it. We can look around for something a little secluded and take a break from driving."

Mel released a blissful moan. "After eight hours in this truck today, the idea of a late picnic under a tree with my baby is extraordinarily appealing."

"Great minds..."

Regan turned her truck down the dirt road, driving them only a half a mile before they found a large oak tree surrounded by an endless field of green. She parked, and was pushing open the door and walking to the back before Mel could say another word.

Mel joined her at the tailgate in time to carry the heavy cooler.

"I love that you're always prepared for these things," she said.

"You never know when there'll be an emergency picnic." Regan walked to the impressive tree and spread out her picnic blanket in the shade. The massive trunk completely screened them from the road.

Mel deposited the cooler onto the blanket next to Regan and plopped down next to her to sit with her legs crossed. "Perfect spot." She batted her eyelashes innocently. "Are you going to make me a sandwich?"

Regan snorted. "How could I refuse a sweet face like that?"

"You can't." Mel lay back on the blanket, lacing her hands behind her head and staring up at the branch-filtered sky above them. "Remember that, okay?"

"Okay." Regan rubbed her palm over Mel's belly, then reached over to flip open the cooler. She pulled out the flatbread wraps from the top, grabbing the package of turkey and a plastic bag of tomato slices from on ice beneath it. "Mustard or mayo?"

Mel rolled over on her side, propping her head up on her hand. "Mustard. I'm not so sure about mayo in general. It's a little freaky."

"My kind of woman," Regan said. She upturned a small bottle of mustard and applied a generous amount to each sandwich.

For a few moments, Mel watched Regan's sandwich-making with distant eyes, then she crawled over to rest her head against Regan's thigh. Regan dropped her free hand to tangle in her lover's dark hair. She could feel Mel's mind racing beneath her fingers and wondered if she was as sad as Regan was that their trip was winding down.

"What's wrong, baby?" Regan asked as she put the finishing touches on each sandwich.

Mel shook her head. "Nothing. Just hungry."

"You're in luck. I happen to have two turkey sandwiches right here."

"Cool." Mel sat up and quirked an eyebrow at her. "Didn't you want to eat anything?"

Regan snorted and handed Mel the plate in her hand. "You're so clever."

"That's what they tell me." Mel folded up her sandwich wrap and brought it to her mouth for a healthy bite. "Have you ever noticed how much better things taste when you're eating outdoors?"

"Yeah, I have. I've always thought...isn't that weird?"

Mel broke out into an evil smirk. "I wonder if that holds true for everything?"

Regan stopped her hand halfway to her mouth, jaw still open in readiness for her bite. *Damn, I love this woman.* "Please. The last thing I want is to get caught naked in a field by some Kansas farmer."

"Who said anything about being naked? Just what were *you* thinking about? Pervert." Mel polished off her sandwich, licking a stray drop of mustard off her thumb.

Regan gaped at Mel's empty hands. "My God, woman, did you stop to breathe?"

"Job hazard. I'm used to eating fast because we always get interrupted at lunch, no matter how slow the day is." Mel lay back on the blanket again, propping herself on an elbow. With a wistful sigh, she said, "I'm going to miss lunch with Hansen. Even despite the crap he always wanted us to eat...I'll miss working with him."

"So you're really going to quit?" Regan wiped her hands on the blanket beside her thighs.

"Yeah, I am," Mel said. "It's time to do something new. I want to like what I'm doing every day."

Regan gave Mel a sidelong glance, then stretched out beside her. Lacing her fingers behind her head, she stared at the clouds.

"But you know," Mel continued, shifting gears. "The only thing I am sorry about is that I don't have more to offer you right now."

Regan turned her head so that she could stare at Mel. "Don't ever say that again," she said. At the almost imperceptible quivering of Mel's lower lip, she gentled her tone. "Please, baby. Not after everything we've been through."

"You're right. That was insensitive."

"I'll live," Regan said. "Try to remember that I love you. Okay?"

Mel took her hand. "I wish my uncle was still alive. I would've loved for him to meet you. He was a good guy. I'm not sure how he and my dad came from the same place...They were as different as night and day, even if they were both cops."

"When did he die?" Regan scooted closer to Mel, laying her head upon a strong shoulder.

"He had a heart attack about two years after I went to college." Mel bent her face to kiss the top of Regan's head, tightening her embrace. "It was one of the hardest things I'd ever gone through. He took me in when Dad kicked me out, no questions asked. I lived with him until I graduated high school, and I don't know what would have happened to me if I hadn't. I've seen too many kids on the streets—" Mel paused, and then cleared her throat. "I didn't even go to his funeral because I was so scared of seeing my father. I've always regretted that."

"He knew you loved him," Regan said, filing another piece of Mel's life story into place.

"Yes, he did. Even if I never knew how to tell him so."

"Did he know about you being gay?"

"I didn't tell him at first. He took me to the hospital—Dad broke two of my ribs that night—but he didn't push me to explain what had actually happened." Mel pulled Regan even closer. "The last couple of months at school were pretty rough, though. Rumors started spreading. I don't know if it was Lauren, or Mike, or even my dad, but somehow it got around that I'd gotten kicked out of my house for being a dyke."

"God," Regan breathed. She had a painful flash of that very epithet—*dyke*—being hurled in her direction on so many days of her adolescence.

"It was pretty much social poisoning, you know? I lost a lot of friends, lost Lauren. One day a couple of guys in my class confronted me and I got into a fist fight." Mel's tense body relaxed when Regan's fingers found her lower back. "I went home and just lost it, totally. All the pressure...I just exploded. I was busy trashing the room Uncle David had set up for me when he came home...God."

"What happened?"

"I thought he would kick my sorry ass," Mel said. "I think I wanted him to, even. Instead he just grabbed me and hugged me. He still didn't push me to tell him what was going on, but it all kind of spilled out, you know? He told me to hang on for just a few more weeks, that everything would be so much better when I went to college."

"And he was right," Regan murmured. "It *is* easier at college. I'm glad you had someone to tell you that. I could have used the reminder, once or twice, myself."

A dark memory of high school crept into her mind. She had never found the courage to tell anyone this story before, and even now, even with Mel, she hesitated. *But I want her to understand me.* "I don't know why the kids at school decided that I was a lesbian. Maybe it was just because I was different and it was something easy to call me. Maybe they saw something I was only just beginning to see." Regan burrowed deeper into Mel's embrace.

"When did it start?" Mel asked.

"Sophomore year. The end of the year, thank God," Regan said. "The other girls never paid a lot of attention to me before that started, but once I was labeled 'dyke' it got pretty bad with them."

Regan closed her eyes, seeing Nicole Bergman's look of disgust almost as if it had happened yesterday.

"Are you looking at me, dyke?"

Regan's gaze was in fact fixed on her own sock-covered feet as she retied her shoes after gym class. She never lifted her eyes from the floor when her classmates were changing in the locker room; she was terrified of being accused of what Nicole now implied.

Regan stayed quiet, pretending like Nicole hadn't been talking to her.

"Yeah, you, Regan. Were you looking at my breasts?"

Regan knew her face was beet red, as if she were guilty. Her tongue felt thick and useless in her mouth, unable to form even a weak defense.

"I don't think they should let lesbians change with the rest of us. Do you, Nicole?"

Regan recognized Julie's voice and suppressed a shudder. She stood up, facing her locker, and fumbled with her backpack. She had to get out of there.

"Especially not the ugly ones," Nicole said, laughing. "Regan, who said we wanted you in here with us?"

Regan turned, ready to flee from the locker room. But Nicole and three groupies were standing in a semi-circle around her. They were all dressed now, though all four never hesitated to walk around barely-clad most of the time.

"Maybe I should tell Mr. Schultz about you," Nicole said. "That you're a fucking pervert."

Regan gasped at the idea of Nicole going to the principal and telling him anything. He would call her parents.

Randa, a willowy brunette, gave Regan a cruel grin. "I'll tell him, too. That you were hitting on Nicole."

"Yeah," Jamie piped up. "I think you need to learn to keep your eyes..." she looked around at her friends, smiling wide, "...and your hands...to yourself."

Regan felt a droplet of sweat travel down her side beneath her T-shirt. She felt sick to her stomach, frozen in terror. She opened her mouth in an effort to voice her defense, but she couldn't make a sound. She watched two of her more quiet classmates slip out of the locker room behind her group of tormenters.

Nicole leaned towards Regan, giving her a disdainful once over. "Do you really think any girl would want – "

The locker room door banged open behind Nicole, stopping her words and drawing her attention over her shoulder. Regan nearly wept in relief at the sight of her gym teacher stalking into the room.

"What's going on here?"

"Nothing, Ms. White," Nicole answered. She looked back to Regan with hard eyes, and then took a step back away from her. "We were just getting ready to go to our next class."

"Regan?" The stocky gym teacher stopped next to the row of lockers, settling her hands on her hips.

Regan ducked her head, fighting not to let her tears spill over. She could feel silent menace radiating from the four girls that still stood near her.

"I'm fine," Regan said. "I was just leaving, too." She didn't look up.

"Regan, I need to see you in my office. You other girls, get going, why don't you?"

A chorus of "Yes, Ms. White" followed Regan's classmates out the door. Regan remained standing where she was, shamed eyes pinned to the floor. She was shaking now that the threat was gone and the tears she'd tried so hard to suppress were rolling down her cheeks.

"Come on, Regan," Ms. White said. She didn't approach, but took a step away from the lockers. "Let's get you a glass of water before you get back to class."

"And the worst part of all," Mel said after Regan stopped talking, "is that I'm sure you didn't have the slightest interest in any of them."

Regan snorted. "Of course not. They were stupid." She paused a moment, and then said, "You know, I'd bet you anything that Ms. White was a dyke. She didn't say much to me. Just had me drink that glass of water then sent me back to class. I went home instead."

"Your parents didn't notice any of this? You couldn't have been acting very happy at home."

"Maybe it was my fault," Regan admitted. "I kept myself pretty distant from them. I couldn't stand for them to know what was happening. How could I go to them and tell them that girls were accusing me of trying to touch them...or look at them?" She shook her head, burying her face in Mel's neck. "I couldn't. I stayed in my room and played with my computers and video games and prayed that I'd be an adult soon, so I could go live by myself and maybe find other people like me."

"I love you," Mel said.

Simple, but it meant so much.

Regan lifted her head and smiled at her lover. "I didn't tell you all that for sympathy, you know. I told you because I want you to understand me. Everything about me."

"I know. It's the same reason I want to tell you everything. It's so comforting to have someone who knows you. At first it seemed scary, but now that I know it is real, I like it."

"So do I. I never dreamed I would ever meet someone who would really know me or understand me." She reached over and traced the lines of Mel's face. "I feel like you complete me."

"Me, too." Mel closed her eyes, a lazy, crooked smile on her face.

Regan's heart raced in her chest and breathing felt like an effort with the all-consuming love she felt in that moment. She moved her fingers down to Mel's chin and her throat, and then further to rub circles on Mel's stomach. After only a moment she worked her way beneath Mel's T-shirt, tickling the soft skin of her belly.

Mel gasped in surprise. "Regan—"

Regan cut her off with a soft shushing noise. "We're all alone out here, sweetheart. Let me make you feel good."

She unbuttoned then unzipped Mel's blue jeans, enjoying the way Mel's eyes grew hooded and her breathing went ragged. She slipped her hand inside Mel's boxer briefs, grinning as her lover's long legs parted in anticipation.

Regan dragged her eyes down to stare at her arm as she found Mel's wet heat. Her pale skin looked even creamier in contrast with the copper color of Mel's belly. Her attention jerked back to Mel's face when her lover hissed in pleasure at the first contact of Regan's hand with her center.

"I love watching myself touch you," Regan said. She brought her mouth closer to Mel's ear, dropping a soft kiss on the lobe. She looked down Mel's body again, watching in rapt fascination as her hand moved inside Mel's jeans.

Mel groaned, fanning Regan's desire. "Watch me," Regan whispered, nodding at her hand.

Mel did as she was told.

MEL LAY STARING up at the blue sky and thick branches above them, and cradled Regan in her arms. Her lover's auburn head rested heavily on her chest, her breathing deep and even, and Mel wondered if she had dozed off.

Regan let out a sudden giggle, answering Mel's unspoken question.

"What do you sound so self-satisfied about?" Mel teased. She gazed down at Regan with heavy-lidded eyes.

Regan lifted her head from Mel's chest and shot her a dazzling smile, then laid back with her head next to Mel's. She pointed up at the sky at a cluster of fluffy white clouds to their right. "I was just thinking that that cloud right there looks remarkably like you do when you come."

"What?" Mel asked. "Beautiful and tranquil?"

"Nah. I was thinking more along the lines of goofy. It's kind of a goofy cloud." Gesturing at the sky again, she asked, "Don't you agree? Goofy like you?"

Mel rolled onto her side and propped her head up with her hand. "Goofy?" She reached out and tickled Regan's stomach. Regan curled her body around Mel's hand, convulsing with laughter. "You're saying I look *goofy* when I come?"

"I-I—" Regan sputtered, shaking with laughter. "I...no, it's—"

Mel moved on to torment her lover's hips, belly, and thighs with tickling fingers. "How will I ever be able to come again without feeling self-conscious?"

Regan squirmed, braying and bucking, howling up at the sky. "Oh," she managed. "I don't really...think you're...going to have any p-problems, do you?"

"You do realize that it's probably going to take a *lot* of therapy before I feel comfortable again, right?" Mel crawled on top of Regan, pinning her hands above her head, and lowered her face to within inches of her lover's. "You may have just screwed me up forever, you know."

Tears streamed down Regan's red-cheeked face. Her mouth hung open, gasping uncontrolled laughter. Mel transferred Regan's left hand to her right, holding both slim wrists down so she could continue to tickle the squirming, shrieking woman with her free hand.

"I'm sorry, baby!" Regan yelped. "I didn't mean it! I'll do anything to make it up to you."

Mel could barely understand the words through the hysterical giggles.

"Let me go! I'll be nice, I swear!"

Mel kept up the casual tickling, holding the writhing body beneath her with negligent ease. "I don't know," she said with a yawn. "It just doesn't sound sincere to me."

"No fair!" Regan howled. "You're too strong!" She bucked beneath Mel in an attempt to wriggle free.

Mel chuckled and relented, allowing Regan to tear her wrists out of her grasp and wrap her arms around her middle in a fierce bear hug. "You're telling me you're just a helpless, delicate little flower?" Mel guffawed out loud when Regan attempted to forcibly roll them over.

Mel allowed the little powerhouse to reverse their positions and straddle her thighs with a triumphant growl. Regan grabbed Mel's wrists and slammed them to the ground above her head.

After a moment of holding Mel down, her smug grin faded. "Are you letting me win?"

Mel gave her an indulgent smile.

With a crestfallen expression, she released Mel's wrists and sat back to fold her arms over her chest. "You were, weren't you?"

"No, honey." Mel dissolved into helpless chuckles. "That little maneuver was a product of your sheer indomitable will. I swear it."

Regan arched an eyebrow in warning. "You're making fun of me?"

"No." Mel's laughter intensified, and she felt weak and desperate to stop the delicious torment of Regan's weight across her hips and the helpless convulsing of her body. "No, no, no. Never." She brought a limp hand down from above her head to wipe away the tears that had leaked from her eyes. "I'm just the goofy one, remember? Don't mind me."

Regan's lips quirked into a reluctant grin, and she lowered her upper body on hands planted beside Mel's head, coming to a stop only inches away from her face. "You know I was lying, right?"

Mel swallowed and looked up into sparkling green eyes. "Lying?"

"The last word I'd describe how you look when you come, baby, is goofy. You make me wet, you look so beautiful."

Mel's hands came to rest on Regan's hips as she listened to the softly spoken words, and she shivered at the feeling of warm breath caressing her ear. "Kiss me," she whispered into the mouth that was already descending upon her own.

Squeezing soft hips, pulling Regan into her again and again, Mel lost herself in the tenderness of their embrace until Regan broke the kiss with a regretful sigh. She sat back up to straddle Mel's hips.

Mel grinned up at Regan and ran her hands down her upper thighs. "God," she breathed. "I guess I'm glad I let you win."

Regan gave her a playful glare. "I'm going to let that one go. But only because I'm too exhausted to manhandle you anymore."

Mel leered and waggled her eyebrows. "That doesn't sound good. We don't want that to happen."

"I won't let it go for long."

"Good."

"That's what you think," Regan said, then leaned over to wrap Mel in a tight hug. "I have so much fun with you."

"Me, too," Mel said, beaming.

"I love this T-shirt, by the way." Regan drew a line down the center of Mel's chest with one finger, over the green cotton of Mel's souvenir from Denver.

"Thanks." Mel grinned, looking down at her chest. "So do I."

A hand-drawn caricature of a girl with medium-length hair and a pair of black-framed glasses was printed in the center of the shirt. When she had first seen it, the drawing had so reminded her of Regan she knew she had to buy it. The slogan printed at the top had sealed the deal.

"'Nerdy Girls Make Me Hot,'" Mel read, then looked up into Regan's laughing eyes. "It's true, you know."

"It better be," Regan said. "I'm just glad that my e-mail addiction led us to that Internet café."

"Me, too," Mel said. She'd not only gotten the T-shirt, but also a lot of good ideas for tattoos. The Internet really was a wonderful thing.

"We should get going soon, shouldn't we?"

Mel glanced past Regan to the late afternoon sun. "Probably," she admitted. Still thinking about tattoos, she asked, "What's the plan for the next couple days?"

Regan twisted her lips into a bittersweet smile. "I figure we've got about two days of driving left. We can stretch it out for three if we'd like." She reached up and played with Mel's collar. "We'll probably hit Des Moines tomorrow. Chicago not too long after that."

A little distraught about the idea that their road trip would soon end, Mel seized upon an idea to stretch it out. "Your parents live in Chicago, right?"

Regan rolled off Mel's hips with a sigh. Mel frowned and propped herself up on her elbows.

"Yes. Just outside of Chicago."

"Do you want to stop and see them? We have time, I mean—" Mel trailed off at Regan's wary gaze, and took a breath before she lost the nerve to conclude her thought. "And I'll bet you haven't seen them in a while, right? They'd probably really enjoy it."

Regan exhaled tiredly, and Mel frowned at her obvious hesitation.

"They're not as horrible as I make them out to be, honestly," Regan said. "I just feel so awkward around them sometimes. Like a whole part of who I am becomes invisible, you know?"

"I know. But they're still your parents. And they would be thrilled to see you, wouldn't they?"

"Probably," Regan admitted. "Goddamn it." She picked at the blanket with absent fingers for a moment before looking up at Mel with thoughtful eyes. "You know, I've never brought anyone home before."

"They never met Sarah?" Mel asked. All of a sudden, she wondered what she'd gotten herself into.

"They met her when they came to see me up at school. They thought we were just friends at the time and we broke up shortly after I came out to them. So you'll be the first." Regan gave Mel a brief, knowing look. "You think you're up for that?"

Well, it had to happen at some point. "No time like the present." Mel forced confidence she didn't quite feel into her voice. "How did they react when you came out?"

Regan shrugged. "It actually wasn't that big a deal. My mom cried a little bit, but I think part of it was knowing that I trusted her enough to tell her." She cast shamed eyes to the blanket. "We never talked much."

"How about your dad?"

"He didn't say much at all. I think he was uncomfortable. Overall, I think they both chalked it up to just one more thing they didn't understand — or want to understand, really — about me."

"But they're cool?" Mel asked.

Regan shrugged again. "We've never really talked about it since I came out to them. We dance around it. They never ask me about my love life."

"So how do you think they'll react to your bringing home a girlfriend?"

"I'm not sure," Regan admitted with a small grin. "But now I'm a bit curious."

"That whole confounding your parents thing?" Mel asked.

Regan shook her head, giving Mel a shy smile. "A little," she said. "But it's mostly that you're pretty important to me and if I plan on keeping you around, I should probably introduce you to the family. Tradition and all."

"I really hope they like me."

Regan gave her a half-smile, leaning forward to press a soft kiss to Mel's cheek. "They will," she murmured. "You're perfect."

Mel rolled skeptical eyes and opened her mouth to protest, then snapped it shut when Regan reached over to grip her chin with a gentle hand.

"Perfect for me," Regan said. A beat, long enough for the words to suffuse Mel with a warm glow, and Regan added, "Am I right?"

Mel gazed into green eyes, utterly at peace with the question and only mildly surprised with her certainty at the answer. *I'll never feel totally worthy of the love I feel from her and I'll never understand how I got so lucky as to find her, but I know...I belong to her. I belong with her. Nothing is more right in this world than the two of us together.*

"You're right." Mel lifted a hand to trace Regan's jaw with the barest of pressure. "And you're perfect for me, too."

Blushing, Regan shot her a goofy grin. "We're a couple of sappy, lovesick fools, aren't we?"

Mel chuckled, then reached forward to slide her hands around Regan's waist, pushing underneath her T-shirt. She moved her hands to caress Regan's stomach before sliding them up to palm full breasts through her cotton bra.

"These are perfect, too," Mel said.

Regan snorted and shot an amused smirk at Mel, who stared at the breasts she cupped in her hands with happy eyes. "There's the pervert I know and love."

Mel tore her gaze away from Regan's chest to stare up into green eyes. "I can't help it if your breasts turn me into a drooling, horny fifteen-year-old boy." She lowered her eyes again as she rubbed reverent thumbs over cloth-covered nipples.

"I was under the impression that you've *always* been a drooling, horny fifteen-year-old boy," she murmured.

"Not like this," Mel said, and squeezed Regan's breasts gently. "I swear. They're addictive. Like crack."

Regan tipped back her head and produced a laugh that sent shivers of pleasure to the tips of Mel's toes. Hearing Regan's joy was her new favorite thing in the world.

When Regan stopped laughing, she wiped her eyes and shook her head. "Baby, we really should think about getting going if we want to make it to Des Moines relatively soon."

Mel scowled and dropped her hands from Regan's breasts with a frown. "All right."

"Don't look so sad. I let you play with them all the time."

Mel nodded and moved as if to stand, but stopped before she pushed off with her hands, giving her lover a careful look. "Hey, Regan?"

"Yeah?"

"May I suggest something to do in Des Moines?" Mel asked.

Regan looked surprised. "There's something specific you want to do in Des Moines?"

"Actually, yeah," Mel said. "Um, when we were in that Internet café?"

"Yeah?"

"I was kind of looking up some stuff. Well, you know how I said I wanted to get a tattoo?"

"Yes," Regan said. Smiling, she gestured at the air around them. "To remember all of this."

"Yeah, so I read some reviews for tattoo shops in and around

Des Moines and I've got the name of a place that's supposed to be really nice."

"You want to get a tattoo tomorrow?" Regan asked. She looked intrigued.

"I do," Mel said. "I've been thinking a lot about this." For whatever reason, she had decided that this was important to do.

"Do you know what you want to get? And where?"

Pointing at the truck, Mel asked, "Can I get my drawing pad out of...It'll just take a minute or two..."

Regan nodded and shooed Mel away with an eager hand. "Yes! Go, definitely. You drew something?"

Mel was on her feet and jogging to the truck by the time Regan got the question out there, and she called back over her shoulder, "I found a bunch of websites on symbols and Celtic imagery online. I sketched a couple of ideas out."

"That's awesome, Mel," Regan said. "I can't wait to see them."

She found her drawing pad in the truck and rejoined Regan on the blanket. Sitting cross-legged, she settled the drawing pad on her lap and tried to ignore a familiar twinge of anxiety at the thought of sharing her work.

"This is so great," Regan gushed. "You're such a good artist, Mel, I think it's a wonderful idea to design your own tattoo."

The heartfelt words bolstered her confidence, and she gave Regan a pleased smile. "Thanks. I told myself I'd never get a tattoo unless it would really mean something to me. And it's incredibly meaningful to me to draw it because you've given me back my art."

Regan's eyes shone with emotion. "Given you back—"

Mel ducked her head and flipped open her drawing pad to the page where she had sketched out some designs just the night before. "What do you think about this one?"

Regan accepted the interruption, and leaned over to examine her drawings; all but one on this page were light, incomplete, but in the lower left hand corner she had drawn a dark, bold design. Mel glanced up and watched Regan's eyes find the final product.

"What is it?" Regan asked.

"It's called the Druid Spiral of Life," Mel said. It was an almost triangular design with three distinct spirals, all meeting in the center, drawn with one line without a beginning or end. "It's supposed to represent life, death, and rebirth." Mel pointed at the Celtic knotwork she had drawn branching from either side of the symbol. "I added that because I thought it might look better if it were a bit longer."

Regan hummed in approval. "It's beautiful, baby, perfect. Appropriate." She bumped Mel's shoulder with her own, giving her a light smile. "Look better, where? Where do you want to get it?"

"At first I was thinking one of two places," Mel said. "My upper arm or lower back. When I added the knotwork, it was because I'm leaning towards doing the lower back and I thought that would look nice. I've always wanted one there."

Regan uttered a low, throaty groan, shifting where she sat. "Lower back," she said in a voice hoarse with familiar arousal. "That sounds so painful, but I can't think of anything sexier."

On the basis of that moan alone, Mel decided that she was willing to take a little pain for the greater good. "So you approve?"

Regan shot her a lecherous grin. "I'll enjoy looking at it whenever I'm behind you. Among other things."

Mel poked Regan in the ribs lightly and returned her grin. Then, sucking in a breath, she said, "I have a few more drawings."

"Yeah? Let me see."

She flipped to the next page, and nodded in approval when Regan reached to take the pad onto her lap.

"Oh, my God, Mel." Regan moved her eyes up and down the page, taking in various half-sketches and outlines, and then the finished design at the center of the page. "Oh, this is so cool!"

Mel beamed over at Regan, studying the freckles on the bridge of her lover's nose. "It's for you."

After a brief, startled look, Regan dropped her eyes back down to the page. The culmination of Mel's work, the final drawing, was a relatively simple labrys, light on detail, but drawn with bold and powerful lines. She tried to gauge Regan's reaction to the sight of the double-headed axe.

"For me?" Regan looked up at Mel for a moment, then down at the page again. "I don't—"

Mel winced, rushing to cut off Regan's speech. "I'm not trying to...I mean, you sounded like you might be interested in a tattoo and I saw some labrys designs online and thought of you. But you don't have to use it. You don't even have to get a tattoo, if you don't want one, it's just that you said before—"

Regan stopped Mel's rambling speech with soft fingers pressed against her lips. "Baby, I am interested in getting a tattoo. Scared, yes, but definitely interested. And this..." she looked back down at the labrys, shaking her head as an awed smile tugged at her mouth. "I've fantasized before about getting a labrys tattoo, actually. I couldn't believe it when I saw your drawing. And I would be honored. This is amazing, baby, but I don't know—Don't you think it's a little *strong* for someone like me?"

"Strong?" Mel reached out and traced her fingers over Regan's hot cheek. "That's why it made me think of you, baby. You're my strong, independent, beautiful woman and I think it fits."

"I don't always feel strong."

"Then let it be a reminder," Mel whispered. She leaned forward and gave Regan a gentle kiss, then murmured against soft lips, "Like mine will be."

Regan smiled against Mel's mouth, and Mel smiled back. "Thank you," Regan said. "This is a wonderful gift."

Determined to accept her gratitude with some measure of tact, Mel said, "You're welcome." She reached up to tug on her eyebrow. "So where do you think you'll get it?"

"I thought you said Des Moines."

Mel nudged her until she was off-balance and had to plant a hand on the ground to stop from toppling over. "Where on your body, goofy girl?"

"Ah," Regan said. "Nothing that seems overly painful. I was thinking of my upper arm. The right one."

Mel reached over and placed her palm on a spot near Regan's bicep. "Right here?"

"Yeah. What do you think?"

"It'll be beautiful." Sighing, Mel cast regretful eyes over to the cooler. "We should go, right?"

"Right." Regan stood up, brushing off the seat of her jeans, and offered Mel a hand. "As much as I don't want to."

Mel let Regan help haul her to her feet. "I know."

With some horror, she wondered if she had just missed the perfect moment for the ring she was carrying around in her bag, then decided she couldn't think like that. There was no way there would only be one right moment with Regan. If she could work up the nerve, any moment would be the right moment.

Hell, she's choosing to wear my art forever. Why wouldn't she wear my ring?

Chapter
Eighteen

"REGAN!"

REGAN CRINGED a little at the excitement in her father's voice. Clearly she needed to call home more often.

"It's good to hear from you, sweet pea. What's going on?" he asked.

"I'm okay," she said, grinning slightly at the childhood nickname. "I'm sorry I haven't called in a little while. I've been really busy."

"Yeah? How's the job?"

Regan suppressed a tired sigh. The job, of course. Why would anything else be keeping her busy? With her father, it had always been about school and work. She felt Mel's hand land on her knee, and the contact soothed her frustration. Gazing across the steering wheel to the front door of a Chinese buffet, she said, "It's okay. It's a job."

They were parked in downtown Des Moines, en route to her parents' house.

"So, how's the assistant principal business?" she forged on with the requisite small talk. "Kids eating you alive yet?"

Brendan O'Riley groaned. "You wouldn't believe the group of kids we've got right now. I swear each year brings more discipline problems than the last."

Oh, I'd believe it. I'm no stranger to that particularly evil breed of animal called the high school student. "Well, I don't envy you. The best thing I ever did was leave high school behind." But they'd never talked about that, and she wasn't about to start now. "Actually Dad, I'm calling you for a reason."

"What's that, pumpkin?"

Regan glanced at Mel, smiling at the warm support she saw in her eyes. "I'm actually in Des Moines, Iowa right now, on my way back to Michigan."

"Are you on a business trip?" Her father sounded rather

confused by the idea that she would be anywhere other than where he would have expected her to be.

"No. More like a vacation, really."

She heard her father sigh and stiffened her shoulders, bracing herself for some kind of overbearing comment. He didn't disappoint.

"I hope you let somebody know you were going on a vacation out-of-state before you left."

"I did," she said, unable to keep the irritation out of her voice. She felt Mel squeeze her fingers, and closed her eyes in an effort to regain her calm. *Easy. He just loves you, he's not trying to make a statement about your having a lack of common sense.* She softened her tone. "Adam knows. He's taking care of my mail and stuff while I'm gone."

"Good. I just get worried when I find out that you're running around the country and I had no idea you'd even left home." Her father paused a moment, then said, "Wait, Adam isn't with you? Are you all alone?"

Regan managed a nervous smile as the moment of truth arrived. "Actually, no, I'm not."

"Oh." A vague air of discomfort arose between them, as he seemed to sense what she was implying.

"We're going to be driving right by Chicago on our way home, so I wanted to call and see if I could stop by and visit, maybe overnight."

"That'd be wonderful, honey." There was genuine pleasure in his voice, enough that Regan couldn't help but smile at it. "It's been too long since you've come home."

"I know, I know. And for that I'm sorry." Squeezing Mel's hand for support, she added, "I have somebody with me I really want you and Mom to meet."

For a moment her father said nothing, and then, "This is a girlfriend?"

"Yes. Her name is Mel, and she's someone very special to me."

"I didn't realize you were seeing anyone." He cleared his throat, and continued in a gentle, but hesitant, tone. "That's great, sweetheart. I look forward to meeting someone who means that much to you. If you like her, she really must be something special."

Regan was left momentarily speechless at the genuine warmth in her father's voice. While she could also hear his slight discomfort, he was doing an admirable job of hiding it. "Thanks, Dad. She is."

"Your mother will be thrilled."

Regan couldn't help but snort a little at the idea of Carla O'Riley, every inch the restrained accountant, acting thrilled about anything. "Great. We'll probably get into town tomorrow afternoon."

"Sounds good. I'm sure we'll be around, but if we're not you remember where the spare key is kept, right?"

Regan bit back a laugh. "I remember." She fidgeted in her seat, ready to get off the phone. "Okay, so...I love you and I'll see you soon."

"Love you, too. Be careful and be good."

This time Regan did roll her eyes, looking up with a wide grin at the Chinese buffet in front of which she'd parked her truck. "I will," she promised.

She turned to smirk at Mel after they said their goodbyes. "That was fun."

"It sounded like it went okay."

"It did. He said he was looking forward to meeting you. That if I like you, you must be something special."

Mel's cheeks turned a lovely shade of red. "I appreciate that you warned him about me. I would have been really nervous surprising them, especially being the first one introduced and all."

"I wouldn't say I was *warning* him...more like preparing him." She gave Mel an understanding smile. "Honestly, he seemed a little uncomfortable at first, but then he just seemed *nice* or something. Like he was making an effort." She wrinkled her nose in thought. "I guess it actually went really well."

"Warning, preparing. Either way, thank you."

"I'd never make you a part of an ambush, honey. I would never do that to you. Especially after what happened to you with your father." There was no way she'd ever risk making Mel go through something like that again. The mere thought was painful. "I love you." She leaned over and gave Mel a peck on her cheek, then pulled back with a mischievous smile. "He also told me to 'be careful and be good'."

Mel snickered. "I promise to keep you safe, but I can't in good conscience encourage you to behave. Besides, it would be against your nature."

"And on that note," Regan said, and nodded toward the building a few doors along from the Chinese restaurant. Her nervousness over speaking to her father dissipated in favor of nervousness over where they were. "We're really going to do this, aren't we?"

Mel grinned at the tattoo shop. The building itself was nondescript, but the glass windows were tinted and covered with posters and a neon Open sign. "I am, at least." She gave Regan a serious look. "You shouldn't do it unless you're absolutely sure you want to do it. For real."

"You know, if you'd told me two weeks ago that I'd be sitting in Des Moines, about to get a tattoo, I'd have told you that you were cracked."

Regan could barely imagine walking into the shop, let alone the whole process of talking to the artist and sitting there while a permanent design was torturously needled into her skin. She felt silly about her fears. Mel had been bursting with excitement all morning, and Regan wondered why she couldn't produce the same nonchalance. This wasn't that big a deal, after all.

"I'll be right there next to you and I promise to hold your hand the entire time," Mel said with gentle empathy. "You can squeeze the life out of me if you want. I'll do whatever I can to make it the best possible experience for you."

Feeling her stomach unclench and relax at the soothing timbre of Mel's voice, she set her shoulders and steeled her nerve. "I'm ready. Let's do it."

"You sure?" Mel's eyes were serious, but her mouth quirked into an excited grin.

Regan grinned back. "Yeah. I've always wanted to do that whole young and impulsive thing, so I'm going to try and be brave."

Mel leaned forward and took Regan's mouth in a sudden kiss, running her tongue along the redhead's upper lip before slipping it inside. Regan moaned into the kiss, swept up in the spontaneity and passion of it, and felt fierce arousal mingle with her lingering fear. The heady feeling left her wet and weak.

Mel drew back to exchange a wicked grin with her, then said, "Let's do it."

The store was moderately crowded. Several young women stood together at the counter, poring over an album of artwork, and two men who looked like they were in their early thirties sat in plastic chairs that lined the wall. For a moment Regan stood stock still, flustered at the unfamiliar environment. But before she started to really panic, a strong hand pressed against the small of her back and Mel guided her to the end of the row of plastic seats, in a darker corner of the shop.

"Why don't you sit over here and look at some of the binders, baby?" Mel picked up an album full of photos and hand-drawn pictures that served as samples from the shop's artists and placed it in Regan's lap. "I'm going to go check things out and then I'll come back and sit with you."

Regan took the binder with a tight smile. "Okay."

Her confidence grew at Mel's too-wide grin, and the sight of her strolling to the front counter with an easy air of self-assurance. Absently, she flipped through the album, glancing at photographs of tattoos and hand-drawn ink sketches. Mel's work compared favorably with the best of the store's samples. Playing with that thought, Regan lifted her eyes to search for her lover.

Mel was standing next to the counter, talking to a tattooed woman dressed in a tank top and tight leather pants. The stranger was gorgeous, with short blonde hair and a wide, sexy grin that was fixed on Mel. While Regan watched, the woman tossed back her head and laughed at something Mel said, her eyes sparkling. Idly, Regan wondered if the blonde was more the type Mel would've normally gone after. She was aware of how irrational her train of thought was even as she hopped willingly aboard. *And why not? She looks sexy, a little wild, so fucking confident.*

At that moment, Mel gestured back towards where Regan sat and swung her head around to grace her with a look of pure devotion. The blonde also looked over and gave Regan an amiable wave and an open, easy smile. Regan nodded, blushing, and bent her head again to study the book in her lap.

Okay, so I'm an idiot sometimes.

She was just flipping through the last pages of the thick album when Mel dropped into the seat next to her. She reached over and brushed her knuckles across Regan's cheek in greeting. "How're you doing?"

"I missed you," Regan said.

Mel's eyes lit up. She leaned close and whispered, "I'll never know what I did to have a woman like you miss me. And I missed you, too." Retreating, she said, "I think you're going to like the artist I just spoke with. Her name is Sasha and she seems really nice."

"Cool," Regan said. "When will she have time?"

"Apparently it's our lucky day. Her next appointment called and cancelled. She can see us in about thirty minutes." Mel leaned over and murmured under her breath, "She's family."

Regan chuckled at Mel's sly observation. *I saw the way she was looking at you.* "I figured." *But then I also saw the way she looked at me.* "She's a lot less intimidating than I was expecting. I'm sure she'll be great. Did you show her your sketches?"

Mel looked down at her drawing pad, which she held on her lap. "Yeah. She really liked them, actually. Asked if I ever thought about apprenticing as a tattoo artist."

"Yeah?" Regan asked, snaking her arm around Mel's shoulders. "That's really cool."

Mel cast embarrassed eyes to the floor. "I don't think it was a flirting thing, either. I mean, maybe it was—"

Regan nudged Mel with her shoulder. "While I have no doubt that she couldn't help flirting with such a hot chick, what she said about your drawings was true."

"Thanks." Mel gave her a gooey look. "You're right, she was flirting. And she's cute, but I've only got eyes for this gorgeous redhead I know."

"Lucky her."

"I HAVE TO tell you, this is my lucky day." Sasha looked back and forth between them with a salacious grin. "It's not often that I get not one, but two, beautiful women in my chair. Why don't you two take a seat and we can talk about what to expect?"

Regan sat down on a stool next to a horrifying-looking chair that looked suspiciously like the one she'd sat in the last time she had a tooth filled.

Too bad I can't ask for nitrous here. Regan took in a room that was medically clean and stocked with a number of unfamiliar tools and instruments. It looked like a dentist's office, a comparison that did nothing to calm her down.

Flashing Regan a knowing grin, Mel said, "Good idea, sweetheart. You take that seat, and I'll sit in the scary chair while we talk."

No doubt about it, Mel knew her well. "Sounds good," Regan said.

"Got your sketchbook?" Sasha asked Mel, who handed it over with an embarrassed smile. Flipping to the drawing of the Druid Spiral of Life, she nodded at Mel. "So this one is for you. Lower back, you said?"

"Yeah," Mel confirmed.

Sasha turned the page, briefly studying the labrys, then lifting her smoky blue eyes to Regan. "And this one is for you." At Regan's nod, she glanced toward Mel and said, "This really is a beautiful drawing. Subtle, but very elegant. I'm telling you, from what I've seen here, you could do this professionally."

Mel's eyes were locked on the floor, so Regan took it upon herself to give Sasha a confident nod. "She's an amazing artist. Too modest, though."

"Your work will do justice to my gorgeous subjects, that's for sure." Sasha winked at both of them, eliciting a hot blush from Regan and a quiet snort from Mel.

"So do you need to see our IDs or something?" Mel asked.

Sasha accepted the driver's licenses and debit cards that Mel and Regan offered. "I'll be right back," she said, then retreated into the hallway and closed the door behind her.

When they were alone, Regan turned to regard Mel anxiously. "I'm going to throw up." She was only half-joking.

Mel wrinkled her nose. "Not really, right?"

Regan rolled her eyes in response.

"How are you doing otherwise?" Mel asked. "Is Sasha okay? She's not making you uncomfortable or anything, is she?" She looked slightly shamefaced. "The flirting."

"No. Flirting is fine." Allowing a small grin, Regan added, "So is Sasha. Mighty fine."

They shared a conspiratorial smile, then Mel asked, "So, you're still nervous?"

"Terribly."

"Would you feel better after a kiss?"

The corner of Regan's mouth lifted into a reluctant grin. "Maybe."

"Maybe?" Mel narrowed the distance between their faces, until their breath mingled in the almost non-existent space separating their lips. "Should I check and see?"

Regan's eyes slid shut at the feeling of Mel's lips just barely brushing her own. She felt consumed by the scent of Mel that surrounded her, and the heat of Mel's body leaning into hers. Leaning forward, she pressed her lips to Mel's and slid her tongue inside her mouth, moaning as Mel met her stroke for stroke.

I'm less nervous already.

Regan reached up to entwine her hand in thick dark hair just as the door to the room opened again. She broke their kiss with an embarrassed little gasp.

Sasha chuckled. "It's okay. Last-minute pep talk, right? Happens all the time." Sasha returned their driver's licenses and cards.

"Have we decided who's going to go first?" She directed a gentle smile at Regan. "I take it you're the nervous one. Do you want to go first and get it over with, or watch Mel so you can see what to expect?"

Regan darted her eyes over to Mel. *If I have to sit here and watch her go under the needle, I'll probably never go through with it.* "I'll go first," she answered in as brave a voice as she could manage.

Mel rose from the dental chair with an admiring little grin, and wrapped her in a strong hug. "Feel free to break my hand if you need to," she whispered into Regan's ear. "It's going to be okay. I love you."

"Hey, I need that hand in good working order," Regan murmured. "Thanks for the offer, though." She settled down into the scary chair, and put on a brave face as Mel dragged a plastic chair over so she could sit close. A steady hand claimed hers, and Regan covered their enjoined fingers with the palm of her free hand.

She barely paid attention when Sasha began explaining the safety and sanitary procedures the shop employed, outlining the precautions as she assembled equipment. She tried hard not to think about what was coming as Sasha pushed up her sleeve and prepared her arm for its impending ink. Regan concentrated only on the hand in her own and on the strength she drew from Mel's touch.

She wasn't certain how long she'd been sitting in the chair when Sasha reappeared at her side with Mel's labrys design in her hand, ready to transfer the image to her skin. "Here?" she asked, and positioned the paper over Regan's right upper arm.

"Yeah," Regan croaked. "Right there."

Sasha gave her an enthusiastic smile. "This is gonna be really cool," she said, and pressed the transfer to pale skin.

Mel peered over at Regan's arm, nodding her approval at the placement of the design. "It's going to be sexy as hell," she drawled.

"Definitely," Sasha agreed with an easy smile. "I wouldn't let this one out of your sight when I'm done with her. Cute girl like this, bad-ass tattoo—" As she spoke, she applied ointment over the transfer.

"Oh, I don't plan on it." Mel's serious tone belied the light mood, drawing Regan's eyes to her face.

Regan's warm feelings faded a bit when she realized that Sasha had picked up a wicked-looking little tool, which she wielded with a confident hand.

"Now, Regan, I'm going to make a little dot on your arm with the needle before I put any ink on you, just so you can see what it'll feel like." Sasha laid a comforting hand on Regan's arm. "Now is the time to jump, if you need to."

Well, thank God my initial reaction to that needle isn't going to leave a permanent badge of shame on my skin if I end up chickening out. Regan gave her a resolute nod. "Okay. Thank you." She took Mel's hand in a tight grip.

Sasha turned on the needle, and a foreboding, high-pitched whining noise filled the air. It immediately set Regan's teeth on edge. "Here it comes, okay?"

Regan squeezed her eyes tightly shut and willed her body to relax as she anticipated the first touch of the needle to her skin.

When it finally came, she flinched more out of reflex than because of the sensation. After a moment the painful pressure left and she released a shaky breath she hadn't realized she was holding.

"How was that?" Sasha asked. "Not too bad, right?"

Regan managed a weak smile that grew when Mel planted a loving kiss on her cheek. "I was right," she said. "It *does* hurt. But if I can deal with menstrual cramps every month, then I should be able to get through this."

Mel grinned, showing Regan white teeth. "Who's the tough guy now?"

"Yeah, well, we'll see how tough I look when I start whimpering halfway through this."

"And such a cute whimper, too." Mel gave her a rakish wink, sending Regan into a fierce blush.

"If you're done teasing your poor woman, I'll just get started," Sasha said. She wore a ridiculously big grin.

"Ready, baby?" Mel pressed a kiss to Regan's earlobe. "Remember, you can still back out now. No big deal."

The easy out injected Regan with sudden confidence. There was no way she was backing out now. Not when she'd come this far. "I'm ready."

"Cool." Sasha turned on the needle. "The outlining is going to be the worst of it; the shading won't be nearly as bad." Moving closer, she gave Regan a quick glance before she touched the needle to skin. "Here I come, okay?"

And then it was on her arm, a scraping, scratching pain that made Regan grit her teeth in irritation. Astounded that she hadn't flinched, Regan prayed that she would be able to sit still for as long as the tattoo would take. If only she knew how long that might be. *Are we there yet?*

Mel leaned in close to Regan's ear, talking low enough that she wouldn't be heard over the whining of the needle. "You're doing great, baby. Seriously. I'm prepared to tell everyone what a bad-ass you are."

"That'll make it all worthwhile." Regan could hear the tension radiating from her own strained voice.

"Would it make it worthwhile if I told you how turned on this is all making me?" Mel murmured. She traced the tip of her tongue along Regan's earlobe. "I promise to ease all your pain once we get out of here."

Regan closed her eyes at that happy thought. *Good idea. That's just what I need to distract me right now...a hot fantasy about Mel.* With that, she set to work conjuring up pleasant images to take her away from the needle moving across her arm.

Okay, so I've got Mel...and a pair of fur-lined handcuffs and a blindfold. She frowned in concentration. *Am I restraining her or is she restraining me?*

Mel whispered close to Regan's ear. "What are you thinking about? I can just see evil thoughts flitting through your mind right now."

Regan smiled. *She's restraining me. And she's wearing leather.* "Just puzzling out a string function in my head."

"Uh-huh."

Fantasizing worked wonders for Regan's pain tolerance. Thoughts of Mel sustained her until her endorphins kicked in and the pain receded to a dull, irritating sensation. Sasha moved from outlining to shading, keeping up a light conversation with Mel as Regan sat in silent musing.

It took Regan a moment to realize that she was done when the whining noise ceased and the scraping sensation left her arm. With a smile and a shaky sigh of relief, she opened her eyes. Mel was giving her a proud grin, while Sasha raised an indulgent eyebrow.

"Was that it?" Regan squeaked.

Sasha snorted in amusement. "That's it. Are you telling me that I have a gentle touch?"

"No." Regan wrinkled her nose at the tattoo artist. "But my heart's still beating, so I'm pretty pleased with you at the moment."

Sasha tipped her head back in a full, genuine laugh. Throatily, she said, "Oh, Mel. She's definitely a keeper."

"I know." Mel wrapped a careful arm around Regan's shoulders.

The way she beamed with pride made Regan's heartbeat stutter, and she craned her neck to inspect her new tattoo. The bold black ink looked impressive against her pale skin, despite the reddened, swollen area that surrounded the design.

"I love it," she breathed and looked up at Sasha. "It's beautiful. Thank you, I love it."

"I think that looks awesome," Mel said, releasing a low whistle.

"Another satisfied customer. I'm really happy to hear it." Stripping off her gloves, Sasha stood up and gathered the supplies she had used for Regan's tattoo. "Let me get a bandage on Regan's arm here, take care of this stuff and get some new equipment together, and then I'll be ready for you, Mel." She stood, already in motion on her way through what was obviously a familiar routine. "I'll go through the after-care instructions once you're both done, okay?"

"Okay." Regan couldn't take her eyes off her inked upper arm. Amazed, she whispered, "I really did it. I can't believe it."

"Not regretting it already, are you?" Mel teased in a gentle voice.

"God, no." Regan looked up at Mel, feeling giddy with pleasure. "This is really cool. Thank you."

"You're welcome. It means so much to me to share this with you," Mel whispered, and leaned forward to claim Regan's lips in a quick, hard kiss. "This is something I'll always remember."

Regan looked down at the tattoo with a smirk. "And really, how could you forget?"

Sasha moved to Regan and started a careful wrapping of her upper arm in cellophane and tape. At Regan's interested look, she said, "This way you can show people without taking the bandage off before your twenty-four hours are up."

Great, I can show it to Mom and Dad tomorrow. She caught Mel's eyes and gave her a broad smile. *Of course, meeting my girlfriend and seeing my tattoo in the same night might just kill them.*

"You're all set," Sasha said when she finished securing the protective wrapping over Regan's arm. "Now you can sit back and relax while I do Mel."

Regan coughed at Sasha's word choice, earning her a playful smirk from Mel as they swapped chairs.

"How are we going to do this?" Mel asked. "Should I take off my shirt?"

Regan watched Sasha's lips twitch with evil intent. *Now there's an opening you could drive a truck through.* Instead of taking advantage of it, Sasha gave Regan a contrite smile. "If you're more comfortable that way," she said in a neutral voice. "We can always just push the shirt up if necessary."

Mel hesitated a moment then tugged her T-shirt over her head, leaving her in just a sports bra. Smiling, Regan allowed her gaze to linger on the play of muscles under her lover's skin.

"I'll warn you now, the lower back is probably one of the most painful areas to have tattooed," Sasha said. "I have one myself and while it's not too bad, I just want you to be prepared."

"That's okay," Regan said. "Mel's a self-proclaimed tough guy."

Mel rolled her eyes and settled onto the dental chair on her stomach. "At the very least, I'm sure I'll be okay as long as I have Regan to hold my hand." She shot Regan a crooked grin that made her stomach flip-flop.

"God, you two are sickeningly cute." Sasha shook her head. "I'm going to need an insulin injection after you leave."

Regan laughed along with Mel, her initial discomfort about being in the tattoo shop all but vanished. *Conquering one fear makes the others seem more trivial, doesn't it?*

Soon enough Sasha had Mel's transfer prepared and positioned over Mel's lower back. "Right here, you think?"

Regan stood up and leaned over, studying Sasha's placement. "Yeah," she said, and looked down at the side of Mel's face. "You trust my judgment, baby?"

"Better than my own, sometimes," Mel mumbled. She rested her head on one arm, the other stretched out alongside her body.

Regan sank down to sit in the plastic chair and took Mel's free hand in both of hers as Sasha applied the needle without the ink.

"Okay?" the tattoo artist checked.

Mel gave a cocky grin. "No problem." Raising an eyebrow at Regan, she whispered, "Because I know how you love a tough guy."

Regan leaned in and lowered her voice. "I love you, tough or not. Even if you were the biggest chicken in the world."

"If you're ready, Mel, I'll get started." Sasha sat with the needle raised in a confident hand and a kind smile that she directed at Regan.

"I'm ready," Mel said. When the needle was brought back down onto her skin, she grimaced. "God, that's unpleasant."

"Well, you're putting on a braver face than I did," Regan said. "I'm impressed."

"I'm screaming inside, trust me."

Sasha snickered, but never moved her eyes from her work. Her focus soon drew Regan's attention to the emerging design on Mel's body and once she got over the sight of the needle and ink piercing Mel's skin, she was fascinated. The artwork made Mel's strong, supple back look even more sleek and powerful, and the slow ritual of applying it began to seem erotic rather than painful. At one point Regan became aware that she was licking her lips as she watched Sasha's hand work over Mel's skin, and she gave Sasha a bashful chuckle when the blonde artist cast her a knowing smirk over Mel's head.

When Sasha was finally done with the tattoo, Mel's only visible reaction to the hour or so of intense sensation was a light sheen of sweat on her forehead and the dilation of her pupils.

Regan leaned over and examined the tattoo while Sasha prepared a bandage. "Gorgeous," she proclaimed. Her clit jumped at the eroticism of the design and the way it complemented the strong lines of Mel's body.

"Yeah?" Mel's voice rang with almost child-like excitement.

She stood and stretched, then walked over to a full-length mirror mounted on the wall, peering over her own shoulder at her lower back. Her grin grew impossibly wide as she took in the artwork. "Oh, I love it."

Sasha just grinned. "I live to serve."

Regan smirked, feeling a surge of delicious confidence after the afternoon's activities. "You should be careful about making a comment like that. Between Mel and me, we never seem to miss an easy opening."

Mel turned and opened her mouth to respond, mischief dancing in her eyes, but was cut off by Regan's groan.

"Forget I said that," Regan said. To Sasha, she added, "See what I mean?"

"Pure evil." Sasha beckoned Mel over with one hand. "Come here so I can get something over that ink, okay?"

"Yes, ma'am."

They walked out of the tattoo shop fifteen minutes later. Regan carried detailed after-care instructions in one hand; the other firmly clasped Mel's. She wore a beaming grin that she directed up into the early evening sky as they walked to her truck.

I feel different. Her arm was a little numb, but her mind was sharp and alive with feeling. *I feel...changed.*

Approaching the truck, Mel flipped her the keys with an apologetic smile. "Think you can drive? I'm not sure I'll be able to sit up normally. My back is a little tender."

"Oh, I get it," Regan said. "Woman of steel in front of the hot blonde, but the façade dissolves when we're alone."

Mel shot her a playful glare. "Well, that's because you're the only one I trust enough to show my vulnerable side." Then she gave Regan an imploring look, blinking innocent eyes, and settled into full pathetic mode. After a moment, she poked her lower lip out in a pout.

Regan laughed and closed the distance between them in two steps, wrapping Mel in a gentle hug. "Well, shit. Make me feel bad for teasing you, why don't you?"

"That was my intention." She gave Regan a soft kiss on the cheek. "Now let's go find a bed somewhere. I'm in need of some serious after-care."

Chapter
Nineteen

MEL LEANED FORWARD in her seat, peering into the driver's side visor mirror. "How does my face look? Really?"

"Gorgeous," Regan said. "As always."

Mel rolled her eyes, touching her cheek where a barely visible scratch had nearly healed, and then the cut above her lip that she had spent the morning trying to conceal. "I mean the scuff marks." She tilted her head, running a careful hand where makeup covered a faded bruise. "I don't want your parents to think you're bringing home a complete thug. It's bad enough that I'm their introduction to the big, bad world of lesbian dating. The least I can do is look presentable."

Regan studied Mel's face. Anxiety was rolling off her lover in waves. "You can't tell there's anything wrong anymore, I promise. It was already so faded and the makeup took care of the rest." She gave Mel a gentle smile. "They're going to love you."

Mel dropped her shoulders, sighing, and sat back against the driver's seat. "I'm a little nervous," she admitted in a quiet voice.

"I know," Regan said. *We've been parked a block away from Mom and Dad's house for almost twenty minutes now.* "It's going to be fine, okay? I swear it. They have no issues with me being a lesbian. They may be slightly uncomfortable seeing me as a sexual being for the first time, but I promise they won't be rude to you. They're nothing if not unfailingly polite."

Mel fixed a naked, open gaze on Regan. "It's just that I know I'm not what your parents probably would have wanted for you. Let's see, in the time you've known me, you've ridden on a motorcycle for the first time, smoked pot, gone skinny-dipping, been in the middle of a bar fight, and gotten your first tattoo." She lifted her face, shooting Regan a dry smile. "Oh, yeah. Your parents will be thrilled with me."

Regan couldn't stop her grin of amusement. *She's just described some of the best times of my life.* Sobering, she gave Mel a soft kiss on the lips. "I don't think my parents have a lot of expectations when it comes to a partner for me. If anything, I think they would just want someone who makes me happy. You do that and I'm proud to have you to take home with me."

Mel shook her head, chuckling. "God, I'm sorry. I just never imagined myself in this scenario, you know? I really want them to like me."

"They'll love you because you're just plain lovable." Regan raised a meaningful eyebrow at Mel. "It worked on me, after all."

This coaxed a reluctant smile from Mel. "I'll take your word for it." She took another quick look in the mirror and exhaled. "All right. I'm ready."

"I promise, if they so much as look at you funny, we're out of there." Regan looked Mel in the eye, willing her to see the truth of her words. "I mean it."

"You'd actually storm out of your parents' house for me?"

"I'd do anything for you."

Mel's shy smile was full of innocence and a kind of amazed wonderment. "Thank you." She shifted into drive. "So, where do I go?"

THE STREET WHERE Regan had grown up looked exactly the same as it had when she was a child and a teenager. Nice, mostly bi-level homes, landscaped lawns, and solid oak trees lined the block. She stared out the truck's front window, feeling a bittersweet melancholy sweep over her at the familiar sights.

It didn't matter that she had more happy memories away from Downer's Grove than she did from when she lived here; a part of Regan would always feel a slight yearning for this idea of home. Today she also felt vaguely nervous, now that she didn't have Mel's anxiety to distract her from her own. She was a different person now than she had been the last time she visited. *I wonder if Mom and Dad will see it?*

"You can pull up behind my dad's car," Regan said when they reached her parents' driveway.

Mel took in the brown brick Colonial-style house with interested eyes as she parked. "So this is where little Regan O'Riley grew up," she said in a soft voice, a hint of a smile tugging at her lips.

"If you're lucky, I'll show you where little Regan O'Riley did all kinds of things," Regan said.

Despite her trepidation, Regan found herself strangely excited about the prospect of introducing Mel to her parents. Finally, she could show them a little bit of what was going on in her life. And it was something that made her prouder than any good grade or solid web application ever had.

She met Mel in front of the truck, giving her lover's slightly clammy hand a firm squeeze. "Just focus on all the hugs and kisses and love you're going to get when this is all over."

Mel exhaled. "Hugs and kisses and love."

The same thought helped steel Regan's nerve.

She unlocked the front door with the spare house key that still hung on her keychain, and tugged Mel inside by the hand. Closing the door behind them, she took a deep breath and called out, "Hello? Mom? Dad?"

"Regan!"

Her father's voice answered from a distant room, bringing an immediate smile to Regan's face. *The den, of course. My parents always spent as much time in the den as I did alone in my bedroom.* "Ready?" Regan whispered, turning to Mel.

Mel nodded and took a step backwards, releasing Regan's hand to fuss with her hair. She wiped her palms on her blue jeans, and curled her hands into loose fists at her sides. Regan flexed her own fingers, feeling Mel's absence.

"Ten bucks says this'll be more fun than visiting my father," Mel said. Her lips twitched, and the dry humor helped ease the slight tension in the air.

With a crooked smile, Regan led them to the den. Brendan O'Riley was just rising from his favorite chair when they stepped inside, and her mother was already on her feet and casting an expectant gaze at the door. She watched her parents closely for their initial reaction to the sight of Mel. Even though they'd known she was coming, there was a brief moment of silent surprise before they settled into what looked like subtle discomfort. Mel's hand brushed against Regan's hip, discreet and calming.

Carla O'Riley stood awkwardly and gave Regan a cautious smile. "Regan, it's so nice to see you." She started to move forward and then stopped, as if hesitant to initiate contact.

At Mel's nudge, Regan stepped forward to embrace her mother. "Nice seeing you, too, Mom."

Her mother's hug was tentative and a little reserved, as most gestures of affection between them always seemed to be. Releasing her mom, Regan grinned up at her father and walked forward into his open arms.

"Sweet pea," he murmured, pulling her close against him and dropping a kiss on her hair. "I'm so glad you came."

She withdrew from the embrace after only a few moments, not wanting to let Mel languish in silent anonymity any longer than necessary. Taking Mel's hand, she said, "Mom. Dad. This is my girlfriend, Mel."

For a moment her parents seemed uncertain of how to respond, then her father extended his hand. "Hello, Mel. I'm Brendan O'Riley. It's very nice to meet you."

"It's very nice to meet you as well, sir." Mel shook hands with him then nodded politely at Regan's mother. "Mrs. O'Riley. You have a beautiful home."

"Please call me Carla." Her mother smiled and offered her hand to Mel. "And thank you. I can't tell you how pleased we are to meet you."

Regan took in the scene with a sense of amazement. While she hadn't doubted that her parents would be friendly to Mel, they were obviously making an effort be warm and gracious. Sure, they weren't doing a perfect job of hiding their mild discomfort, but they were really trying.

Regan felt disoriented. *This is still my mom and dad, right?* She glanced over to Mel, feeling the tension thrumming off her lover's body. It was well disguised by a pleasant, relaxed smile just like the smiles Regan's parents were wearing. No one seemed entirely sure where this should go next. Regan wasn't certain, either. *But I think it's time for everyone to decompress for a minute.*

"Listen," she said. "Mel and I are just going to put our bags downstairs in my room, and then we'll be right back up."

Her parents reacted with simultaneous smiles of relief, and she watched her mother glance at her father in much the same way Mel glanced over at her. Regan could see their desire to confer alone almost as much as she felt her need for that very thing with Mel.

"That sounds fine, honey," her dad said, giving them both a big smile.

"Have you girls had lunch yet?" her mother asked. "If not, we'd love to take you out somewhere."

"Antonio's?" Regan suggested with a sudden grin. Just the thought of lunch at her favorite restaurant ever made her stomach growl.

Her father rolled his eyes playfully. "Of course," he said in droll voice. "What a surprise."

"Well, I have to take advantage when I'm here, don't I?" Turning to Mel as her parents chuckled, Regan said, "It's the best place in the world. Trust me."

Mel grinned. "Antonio's it is."

"Come on. I'll show you my old room and we can get rid of these bags." Regan took Mel's arm in her hand. "We'll be right back."

She walked them out of the den towards the stairs to the lower level.

"Your bedroom was in the basement?" Mel asked as they descended the steps.

Regan grinned back over her shoulder. "I moved down here when I was fourteen. I was craving isolation at the time. Mom and Dad weren't so sure about it when I started begging, but I hadn't really given them any reasons to refuse heartfelt requests. I was the perfect kid, never in trouble. No harm in letting me occupy the space, you know?"

Mel took Regan's hand as they reached the bottom landing and followed as she led them to the door of one of two adjoining sections of the basement. "So this is where little Regan O'Riley hung out."

"Yeah. This is where I misspent my youth."

"Very cool." Mel gave her a quick kiss on the cheek. "I wouldn't have minded a little more privacy when I was a kid."

That's an understatement and a half. Regan opened her bedroom door and flipped on the light with a careless hand, unable to suppress a surge of emotion as she looked around at the one thing that hadn't changed a bit since she left for college.

Her full-sized bed sat in the corner of the room, against the wall, and it was still covered with the same cozy blue comforter she'd had since she was twelve years old. An overstuffed green bean bag lay in the other corner next to a bookcase that had once been packed full of books and that still contained a few errant volumes. Next to that was the sturdy wooden desk she had gotten as a Christmas present when she was sixteen years old. Her very first computer, an IBM with a 386 processor that looked like it belonged in a museum, still occupied the desktop. Assorted knick-knacks surrounded the machine. Various posters were plastered on the walls, the most notable a large one of Albert Einstein, which was flanked by slightly less conspicuous shots of different actresses and female athletes.

Mel stepped forward into the bedroom, and turned in a slow circle to survey everything in sight, chuckling in amusement at her blatant shrine to the female form.

"Subtle, I was not," Regan acknowledged.

"I can't imagine your parents didn't have *some* idea about you."

Regan closed the door behind them, grateful for a few minutes alone. "Honestly, they didn't come into my room very often." She tossed her bag onto the carpet next to the bed, then reached out to Mel, who handed over her own black duffel bag, a playful grin on her face.

"This is so you." Mel plopped down on Regan's bed, causing the mattress to bounce gently beneath her.

"I guess I haven't changed much." Regan moved to stand in front of Mel with a hopeful smile. "Wanna make out?"

"Desperately," Mel purred, and pulled her down onto her lap.

Regan leaned up and met Mel's mouth with her own, moaning quietly at the feeling of teeth and tongue and lips. *I could do this all day.* She basked in that thought for a few glorious moments, then pulled away with a resigned sigh. *However, Mom and Dad would probably get suspicious after a couple hours or so.*

Regan trailed a string of kisses across Mel's cheek, towards her ear, forcing her mouth away from full lips that threatened to shatter her resolve to stop. She reached a hand up to play with the silky, shorter hairs at the nape of Mel's neck, keeping her other arm wrapped around her lover's strong back.

"You doing okay?" she whispered.

Mel nodded into her neck. "Your parents are very nice." Her warm breath raised goosebumps on Regan's pale skin. "I think they're a little freaked out, but they're certainly trying. I can tell how much they love you, though."

Regan didn't know what to say to that. "So, you're up to lunch with the folks?"

"Definitely," Mel said. "How about you? Are you doing okay?"

"I'm good." Regan traced her fingers over the back of Mel's neck. "It felt good to introduce you to them."

"It felt good to be introduced."

"At the risk of being redundant," she whispered, "I love you."

"And at the risk of sounding unoriginal, I love you, too."

Regan murmured, a nonsense sound, into Mel's hair. "Shall we move on to round two?"

Mel released Regan from the embrace and shook out her arms as if preparing for a boxing match. "No problem."

"You're almost too charming for your own good, honestly. You're doing great."

"Shaddup." Mel gave Regan a light pinch on the butt as they got to their feet. "Come on. Let's get upstairs before your parents get worried that I'm taking advantage of you down here."

As they reached the top of the stairs, Regan wasn't sure if she was relieved or disappointed by Mel's quick retreat from their usual sensual play. While she didn't want to hide reality from her parents, she also didn't want things to be more uncomfortable than they needed to be. And not just for Mel or her parents. In reality, she was a little hesitant about revealing so much to people who knew her so little.

This is still a new thing, after all. For all of us.

ANTONIO'S WAS ONLY moderately crowded, most of the patrons still dressed in suits and skirts from the business day. The interior was dimly lit, though the sunlight from outside served to illuminate the rows of tables and booths that filled the two dining rooms.

Much to Regan's relief, they only had to wait a couple of minutes before the hostess led them to a booth in a relatively quiet corner. Her mother and father settled next to one another on one side of the table, while Regan crawled onto the opposite seat next to Mel. Her hand found Mel's thigh under the table and strong fingers covered hers, stroking her skin with gentle caresses.

Peering over Mel's shoulder at the menu her lover studied, Regan said, "I'd definitely recommend the spaghetti."

"Of course she recommends the spaghetti," her father told Mel with a fond smile. "We've probably brought her here hundreds of times since she was a little girl, and I can count on two hands the number of occasions when she *didn't* order the spaghetti."

Mel gave Regan an affectionate grin. "It's that good?"

"What can I say? When I find something I like, I stick with it." Regan's eyes sparkled as she said the words, and Mel ducked her head in shy response.

Her father cleared his throat. "Well, I think I'll also be predictable and get my favorite—lasagna." He gave Mel a friendly smile. "That's very good, too."

Mel glanced at the menu for a moment before closing it with a lazy nod. "I've always been the spaghetti sort myself, so I'll follow Regan's lead."

"You won't be sorry." Regan resisted the urge to rub her hands together in delight at the thought of eating her favorite lunch again.

As if sensing Regan's impatience, their waiter came strolling up to their table with a big smile and a perky manner that had Regan wrinkling her nose in immediate irritation.

"Good afternoon, folks," he said. He swept his gaze over to Regan briefly, before moving it over to linger on Mel. "Ladies." His smile widened for Mel alone.

Regan narrowed her eyes as her father started to order. *Oh, pal,* she thought as the waiter directed another flirtatious glance at Mel. *You have no idea how much I want to smack you over the head with my menu.*

Regan was relieved when Hank, as their waiter's nametag identified him, gathered up their menus and left them alone again. There was something quite unbearable about watching someone flirt with Mel while they were dining with her parents. She felt helpless to do anything but sit and stew in her own annoyance.

Her mood lifted a little at the reassuring touch of Mel's hand on her inner thigh. With some effort, she smiled up at her parents. *I wonder when the interrogation will start?*

"So, Mel —" Her father leaned forward and clasped his hands on the tabletop. *Three, two, one...*"How did you meet our daughter?"

Regan rambled through a potential answer in her head. *Well, Mom and Dad, Mel kind of picked me up in a straight bar, drove me back to my place on her motorcycle, and the only reason we didn't end up in bed that night was because I let it slip that I didn't just want a one-night stand.*

Mel's calm answer was a lot better. "Actually, sir, I was attending a bachelorette party at a bar where Regan was out with her co-workers. I noticed her Atari T-shirt and decided to go introduce myself and remind her of one of my favorite video games."

Well, that sounds a heck of a lot more innocent than I think it really was. Regan was surprised at the pleased looks her parents traded at the story.

"Are you originally from Michigan?" her mother asked.

"I was born in Oklahoma. I moved to Michigan to go to college. At Michigan State, actually."

Mel's voice was pleasant but Regan could sense the underlying tension at having to talk about herself. She sat prepared to jump in and change the subject if her parents started to pry too badly.

"Ah," Regan's father said. "So you and Regan are rivals, then?"

"Nah." Regan grinned at her lover. "It can't really be considered a rivalry when Mel knows full well that the Wolverines are superior to the Spartans."

Mel raised a dark eyebrow and gave her an amused smirk. "I know that they always seem to think they are, at least."

Regan merely stuck her tongue out in response. She was half-aware of the uncharacteristic playfulness she was letting her parents see, but being with Mel made her too relaxed to feel awkward about it. Both of her parents chuckled at their interaction, and her mother looked at Regan with a kind of bemused puzzlement.

"What did you study at Michigan State?" her father asked.

"Criminal justice," Mel said.

Recalling how nervous Mel had been to talk about these things on their first date, Regan snuck a glance at her face to gauge her reaction. To her surprise, Mel looked calmer in this scary situation than she had then.

"Well, that's interesting." Her mother smiled. Before she could follow up with another question, their waiter returned to the table with their drinks.

Regan wasn't sure if she was pleased or irritated with his reappearance.

"A diet Coke," he recited, setting one glass down in front of Regan's father. "Two regular Cokes." Hank deposited one in front of Regan's mother, and then the other in front of Regan. "And one water," he finished, holding out the final glass for Mel.

Regan watched Mel's hand as she reached out to take the glass from Hank. She clenched her fists in her lap when she saw the way the waiter deliberately stroked his fingers over Mel's as he handed over her drink. Grey eyes flashed in danger, then coldly conveyed the clear message that she wasn't interested.

I wouldn't necessarily mind if she decided to throw a punch in this instance, Regan mused. *And I'm only half-joking.*

Mel turned her gaze to Regan, ignoring him completely. Regan's fist uncurled a bit and her fingers twitched in her lap.

If I had the nerve, I could just grab her hand. Regan shared a look of irritation with Mel. *I wonder what my parents would think of that.*

As it turned out, Hank left before Regan could weigh the pros and cons of sending that kind of message to everyone at the table. She watched him walk back to the kitchen with narrowed green eyes.

Skinny little bastard.

"So you got your bachelor's degree in criminal justice?" Regan's mother said, recalling the point at which the questions had left off. At Mel's affirmative nod, she asked, "And what do you do for a living now?"

Regan's internal groan was so loud in her ears that she stiffened in her seat, almost afraid that her parents would hear it. *Perfect.* Seeking out Mel with apologetic eyes, Regan was a little shocked to see how calm and determined her lover looked.

"Up until about a couple weeks ago, I was an officer with the Detroit Police Department," Mel said. Her voice was steady and confident, a far cry from the confusion and turmoil she let Regan see. "Now I'm thinking about a career change. I was thinking about graphic design, maybe something computer-related."

Her father's brow furrowed in concern, and Regan could almost see his brain firing away at this information. *At least she didn't suggest that she might become a tattoo artist.* Regan knew her father's philosophy of always doing the safe and sensible thing, and she also knew that changing careers midstream — to become an artist, of all things — would really tie him in knots.

"Why are you quitting?"

Blunt, Dad. Regan sat up, clearing her throat and giving her father a pointed look. "Hey, is the interrogation really necessary?"

Mel turned to Regan with a mellow smile. "It's okay, Regan." She turned back to Regan's father with a polite nod. "After all, he has every right to want to know about the person in his daughter's life." At Brendan's appreciative smile, she continued. "To be honest, sir, I realized that being a cop just wasn't for me. I was very unhappy and I didn't feel like I was doing what I'd joined to do."

"And what was that?" He gave her a sheepish smile, then added, "Oh, and please call me Brendan. I insist."

"Well, Brendan, my dad and my uncle were both cops, and if I want to be honest, that's the main reason I joined. But I also wanted to feel like I was helping people. I wanted to feel like I could change someone's life for the better."

"You don't feel like you were doing that in the police department?" her father asked.

Despite the way her stomach clenched in sympathy at the continued questioning, Regan was aware of the gentle curiosity in her father's voice. She knew he wasn't on board with the struggling artist idea, but he sounded genuinely interested in Mel's experience.

"No, I didn't. I felt like I was always picking up the pieces after someone's life went wrong. I've seen so many senseless things, and I've seen so many of the same senseless things, over and over again. It wore me down, to be honest." Mel looked down at the tablecloth for a moment, then raised serious eyes to Regan's parents. "And then a few weeks ago my partner and I were involved in a shooting. He was hurt and I just — I realized that I couldn't do it anymore. I was miserable. And life is short."

"That it is," her father murmured, giving Regan a quick glance full of something she couldn't identify. "I'm sorry to hear about your partner. Is he all right?"

Mel allowed a brief smile full of so much emotion that Regan felt it in her gut, a moment of instinctive empathy. "He's going to be fine, thank you."

Her father looked at her with sincere compassion. "I can understand where that would be an extremely difficult job. And certainly not something suited for everyone."

"No, it's not," Mel said. "And to tell you the truth, I was pretty terrified by the whole idea — changing careers, starting from scratch — but Regan has really helped me put things into perspective." She shot Regan a warm look. "I'm not sure how I would have gotten through the past few weeks without her."

"So you're also an artist?" Regan's mother asked as soon as Mel stopped speaking. Her slim, pale hands fidgeted with a napkin, and Regan had the urge to still her mother's nervous movement with force.

Mel answered with a shy smile. "I haven't actually been very involved with art for a while, but I spent a lot of my childhood and adolescence drawing. I've just started to get back into it, though, and Regan has encouraged me to get started in digital art."

"What are you going to do until then?" her father asked.

What would he do if I kicked him under the table? Regan wondered, watching her father with defensive eyes. *I know he hates uncertainty, but give me a break.*

"I mean," he continued, looking back and forth from Mel to Regan. "I imagine it'll take you some time to prepare yourself to get a job in that field."

Mel gave him a serious nod. "You're right," she said. "Actually, I've been thinking a lot about that. When I was in college I did some volunteer work with abused and neglected kids. That was the last time I felt like I was really making a positive difference, and it meant a lot to me. I'm friendly with the program director at an organization in Detroit that works with those kinds of kids and she's been hinting around about hiring an activities coordinator for a while now." With a shrug, she said, "I figured I would go talk to her. It wouldn't pay much, but it would be something worthwhile to do. And maybe I can use my experience to do some good."

Regan blinked, moved by Mel's idea. The experience she spoke of could easily be interpreted as her police background, but Regan knew better. *Oh, baby.* The thought of Mel interacting with a group of kids brought a sudden smile to Regan's face. *I bet you'd be amazing at that.*

Her father opened his mouth to say something else, but one look from Regan stopped his words and his jaw snapped shut with an audible click. He sat for a moment, staring at the two of them in contemplative silence, then turned a sincere smile on

Mel. "I wish you the best of luck in whatever you do. And I respect your desire to help others. That's a very fine quality for a person to have."

Regan was stunned silent. *I know she's not his daughter or anything, but he took away my tuition for refusing to change my major, yet she gets praised for her fine qualities after announcing that she wants to be an artist?* She wasn't sure if she was stifling a laugh or a sob at the thought.

When Hank came back this time, it was with four tossed salads, a basket of bread, and a more subdued attitude. "Here you go," he murmured, setting the bread in the center of the table.

I guess Mel's dismissal cooled him down a bit.

Hank's eyes found Mel's face again, then his gaze dropped somewhere in the vicinity of her chest. "Tossed salad with Thousand Island?" he asked, staring at Mel.

Regan's father cleared his throat. "That's me."

Hank set the salad in front of him without glancing away from Mel. "And the rest are ranch," he said, setting three plates in front of Carla, Regan, and Mel in turn. He made no real effort not to let his eyes keep returning to Mel.

Regan sighed in disgust. *All right, that's it.* She reached over and grabbed Mel's hand, bringing their enjoined fingers to rest on the tabletop. Mel seemed startled for a moment before she relaxed and rewarded Regan with a wide grin.

"Honey," Regan said, and glanced up at Hank as she uttered the endearment. "They have the best ranch dressing here. I haven't been able to find anything back in Michigan that even comes close."

Mel squeezed Regan's hand. "Well, then," she drawled. "I look forward to it."

Both Regan and Mel completely ignored Hank as he left the table, choosing instead to meet the startled looks from her parents across from them. For a moment there was awkward silence, and then Regan's father cleared his throat. Regan wasn't finding it any easier to move past the moment than her parents.

Mel released Regan's hand with a final squeeze and picked up her fork to dig into her salad. "I've learned that Regan is a very able guide to the best of all different kinds of food," she said, and speared a piece of tomato. "She's already introduced me to the best breadsticks in the Detroit suburbs."

Brendan chuckled after only a slight hesitation, and nodded his head in agreement. "I know I've heard about the best cheeseburger, the best mashed potatoes, and the best pumpkin pie."

"I still make sure to get the best bagel every morning before work," Carla said, glancing over at Regan with a smile in her eyes.

Everyone shared a good-natured laugh at Regan's expense, then fell silent as they began to enjoy their salads. Regan chewed on a slice of cucumber, watching her parents with interest.

I think they like her. She moved her eyes between her mother and father, trying to read their body language. *I mean...they're being predictable enough, for the most part, but Mel really seems to be winning them over. I know Dad likes her. I think Mom does, too. They're trying so hard and they almost seem...pleased.* She shifted in her seat as she began to grow a little uncomfortable with the continued silence at the table.

Mel seemed to sense her unease and picked up the conversation once more. "So Regan tells me that you're an assistant principal at a high school, Brendan. Speaking of difficult jobs not suited for everyone."

Regan breathed a sigh of relief when her dad smiled at the invitation and launched into a light discussion of the trials and tribulations of working in the public school system. He and Mel were deep into a serious conversation about the importance of extra-curricular activities for teenagers, with Regan and her mother interjecting occasional comments, when their meals finally arrived.

"Here you are," Hank said, sparing only a quick nervous glance at Mel as he set a plate of lasagna in front of Regan's father and a bowl of pasta primavera in front of her mother. "And two spaghettis." He laid out a plate in front of Regan and another in front of Mel, and gave Regan a respectful nod.

Wow, Regan mused. She smiled at Hank, and then met Mel's pleased look from beside her. *Being assertive has real benefits.* She managed a quick glance over at her parents as she picked up her fork and knife. *And it's probably good for them to see, too.*

Mel swallowed a bite of her spaghetti, then turned her attention over to Regan's mother. "Regan mentioned that you're an accountant. I've gotta admit, my financial accounting elective nearly killed me in college. I'm impressed by anyone who can juggle numbers like that."

Carla laughed and fixed Mel with a bright smile. Regan could only sit in awe as her mother picked up the conversation by talking about her job, and then her garden, and then the vacation she and Regan's father were planning to take in two months.

Why the hell was she so nervous about this? Regan wondered as she chewed and watched Mel's easy interaction with her parents.

She's goddamn Eddie Haskell. They're eating her up.

"So, tell us more about this vacation you've been taking, Regan," Carla said after some time. "What have you seen? Have you done anything interesting?"

Regan shared a brief sidelong glance with Mel, a half-second during which she could see Mel reviewing the same journey in her head. *This will obviously need to be edited for retelling to my parents.*

Mel started off with some highlights from their camping trip in St. Louis, after which Regan picked up and spoke about the drive through the Painted Desert and Monument Valley. They traded the narrative back and forth with unthinking ease, bantering and disagreeing on certain details, and before Regan knew it her plate was empty and her parents were sitting across from them with relaxed, amused smiles on their faces.

When Hank came back to deliver their bill, Regan's father held up his hand to protest the debit card she tried to slide over to him. "We've got it, honey."

Despite Mel's hesitation, Regan knew when to give in to her father. "This was really nice, Mom and Dad. Thanks for taking us out." With a grin, she realized just how well the entire meal had gone. Mel fit in almost like she completed their family just as much as she completed Regan.

"So Mel, are you interested in seeing some of Regan's embarrassing childhood photos and memorabilia? We've got a whole stack back at the house and the burning desire to show it off." Her father was giving Mel a conspiratorial smirk that let Regan know that she was in real trouble.

Horrified, she shot a quick look at Mel, who gave her a sly grin in return and said, "That sounds absolutely perfect."

"Oh, no," Regan said. "We don't need to bore Mel—"

"Sure we do." Mel gave Regan a teasing poke in the side.

Regan fixed her parents with an imploring gaze. "Nothing too incriminating, okay? Please?"

"Does that mean we can't show her that picture of you when you stuffed your little bikini top and posed for us when you were ten years old?" Regan's mom shocked her with the question, and then with the wicked grin that accompanied it.

Regan's face burned. *She wouldn't.* "You wouldn't." Her parents dissolved into evil chuckles, confirming her worst fears. *They would.*

"Come on, Mel." Regan's father scooted out of the booth, and reached out to help her mother to stand. "We've got a lot to show you."

MEL STOOD UNDER the hot spray of the shower, eyes closed, thinking again of tousled red hair, wild smatterings of freckles, and pale, chubby cheeks. She was reasonably certain that Regan had been the cutest little girl in the world.

She groaned at the sensation of the water hitting her skin and washing the long day from her body. Facing the spray, she bent forward at the waist in an effort to keep her lower back relatively dry. The tattooed skin wasn't as sore as it had been that morning, but she was still being careful with it. She had been aware of the spot all day, alive with sensation.

And it was hot. It was goddamn erotic to feel, for all the good it would do her tonight. At that sobering thought, she straightened up and turned off the shower, studying the brightly colored fish that decorated the translucent curtain. *Well, it may have started out a little rocky, but meeting Regan's mom and dad wasn't so bad at all.*

Toweling her hair, she stepped out of the shower, shivering a little in the chill of the basement air. Regan's bedroom and the attached bathroom were about ten degrees cooler than the rest of the house, so Mel rushed through tugging on a clean T-shirt and a pair of soft cotton boxer shorts.

When she exited the bathroom, she was confronted by the sight of her naked lover reclining on the bed. Regan's auburn hair was still wet from the shower she had taken upstairs and her black wire-rimmed glasses were the only thing she wore. She held a book in her hands and stared at the pages in thoughtful silence.

Mel shut the bathroom door behind her with a weak hand. *No fair. She's not allowed to look that beautiful at her parents' house.* She took a step forward, running her eyes down the length of Regan's body. To hell with propriety, all she wanted to do was ravish her.

"Hey," she said.

"Hey." Regan's eyes left the worn book in her hand and lifted to meet her gaze. "My parents love you, you know. You've totally won them over. I think they may ask you to Thanksgiving before they ask me this year."

"Yeah? I thought it went pretty well, too." Raising an eyebrow at Regan, she said, "And they love you, too. I could see it in everything they did and said tonight."

Regan's green eyes grew bright with sudden emotion. "You think so?"

Mel nodded. "But I can also see that you're right. They only know a little of the wonderful woman you are." She approached the bed to sit down at the foot of it, stroking Regan's big toe with her fingertip. "Did it feel good to show them more?"

"It did."

"I'm glad."

Regan rolled her eyes. "They went a little overboard with showing you all those pictures, though. I'm sorry if you were bored to death." She raised a leg and planted her foot on the bed, gracing Mel with a most tantalizing view of her body.

Baseball. Think about baseball...or my bike. Just think about anything but that. *Not here, not now.*

Mel struggled to answer. "Not at all. I loved looking at them. You were the cutest little kid in the world." She exhaled and stared at the wall. She had to keep her eyes off Regan, because the only thing she could think about was touching her bare skin.

We're going home tomorrow. She gazed at a picture of Michelle Pfeiffer as Catwoman that was taped up near Regan's ancient computer. *We're going home and I'm scared and all I want to do is be close to her. I'm ready to crawl inside her goddamn skin, I need to be near her so badly right now.*

Instead, she kept talking. "I didn't see animals in any of those pictures. Didn't you ever have any pets growing up?"

Regan shook her head and lay her book on the bedside table. "No. No pets, no siblings. It explains a lot, really."

"Did you want pets?"

"Sometimes. My dad really can't stand animals, though, and he was always against the idea. Eventually I think I realized that I didn't even feel comfortable around other people's animals, so how could I deal with one of my own?"

"So that was one battle you never really fought with him?"

"Nope." Regan rested her back against the headboard. "I told him I'd stop asking for a puppy if he'd buy me a computer." She adjusted her glasses with a lazy hand. "The rest, as they say, is history."

Mel laughed and grinned down at her hands in an effort not to stare at pale skin.

"How about you?" Regan asked after a moment. "Did you have pets?"

"One. A cat, Spike."

Regan interrupted her by bursting into giggles. "Spike? A cat named Spike?"

Mel shot her a scolding look. "I named her when I was seven years old. She was a beautiful cat."

Regan's laughter rose in volume and her shoulders shook with her mirth. Tears leaked from shining green eyes, and Regan wiped a desperate hand across her cheek to dry them. "*She?*"

Mel poked at the bottom of Regan's foot, eliciting a startled squeak amidst the laughter. "My mom brought her home for us, oh, eight months or so before she died. That cat loved Mom."

Regan's laughter faded away at the note of sadness in Mel's voice and she sat up, resting her forearms on her legs, her hands held in loose fists. "What happened to Spike?" she whispered, as if afraid of the answer.

Mel gave Regan a reassuring pat on the knee. "She died when she was about ten years old. Natural causes, I think. She didn't really like people very much. I mean, she did before Mom died, but after...Well, I think she became really timid with all of the yelling, you know, and the commotion in the house."

Regan stared at Mel with gentle eyes. "That's not a good environment to foster trust."

"No." Mel stared down at her hands. "I was the only one she trusted, after a while. She spent so much time hiding under furniture or running when you approached her—" With a disgusted shake of the head, she said, "I think my dad probably took out his frustration on her sometimes, too. Sometimes if I could get in a room alone with her, when it was quiet, and calm, if I just sat on the floor for a while, looking at her, talking to her—" she trailed off.

"You could bring her out?"

Mel smiled at Regan. "Yeah. Those were some of the best evenings of my childhood, I think. When she'd actually crawl in my lap and look at me. Stare at me, really. I just felt like I had something real, a connection, outside of all the bullshit." She shook her head, snorting in self-derision, and tore her eyes away from Regan's again. "Christ, I sound cheesy."

"No," Regan murmured, and touched Mel's arm. "You don't." She leaned back against her pillows and waved Mel closer. "Come here, baby."

Mel could read the intent in dark green eyes and she gave her beautiful, naked lover a sheepish shrug. "I'm not sure. I know it's silly, but I'm a little superstitious about the whole sex-around-parents thing—"

"I have locks on my bedroom door," Regan said. "We're two floors away from my parents, who are probably sleeping anyway." She fixed Mel with imploring eyes. "Please, baby. I need to feel you tonight."

Mel exhaled and tossed a look at their packed bags sitting near the door, ready for their return home tomorrow. She needed it, too. Tonight, it felt like the most important thing in the world.

"You're lying here naked on purpose to convince me, aren't you?" Mel accused, giving Regan a lazy sidelong smile. "That's pure, evil genius, you know."

"I know." Regan beckoned to her with a seductive smile. "Did it work?"

Mel took a few moments to look at Regan. Really look. At her shape, her curves, and the color of her skin. Mel had seen so many female bodies in her life — some almost physically perfect, each appealing in their own way — but she had never seen anyone as beautiful as Regan. The unselfconscious way that Regan presented herself set her heart pounding and her head spinning with raw arousal.

"Of course it did." Mel's eyes strayed to the bedroom door, then back to Regan's face. "You're sure the door is locked?"

"They know I'm in here with my lover. They're not coming down any time soon." Regan gave her a slow smile. "Take off your clothes, baby. I want to see you."

Without a word, Mel stood up and tugged her T-shirt over her head. Skin tingling beneath Regan's intense gaze, she tossed her shirt down on top of her duffel bag.

"Now the boxers," Regan murmured.

Grinning crookedly, Mel hooked her thumbs in the elastic waistband of her shorts and eased them down over her hips. She watched Regan's eyes darken with desire as her body was bared, and her smoky desire stoked Mel's own need. Shifting her weight, she let out a soft moan when she felt slick arousal covering her thighs. A light kick of one foot and her boxers went flying towards her duffel bag.

Regan made her stand for another few moments before speaking again. "Turn around. I want to see your tattoo." When Mel started to turn, smiling hard, Regan stopped her with another command. "Come here first."

Mel obeyed, walking within Regan's reach before turning around to face away from her. She listened to Regan's murmured approval, then felt soft fingers trace light patterns around her tattooed flesh.

"Does it still hurt?" Regan's fingertips just barely grazed the slightly upraised skin, sending a jolt of sensation skittering throughout Mel's body.

"No." Mel spoke in a hushed voice and kept her eyes forward. "It's a little sensitive, but it doesn't hurt."

"It's incredibly sexy," Regan whispered. The hand that was stroking her lower back moved further down, and Mel exhaled when she felt blunt fingernails scrape against her buttocks. "Everything about you is so incredibly sexy. I get wet just looking at you."

"Are you wet right now?" Mel asked.

"Would you like to see for yourself?"

Mel grinned at Regan's voice, quiet and teasing, and at the confident game they fell into so easily. She got onto the bed. "Yes."

"I'd like that, too," Regan said, naked and smiling and gorgeous. She rolled onto her side so that they could face one another.

For long moments Mel stared into green eyes so close to her own; looking into their depths, she reached out and laid her hand on Regan's bare hip. "I love touching your body," she whispered. "I love your skin. So pale, and soft, and smooth." She slid her hand over the curve of Regan's hip, around to the silky skin of her ass. "I love your curves, your shape." Mel leaned forward to nibble on Regan's collarbone, and suck on the pulse point that jumped beneath her roaming lips. "I've never found anyone as beautiful as you are to me."

Regan closed the distance between their mouths. Mel could feel the heat of Regan's face on hers, and she groaned and parted her lips in anticipation. Her groan rose in volume when Regan's tongue filled her mouth. She tightened her hand on Regan's ass, pulling her lover into her so their bodies touched along their lengths. A small hand tangled in Mel's hair and scratched at her scalp, and she nearly came right then from the sheer pleasure of it all.

Christ, not yet!

Gasping for air, Mel drew back and raised a stern eyebrow at Regan. "Not so fast," she breathed. "I want to take my time with this. I want to show you exactly how much I love you."

"I was just saying hello." Regan's wide, innocent smile was in direct contradiction to the flush of her skin and the desire in her eyes.

Mel pinched her lightly on the bottom. "Is that how you say hello to everyone?"

"Just you." Regan's voice was serious, and her words grabbed hold of Mel's heart and gave it a painful squeeze. "Only you."

Mel blinked back sudden tears. Goddamn, she'd done it again. She could feel the love pouring from Regan, raw and boundless and unconditional, and she could only stare at her lover in awe. Lifting a hand to trace the lines of Regan's face in reverence, Mel smiled when she closed her eyes and leaned into the touch.

"Look at me." Mel slid her fingertips across Regan's chin, then down onto her throat. "Please."

Green eyes blinked open and captured hers in a silent exchange of feeling and affection. At first the naked adoration she saw in Regan's gaze took her breath away; when she remembered how to breathe again, she resumed her gentle exploration of warm skin. She took a lazy tour of Regan's body with her hand; she touched her throat, her collarbones, the slope of her breast. She circled a stiff pink nipple, then moved lower still to trail her fingers over Regan's stomach.

Mel watched her lover's eyes as she attempted to memorize every inch of creamy skin. The pupils narrowed and contracted when she hit a particularly sensitive area, and the color of the iris shifted and changed to reflect her rising emotion. Fascinated, Mel stopped her gentle worship only when she realized that Regan was panting, skin flushed, and that she herself felt wet and ready for more. She lifted her hand from Regan's hip, and pressed a kiss against a delicate earlobe. "Can you be quiet?" she whispered. "We need to be quiet."

"I promise."

Mel rolled over and climbed on top of Regan, holding her body above her lover's so that their skin didn't connect, and it looked almost as if she were ready to do push-ups.

"I want to feel you," Regan whispered, sliding her hands up Mel's biceps and around to her back, attempting to force her down.

Mel held her body above Regan with ease, and tried not to laugh at the desperation in her eyes or the whimpers of frustration. "I love you *so* much, Regan," she said.

"Yeah?" Regan returned her grin, and the look on her face was so genuine and happy that Mel once again fought back tears.

"Yeah."

"Well, good. 'Cause I love you, too. More than I know how to tell you." Regan rubbed the backs of her fingers across Mel's cheek. "I'm gonna spend every day trying, though."

The strain of holding her body above Regan's finally registered just as Mel decided that she absolutely needed to feel Regan, too. She lowered herself slowly, and sighed when she felt Regan's warm skin touch her own. Her breasts pressed against Regan's, their hard nipples meeting and sending shockwaves straight to Mel's center.

Their sighs mingled at the feeling of being connected once again.

"Your skin feels perfect against mine," Mel murmured in a solemn voice, and eased a firm thigh between Regan's legs.

"It looks perfect, too," Regan breathed. She held her arm up next to Mel's so they could both admire the contrast of pale skin with tan.

Her green eyes and dreamy smile made Mel blink in

wonder, and she pressed her thigh to Regan's center, coating her skin with Regan's arousal. "You're wet," she said. Her throat felt tight, the words emerging only with difficulty.

"I told you so." Regan moaned and moved against the thigh that pressed into her wetness. "It's your fault."

Mel kissed her, then, with her lips, trailed a whole series of feather-light caresses on her face and neck.

"Please," Regan murmured when Mel kissed her way down her throat and lingered at her upper chest. "Please."

Mel licked down the slope of a pale breast, pausing to suck the nipple into her mouth. Eyes slipping shut, she savored the taste of Regan's skin, the softness of her breast. As Regan whimpered and squirmed beneath her body, Mel could feel her own wetness grow. Ignoring whispered pleas, she worked her way over to the other breast with another trail of lingering kisses. Again she wasted no time claiming a hard nipple between her lips and stroking the erect nub with a firm tongue, drawing out a series of hushed whimpers and pleas from her writhing lover.

She loved getting Regan to make those noises. Knowing that she was making Regan feel good took her breath away. Impatient for more noises, Mel released the nipple she held between her teeth and slid her lips from breast to stomach to abdomen. She could smell Regan's arousal; it was a heady scent, and it struck her hungry with need.

"You smell so good," she whispered, running her tongue across Regan's hip and down over her inner thigh. "And I love how you taste."

Regan's body was in almost constant motion beneath Mel's mouth, forcing her to press a hand on each of her lover's hips to hold her in place against the mattress. She traced her tongue to the juncture of hip and thigh. She kept her mouth moving and groaned at the wetness she found with ease.

"No fair." Regan was gasping and trembling; whether it was from the pressure of Mel's tongue against her or the effort of staying quiet, Mel wasn't sure. She swiped the flat of her tongue up the length of Regan, then down again to press the tip just inside of her, where she tasted sweetest. Desperate fingers tangled in her hair and blunt nails scraped across her scalp, and Mel hummed her pleasure into Regan's center. "No fair," Regan whimpered again, and pulled at Mel's head weakly.

Mel looked up from her task. "What's not fair?" She grinned and bent again to Regan. "This isn't fair?" She lapped at her with a teasing tongue.

Regan moaned low and deep in her chest. The sound sent a

jolt through Mel, delivered right between her legs. Without a doubt, that was a very good noise. She squeezed her thighs together and closed her eyes to concentrate on licking Regan.

Fingers tugged at Mel's hair, and she allowed her face to be lifted from between Regan's legs. Mel looked up at Regan with imploring eyes.

"I know, baby," Regan answered the silent plea, breathless. "But I want to touch you, too."

Mel brought her finger up to swirl through the wetness at Regan's entrance. She lifted her eyes to capture Regan's before pushing inside of her lover with a soft groan. "Touch me like this?" Mel asked, delighting in the snug fit.

"Stop teasing me," Regan whimpered. "And come up with a solution, okay?" She wiggled her body on Mel's finger and Mel obliged with some counter-movement of her own. "Please, Mel."

"Oh, all right."

Mel crawled up the length of Regan's body and kissed her, hard, before facing the other way and straddling Regan's face. Exhaling at the feeling of her breasts pressing against Regan's hips, she lowered her face to again stroke swollen folds with her tongue. After a moment soft hands gripped Mel's hips and she was drawn down, her center enveloped in wet heat. Mel moaned into Regan and felt Regan moan into her body in response.

She felt totally connected with Regan like this. Again she pressed her finger inside Regan, only to feel herself filled a moment later. She muffled her moan into Regan's flesh, the fullness she felt shutting her brain down and pushing her closer to the edge.

Mel worked her mouth and hand without conscious thought. Her actions were driven by instinct alone, by the noises Regan made and by the movement of their bodies against each other. The feeling of Regan below her was creating wonderful pressure low in Mel's belly, radiating upward from her clit and guiding her hips in their frantic rhythm above Regan's tongue and fingers. She felt desperate to come.

"Oh, yeah," she mumbled. Her words were unintelligible, but her meaning was apparently clear to Regan, who began touching and licking at her in the most perfect way. A moment later she was sucking at Mel until her thighs began to tremble with the effort of holding her body over Regan's.

She squeezed her eyes shut while she licked and fucked Regan. She could tell by the way her lover moved that she was as close as Mel to release, and she was determined to hold out until they could come together. She sucked Regan into her mouth, moaning at the texture and taste of her. Regan shook and whimpered, and then Mel felt her lover stiffen and cry out against her wetness.

When she heard that noise, when she felt Regan orgasm beneath her, Mel tightened around Regan's fingers in sympathy, and then she was also crying out, overcome by wave after wave of pleasure. For long moments they both licked and touched one another, driving each other to greater heights, each of them trembling and straining to continue their sweet torture of the other's body. Finally Regan pulled her mouth away from Mel and buried it in her thigh, squeezing at her hips with weak hands.

"I'm going to pass out," Regan warned in a whisper.

Mel lifted her tongue from Regan's clit and lay her head on a pale thigh, panting in blissful exhaustion. "Good," she said, and swallowed. "So was I."

They lay together for some time and recovered in silence, unmoving. Finally, it was the need to kiss Regan that compelled Mel up. With shaky arms, she changed position and settled down against her, marveling at the way their bodies fit together — breast-to-breast, thighs interlocked.

"Welcome home," Regan whispered with a grin.

Mel blinked in surprise. *Fuck. At this point, I can either kiss her or start crying.* She leaned down and took Regan's mouth in a deep kiss, pouring every ounce of her love for her into their joining, never breaking the contact of their lips and tongues. She needed more. She needed everything.

"I want to be inside you," she whispered. "I need to feel you against me when I'm inside you."

Regan nodded, gasping for air. "Yes."

Mel stood on shaking legs, then strode over to search through her duffel bag. Her hands were trembling, her knees weak, and she was breathing hard from her sustained arousal. If it didn't feel so damn good, it would be scaring the hell out of her. She located her harness, dildo, and box of condoms and quickly readied herself, aware all the while of Regan with her hand between her thighs, stroking herself as she watched.

"Hey." Mel secured the harness around her hips and adjusted the straps so that the base of the dildo was snug against her sex. "What do you think you're doing? Stop that."

"I can't help it. If you'd stop bending over right next to me —"

"Regan," Mel said, and raised an eyebrow in warning at the hand that hadn't ceased its movement. "I want your hands above your head. You're not allowed to start without me."

Regan obeyed, stretching her hands over her head and giving Mel an innocent smile. The motion caused her to thrust her bare breasts outwards, and elicited a wolfish smile from Mel.

"Beautiful." She studied Regan's body, flushed and soft and perfectly curvy. "Now stay that way until I say otherwise."

"Yes, ma'am."

Mel tore open a condom and eased it over the dildo.

"That harness isn't rubbing against your tattoo, is it?" Regan asked. She wrung her fingers above her head in an effort to keep still.

"It's okay." Mel settled between Regan's spread legs and leaned up for another kiss. "I've been wanting to be with you this way for so long."

Regan brought her hands down to rest on Mel's shoulders, kneading the muscles there with firm fingers. Mel recaptured her lips and groaned into her open mouth. She shifted her hips to press against Regan, creating delicious pressure between her own legs, and moved her mouth from lips to jaw to throat. She was on fire.

"Just—" Regan whimpered into Mel's hair, and clutched at her broad shoulders. "Just go slow, okay?"

Mel touched the side of Regan's face with a tender hand, then traced her fingers up and over her eyebrow. "Of course, baby."

She held herself up on one arm and slid her hand between their bodies. She ran her fingers through the wet curls between Regan's legs, then further down to stroke her hot, swollen labia. Regan was unbelievably wet; liquid covered Mel's hand and she pressed a finger inside of her with ease.

"I love how you feel," she whispered into Regan's ear. She slid her finger in and out, listening to Regan's breathing and delighting in the way Regan grabbed at her back and shoulders with frantic hands. "So hot and wet and tight."

Mel withdrew, then pressed into her again with two, muffling Regan's cry with a kiss. She lifted her head when she felt Regan's hips begin to move in rhythm with the motion of her hand. "Does that feel good?"

"Yes. Yeah."

"Are you ready for more?" Mel stared into Regan's eyes in awe even as she asked the question. "I love you," she whispered before Regan could speak. "I love you so much and you feel so good."

"I love you," Regan gasped back, her voice hushed. "Give me more, baby. I want you inside me."

Mel eased her fingers out of Regan, and reached down to grasp the dildo so she could guide the head to Regan's entrance. She rubbed it back and forth through the wetness she found there before pressing the tip just barely inside. Inflamed, she looked up at Regan for a moment before glancing down again to watch the dildo slide into her lover.

"I love watching my cock disappear inside of you." Mel whispered the words into Regan's ear, grinning when she heard the expected intake of shaky breath and felt Regan squirm beneath her. She laid her forehead on Regan's shoulder when strong legs wrapped around her waist to pull her deeper inside.

"It feels so good."

Mel turned her head and kissed Regan again, thrusting her tongue into her mouth in the same lazy rhythm that her hips thrust the dildo in and out of her body. Regan's bare skin was damp and slightly sticky against her own warm flesh, driving Mel mad. Knowing it wouldn't be long before she came again, she fucked Regan with gentle strokes, loving strokes, and alternated between staring into hazy green eyes and kissing and sucking on full lips. They traded quiet moans into one another's mouths, both muffling their cries in an effort to stay as silent as possible. The need to keep quiet created in Mel a razor-sharp attunement to Regan's responses — her body language, the way she was sweating, the soft noises that managed to escape her mouth — and she was aware that Regan was getting close to orgasm.

Mel began to thrust her hips in earnest, emboldened by the way Regan tightened her thighs and slid her hands down to grab at her ass and urge her harder and deeper. She could feel her own climax building deep in her belly, and lifted her upper body on planted hands, moving against Regan in a deliberate cadence.

Regan raised her head and captured a nipple that was suspended inches above her mouth, sucking hard on Mel's breast. Mel ground her clit against the base of the dildo strapped to her, gritting her teeth in an effort to stave off the orgasm that threatened to overwhelm her.

It was going well, and she thought she could last until Regan released her nipple and looked up at her with stormy green eyes, murmuring, "Come inside me, Mel. I want to feel you come inside of me."

Mel came. Those words — whispered and passionate — were all it took. She came and shook and cried out into Regan's mouth, against Regan's tongue, and she lost herself in the feeling of soft skin and hot wetness and gasping, clutching hunger.

Just when she could breathe again, when she began to feel in control of the erratic thrusting of her body, Regan quivered and cried out as well. Her body stiffened beneath Mel's, her blunt nails dug into Mel's back, sending Mel crashing over the edge again.

She buried her face in Regan's neck and absorbed the pleasure she felt wracking her lover's body, allowing it to unleash a new wave of sensation throughout her own. She held Regan tightly against her, basking in the feeling of her soft hands moving against her skin in mindless patterns, stroking and reassuring. She knew she was doing the same thing to Regan, touching and pulling at her, delighting in skin against skin, wishing she could consume her to sate the need that pounded through her body.

Mel couldn't form a coherent thought in the aftermath of their climaxes; she was all instinctive feeling and emotion. When at last she could breathe again, she raised her head to stare into familiar green eyes. "That was fucking amazing."

Regan tipped back her head on the pillow and laughed, low and throaty. "It was, yes." She lifted her head and pressed a soft kiss to Mel's chin. "You are."

Mel closed her eyes in silent appreciation of the woman wrapped around her body. She made a decision. "I want to give you something, Regan."

Regan laughed again, sliding her hands down to cup Mel's buttocks and pull her even more tightly against her. The dildo that still rested inside of Regan shifted a little at the movement. "I thought you just did."

Mel took a moment to steel her nerve. "I mean it, Regan. I want to give you something."

Regan's eyes grew tender at her serious tone. "All right."

Mel kissed her again as she withdrew from her body, swallowing Regan's groan. She stood, legs weaker than ever, and left Regan lying on the bed. Without a word, watching Regan's face, she unhooked the harness and escaped to the bathroom to clean up.

Her mind raced as she washed the dildo with soap and water. *This is no big deal. It's just a present...It doesn't have to mean anything.* Mel scoffed, looking up at her face in the mirror. She looked scared to death. She leaned closer, inspecting. At least the bruises really had faded.

It's a ring, though. She stared into her own eyes. *Everyone knows that means something.*

She wasn't going to let anything deter her from this. Regan loved her just as much as she loved Regan. She knew it deep in her soul.

Regan was still lying in bed when she emerged from the bathroom, a haphazard sheet pulled up to cover her hips. She sat up, looking concerned. "Are you okay, baby? All of a sudden you seem...upset."

"I'm fine, I promise." Exhaling shakily, Mel crossed the room to kneel next to her bag, tucking the dildo and harness back inside and, after a momentary pause, unzipping a smaller pocket to retrieve a little black box.

With the ring in her hand, she was beset by new doubts. *I should've bought something better, right?* She turned the fuzzy black box over and over in her hand, staring down at what suddenly seemed like a sorry token. *Is this even good enough to mean anything?*

"Get a grip," she mumbled under her breath the moment the irrational thought took hold. "Jesus."

"Mel?" Regan's voice was tentative. "Are you sure? You don't have to give me anything if it's making you upset."

When Mel looked up, her fear and nervousness vanished. She could see the depth of love in Regan's gaze, and she felt her soul filled with the love she felt in return.

She walked to the bed and sat next to Regan, who scooted back on her elbows to sit up against the headboard, hands folded in her lap. Looking down at the black box in her hand, then back up at Regan, who had also noticed the box, Mel gathered her words.

"I want you to know that the time I've spent with you, especially this road trip, has been the best experience of my life." She took Regan's hand in hers and stared into eyes that shone with deep emotion. "I bought something for you in Santa Fe, the day after you told me you love me." Sheepish, she added, "The day I told you that I love you." Looking up, she saw Regan had the most indescribable expression on her face, which brought a smile to her own. "It really isn't much. I mean, it's nothing very special. And it doesn't have to mean anything, but—"

Regan pressed her fingertips against Mel's lips to interrupt her rambling. "Mel."

Mel leaned into the caress. "I just want you to know, I love you." She offered the box she held to Regan, who took it with a trembling hand.

Regan made a small noise when she opened the box, and her lips worked in silent effort for a moment before stopping, still parted. Mel looked down with Regan at the thin 10-carat gold Claddagh ring, and felt her chest flutter when Regan reached out to trace the design with her fingertip.

"Like I said, it isn't anything much. And you don't have to wear it if—" Mel took a deep breath. "If you don't want to. But it doesn't have to mean anything, really, I just—"

Regan lifted the ring out of the box and held it in two

fingers, staring at it with a tiny smile. "I love it." She paused, then murmured, "What does it mean to you?"

"It means...I know the beginning of us has been intense, but I'm looking forward to spending all my more mundane days with you." Mel locked eyes with Regan as the words poured from her mouth. "It means I never want to be with anyone else again, for the rest of my life. It means you're my best friend and the most incredible lover I've ever had." Leaning forward, she took Regan's hand again. "It means I want to hold you at night when we go to sleep and be the first thing you see in the morning when you wake up. It means I want things from you that I'm afraid to ask, because I know it must be crazy, how fast all of this has happened." She gave Regan a rueful smile and squeezed her hand. "It means I make long, heartfelt speeches that make me feel silly, all because I can't let you drive us home without telling you that I don't want all of this to end tomorrow. I want to be with you all the time."

Regan launched herself into Mel's arms, knocking her backwards onto the bed. She dropped tender kisses all over Mel's face, on her eyebrows and cheeks, lips and chin. "Thank you," she breathed. "Thank you for being brave enough to say what I've been wanting to say. I don't want this to end tomorrow, either. I want to always be with you. Every day."

Mel wrapped her arms around Regan and shifted them so that she was lying back against the pillows, Regan snuggled on top of her chest. "You don't even understand how nervous that all just made me."

Regan smiled. "Actually, I think I do. That just makes it even more special to me."

"I thought for sure you'd think I was moving too fast."

Regan shook her head and brought her left hand up so she could poise the ring she still held over the ring finger. "No," she whispered. "When it's this right, I'm not sure there's such a thing as too fast."

Mel reached out and took the ring from Regan before she could put it on. Then, holding Regan's gaze, she slipped the gold band over her finger. They clung together in a tight embrace, and Mel enjoyed the peace she felt at the sound of Regan's heartbeat thumping beneath her ear. When the steady rhythm picked up after a couple minutes, Mel raised her head.

"So would I be moving too fast if I asked you to think about living with me?" Regan asked.

Mel blinked in surprise at the question. She opened her mouth to respond, elated, only to deflate a little when familiar worry took hold. Everything was still so uncertain in her life, and the last thing she wanted was to feel like she was taking advantage of Regan. But she had to live somewhere, right? And why not go where she wanted to be? "And I'll pay for half of everything?"

"Does that mean you'll think about it?" Regan asked with a beaming grin.

"If I can afford it, and not be a burden to you, then yes. I'll more than think about it."

"Let's worry about money and reality later, okay, baby?" Regan laid her head down on Mel's shoulder. "I'll just focus on the 'yes' part of all that."

"Deal." This was crazy, Mel was sure, but at least they were crazy together.

When she realized that Regan was struggling not to fall asleep, she rolled them onto their sides and spooned against her lover, wrapping an arm around Regan's middle.

"Go to sleep now, baby." She kissed the back of Regan's neck. "I love you."

"Love you, too," Regan murmured. She pressed her bottom into Mel. "This has been the best experience of my life, too."

Mel waited until she felt Regan's body relax, then whispered one final promise in her lover's ear. "I'm gonna try to make you so happy."

MEL COULDN'T SLEEP. She stared at a glowing alarm clock, holding Regan in her arms. It was almost three in the morning and she felt as restless as a caged animal. Regan was sleeping hard, her body limp and heavy in slumber, but her measured breathing did nothing to calm Mel's mind. She was wired from their lovemaking and the intense moments that had followed it.

Sleep wasn't coming to her, she was sure of it. She was full of energy. In fact, she really wanted to draw. With that decision, she maneuvered out from under Regan's body with as much care as she could manage and rose from the bed in silence, replacing her body with a pillow. Placing a gentle hand on Regan's shoulder, she left her with a subtle squeeze.

Her drawing pad was nowhere to be found. *Because it's in the truck.* Mel stifled a loud groan when she remembered that little detail. She hadn't put it back in her duffel bag after taking it out the day before.

Glancing at Regan's bedroom door, she engaged in an internal debate. If she went outside to get it, she'd have to get dressed. And make noise on the stairs. She thought of the half-finished sketch of Monument Valley she had been working on for the past couple days. Damn, she wanted to finish it. And it wasn't like she could sleep, anyway.

When she reached the top of the basement stairs, tiptoeing in boxer shorts and a T-shirt, she opened the door as cautiously as she could. Though the house was silent and everyone was surely sleeping, she didn't want to take the chance of disturbing anyone. The side door of the house was directly across from the top of the basement stairs, set in a small enclave adjacent to the kitchen, and Mel was grateful for the muted glow coming from the adjoining room that lit her way. She slipped out into the night, drawing a deep breath as she shut the door behind her.

Her drawing pad was exactly where she'd left it, tucked in between the passenger seat and the center console. Her pencils and other supplies were in a box that she had stowed under the seat. Mel couldn't help but grin as she held the tools of her art.

She still couldn't believe how much everything had changed since she'd met Regan. She never thought she'd be drawing again.

The light in the kitchen almost seemed brighter as she eased back into the house. It illuminated the top of the basement stairs, and Mel began to panic when she heard a noise from the other room, then a whispered, "Regan?"

She froze in her tracks. For a moment, she had no idea what to do. She cast a longing look at the basement stairs and the inky darkness at the bottom, but immediately dismissed the idea of fleeing to Regan's room. Running in terror probably wouldn't make the best impression.

Swallowing, she gathered her courage and peeked around the doorframe. Carla sat at the kitchen table in a pair of cotton pajamas with both hands wrapped around a red ceramic mug.
Mel shot her an awkward grin from the doorway. "Sorry. It's just me. I couldn't sleep and I was just getting something from the truck."

Carla gave her a nervous little smile. "No, I'm sorry. I didn't mean to startle you. I can't sleep, either."

"Likewise. About startling you, I mean. I hope I didn't." She mentally slapped her forehead at how bumbling she sounded.

Carla relaxed into an easier smile. "Do you want to sit down? I can get you some tea or water."

Mel hesitated. The idea of sitting down for a late-night chat with Regan's mother was uniquely terrifying, especially with the memory of how she had just made love with Regan as fresh in her mind as her lover's scent was on her hand. She fought not to twitch at that thought. Building a relationship with Regan's parents was important. She just hoped to God that she didn't reek of sex.

"Sure," she said. "A glass of water would be great."

Carla watched as she crossed the room, shifting her drawing supplies from one hand to the other, trying not to squirm under the older woman's scrutiny. She dropped into a chair and laid her drawing pad and pencil box on the table. She could feel an uncharacteristic shyness creeping over her.

Carla was up and on her feet as soon as she sat down. She went through the motions of getting Mel a glass of water without a word, and Mel knew that neither of them were quite sure how to start a conversation.

When she returned with the drink, Mel accepted it with a grateful smile and took a long sip. Another stalling technique, because she still didn't know what to say.

Carla moved as if to sit, then stopped to grab something from the countertop. She returned to her chair with a package of Oreo cookies, cocking an eyebrow at Mel when she smiled at the sight. "If I were the ideal mother, I suppose I would have homemade cookies to give you," she said in a light voice. "As it is, I can present you with the very best that the local grocery store has to offer."

Grinning, Mel took a cookie from the open package. "Homemade cookies are overrated. Give me Oreos any day."

Carla chuckled as she took a cookie for herself. At first they both sat, chewing in silence, then Carla broke the ice.

"Regan also used to have trouble sleeping, sometimes. I can remember a couple of nights we met in the kitchen during our bouts with insomnia to talk and snack like this. It didn't happen often, really. She usually preferred to stay in her room most of the time. Playing with her computers, I guess. But those were some of my favorite times with her, late at night." Carla looked down at her hands on the table, folding her fingers together in silent contemplation.

Mel smiled at the thought and at the bittersweet feeling Carla's memory evoked. She tried to imagine sitting with her own mother in the middle of the night, pouring out her teenage fears and worries and triumphs. It wasn't a new wish, but it was made more poignant sitting across from Regan's mother.

"I'm sure Regan appreciated those times, too," she said. For all the distance and frustration she sensed between Regan and her parents, she also saw in Regan an intense longing for more.

With a sad smile, Carla said, "I don't know. I hope so. The truth is, I've always wished that Regan and I were closer. I think every mother wants to be close with her child, no matter how inept she may be at developing that kind of relationship." A moment of silence, and then the inevitable, "Are you close with your mother, Mel?"

Mel stared down at the cookie in her hand, feeling the shameful sting of unshed tears in her eyes. With a mental shake of her head, she pushed back her emotion and met Carla's gaze. The older woman stared at her tentatively, as if she already knew what Mel was going to say.

"My mother passed away when I was very young." Mel breathed a sigh of relief when her voice came out strong and steady, even when her heart and her head were reeling. "We were very close before she died, but I think most kids are close with their mom at eight years old."

Carla reached out and took Mel's hand without hesitation. "I'm sorry."

Mel shrugged, embarrassed by the sorrow in Carla's eyes. She looked down at their enjoined hands with burning cheeks. "So am I. It was a long time ago."

Carla nodded and released Mel's hand, taking a sudden drink of tea. When she set the mug down again, she looked across the table at the drawing pad.

Mel answered the unspoken question. "I decided I might try drawing, since I couldn't sleep. This trip has been pretty inspiring. I hadn't drawn in years before this past week and a half, and now I find myself thinking about it all the time."

She waited for the recrimination to color Carla's eyes at the mention of her art, but it didn't happen. Instead, there was polite interest.

Carla leaned forward in her seat and opened her mouth as if to speak, then stopped. An instant later, she sat back and gave Mel a friendly smile.

Ah, hell, Mel decided. It wasn't like she'd drawn Regan naked or anything. Yet. She sat up straighter in her seat, exhaled, and pushed the drawing pad over to Carla.

"Oh, no, it's all right," Carla said, and shook her head as she held up a hand to forestall Mel's movement. "You don't have to show me your work—"

Mel slid the pad in front of the older woman with a crooked smile. "You looked curious. I can't blame you. I'm sure you're wondering if I have any talent after hearing my career plans." She kept a calm face even as her insides twisted in knots.

Carla opened Mel's drawing pad without hesitation. She started from the end, flipping open the back cover and skipping a few blank pages until she revealed the unfinished sketch of Monument Valley that had drawn her out to the truck so late at night. She stared at it with her jaw hung slightly open, as if struck dumb by Mel's work in progress.

"I'm not finished with that one yet," Mel said, stating the obvious. "So it's not very good at this point."

"On the contrary," Carla murmured, clearly impressed. "You obviously do have a lot of talent."

Mel shrugged and folded her hands on the table, a little uncomfortable about just how important this approval from Regan's mother felt.

Carla gave her a reassuring smile and flipped back another page, glancing down to stare at a finished drawing of an old man Mel had seen sitting at a gas station on their way through Kansas. She'd sketched him as Regan ran inside to pay for gas and fill up the truck, hurrying to get down the lines and details of his craggy face and the bent posture of his aged body. It had been one of Regan's favorite pieces.

"You capture the human form so well," Carla said. "This is really amazing, Mel."

"Thank you." The compliments made her chest hurt with pleasure and her face burn bright red. She scrubbed at her cheeks with her hand, deciding then and there that she really needed to learn how to accept praise. Blushing wasn't in her nature.

Carla flipped back another page, taking in a drawing that had come entirely from Mel's mind. Two women leaned across a table engrossed in deep conversation. Their hands were frozen in enthusiastic expression, the looks on their faces intense, and Mel implied a certain level of intimacy between them through the positioning of their bodies in their chairs. Carla stared at this drawing in silence for what felt like forever to Mel.

"Remarkable," she finally said, and flipped to the first drawing in the pad.

This was the drawing of Regan that Mel had sketched from memory during their morning in Amarillo. Carla gasped and brought her hand up to cover her mouth, and Mel watched her eyes brighten with emotion.

"Oh, my."

Mel swallowed and looked down at the picture that Carla studied with an intense gaze. She wondered how much of her feelings for Regan could be seen just by gazing upon the sketch. Choice adjectives came to mind—love, desire, devotion—and Mel squirmed in her seat at the thought that they were visible in the loving strokes of her pencil.

"Oh, Mel." Carla raised shining green eyes to give her a watery smile. "This is absolutely beautiful."

Mel glanced down at the tabletop, her hands. "Regan is beautiful," she said. "I think the subject can take most of the credit there."

"She is that. And you captured her beautifully. Lovingly." When Mel met her eyes, she asked, "You really love her, don't you?"

"Yes." Mel squeezed the back of her neck with one hand, unable to say what she felt. "More than I've ever loved anyone. Your daughter's an amazing woman."

Carla gave her a smile filled at first with unrestrained joy, and then with a hint of melancholy. "She is," she agreed in a quiet voice. "And I know that I don't even know half of who she is. I wish I did, though."

"I think Regan wishes that, too." Mel paused a moment, then said, "It's not too late, you know."

"I guess I'm just not sure how to do that." Carla twisted her wedding band around on her finger nervously. "I've always wanted it. We were so close when she was a little girl, all three of us. It seemed like we did everything together. And then when she got a little older something changed. I don't know what, but it was like where she used to be bold and precocious she became so quiet, so shy. By the time she hit puberty I felt like I didn't know her at all."

"For what it's worth, I think that's not entirely uncommon with teenagers and their parents."

Carla traced her finger over the rim of her red mug. "I know you're right. But I always felt like I was doing something wrong. She spent so much time in her room, reading, and then on her computers. I always knew there was so much more going on in her head than she was letting us see, but I didn't know how to act with her." Her quiet sigh hinted at disgust. "I didn't know how to deal with it; how to relate to my own daughter. I think sometimes I'm a little too reserved for my own good."

Mel's heart hurt at the sadness in Carla's words. It was so clear to her that everyone in Regan's family wished for greater closeness, but nobody knew how to attain it. So Regan's self-imposed isolation from her peers kept her parents away, too. They were all just so scared and uncertain about how to talk to one another they had ended up in a self-defeating pattern. Poor Regan. Her poor mom. Mel sighed, unsure of what to do about her perspective on the situation.

"I've never met anyone quite like Regan before," she said after a moment's consideration. "I can imagine that she could be quite a challenge at times."

"Has she been a challenge for you, Mel?"

Mel thought about that for only a moment before shaking her head, her lips curled into a shy smile. "No. No, she really hasn't. Somehow everything has been so easy with her, even though I think I have a natural tendency to make situations more challenging than they need to be sometimes."

"Do you feel like she really lets you inside?"

Ignoring the unintended double entendre, she gave Regan's mother the truth. "She does. I've never had a friend like her before. She's...well, she's my best friend. There is so much honesty and communication between us. I've never felt so comfortable with someone in all my life." Quietly, she added, "She lets me know all of her."

Carla's eyelashes fluttered in rapid reaction, and she looked down into her mug with a wry little smile. "I'm glad she has a friend like that. Like you." She hesitated, took a sip of her tea, then said, "I apologize if I've seemed a little uncomfortable seeing the two of you together. It has been a little strange for me, I'll admit, to see Regan so obviously intimate with someone."

Mel's stomach dropped as she tried to decide what she could possibly say to that. "I—"

Carla stopped her words with an upraised hand. "It's a mom thing and I'll deal with it. What's important is that Regan seems really happy, happier than I can ever remember. And I can see how much you care for her." Gesturing to the drawing pad, she said, "Especially now."

"I do."

"Is she happy?"

Mel barely hesitated before answering the earnest question. "I think so, yes. I hope so. I hope I can always make her happy." She flashed on a couple of images from the past few days— Regan smiling and laughing as they left Dave and Buster's, the look in Regan's eyes when she saw her new tattoo for the first time, giving Regan the Claddagh ring earlier that evening. Her grin turned confident. "Yes, she is," she amended. "She's happy."

"Good. I always worried for Regan. That she would be lonely or unhappy. I never worried that she'd be successful, because I always knew how brilliant she was. I only worried for her happiness."

Having made the same promise to herself and to Regan, Mel didn't hesitate to make it now. "I will always love and protect her, and above all else, I'll try and make her happy."

"I'm a lucky mother, then, because that's all I ever wanted for her," Carla said. Her eyes sparkled with unshed tears, and she seemed uncomfortable with the emotion she was showing. "And I know you will, Mel. The way she was acting with you tonight, I swear I've never seen her like that before. She was glowing."

"I'm the lucky one," Mel said. "Regan and I have had the argument about who's luckier many times, so I won't get into it again."

Carla chuckled. "Ah. And have you figured out yet that it's best not to argue with Regan if you can avoid it?"

Mel sighed and planted her elbows on the table, resting her chin on her hands with a happy nod. "She does have a habit of making rather salient points in the most infuriating of ways."

"She gets that from her father." With a glance at the clock on the wall, Carla said, "I should probably get back to bed, honey. It's late and Brendan tends to get a little lonely when I leave for too long."

"I should probably get back, too. I'm sure Regan would really wonder if she woke up and I'd disappeared."

"It was very nice talking to you, Mel." Regan's mother gave her a tender smile as she stood, and stepped over to lay a warm hand on Mel's shoulder. "And thank you for sharing your art with me."

"No problem." Mel looked up at Carla with a crooked smile. "It was nice talking with you, too."

Mel helped Carla clear the table, then, gathering her drawing supplies, she turned to the basement stairs.

"Oh, Mel?" Carla's voice stopped her at the top of the stairs.

Mel looked back. "Yes?"

Carla gave her another smile, one that warmed her insides with its unrestrained warmth. "Welcome to the family."

Chapter
Twenty

"YOU'VE GOT TO get out of here," Mel protested as Regan's lips found her nipple. She pushed back on Regan's shoulder with one hand and used the other to pull insistent fingers away from the back of her upper thigh.

Reluctantly, Regan released Mel's nipple and looked up, squinting when her face was assaulted with warm spray from the showerhead. "But, Mel —"

"No. It's one thing when your parents are asleep, but I know they've woken up by now. I heard them walking around upstairs."

"They'll never hear us in the shower —"

"Go." Mel giggled as she pushed Regan backwards a step. "I've washed your hair, you're all set. Go upstairs and say good morning to your mom and dad. I'll be there in a few minutes."

"Fine." Regan produced a dramatic sigh. "But I'm coming to collect soon, sweetheart."

"Fair enough." Her lover waggled her eyebrows and disappeared back into the shower.

When Regan made her way upstairs, after throwing on her clothes, she found her father sitting in his favorite leather easy chair with the local paper in his hands. *Just the beginning of another typical day at the O'Riley household.* The sight of him in such a familiar pose sent a warm rush of affection through her entire body. The desire to bond with him tugged at her insides, drawing her into the den on quiet feet. She cleared her throat and her father looked up from his reading with a smile.

"Morning, sweet pea. Did you just wake up?"

"Good morning," Regan crossed over to his chair and leaned down to kiss the top of his grey head. "I woke up not too long ago."

"Is Mel still asleep?"

Regan settled herself onto the arm of the chair, curled up next to her father, and peered at the paper over his shoulder.

This, too, was a familiar pose, and Regan fell into it comfortably. She watched her father's grin from the corner of her eye.

"No. I think she's in the shower." *Or she was when I left her.*

"Hmm," her father murmured in response.

They sat in silence, reading the newspaper together. Her father waited until she nodded at the end of each page before turning it. It was a quietly intimate routine only broken when Regan reached up to scratch her nose with a lazy hand. She immediately became aware of the way her father's attention had shifted from the paper to the small Claddagh ring on her finger. She resisted the urge to blush and the even stronger urge to excuse herself from the room.

"That's a very pretty ring." He gave her a sidelong glance. "I don't think I saw it yesterday."

"I wasn't wearing it yesterday." Regan took a fleeting glance at the gold band, her hand still poised in front of her face, then dropped her arm to rest along the length of her body again. "It's kind of new."

"Hmm." He turned his face back to the paper and so Regan did, too, and for a minute she thought he wasn't going to say anything else. She was both saddened and relieved by that thought. Then he spoke. "You need to hang on to that girl. She seems like a wonderful young woman."

"She is," Regan whispered. The newsprint on the page in front of her blurred grey with the tears that welled in her eyes. She could feel her hand trembling against her thigh at the turn of their conversation.

Her father turned look at her with a small grin. "And very beautiful, too."

Regan blushed and met his gaze for just an instant. "She is that, yes."

"Keep us posted on the art career, okay?"

Regan nodded, turning her face back to the paper. *I knew that one was coming.* "We will."

Her father gave her an amiable grunt and turned his attention back to the paper. Regan continued reading, as well, relishing their time together. She was so involved that she didn't even notice that they had company until her father raised his eyes from the paper and said, "Good morning, Mel."

Regan grinned up at her lover. Mel was standing in the doorway with her hands stuffed deep into the pockets of her blue jeans. Her hair was still damp and her feet were clad only in socks.

The smile Mel gave her in return was a little restrained under her father's observation. "Good morning. You two were so quiet that I wasn't sure I was going to find you."

"Here we are," Regan said with a nervous chuckle. She stood and walked to meet Mel in the doorway. "Are you hungry? Do you want some breakfast?"

"You're welcome to any of the cereal we have out there, and we have jam for toast, or eggs," her father offered from his chair.

Regan raised an eyebrow at Mel. "What do you say? Shall I make you something to eat?"

"That sounds good, thanks." Mel gave her a smile that warmed her from the inside out.

"Do you want anything, Dad?"

"I had some toast an hour ago." He rearranged his paper to continue reading. "I'm fine, thanks."

Regan smiled and took Mel's hand to tug her out of the den. She led them through the dining room in silence.

"I didn't mean to interrupt you guys."

"You didn't. I was getting hungry, too." Regan tugged Mel into the kitchen behind her, then turned and continued to pull her into a tight hug. She sighed when she felt Mel's arms come up around her waist. "Are you ready for the drive home?" Regan whispered into Mel's ear.

"More than I was yesterday."

Regan could feel Mel's smile against the sensitive skin of her neck and she smiled as well. "Me, too."

She heard a throat being cleared behind them. Regan stepped back from their embrace and turned, already blushing, to see her mother standing at the kitchen door with an embarrassed look on her face.

"I'm sorry —" her mother started.

Regan shook her head. "No, I'm sorry."

With a careful smile, her mother said, "Don't be silly, dear. You have nothing to be sorry about." She stepped into the kitchen, past a surprised Regan, and gave Mel a nod. "Good morning, Mel. Did you sleep well?"

"Eventually," Mel said. "And not long enough."

Carla chuckled and lightly patted Mel on the arm as she passed. "I know the feeling."

Regan watched their interaction with a sense of awe. *What's going on here?*

"Do you girls want some breakfast?" Her mother opened the cupboard door and encouraged Mel and Regan to look at the boxes of cereal within. "I could make you some toast, too, if you'd like."

"Oh, that's all right, Mom." Regan stepped over to her mother, giving her an awkward smile. "You don't have to get us anything. We were already on a mission for food, anyway."

"No, really, I don't mind. Go ahead and sit down, girls." She glanced over Regan's shoulder. "Did you want cereal, Mel?"

"Cheerios would be great, thanks."

Regan watched as Mel ambled over to the kitchen table and plopped down in one of the chairs there. She frowned a little at how surreal the entire scene felt, especially how her mother was acting. Gone was the nervous woman of the night before, but Regan didn't understand how or why. "Do you still like Frosted Flakes?"

Regan nodded for a moment before finding her tongue. "Thanks, Mom." She walked over and sat down next to Mel, raising a curious eyebrow at her lover, who only smiled at her unspoken question.

First her mother laid out two glasses and a carton of orange juice, which Regan poured for each of them. A moment later Carla was back with two bowls and spoons, two boxes of cereal, and a half-gallon of milk. She arranged the bowls and utensils in front of Mel and Regan, then stepped back and wiped her hands on her thighs with a tentative nod.

"Did either of you want toast?" she asked.

"No, thank you," Mel answered in a polite voice. "I'm fine."

"I'm fine, too," Regan said. "Thanks." She didn't reach out to start pouring the cereal, uncertain of what to do next.

"Have you eaten yet, Carla?" Mel asked, apparently at ease.

"No, not yet. I was thinking that maybe I'd do my workout first."

Mel gave Regan's mother an uneven grin. "Why don't you get a bowl and pull up a chair?"

Regan blinked in surprise as her mother's face dissolved into a bright and genuine smile. "I'd like that." When Carla sat down at the table with the extra bowl, she poured some cereal and gave Regan a mildly wicked smile. "So, Regan, why don't you tell me something about your trip that didn't make it into the parent-friendly retelling last night?"

Regan blinked in surprise, caught Mel's eye, and then grinned.

"CALL AND LET us know that you've gotten home okay, will you, sweet pea?"

Regan wrapped her arms around her father, and he planted a fond kiss on top of her head. "Sure, Dad." She stepped back from his embrace and gave him a nose-crinkling smile. "It was really nice seeing you. I'm sorry we couldn't stay for very long."

He reached out and tousled her hair, drawing a playful little growl and a swipe of her hand across his extended arm. It was uncharacteristic behavior from both of them, but Regan threw herself into it with abandon. *It feels like I remember it used to feel back when I was little.* She gave him a bright smile.

"We were just glad you came to see us old folks at all," he said. "I know we weren't as exciting as most of what you've seen on your trip."

Regan smirked and bent down to pick up her bag from the floor, shouldering it with ease. "Not as exciting, maybe, but a highlight just the same."

"Smart-ass." He offered his hand to Mel. "Mel, it was really wonderful to meet you."

She gave his hand a firm shake. "It was great meeting you, too, Brendan." She looked over to Regan's mother, who stood beside her husband in the foyer. "Both of you."

Regan watched, still confused by the undercurrent of emotion in their interaction as her mother gathered Mel into a sudden, gentle hug. "It was good meeting you, Mel. I hope we'll get to see you again soon."

Mel looked slightly less surprised than Regan felt, and said, "Thank you, Carla. So do I."

After releasing Mel, she drew Regan into a similar embrace. Regan returned the hug with tentative arms, a little unbalanced in the face of her mother's confidence.

"Let's not go so long before our next visit, huh?" she whispered into Regan's ear. "Maybe we can come visit you two in Michigan sometime?" At Regan's nod, her mother added, "I really like this girl, Regan. You take care of her, okay?"

"Okay." Regan eased her way out of her mother's arms and gestured at Mel. "Ready to go?"

"All set."

Her parents followed them out to the truck and stood with their arms around one another's waists.

"Love you guys," Regan called, a few feet from the truck.

"We love you, too, honey." Regan's father waved with his free hand. "Now get going. I'm sure you girls are looking forward to putting all this driving behind you."

Regan nodded even though he couldn't have been further from the truth. *I'm not looking forward to ending the most amazing experience of my life, no. Then again, nothing about this really feels like an ending.*

She turned to Mel, beaming at her. "I'll drive, stud. You look tired."

"Thanks. I did have some trouble sleeping last night." Mel

climbed into the truck, and waited until Regan buckled herself into the driver's seat before continuing. "I went upstairs to get my drawing stuff and ended up meeting your mom in the kitchen for a late-night snack."

That might explain some things. With a final wave to her parents, Regan backed out of the driveway. "That must've freaked you out."

"At first, yeah. But I really like your mom. She's very cool."

Regan laughed. "Cool?"

Mel nodded, reaching over to tuck a lock of auburn hair behind Regan's ear. "Yeah. She loves you a lot, baby."

"Yeah," Regan said, shrugging. "I know she does."

"She does. She told me she wishes you two were closer."

Regan looked at Mel in amazement. "She told you that? You've known her for less than twenty-four hours and you actually had a conversation like that?"

Mel grinned. "I told her it's not too late."

"I guess this *does* explain a lot," *All of a sudden this morning makes a lot more sense.* She gave Mel a sidelong glance, impressed. "What ever happened to the chick who would have run screaming from something like that?"

"She graduated from Sensitive Chats 101?" Turning in her seat, Mel reached over and gripped Regan's thigh with a possessive hand. "Speaking of which, when do I get my diploma?"

Regan arched an eyebrow at her lover. "Baby, I've got all the diploma you need once we get home."

"That sounds promising."

"It should."

They fell into a comfortable silence for a few minutes and Regan watched the familiar landscape around them. Already she missed the reds and purples of the Southwest.

"Hey, Mel?"

Mel turned away from her study of the passing traffic. "Yeah?"

Regan quirked a hopeful grin. "Do you want to spend the night at my place?"

"I don't have anything waiting for me back at my place, so there's no place I'd rather be. I don't even have a plant to kill if I don't get home."

"Cool," Regan said, and beamed out the front windshield.

The silence between them was comfortable and easy, as it had been from almost their first night together.

Just when Regan thought that Mel had fallen asleep, her lover turned her head and said, "Um, Regan?"

"Yeah, baby?"

"Um, I was just wondering...well, I don't want to totally disrupt your life or anything, but, I mean, after I move in, whenever that will be—"

In a stroke of mercy, Regan put an end to Mel's rambling speech. "The sky's the limit, baby. What do you want?"

"Can we get a kitten?"

Did I say the sky? Regan despaired in silence. "A what?"

"A kitten." Mel shot a hopeful grin over at Regan. "You know...four legs, plays with little furry mice, meows on occasion?"

Regan's apprehension must have been plain on her face, because Mel instantly beseeched her with wide, sad eyes and a full lower lip that poked out in shameless pleading. When dark eyebrows furrowed to complete the pathetic expression, Regan groaned in defeat and turned her eyes back to the road.

"That's a cheap tactic."

"I'm just saying please," Mel said. "Please?"

"What's wrong with a nice puppy?" Regan asked. *It's worth a try.*

"A puppy?" Mel scoffed. "Puppies are loud and messy and very high-maintenance."

Regan shot Mel a warning look. "The same could be said of me, on occasion."

"You, I'll keep. Besides, I can't respect the kind of blind, unthinking loyalty that a dog gives you. Cats are more intelligent. You have to earn their love and trust, and I appreciate that."

Mel began stroking her inner thigh in the most distracting way. Regan dropped her eyes for a half second to watch the seductive play of manipulative fingers on her body. *Not that I mind her little technique one bit,* Regan mused, *if I'm being honest here.*

"Yeah, great," she grumbled. "Fantastic. Just what I need— feline rejection."

Mel chuckled. "Why do you assume it would reject you?"

Without answering the question, Regan said, "I have no problem with unconditional love, by the way."

"But that's why you've got me."

She tore her eyes away from the road to study Mel's pleading face for a beat. "I guess I *do* see the puppy resemblance, now that you mention it."

"Come on. Kittens are cute!" Mel gave Regan's arm a playful slap.

"In an evil sort of way." Looking over at Mel and seeing the pout still firmly in place, Regan expelled a long-suffering sigh. "All right. We'll get a kitten."

Mel leaned over in her seat with an excited little yelp, wrapping strong arms around Regan in a tight hug. "Awesome!"

"Can I name it?" Regan asked.

Mel pulled back, giving the redhead a suspicious look. "Maybe. It depends."

"Hey, I just want to make sure this poor thing isn't going to be called something as dysfunctional as Spike."

Mel snickered. "So what are you thinking? What's the perfect name?"

"I don't know. Something cute. How about Pixel?"

Mel's beaming smile said it all. She looked out the front windshield and shook her head. "Geek."

"Yup." Regan looked over at Mel with an amused smile. "Hey, I bet you never would have guessed just a month ago that you'd be sitting here now, thinking about moving in with your girlfriend and excited about the idea of adopting a kitten, huh?"

"The very picture of lesbian domestic bliss, right?"

Regan tilted her head back to smile up at the sun. "Right," she answered, and she continued to steer them onwards towards home.

Epilogue

MEL OPENED THE side door of Regan's house with the new silver key that hung from her familiar Harley Davison keychain. Regan had given it to her almost two months ago, but it still felt new every time she slid it into the lock.

I wonder how long I'll have to live here before I think of it as something other than Regan's house.

She hung her black motorcycle helmet on a peg next to the door, walked into the kitchen, and dropped her backpack to the floor. She didn't have to wonder where Regan was; the noise of a loud video game sent her through the kitchen and down the hallway in search of her lover.

It still felt like Regan's house, even after two months, but Mel could already feel her growing presence here. She passed by a second-hand book on Flash animation and web development that sat on the kitchen table, a loaner from Regan's co-worker Dan to supplement the texts assigned by Mel's new professor. In the hallway leading from the kitchen to the living room, Regan had framed and hung Mel's portrait of the old man at the gas station in Kansas.

Mel directed a smile at the piece as she passed it by. That one was Regan's favorite. Mel's favorite was the portrait of Regan, and that was hanging in the bedroom.

She entered the living room and found Regan and Adam sprawled in their favorite positions on each couch, completely engrossed in what looked like an intense game of Halo. Mel grinned at the screen and at the running dialogue that Regan and Adam kept up as they strategized against their mutual enemies.

"Sniper on the ridge, Regan," Adam said.

A single gunshot, then Regan chuckled in victory. "Got him. Go get the flag."

"I'm on my way. Keep sniping as they respawn."

"Not a problem."

Mel came up behind the couch and grinned down at another recent addition to the house. Pixel the grey wonder kitten sat perched on Regan's shoulder, watching the television screen in rapt fascination.

"That cat is going to grow up to be a gamer. I just know it," Mel drawled.

"Hey, baby." Regan managed a quick glance back at Mel. "I didn't hear you come in. How was class?"

Adam also gave her a quick look, then returned his eyes to the screen to continue running through a grassy field carrying a red flag. "Hey, Mel."

Mel approached the couch and bent to kiss Regan on the cheek, then nuzzled one of Pixel's fuzzy ears with her nose. "Class was good. I like the professor. And I think I'm getting all the computer stuff so far."

"Cool." Regan's eyes stayed glued on the screen as she provided cover for Adam's mad dash back to their fort with the enemy's flag. "Adam's running in the winning point and then I'll get ready to go."

"No problem." Mel stroked Regan's hair. "Annie said dinner would be at about six-thirty. You've got time. I'm just going to go get changed, okay?"

Regan nodded, giggling when Pixel stretched out and nearly fell off his seat on her shoulder. "Help this kitten, would you?"

Mel scooped up the boneless little body and repositioned Pixel next to Regan's neck. "And you said this little guy wouldn't love you."

"Score another point for you. A week and a half and I'm a changed woman. Cats are definitely better than dogs."

Mel chuckled and tugged on a lock of Regan's hair as Adam whooped with joy at Regan's flipping a truck that was chasing after him with a well-thrown grenade. She shook her head. "Come see me when your game is over," Mel said.

Regan nodded. "We're about to send these boys home with their tails between their legs."

Mel was still grinning when Regan joined her in the bedroom ten minutes later, flushed with the afterglow of a well-played game, a state not unlike the afterglow of great sex. Mel enjoyed seeing her like that, fully engaged and excited. Especially when she knew the upcoming hours would be nerve-wracking for Regan.

"You ready for this?" she asked.

Regan walked to the closet and threw open the door, releasing an anxious sigh. "I've been trying not to dwell on it."

Mel sat down on the bed, and grinned when Pixel followed Regan into the bedroom and launched himself up onto the mattress. She stroked his head, then rubbed a slow hand over his belly when he flopped over on his side to give her access.

"You did so great at Jane's wedding, though," Mel said. "Seriously, you were so charming. Jane thinks you're the best thing since sliced bread."

"She's just happy someone has settled you down."

Mel shot her a firm look. "I mean it, you did great. I know you were nervous and everything, but everyone loved you." She leaned down and kissed Pixel's tummy. "Everyone will love you today, too. You're great."

Regan stared into her closet. "But this is Hansen. This is really important."

"And you'll do fine. Just be yourself, Regan. You're the most likeable person I've ever met. You just don't realize it most of the time."

"What should I wear?"

Mel's lips twitched into a sympathetic grin. She stood up from the bed, ignoring Pixel's outstretched paws that flailed about in protest, and approached Regan from behind. Wrapping her arms around the redhead's middle, she said, "How about that cute little T-shirt with the old-school joystick? And those jeans that make your ass look so hot."

Regan snuffled a little at the suggestion. "That's not too geeky for this?"

"It's you," Mel said with a shrug. "He's barbecuing out, baby. It's totally casual."

Regan nodded and turned in Mel's embrace. Mel looped her arms around Regan's waist and pulled her close.

"If you say so."

"I say so." Mel dipped her head and kissed Regan, lingering for long moments in the enjoyment of her taste and feel. "Is Adam gone?"

Regan nodded. "We won. He went home to celebrate."

"You two are so cute together. It's unbelievable."

"We're a well-oiled machine." Regan gave Mel a cocky smile. "I'm serious. We're a force to be reckoned with. Enemies tremble in our wake."

Mel released Regan with a gentle pat on the behind. "I think it's great that you've got a little boyfriend to play with."

Regan frowned. "He's not my *boyfriend*."

"Sure he is," Mel argued. "He's a guy. He's your friend. You're a cute little team...uh, I mean *well-oiled machine*. He's your boyfriend."

"Whatever," Regan said, rolling her eyes. She gave Mel a pleased grin. "I'm glad you like him. I'm glad he likes you."

"Me, too. Now get dressed. We've got places to go, people to meet." She watched the blood drain from Regan's face.

"Right," Regan murmured. "I can do this." She pulled off the T-shirt she wore, revealing a black bra underneath.

Mel leaned forward and traced gentle fingers over the design on Regan's upper arm. "Yes, you can do this."

Regan closed her eyes and exhaled nervously, then her face relaxed and grew peaceful. Nodding, she looked up at Mel with determined green eyes. "I can do this."

HANSEN STOOD AT an impressive grill, an apron tied around his waist and a baseball cap on his head. Annie and Katie sat at a table on the deck behind him, their heads bent over coloring books with a large box of crayons open between them.

He looked up from the grill as soon as Mel and Regan came into view, and pinned her with a wide grin. "I hope you're ready to eat, Raines, 'cause I'm making enough to feed an army."

Mel covered her stomach, groaning. "Are you on a mission to kill me with food, Hansen?"

"Nah," Hansen said. "Just trying to toughen you up a bit."

"Well, thanks. I guess if that taco joint you like never killed me, nothing can."

Hansen curled one arm over his stomach to take a bow, and raised a pair of tongs in the air. "You're welcome." Straightening up, he moved his gaze behind Mel and dissolved into a warm smile. "You must be Regan."

Mel led Regan over to him by the hand, stroking her thumb over her lover's knuckles in reassurance. "This is Regan," she confirmed, and tugged Regan close. "Regan, this is Peter Hansen."

"Regan, you have no idea how long I've wanted to meet you." Hansen offered his hand to Regan, who took it without hesitation. "I had to see the woman who turned the unflappable Officer Raines so inside out."

Mel reached out and poked Hansen in the side without thought, then winced when he sucked in a breath in reaction. "Sorry, partner."

Hansen shook his head, chuckling. "No, I deserved it. Don't worry, I'm in perfect health and wholly capable of accepting a jab for bad behavior." He grinned past Mel, to his wife. "Just ask Annie about that one."

Annie Hansen rose from her place at the table to join the small group, and wrapped her arm around her husband's middle. "Only in the most extreme circumstances. And for the record, I think that one was justified." She smiled over to Regan, offering her hand in greeting. "Hi, I'm Annie."

Regan returned her smile, giving her hand a polite shake. "Well, you know who I am by now. It's nice to meet you."

"Likewise," Annie said. "We're thrilled to finally meet you."

Hansen looked back at the picnic table, extending his hand with a patient smile. "Katie, honey, come here and say hello to Aunt Mel and her girlfriend Regan."

Mel blinked at Hansen's easy handling of the introduction, and turned nervous eyes on his daughter as she stood up and walked over to her father. The girl kept her gaze down, shy, until she stood in front of Mel. Then she raised innocent hazel eyes, and gave Mel a timid smile.

"Hi, Aunt Mel." She darted a quick glance over to Regan, cheeks turning pink. "It's nice to meet you, Regan."

"You, too," Regan said, staring at Katie with something akin to empathy.

Mel smiled at the realization that Regan was seeing a piece of herself in the red face and quiet timidity of Hansen's daughter.

"Did you want to give your present to Aunt Mel, sweetie?" Hansen asked, stroking Katie's hair with a large hand.

Mel looked at Hansen in surprise, and then at Katie, who nodded and fumbled with a piece of paper. For a moment she didn't look like she would manage to say anything, but finally she gazed up at Mel and offered what she held in her hands.

"I drew you a picture." She wrung her hands together when Mel took the paper. "My dad said you like motorcycles."

Mel grinned at Katie, eyes watering with sudden tears, and gazed down at the colorful drawing in her hands. Her grin grew wider when she took in what she had been given. It was a picture of her, she supposed, in full comic book style. She sat astride an elaborate motorcycle, every inch the female superhero. She wore a colorful costume with a simple insignia on the front. One muscular arm was flexed in a display of strength.

Regan chuckled. "Katie, this is great!"

Mel looked at the girl, who had dissolved into a look of embarrassed pleasure. "You're a really good artist. I'm impressed." She hesitated only a moment, then crouched down to pull Katie into a gentle hug. "I'm also flattered, Katie. Thank you for the gift."

With a flustered grin, Katie murmured, "You're welcome," and retreated to her mother.

For a moment nobody said anything, and then Annie asked, "You like video games, don't you, Regan?"

Regan gave Annie a shy grin. "I love them."

Annie put her hand on Katie's shoulder, drawing the girl's attention up to her, and gave her daughter an encouraging nod. "I thought so. I told Katie that maybe you could help her with a new game she's been working on with Peter. They're both stuck and desperate on this level of *Super Monkey Ball 2*."

"You've got a Game Cube?" Regan asked Katie.

The girl nodded in excitement. "Dad got it for us when he got out of the hospital. We play together when I get home from school sometimes."

Regan nodded, already looking more relaxed. "*Super Monkey Ball 2*, huh? That's a tough one. I've played it a lot, though, so I can try to help you out."

"Cool." Katie looked up at her mom with a hopeful smile. "May we play games, Mom?"

"Sure, honey. Why don't I go help you guys get set up?"

Mel checked in with Regan. *You're okay?* Regan gave her an easy smile in reply. Video games. Worked like a charm, every time.

She watched Annie lead Regan and Katie to the sliding glass door at the other end of the deck, and toss a loving smile back over her shoulder to Hansen. He waved his tongs in parting.

"Was that planned or is it just my lucky day that we're getting a chance to have another of these one-on-ones you know I live for?" Mel muttered.

Hansen tossed her a playful grin. "A little of both?" He reached out and turned a piece of chicken with the tongs. "She's really sweet, Mel. Really cute."

"She's everything," she said, jamming her hands into her pockets. After a moment, she bumped Hansen's arm with her elbow. "I'm going to have to get used to the whole Aunt Mel thing, I think."

"Is that okay?"

"More than okay," Mel said. "Just new."

Hansen smirked down at the chicken, then up at her. "Katie thinks you're wonderful, by the way. Saving her dad's life and everything—"

"I didn't save your life," Mel mumbled. She stared through the smoke coming off the grill. After a beat, she knelt and snagged a can of Coke from the cooler that sat at her feet. She straightened up with the freezing can in her hand, and struggled to fight off her emotion at the subject.

Hansen didn't respond to her denial. Instead, he chuckled. "I think she may have a crush on you. Hero worship, crush...at that age it's all the same, isn't it?"

Mel's mouth dropped open. "Hansen, I—" She stopped,

uncertain of how to respond. Finally, she gave him a cautious smile. "It was cool of you to introduce Regan like you did. As my girlfriend, you know." She wished she could verbalize why his acceptance was so important to her. "I appreciated that."

Hansen chuckled in amusement. "We had the women can love other women and men can love other men talk with her last week. We figured it was best, you know, before you brought Regan over for the first time."

"That's really...that's really cool of you."

He shrugged. "That's the great thing about kids, you know. You tell them stuff that puts some adults in a tailspin and they just accept it in the blink of an eye."

"You're a good father. I wish I'd had a father like you."

Hansen turned away from the grill, pinning her with tender brown eyes. "And that's the great—and terrible—thing about being a parent. You have a lot of power over your kids. They learn what you teach them. I want to teach Katie to be a good and tolerant person."

"She's lucky to have you."

Hansen grunted in agreement, reaching up to touch his neck. An angry pink scar stood out in stark relief against his tanned skin. "We're all lucky."

Mel turned her eyes towards the door where Regan had disappeared. "You can say that again."

"So couplehood is agreeing with you?" Hansen smiled down at his chicken, then took a sip of ginger ale from an open can that sat next to the grill.

"Yeah," Mel said, still with a touch of wonder. "It really is." Hansen's knowing eyes held an intensity that made her break their gaze. "I mean, I'm still getting used to being in Regan's house. But even though a lot of things are changing for me right now, it doesn't really matter. Because when I'm with Regan, I'm home."

"Then, my friend, it sounds like you've really found it." Hansen's voice was so full of love that it lulled Mel to peace.

"What's that?"

"A family."

Mel looked at him with unrestrained joy. "For once in my life, there's no doubt in my mind." Remembering the can of Coke she still held, she opened it and held it aloft to Hansen in a one-sided toast. She couldn't have stopped her too-wide grin if she'd tried.

"A family," she repeated. "Yes, that's exactly what I have."

Meghan O'Brien lives in Brighton, Michigan with Ty, her partner of over six years. Though she graduated from the University of Michigan Business School with a degree in CIS and currently works as a software developer, her real passion is writing fiction. And video games—we can't forget video games.

When she's not writing or playing Halo 2 online, Meghan enjoys spending time with her friends, wrangling her six cats, and taking road trips. She is 26 years old, and hopes to keep writing lesbian fiction into the indefinite future. *Infinite Loop* is her first published novel, but by no means her last.